Southern hospitality can kill you...

Roxanne Scarbrough is renowned for her Southern charm and taste. She has built an empire that already includes magazines, videos and bestselling books. But now someone is out to take it all away from her....

Dorothy Landis: Roxanne's overworked and underappreciated personal assistant. She'd once said, "Someday someone's going to do the world a big favor and kill Roxanne Scarbrough."

George Waggoner: blackmailer. He knows too much about how Roxanne created herself...and the secrets she left behind.

Jo McGovern: documentary filmmaker. She is supposed to film a pleasant piece of fluff, but sometimes Roxanne wonders if Jo has ulterior motives.

Chelsea Cassidy: the handpicked biographer hired to perpetuate the Roxanne Scarbrough myth. But Chelsea is too sharp. And too interested in Cash Beaudine, a man Roxanne wants for herself.

Cash Beaudine: Southern charmer and rebel. His independence makes him appealing to women who control everyone and everything.

Which of them is determined to kill her?

JoAnn ROSS

Southern Comforts

MIRA

MIRA

ISBN 0-7783-2040-5

SOUTHERN COMFORTS

Copyright © 1996 by JoAnn Ross.

Visit us at www.mirabooks.com

Printed in U.S.A.

To Jay

Prologue

1989

It was a night made for romance. Outside the ballroom of the Hillcrest Country Club, sparkling stars filled the night sky like diamonds scattered over a jeweler's black velvet cloth. Music drifted on air perfumed with the scent of lilacs, accompanying the soft sighs and whispers of lovers who'd slipped away to steal kisses in the shadows of spreading chestnut trees.

Inside the ballroom, seated at a damask-draped table, Chelsea Cassidy watched her cousin, Susan Lowell, dance with her groom.

The bride was, as brides are supposed to be, beautiful. She also looked as if she were dancing on air.

"I still don't understand." Chelsea's date, Nelson Webster Waring complained for the umpteenth time that night. He shook his head as he cut into his prime rib. "Why did you feel the need to actually have your name on that tacky story?"

For the umpteenth time that night, Chelsea tried to explain. "In the first place, I don't consider it a tacky story—"

"A woman baring her breast in public?" Nelson arched a patrician brow that reminded Chelsea too much of the way her mother had looked at her so many times over the years.

"To feed her child, Nelson." A champagne bottle, nestled in ice cubes in which pink rosebuds had been frozen, awaited the wedding toast. Tempted as she was to open the dark green bottle, Chelsea reached instead for her water goblet, only to have it taken away by a tuxedo-clad waiter.

"The woman unbuttoned her blouse to feed her infant daughter," she said. "As women have, thank God, been doing since the beginning of time."

"Hopefully not in public parks." He took another bite, annoying her further by chewing his usual ten times, as he'd been taught by some nanny. Chelsea wondered if Nelson would actually choke to death if he swallowed the damn piece of meat after only six chews.

"Kathy Reed pays taxes." Chelsea snatched the refilled glass from the waiter's hand before he could return it to the table. "That makes her the public."

She took a long drink of ice water she hoped would help calm her. It didn't. "Which, in turn, makes it her park. And it wasn't as if she tore off her clothes and went skinny-dipping in the fountain, Nelson. She was behaving quite discreetly. People didn't have to look."

"We're getting off the point." His own irritation beginning to show, he stabbed a piece of potato. "The issue is not whether the woman's behavior was proper. The issue is why you insisted on having your name linked with hers."

"Because I'm a journalist."

"You're merely an intern at the *Register*," he reminded her.

"I start getting paid next week. When I begin working full-time."

"As a Sunday life-style reporter. Which doesn't exactly put you on a par with Woodward and Bernstein."

"Thank you for pointing that out to me."

He appeared unmoved by her sarcasm. "Why can't you cover the summer social season?"

"The job of society reporter's already filled. Besides, covering weddings and yacht regattas would bore me to tears. I want to write important stories, Nelson."

"Like that unsavory date-rape series?"

"That unsavory series, as you call it, received a great deal of national attention, Nelson. I'd hoped you would be proud."

"Of course I'm proud of you." He lifted his gilt-rimmed coffee cup, signaling for a refill. "That goes without saying."

Exchanging the water pitcher for a sterling pot, the waiter obliged. When his mocking dark eyes met Chelsea's, she glared at him.

"But if you're going to insist on writing about such distasteful topics," Nelson continued, oblivious to Chelsea's silent exchange with the dark-haired man standing behind him, "couldn't you at least use a pen name? Like George Eliot?"

"Pseudonyms are for fiction writers."

"Honestly, Chelsea, I don't understand why you can't be like other women. Like your mother. Or mine."

Nelson's mother was, if possible, even more rigid than hers. Margaret Waring clung to the old WASP belief that there were only three times a woman should have her name in the paper: when she was born, married and died.

Chelsea sighed. "I know."

"Know what?"

"That you don't understand." She stood up and placed her napkin on the table. "Excuse me. I need to freshen up."

The women's lounge was deserted, allowing Chelsea the chance to try to regain her composure. During the past four years, while working hard at her studies, along with writing for the *Yale Review,* she'd managed to build a lucrative free-lance career working as a stringer for a syndicate providing news copy and interviews for a group of small weekly papers along the eastern seaboard. If all that wasn't enough to keep her busy, she'd also talked her way into an intern job on the local *New Haven Register.*

And then a close friend had made the mistake of getting drunk at a party after the annual Harvard-Yale football game.

The series of date-rape articles Nelson found so objectionable had not been easy to write. Many of the victims had suffered feelings of shame and guilt and it had taken Chelsea time to convince them that only by bringing the issue to the bright light of day could the stigma be burned away.

Although the intensely personal interviews had definitely not been popular with her mother or Nelson, they *had* been met with ego-boosting approval on campus and won her the offer for a full-time position at the *Register* after graduation. They'd also been picked up by a few weekly papers around the country, technically establishing her as a national journalist.

Which was, Chelsea thought as she dried her hands and began energetically brushing her hair, a pretty good start for someone who'd just graduated from college. Her famous father, Dylan Cassidy, had been a year older—twenty-two—before he'd gotten his first national byline.

She left the lounge and was walking down the hall on her way back to the ballroom, when, without warning, a hand reached out of a doorway, snagged her wrist and pulled her into a narrow dark room.

Before she could utter a word of protest, her mouth was covered by another in a deep, punishing kiss that literally took her breath away.

There was no light in the room, which, from the scent of disinfectant, she realized was a janitor's closet. Since her eyes had not adjusted to the dark, she could not see the man whose lips were grinding against hers.

But Chelsea didn't need to see. Because she had everything about him imprinted on every inch of her mind and body. It was as if she'd been bewitched by some black magic, she thought wildly, as she dragged her hands through his dark hair and pressed her body even tighter against his. From the first day Cash Beaudine had shown up in her dining hall, hired to bus tables at mealtimes, she'd fallen under his spell.

Unlike any of the boys she'd grown up with—boys groomed from infancy to take their places in boardrooms all over America—Cash was a rebel. He was Heathcliffe, James Dean, Billy the Kid and Butch Cassidy all rolled into one dark, dangerous, smoldering package.

Other than the fact that he was from the South and was attending the college of architecture on a work-study scholarship, Chelsea didn't know very much about him. She had no idea about his family background, what religion, if any, he practiced, or his political affiliation. Their relationship was not based on any high level of communication.

It was lust, pure and simple.

And it was wonderful.

"Why the hell do you put up with that guy?" Cash growled as he thrust his hands beneath the full-skirted bridesmaid dress.

"I've known Nelson for years." Although talking was

never at the top of their list of things to do when they were together, this was not the first time Cash had asked that question. Her answer was always the same. "I'm going to marry him. When I turn thirty."

If she married earlier, she'd lose the inheritance bequeathed to her by her great-grandmother Whitney. But marriage and money were the last things on Chelsea's mind right now. She gasped with a combination of pleasure and anticipation as Cash pressed his palm against the already damp crotch of her seashell pink panty hose.

"You might be able to fool *Nelson*. You might even be able to fool yourself, sweetheart." His mouth scorched a trail of flame down her neck. Chelsea tilted her head back, giving him access to her throat. "But you sure as hell can't fool me."

There was barely room for one person in the close confines of the closet, let alone two. Chelsea was firmly wedged between a wall of wooden shelves and Cash's rock-hard body.

"You'll never marry that cold-blooded, self-righteous yuppie creep." As if staking his claim, he yanked the waistband of her panty hose down. His long dark finger combed through copper curls before probing moist feminine folds. "Not after being with me."

"Is that a proposal?" If he were the last male on earth, Chelsea couldn't imagine marrying a man like Cash. Of course, she considered as his intimate caress made her head spin, the thought of bringing Cash home to her mother, then sitting back and watching the fireworks, was definitely appealing.

"Hell, no." As forceful a lover as he was, Cash was not without finesse. Two fingers had replaced the one and his thumb was doing incredible things to her tingling flesh.

"I've already told you, baby, I've got too many things I

want to do before I tie myself down with a ball and chain. And even if I ever do decide to get married, it damn sure won't be to any uptown Yankee girl.''

Despite her disinterest in marrying Cash, the Yankee reference stung. Refusing to give him any more power than he already held over her, Chelsea chose to concentrate on his unflattering description of matrimony.

''A ball and chain. What a lovely original metaphor.'' Her voice dripped with sarcasm. Wanting to make him as desperate, as hungry as he was making her, she managed to snake her hand between their bodies and unzip his black waiter's slacks. ''I must remember to write it down.''

''You do that.'' He was hard as marble in her hand. But much, much hotter. ''When you can think again.'' One last flick of that wicked thumb sent her over the edge. Even as she felt the first orgasm ricocheting through her, Chelsea knew there would be more.

Chelsea had never thought of herself as a particularly sexual person. Oh, she'd slept with Nelson, of course. After all, she'd known him all her life.

But this crazy time with Cash Beaudine had changed something elemental inside her. Since their first stolen time together, she couldn't stop thinking of Cash.

Wanting him.

And heaven help her, needing him.

He'd filled her mind as completely as he'd filled her body. The more of Cash she had, the more she wanted.

Before the last of the ripples had faded, he'd set her away from him and was zipping up his slacks. ''Let's go somewhere there's room to do this right.''

Now that her eyes had adjusted to the light, she could see his devilish grin. It was arrogant, mocking and sexy as hell. ''An uptown girl like you deserves more than a quick stand-up fantasy fuck in a broom closet.''

"Once again your mastery of the English language overwhelms me." Chelsea was not by nature a sarcastic person. She had, however, recently resorted to snapping back at him in order to maintain some small sense of balance in this relationship.

Not, she reminded herself firmly, that two people having sex at every opportunity could be considered a real relationship.

"Besides, Susan will be throwing her bouquet soon. I have to be there."

"Which would you rather have?" His deep voice heated her blood all over again. "A bunch of overpriced hothouse roses tied up in pink-and-white satin ribbons?" Taking hold of her wrist, he pressed her hand against his swollen groin. "Or this?"

What should have been an easy question was anything but. Chelsea thought of Nelson, waiting back at their table, armed with new arguments he'd undoubtedly worked out during her absence.

She also thought of tomorrow when she'd be off to her mother's summer home at the Hamptons for a week's visit before beginning work at the paper, and Cash would be on his way across the country to San Francisco. He'd landed a job with a famed international architectural firm whose name she recognized.

And even as she wondered how this rebel would fit into the buttoned-down world of designing high-rise office buildings for the corporate elite, Chelsea couldn't help being impressed.

"You'd better make up your mind quick." The thick, south-of-the-Mason-Dixon line drawl was the same one he pulled out whenever he sensed her wavering. "Before we croak from inhaling too much Pine-Sol. Or your boyfriend suddenly stops thinking about himself long enough to notice you're gone and sends someone to find you.''

Leaving with Cash Beaudine would not only be wrong, it would be the most outrageous thing she'd ever done. And for Chelsea, that was admittedly saying something.

She hesitated another heartbeat. Then, as she drank in the mysterious male scent emanating from Cash's dark neck, Chelsea pictured the rumpled, unmade bed where she'd discovered the true meaning of passion.

Heaven help her, she was going to do it!

Five minutes later, she was sitting on the back of Cash's jet-black Harley, racing down the road away from the country club. The wrinkled pink taffeta skirt was hitched up around her thighs, her arms were wrapped around his waist and her hair streamed out like a copper flag from beneath the black motorcycle helmet he'd stuck on her head.

It was a night made for romance.

A night when anything was possible.

A night Chelsea knew she'd remember for the rest of her life.

Chapter One

New York City, Seven Years Later

The Power Behind The Pretty Face

Roxanne Scarbrough is the doyenne of decoration, the maven of modern style. In addition to her monthly magazine, *Southern Comforts,* several *New York Times* bestselling how-to books, videotapes and a syndicated weekly television program, America's favorite Steel Magnolia has inked a six-figure deal with Mega-Mart stores. Middle-class shoppers frequenting the booming, 347-store chain can now live and shop the Scarbrough way.

Mega-Mart's budget for the new advertising campaign announcing their Southern Comforts line is $12 million, which should make the folks over at Chiat/Day a great deal more comfortable. Whatta deal! Whatta gal!

Adweek, March 26, 1996.

For a woman whose public image made Donna Reed look like a slacker, Roxanne Scarbrough proved to be a dragon lady extraordinaire.

Chelsea had never met anyone like America's most famous southern belle. Which, for someone who had managed to survive interviews with both Madonna and Roseanne, was saying something. As she sat on the sofa in "Good Morning America"'s greenroom, waiting for her interview with Charlie Gibson, Chelsea watched Roxanne's off-screen theatrics in amazement.

Since the limousine had delivered America's most famous life-style expert to the studio from her suite at the Plaza an hour ago, she'd thrown a brush at the hairdresser who had quick reflexes and ducked just in time, stomped out of the room when the makeup woman had made the fatal mistake of suggesting a concealer to cover the faint scars from recent eyelid surgery, and managed to deride her personal assistant at every possible opportunity.

The makeup room was too hot. The greenroom too cold. The orange juice was frozen. And the Danish, horror of horrors, were cold.

"Honestly," Roxanne huffed with a brisk shake of her sleek blond bob, "you Yankees have absolutely no sense of style!"

"I expect that's why you've been invited on the program," Chelsea replied blandly. "To bring culture to the philistines."

Only the sharpest ear would have caught Chelsea's veiled sarcasm. The glint in her green eyes would have warned anyone who knew her. As it was, the other woman was so wrapped up in her pique, it flew right over her head.

Roxanne's gaze flicked over Chelsea like a medical researcher checking out the dog pound for potential experimental material.

"A hopeless task," she asserted between bonded teeth,

then announced to no one in particular, "This is a shitty time of day."

When she pulled a cigarette from a crushed gold mesh pack and planted it between her lips, her assistant, a harried, pleasantly plump thirty-something woman leaped to light it. Chelsea noted the lack of a thank-you. Perhaps no one had bothered to inform the southern doyenne of domesticity that slavery had been abolished.

"It fucks up my biorhythms." The proclamation was exhaled on a cloud of noxious blue smoke that came puffing out of both nostrils like dragon fire. Chelsea said nothing. But she did wonder what the Steel Magnolia's legion of fans would think of such earthy language escaping their guru's glossy pink lips.

Roxanne glared around the room, which had nearly emptied; the third guest of the hour—an economist from Harvard scheduled to discuss the potential impact of baby boomers reaching Social Security age—had already sought sanctuary in the rest room down the hall.

"Where the hell is that boy with my tea?"

A moment later, one of the interns returned to the greenroom. His name was Brian, Chelsea had learned. The son of a West Virginia coal miner and truck stop waitress, he was a scholarship student from Penn. He was, he'd told her earlier, thrilled to have won this highly coveted internship. But of course, he'd shared that little nugget of personal information *before* he'd met Roxanne Scarbrough.

When she glimpsed the red-and-white tea bag tag hanging from the rim of the foam cup in Brian's hand, Chelsea braced herself.

"What the hell is this?" Roxanne demanded.

"Roxanne," her beleaguered assistant, Dorothy Landis, murmured, "it's the tea you asked for."

"This is not tea." Roxanne crushed her cigarette out into

a GMA ashtray with enough force to break the slim cylinder in two. Blazing blue eyes hardened to sapphire as they raked the cup the young man was holding.

"Tea is properly brewed in freshly drawn soft—but never chemically softened—water which has been heated in an enameled vessel. The leaves—preferably Imperial Darjeeling—should be dropped into the water just as it arrives at a brisk rolling boil, giving them a deep wheel-like movement, which opens them up for fullest infusion."

Her voice, as it slashed away at the intern, was as sharp and deadly as a whip. "After which time it is poured into a scalded, preheated pot to allow the essential oils to circulate through the liquid."

A very good four-carat diamond sparkled in the overhead fluorescent light as Roxanne reached out and plucked the white cup from the intern's hand. "This is not tea," she repeated. Turning her wrist, she deliberately poured the brown liquid onto his shoes.

Chelsea watched the bright red spots appear on his narrow cheeks. Fortunately, before the young man could make a mistake that might cost him his job, another intern appeared in the doorway.

"Ms. Lundon is ready for you now, Ms. Scarbrough," she said.

Roxanne immediately stood up. Chelsea watched, fascinated in spite of herself, at the woman's metamorphosis. Her perfectly made-up face softened, the hardness left her eyes and her lips curved into her signature smile. She ran her hands over her spring suit—pink with black piping, from this season's Chanel collection, Chelsea noted—smoothing nonexistent wrinkles.

Then, without a backward glance, she swept from the room.

"Christ," Brian muttered. He grabbed a handful of paper napkins and began swiping at his previously white Nikes.

Roxanne Scarbrough's assistant's brown eyes hardened. Brackets formed on either side of her thin lips.

"Someday," Dorothy Landis said in a coldly furious, tight voice, "someone's going to do the world a big favor and kill that bitch."

Chelsea waited in the greenroom, watching the television as Roxanne taught Joan Lundon how to paint Easter eggs and decorate *darling* little baskets with organza ribbons and real grass, even though she had no interest in such overwhelming domesticity. She knew she should be concentrating on her own upcoming interview.

When inviting Chelsea to appear on the program, the "Good Morning America" producer had explained that the focus of the five-minute segment would be Chelsea's recent magazine article profiling Melanie Tyler, an Oscar nominee who was currently dating a U.S. senator. A very popular senator rumored to have a good chance at the White House in the next election.

The idea that the outspoken, drop-dead gorgeous actress, known for her femme fatal roles, could actually end up First Lady had captured the interest of even those Americans who wouldn't be caught dead watching "Entertainment Tonight," or glancing at a tabloid newspaper.

The cover article had escalated interest in the actress while drawing additional attention to Chelsea. After the magazine first appeared on newsstands two weeks ago, she'd received calls from three publishing houses expressing interest in a book about her experiences rubbing elbows with the rich and famous.

Since graduating from college, Chelsea had been steadily making her way up the New York publishing ladder. Although she'd initially planned to follow in her father's footsteps as a serious journalist, she'd come to realize she possessed a talent for making people comfortable enough to open up and share life experiences and insights.

She also possessed a natural curiosity that had been encouraged by her journalist father.

"Curiosity steams the engine of progress, Chelsea," he'd told her time and time again whenever he'd return home from a assignment in some far-off locale. "Why do you think Columbus set out for the New World?"

"Curiosity," she had answered from her favorite perch on his jean-clad knee.

"That's right." His voice, deep and rich and booming, was a welcome change from the usual hushed quiet of their Park Avenue apartment. "And what made doctors think common old mold could lead to the miracle of penicillin?"

"Curiosity!" It had been, hands down, her favorite game. "And what made man set out to discover that the moon wasn't really made of green cheese?" she'd ask him in return.

"Curiosity!" they'd both shout, then laugh at the shared joke.

At the time, she'd had no way of knowing that the beloved game would lead her to a career writing celebrity profiles for *Vanity Fair*.

With a self-honesty that had always served her well, Chelsea realized her illustrious family name opened more than a few doors. But once they were opened, she had to work even harder to prove herself to those skeptics who believed her to be little more than just another connected society girl, playing at being a writer in between planning charity balls.

Having worked hard to get where she was, Chelsea should have been pleased with how far she'd come. After all, how many people had an opportunity to sit in the copilot's seat while John Travolta flew his jet one day to Aspen, then discuss love and life with Brad Pitt over pizza at Spago the next? Although she knew writers who'd kill to be in her position, lately she'd been feeling as if she were in a rut. Or more accurately, a treadmill.

Deciding to straighten out her life later, when she had a moment to think, Chelsea focused her attention on the monitor. As she compared Roxanne's bright spring suit to her own subdued outfit, she wished she'd stuck to her guns this morning when she'd come out of the bathroom and found Nelson laying out her clothes.

"I thought your taupe linen slacks and cream silk blouse would provide the perfect look," he'd informed her with the easy confidence of a man accustomed to getting his way. "Casual enough for morning television, while being classically elegant at the same time."

"I was planning to wear my new suit." She'd found it last week at Saks, and although it was ridiculously expensive, she'd fallen in love with it at first glance.

"The peplum is too fussy for this time of the morning. Besides, the color clashes with your hair."

"Red gives me confidence."

"That may be. But this outfit will make you *look* confident."

Swallowing her frustration, Chelsea had taken the blouse he held out to her. Lord knows, as her mother was always telling her, when God had been passing out style, she'd been at the back of the line, reporting on the event.

The fact that she could never live up to Deidre Lowell's fashion-plate standard had never bothered Chelsea. Just as she usually didn't mind allowing Nelson—whose intrinsic fashion sense rivaled her mother's—to select her outfits for important occasions.

She might look elegant, Chelsea thought now. The problem was, she didn't *feel* elegant. What she felt was irritated. And drab. Dammit, she considered with a burst of frustration, she knew she should have worn the red.

Raintree, Georgia

There was nothing finer than sex first thing in the morning, Cash considered as he engaged in some slow, postcoital caresses with the lushly endowed blonde lying beside him.

The bedroom was dark, lit only with the pale, silvery pink light of a new dawn. The sweet fragrance of Confederate jasmine wafted in through the open window, mingling with the woman's perfume and the redolent scent of lovemaking.

"Nice," he murmured as he nibbled luxuriously at her throat.

"Much, much better than nice." Melanie Tyler linked her hands around his neck and treated Cash to a long, wet kiss. "If I'd only known southern men were so good in the sack, I'd have joined the Confederacy a long time ago."

He chuckled warmly. "It takes two."

Cash liked Melanie Tyler. A lot. And for more than great sex, although, he admitted readily, compatibility in bed was always a plus. He'd met her at the Magnolia House, an inn where her movie company was staying while filming a sprawling Civil War epic. Within fifteen minutes of meeting the actress in the lobby bar, they'd been tangling the sheets in her room. The affair had been going on for a month now and both accepted that her time in Georgia was at an end.

Melanie treated sex as a man did. She enjoyed it for what it was, took what she wanted, gave what she could, and when it came time to move on, she did. With no regrets.

"Oh, hell." She leaped from the bed as if burned.

"What's the matter?"

"I almost forgot. Marty called yesterday." Marty, Cash

knew, was her agent. "That writer who interviewed me for *Vanity Fair* is going to be on "Good Morning America" today."

Cash leaned back against the headboard and enjoyed the view of Melanie fiddling with the television dial. The remote had disappeared early last night amidst the sheets. As much as he genuinely liked her, Cash could not imagine this free-spirited sex goddess living in the White House.

"You're not really going to marry that stuffed-shirt senator, are you?"

"That's for me to know and you to guess, sweetheart." She returned to the bed and snuggled up beside him as they waited through the segment where Roxanne Scarbrough was demonstrating how to prepare a proper southern Easter brunch.

The life-style demonstration ended. A commercial for a new, improved detergent was followed by another pushing the wonders of quilted toilet paper.

"How would you like to sleep in the Lincoln bedroom?" Melanie asked.

"I suppose it depends. Would I be sleeping there alone?"

She laughed. "Don't be silly."

Across the room, on the nineteen-inch television screen hidden away in an antique armoire, the commercials faded away.

When the camera focused in on a close-up of Charlie Gibson introducing the magazine writer, Cash knew he'd lost Melanie. Her sudden alertness reminded him of the way Blue, his old German shorthaired pointer, had reacted upon sniffing out a covey of quail. Looping his arm around her smooth, nude shoulders, he settled down to watch the interview.

From what Melanie had told him about the importance of this interview, Cash realized he'd formed a mental image of some hardened, thin-lipped, cynical Yankee journalist who'd seen it all and didn't like much of what she'd seen.

As the camera shifted to the young woman seated across from Charlie, Cash experienced a white-hot jolt of recognition.

Although she was as beautiful as ever, Cash thought Chelsea looked tired. And if she'd chosen those obviously expensive sedate clothes to appear older and more sophisticated, she'd failed. Because the subdued colors only called attention to the gleaming copper penny hue of her long straight hair.

Her bright eyes—the color of new money—were wide and warm; her mouth smiled easily. The way she answered Charlie's questions with brief, but thoughtful answers, revealed she'd matured. She'd also revealed a vulnerable, intelligent side of Melanie that even Cash, who prided himself on being able to read women, hadn't discovered.

"I didn't know you had a degree in economics from Johns Hopkins."

"When I first started out in Hollywood, being smart wasn't sexy." Melanie didn't take her eyes from the screen. "Hush. I want to hear what she's saying."

So did he. Chelsea Cassidy's voice was still as smooth as heated honey. He could have listened to it all morning.

All too soon, the interview was over. When Cash found himself wishing they'd thought to tape it, so he could listen to those dulcet tones again, he decided that lack of sleep and too much champagne at last night's wrap party for Melanie's film must have killed off a few too many brain cells.

"Well, what did you think?"

"She was pretty good."

She hadn't known him long, but her next words proved that she'd come to know him well. "Christ, Cash, trust your hormones to leap to attention at the sight of a beautiful woman. I was talking about what Chelsea Cassidy had to say. About *me*.''

It was not Cash's style to ignore one woman for another. Since he'd first lost his virginity in an upstairs bedroom of Fancy Porter's whorehouse, Cash had prided himself on being an attentive, thoughtful lover. Fancy had taught him a lot of things that long hot summer of his fifteenth year. But the two most valuable lessons had been that a slow hand was worth a dozen quick fucks and treating a woman as if she were the only female in the world invariably paid off big time.

Concentrating on the woman who'd warmed his bed so well and so often these past weeks, Cash pulled Melanie closer. ''You're a lot better than damn good, sugar.''

''Well, I know that.'' She pouted prettily and brushed some dark hair back from his forehead. ''And, by the way, I think Chelsea is married. Or, if not married, seriously involved. While we were doing the interview, she got a call from some guy she was living with. Nelson somebody.''

So she'd actually gone and done it, Cash thought with a burst of cold, angry derision. She'd actually married that arrogant, pompous jerk.

''Not that I imagine a little detail like marriage vows would much matter to you,'' Melanie said.

''I never sleep with married women.''

It was true. These days, anyway. Well, almost true, Cash amended as Lilabeth Yarborough came to mind. But hell, Lilabeth's husband had left the former high school cheerleader and their three kids to seek his fortune on the NASCAR racing circuit, and although they'd never actually gotten around to signing the papers to make the divorce legal, Billy Yarborough hadn't been back to Raintree for two and a half years.

"Besides, why would I want her?" He nibbled seductively at Melanie's earlobe. "When I have you?"

"Damn. I don't know what's wrong with my mind today." She was out of bed again like a rocket, scooping up last night's discarded clothes which made a path from the doorway to the bed. "I'm sorry, Cash. But I'm booked on the ten-thirty flight back to L.A."

Cash drove her the thirty miles into Savannah. After watching her disappear down the jetway he stopped at a newsstand in the terminal and bought a copy of *Vanity Fair*.

Over the intervening years, he'd managed to convince himself that those crazy six months with Chelsea had been nothing more than a particularly virulent attack of lust. He'd gotten over it. And her. He survived the uptown Yankee girl in the same way he might have survived some rare fever that having run its course, never returned.

As he sat in his Ferrari in the terminal parking lot, flipping through the glossy magazine to the article, Cash assured himself that he was only moderately interested in seeing if Chelsea had turned into as good a writer as she was a talker.

He hadn't bought the magazine because he was interested in her personally. Because he wasn't.

Not even a little bit.

The hell he wasn't.

Casa Grande, Arizona

In a Motel 6 off Interstate 10, George Waggoner lay in bed, drinking from a can of Budweiser in an attempt to take the edge off the blinding hangover he was suffering.

Since the cut-rate motel didn't feature dirty cable movies, he'd been forced to settle for network fare. As he made his way through the six-pack, he was only vaguely aware of the early morning newscast. He'd been in this motel room for most of the six weeks since his release from the prison.

The money he'd managed to stash away during seven years in the pen was almost gone, eaten up by rent, cigarettes, booze and the occasional hooker. It was time to come up with a new plan.

Which was difficult to do when his eyes felt as if they were bleeding and some shitass maniac was breaking rocks inside his head.

And then he saw her.

George blinked and rubbed his hand over his aching eyes, at first thinking she was some sort of hallucination left over from last night's binge. Like those bats in *The Lost Weekend* he'd watched on late-night television.

But no. The image flickering on the snowy television picture was unmistakable. Oh, she'd changed her hair. Her clothes may not be Kmart blue light specials anymore and her accent was a helluva lot more fluid than he remembered. But having known her intimately, George wasn't fooled. Not one damn bit.

"Roxanne Scarbrough." He barked a tobacco-roughened laugh as he watched her pour some unpronounceable French liqueur into a white bowl. "Where the hell did she come up with a name like that?"

Tossing back the rest of the beer, he climbed out of the too soft bed, retrieved his unwashed jeans from the floor, and yanked them on over his briefs. A black Harley-Davidson T-shirt followed. Then his boots.

Since the motel wasn't the kind to put out fancy writing paper for its guests, he went next door to the 7-Eleven, bought a tablet, a package of envelopes, a stamp and another six-pack. Then, on impulse, having already decided that his luck had just taken a decided turn for the better, he spent ten bucks on Powerball lotto tickets.

Not that he needed them, George told himself as he walked back to his single room. Because, hot damn if he hadn't just hit his own personal jackpot!

He opened the tablet to the first page and began to write. "Dear Cora Mae…"

Chapter Two

New York

While Chelsea knew her "Good Morning America" interview had gone well, the old feeling of dissatisfaction that haunted her too often these days returned as she arrived home.

"You were terrific," Nelson assured her. "You were clever, intelligent and beautiful." He touched a fingertip to the pearl gleaming at her earlobe. "In fact, you radiated a cool sex that reminded me a lot of Diane Sawyer."

Chelsea viewed the gleam in his eyes and guessed what was coming.

"You know," he suggested, rubbing his chin thoughtfully, "I just had an idea."

"No."

"No, what?"

"No, I do not want to become a television personality."

"Why not? The money would be more than you'll ever make at the magazine."

"In the first place, I'm a print journalist—"

"At a time when papers and magazines are folding all over the country."

She may be willing to let him choose her wardrobe. But her career was an entirely different matter. "I love writing, Nelson. And I'm good at it."

"I'll bet Diane Sawyer writes her own copy."

Chelsea shrugged and tried to ignore the headache that was threatening behind her eyes. "It's a moot point. Since I have no intention of even trying to break into an already overcrowded television market."

"If it's good enough for Barbara Walters—"

"When you go on television, suddenly *how* you look becomes every bit as important, sometimes even more so, than what you're saying. And while we're talking about Diane Sawyer, I read she received more viewer mail about cutting her hair than any story she'd ever done. You know I'm no good at things like clothes and jewelry and the latest hairstyle, Nelson—"

"Granted, you weren't gifted with a plethora of style sense." His blue gaze swept over her, approving of what he saw. "But that's what you have me for, darling. Together, we'd make one terrific team."

Looking at him looking at her gave Chelsea a very good idea of how Eliza Doolittle must have felt while undergoing Henry Higgins's intense scrutiny.

"I never thought I'd find myself wishing for the old days."

He arched a brow. "Old days?"

"Back when we were in college, and used to fight over the idea of my having a career."

Like everyone else in his family, Nelson Webster Waring didn't work. No Waring had worked for wages since great-great-grandfather Warren Waring, an old-fashioned robber baron, had made a fortune in railroads and western mining claims.

"Warings never fight. We have discussions." He smiled. "And in defense of my behavior, most young men are horribly chauvinistic. Some of us are fortunate enough to have a clever woman who insists on dragging us from our caves into the modern world."

Chelsea sighed and cast a quick, surreptitious glance at her watch. She was running late. As always, these days. "Could we discuss this later?" she suggested, even as she knew that on this issue, she would never budge. "I have a meeting at the office in thirty minutes."

"How about over lunch at the Pool Room?" he suggested, knowing the Four Seasons restaurant to be one of her favorites.

"I'm flying to Toronto to interview Sandra Bullock this afternoon," she reminded him. There were rumors of a romance with a recent costar she wanted to check out. More than that, she was interested in how the actress appeared to remain so centered as she rode the comet her acting career had become.

There had been a time when Chelsea would have braced herself for his complaint that she was working too hard. Strangely, since they'd gotten back together after an eighteen month separation—during which time she'd concentrated on establishing her career while he'd seemed determined to date every deb in the city—she'd heard not a negative word about the hours she spent away from home.

"I'll bet Diane Sawyer flies first-class," he pointed out.

Giving him points for tenacity, Chelsea laughed. "Good try. But the flight's not that long. And, since I'll be writing the entire time, I wouldn't notice the difference anyway."

She scooped up the duffel bag she used as a purse. And, more importantly, with her hectic schedule, as an office in a bag. She kept it filled with pencils, notepads, a mini tape recorder for interviews, a toothbrush, makeup, tampons, and an extra pair of panty hose. So long as she kept the bag with her, she could be on a plane to anywhere within minutes. Chelsea would have felt naked without it.

She gave him a quick kiss. "Wish me luck."

"You know I do."

Although his tone was pleasant and matched his winning smile, Chelsea knew that the subject was far from closed. Once again she had a fleeting wish for those days when the only thing they argued about was whether she *would* work.

More and more lately, it seemed that not only was Nelson determined to act as her advisor and manager, he was also even more ambitious when it came to her career than she was.

As she sat in the back of the cab crawling through the crush of morning traffic, Chelsea decided that one of their problems was that Nelson had no career of his own to focus on. Perhaps, if she broached the subject carefully, she could make him see that by going to work, he'd be more personally fulfilled.

Today was Thursday. They had a long weekend ahead of them after she returned from Toronto. Plenty of time for an overdue, calm discussion. About her work, his lack of work, and where, exactly, their relationship was going.

Perhaps, she thought with a renewed burst of her typical enthusiasm, Sunday morning she'd make Nelson French toast. The fancy kind, with Grand Marnier, that Roxanne Scarbrough had demonstrated for Joan Lundon on the show.

Not to soften him up. But to show him how much she cared. How much she wanted things to work out.

Feeling reassured, Chelsea pulled a notepad out of her

bag and began composing a list of questions for her interview with the woman Hollywood insiders were touting as
the new Julia Roberts.

"I have your tickets," Heather Van Pelt said, handing
Chelsea an envelope as she exited the editorial meeting.
"Your boarding pass is attached—you're on the aisle, in the
first row of first class. A driver and car will be waiting for
you as soon as you clear customs, and I've upgraded your
room at the Four Seasons to a suite.

"I thought it would give you more room to work," she
continued as she easily kept up with Chelsea's dash toward
the bank of elevators. The meeting had run long; if Chelsea
didn't leave now, she'd miss her plane.

"Did you clear the extra expenses with accounting?"
Chelsea asked as she dug through her bag and pulled out
the roll of antacids she was never without these days. Although the magazine had generous travel allowances, she
wasn't accustomed to a suite for overnight turnaround trips
like this one.

"Of course." Heather's smile was calm and self-
confident, befitting a young woman who'd grown up in the
lap of luxury in Greenwich, Connecticut. "At first they
weren't all that enthusiastic about the idea. But I can be
very convincing when I put my mind to it."

Chelsea had not a single doubt of that. From what she'd
seen, Heather's talent for persuasion rivaled Chelsea's
mother's. Since being hired after her graduation last June
from Bennington, she'd made herself indispensable, even
volunteering for personal errands, which made Chelsea feel
a bit guilty. But not so guilty that she'd turn down any
assistance that came her way.

"You really are a wonder," she said with honest appreciation. "If things go well, I may actually manage to get
another chapter done on my novel." She'd been slogging

away at the suspense story centered around the murder of a thoroughly unlikable movie star for the past two years; trying to squeeze time in between her hectic work schedule and her on again, off again, and now on again relationship with Nelson.

"That's what I was thinking," Heather said with another of those smiles that was as smooth as her sleek blond hair.

Although the job of editorial assistant paid starvation wages, Heather always managed to look as if she'd stepped right out of the pages of *Town and Country* magazine. Once, after Liz Smith had shown up at the office for a lunch date with Chelsea, the gossip columnist had declared that the new editorial assistant was *Vanity Fair*'s answer to Princess Di.

The difference, Chelsea had considered at the time, was that Heather Van Pelt possessed far more self-confidence than the most celebrated member of Britain's royal family. She was also more ambitious. Chelsea knew Heather wanted her job. Since she didn't have any intention of giving it up anytime soon, such single-minded zeal didn't disturb her. Especially when it resulted in upgraded plane tickets and hotel reservations.

Raintree

Amidst the Camelot environs of her lushly wooded landscape, Roxanne Scarbrough sat in the library of her Tudor-style home leafing through the mail her assistant Dorothy Landis had left on her Louis Quatorze desk. On the corner of the desk, an electric fan was ineffectually attempting to stir the moisture-laden air.

Roxanne was not happy. Trust the air conditioner to choose today of all days to give out! The temperature outside was unseasonably warm for April. Although it was not

yet noon, a thick, wet heat had seeped into the house
through the window screens, permeating everything, making
her sweat.

No. Ladies never sweat, she reminded herself with a brisk
mental shake. As moisture beaded on her forehead and between the cleft of her breasts, she remembered telling Oprah
about her southern grandmother's stern edict that horses
sweat, men perspired and ladies glistened.

Of course, beloved old Maw Maw, with her infinite
wealth of southern aphorisms, was, like so much of Roxanne's outwardly perfect life, a fictional invention. Still, the
stories she'd spun during that afternoon taping had added a
charming southern warmth to the interview.

The bundled-up Yankee audience, still shivering from the
Chicago blizzard raging outside Harpo Studios, had, as always, eaten it up, and her clipping service subsequently re-
ported that the "glisten" quote had appeared in sixty-five
papers around the country over the next week.

It wasn't always easy being Roxanne Scarbrough. But,
she considered with a self-satisfied smile, no one did it better.

The breeze from the fan stirred the fragrance of potpourri
she'd created from pink freesia and Lady Banks roses growing in the formal gardens.

When she'd first planted the garden, several members of
the Raintree garden club had warned her against including
the old-fashioned rose bushes. Local legend prevailed that
when a Lady Banks got old enough to shade your grave,
you'd die. Not the least bit superstitious, Roxanne had ignored the caution. But knowing a good story when she heard
one, she'd included the myth in her latest life-style book,
Strolling Through Grandmother's Southern Garden.

She skimmed a fax she'd received this morning from her
agent regarding Chelsea Cassidy. Although at first glance,

she'd considered the writer to be a definite lightweight, the deft way she'd handled her interview and the *Vanity Fair* article Roxanne had read on the flight back from New York proved that appearances were definitely deceiving.

Roxanne had no concerns about the writer rejecting the proposal her agent was going to make. People did not say no to Roxanne Scarbrough.

Especially men, she considered with a slow smile ripe with feminine intent as she glanced over at the mantel clock. She should have left a half hour ago for her luncheon engagement. Not that she was in any particular hurry. It was, after all, a lady's prerogative to keep a gentleman waiting.

However, in this case, it would be a blessed relief to leave the house. The stifling humidity clogged Roxanne's lungs, making her feel as if she were trying to breathe underwater. Her dress—a silk wash of watercolor flowers with a dangerously plunging neckline, selected specifically for today's lunch with Cash Beaudine—already seemed too hot and heavy against her heated skin.

Deciding to open one more piece of mail, she picked up a sterling silver letter opener in the Francis I pattern she claimed she'd inherited from her unfortunately deceased mother, and slit open a cheap dimestore envelope marked Personal that had been forwarded from the staff of "Good Morning America." Obviously another piece of fan mail. Considering the inferior stationery, this was a person in dire need of life-style training.

The paper was badly ink stained, as if the letter had been written with one of those horrid plastic ballpoint pens one saw everywhere these days. As her eyes skimmed down the wrinkled page, Roxanne's heart clenched. The scrawled handwriting was all too familiar.

"Dear Cora Mae..."

She pressed a beringed hand against the front of her silk

dress and wondered if she could be having a heart attack. Black spots danced like whirling demons in front of her eyes.

Belying the fictitious Maw Maw's now famous axiom, it was, indeed, sweat that puddled beneath Roxanne's armpits and slithered wetly down her sides.

Cash was suffocating. The restaurant Roxanne Scarbrough had chosen for their luncheon meeting was one of those precious southern tearooms that had sprung up in plantation mansions all over the state, catering to a female clientele who preferred to pretend that William Tecumseh Sherman—or, as he was known around these parts, "that low-down Yankee pyromaniac"—had never set a booted foot in Confederate Georgia. Decorated in shades of peach and mint green, it boasted translucent china, sterling cutlery, glittering crystal, hanging plants and lace-covered windows. He'd been at the tearoom for nearly an hour. During which time Roxanne had pulled out all the stops in her attempt to convince him that he was the only man in Georgia, indeed, on the planet, capable of restoring her antebellum plantation house.

Located just outside Raintree, on the road to Savannah, if the woman could be believed, the mansion was a combination of Twelve Oaks and Tara, with a little Xanadu's pleasure palace thrown in for good measure. To demonstrate she'd done her homework, she'd also brought along an attaché case of engineering reports, proclaiming the home to be structurally sound.

Roxanne tried tempting him with fame assuring him that the project would end up featured in yet another of her bestselling books.

"You've no idea how many people buy these books," she stressed over salads of spinach, bay shrimp, watercress and artichoke hearts. There was not a single offering of red meat on the menu. "People with quality who need my guidance when it comes to creating a stylish ambiance."

She shared a conspiratorial smile. "And just think, when they read that you're the man I've selected to create my dream home, why, your phone will be ringing off the hook."

There'd been a time, not so long ago, when Cash might have found the idea enticing. But no longer. Not after his years in San Francisco.

"As attractive an idea as that might be," he said mildly, "I currently have about as much work as I can handle." His own smile did not reach his eyes. "Some people, it appears, have heard of me without the media hype."

"Well, of course they have," Roxanne said quickly. Switching gears with an alacrity that Cash found impressive, she appealed again to his ego. "But if you were to work for me—"

"With," he interjected.

She arched a perfectly shaped eyebrow. "Excuse me?"

"*If* I were to agree to do the job, which I'm not saying I am," he drawled, "I'd be working *with* you, not *for* you. It would be a joint project, based on your vision, but I'd insist on input on all decisions."

"Oh." Cash was not all that surprised by the way she managed to frown without causing a single line in her forehead or her lips. Southern women had such frowns down to a science. "I'm not accustomed to collaborating."

"I can understand that." He braced both elbows on the table and eyed her over his linked fingers. "However, remodeling a house is not exactly the same as baking petit fours or creating gilded mistletoe Christmas wreaths. It's a major construction project, often more difficult than the

original work. It also requires the art of compromise between architect and home owner.''

"Compromise.'' Her sigh caused her breasts to rise and
fall beneath the flowered silk dress. Cash watched her mull-
ing the idea over and decided it was not something she was
accustomed to doing. "I could live with that,'' she decided
after a long pause. "So long as I had the last word.''

"Unless it involved structural integrity.'' The words were
no sooner out of his mouth than he realized she'd obviously
take them as encouragement. "Then the decision would be
mine.''

"Agreed.'' She sat back in the velvet chair and crossed
her legs with a satisfied swish of silk on silk. "So, when
would you like to look at the house?''

"I haven't said I'd take the job,'' Cash reminded her.

"If you'd just look at Belle Terre, you might be more
amenable. It's horribly run down at the moment. I swear, it
looks as if Sherman's entire army had just finished sacking
it. But I'm sure an artistic man such as yourself—'' her
voice lowered, thickening to molasses "—will be able to
see its true potential.''

She was definitely not a lady accustomed to hearing the
word *no*. Cash had known women a lot like Roxanne Scarbrough in San Francisco, but most of them had been society
wives, married to wealthy, usually much older men. Men
more interested in making money than paying attention to
their blond and bored trophy wives.

Which was where he'd come in. The same women who'd
married for money and ended up being corporate widows,
were often desperate for male companionship. Being male
and available, Cash had done his best to oblige them.

Until one night when he'd been forced to climb out the
bedroom window of a Pacific Heights mansion because his
current lover's stockbroker husband had arrived home early.

Shortly after that, realizing he was in danger of becoming a cliché, he'd resigned his partnership at the Montgomery Street firm and returned home to that very same place he'd worked like hell to escape.

Growing up on the wrong side of the tracks, he'd found Raintree creatively and personally stifling. Every conversation began with the opening line, "Who are your people?"

The answer to that had routinely kept him barred from country club dances and fraternity mixers. In a part of the country where family roots tended to predate the Revolution, having a sharecropper for a daddy and a mama who'd come from a Blue Ridge family known primarily for the high quality of their bootleg whiskey, kept him out of the social register.

His daddy had died when Cash was thirteen. Although his mother had done her best to look after them, money had become even harder to come by, which is how he'd ended up doing odd jobs at Fancy's whorehouse on the outskirts of town.

It was there Cash had received a first-class education on how to sexually please a woman. Such insight had allowed him to coax more than his share of fascinated, daring debs into the back seat of his black Trans Am. The same belles whose fathers would have bolted the door and gotten out the shotgun if they knew a renegade like him was sniffing around their precious baby daughters.

Chelsea Cassidy had been one of those girls. He'd been thinking a lot about her since seeing her on that television program. Oh, Chelsea's roots were deep in the rocky soil of New England, instead of the rich loam of the South, but she'd grown up pampered and privileged, and sexually repressed. It had, of course, taken no time at all to break down her sexual barriers. But the social parapets had proven a different story. Their entire relationship, if it could have even been called a *relationship* had been a clandestine one, consisting of quick, frantic couplings like the one in the broom closet of the country club, or more leisurely love-making in his cramped rented room.

But she'd never—not once—allowed herself to be seen in public with her secret lover. And when the time came to choose a lifelong partner, it sounded as if she'd actually ended up with that self-centered prig she'd been unofficially engaged to since childhood.

"Mr. Beaudine?"

Roxanne's annoyed tone brought Cash back to the subject at hand.

"I'm sorry." He managed a smile much friendlier than his mood. "I was just thinking about your offer."

Her eyes swept over his face. "I do hope your expression isn't a true indication of your thoughts."

"Not exactly."

Forcing his mind back to business, Cash reminded himself that he'd always been fascinated by old houses. He loved their architectural individuality—so different from the cookie-cutter homes found in even new multimillion dollar neighborhoods. He was intrigued by their history and believed that, like dowager queens, even the oldest, most lived-in home enjoyed a certain inimitable dignity.

A man easily bored, he also enjoyed challenges. And from the way Roxanne had described the condition of her dream house, he suspected that the proposed remodeling project could provide the challenge of a lifetime.

"I suppose it wouldn't hurt to look at the house."

"You'll love it," she promised.

Her eyes glittered with a satisfaction she didn't bother to conceal. And something else. Something Cash recognized as a feminine interest he had no intention of encouraging. She leaned forward, giving him an enticing glimpse of cleavage and placed a hand on his arm in a way that confirmed his instincts.

"So, when would you like me to give you the grand tour?"

"No time like the present, I suppose," he decided. "As it happens, I've got the rest of the afternoon free."

Her lips, painted a bright pink that had left a smudge around her teacup, turned upward in a satisfied smile that suggested she'd never expected any other outcome. "How perfect. I can't wait to show you all my ideas."

"It's a little early for that. First I have to determine whether or not I think the house is salvageable. And whether I find it enough of an artistic challenge."

"I don't believe the second of your concerns is going to be a problem."

"Why don't we let me be the judge of that?"

There was a tug of war going on. As surely as if they'd suddenly begun pulling at opposite ends of the cream-hued damask tablecloth. As she viewed the steely determination in his dark eyes, Roxanne considered yet again that this man could prove a challenge.

At a time when she definitely didn't need any more problems.

Still, she'd noticed how the young restaurant hostess kept looking at Cash and asking him if everything was all right. And after the past hour in close proximity to his dangerous masculinity that was proving overwhelming in such feminine surroundings, she found herself looking forward to the sexual perks of working intimately with this man.

"You're going to love Belle Terre," she assured him again, rising with a lithe grace that was the product of years of practice. "It's marvelous. Even without the ghost."

Cash was not surprised the house came with a resident

ghost. It was de rigueur for homes of its era in this part of the country to boast of at least one.

Yet as he left the restaurant with Roxanne Scarbrough, passing the table occupied by a young woman whose flaming hair reminded him of Chelsea, it crossed Cash's mind that he already had one too many ghosts in his life.

Chapter Three

New York

"So, how was Toronto?" Mary Lou Wilson asked.

"I'm sure it was delightful." Chelsea's irritated expression said otherwise. "All I saw of it was the airport and the hotel. I was hoping to interview Sandra on location, but a stupid rainstorm shut down shooting."

The same rainstorm, it seemed had followed her home. She scowled out the floor-to-ceiling windows of her agent's Madison Avenue office and pretended interest in the Manhattan skyline. An icy spring rain streaked down the tinted glass.

While working with the actress's publicity people to move the interview to Chelsea's suite, it had crossed her mind that she should have asked the overly efficient Heather to arrange for the sun to shine.

"I'm sorry it didn't turn out well."

Chelsea shrugged. "It was a good interview. I just wanted

more. But cutting things short did allow me more time to work on my book.''

Mary Lou smiled at her client. ''Now that is good news. And speaking of good news,'' she segued smoothly into the reason for having called Chelsea to her office, ''it appears that interview with Charlie Gibson may just change your life.''

Chelsea opened her mouth to point out that her life was just dandy, thank you. But of course, that wasn't exactly the truth. She wasn't happy, dammit. And, despite her growing success—success that Heather would undoubtedly be willing to sell dear old Grandmother Van Pelt to achieve—she hadn't been for a long time. Once again she felt as if she were spending her life on a treadmill.

No, Chelsea considered, she felt more like Lucille Ball in that old chocolate factory episode. The more she achieved, the faster and faster she needed to work to stay ahead.

''All right,'' she said when her agent paused for an unnecessarily lengthy time, ''I'll bite. What are you talking about?''

''I had an interesting offer for you after the interview aired.''

Chelsea thought about Nelson's ongoing argument that she belonged on television. ''If it's from the network, suggesting I replace Joan Lundon, tell them the answer's no.''

''Actually, the call was from Roxanne Scarbrough.''

That was a surprise. ''What in the world could America's Diva of Domesticity want with me?''

''She's looking for a biographer.''

''No way.'' Chelsea folded her arms across the front of her silk jacket. In defiance of the weather, her suit was a splash of bright, sunshine yellow. ''I'd rather swim naked in the East River with a bunch of killer sharks than work with that woman.''

Mary Lou's eyes narrowed, revealing surprise at Chelsea's adamant refusal. "Am I missing something here?"

"Let's just say that Roxanne Scarbrough and I had a slight personality clash and leave it at that." Actually, it had been dislike at first sight—as clear and strong as one hundred proof grain alcohol.

"Roxanne thinks the world of you."

Chelsea seriously doubted that Roxanne thought of anyone but herself. It also did not escape her notice that her agent and Roxanne Scarbrough seemed to be on a first-name basis.

"Tell me you're not that Steel Magnolia from hell's agent."

It was no secret that Mary Lou Wilson had migrated to Manhattan from somewhere in the deep South. Indeed, the agent, while outwardly appearing the epitome of New York chic, went out of her way to cultivate her image as a publishing outsider. Chelsea had noticed, on more than one occasion, that the more prolonged the contract negotiations, the more Mary Lou's voice took on a sultry slow cadence of the South, causing more than one misguided editor to let down her guard. Which with Mary Lou, Chelsea reminded herself now, was *always* a mistake.

"As it happens, Roxanne is one of my oldest clients," Mary Lou confirmed.

"And one of the most profitable, too, I'll bet," Chelsea muttered.

She glanced around the professionally decorated office, seeing it with new eyes, now that she realized the attractive furnishings she'd always admired had undoubtedly been selected by the most vicious mouth in the South.

"You know I never discuss other clients' earnings," Mary Lou said mildly.

"I can't believe you can even stand to be in the same

room with that woman.'' Chelsea studied the exquisite Ming vase on its ebony pedestal she'd always admired and wondered if it had been purchased with Mary Lou's fifteen percent of Roxanne Scarbrough's latest bestselling cookbook, *Just Desserts.*

''Roxanne is a bit of a challenge from time to time,'' Mary Lou admitted with what Chelsea decided had to be the understatement of the millennium. ''But she's garnered the major percentage of the life-style market, and her fans love her.''

It crossed Chelsea's mind that were she to write the truth about the beloved life-style maven, all those fans would disappear like Roxanne's famous beer-battered popcorn shrimp at a Super Bowl party.

Although she'd throw herself off the top of the Empire State Building before admitting it, she'd actually tried the recipe at her last party and earned raves from all the guests. Even Nelson, who considered himself a gourmand, had been impressed.

''Why doesn't she have her usual cowriter do the book?''

''Glenda Walker is excellent at interpreting Roxanne's creative vision to the written word. But something like an autobiography is, quite honestly, beyond her talents.''

''You know I don't want to ghostwrite.'' And even if she did, Roxanne Scarbrough would not be on the top of her list of potential subjects.

''Roxanne has already agreed to give you coauthor credit.''

''Which still means she'd get fifty percent of a book I wrote.'' Fifty percent less Mary Lou's agency percentage of both their earnings, Chelsea amended, growing more and more uncomfortable with this entire situation.

''Actually, Roxanne suggested an eighty-twenty split. With you getting the larger share.''

"I don't get it." Chelsea blinked. Her fingernails drummed a rapid staccato on the wooden arms of the cream suede chair as she tried to figure out Roxanne Scarbrough's angle. From what she'd witnessed in the greenroom, generosity was not the woman's strong point. "What's the catch?"

Mary Lou frowned. "You and I have a seven-year relationship." There was an unfamiliar edge to her usually smoothly modulated drawl. "Surely you aren't implying I'd suggest anything that wouldn't prove beneficial to your career?"

Chelsea winced inwardly. *Terrific career move, insulting your agent.* "I'm sorry. Of course I'd never imply any such thing."

Her recent restlessness made it impossible for her to think while sitting still. She stood up and began to pace, her short pleated skirt swirling around her thighs.

"It's just that I can't figure out why Roxanne would want me to work with her on her autobiography."

"That's simple. Thanks to the Melanie Tyler interview, you're currently the hottest young writer in town. She also read your *Vanity Fair* article and decided that you're very good at what you do."

"I suppose I should be flattered," Chelsea said reluctantly, pausing in front of the Ming vase. It really was lovely.

"This isn't about flattery. It's about money. As I told Roxanne, you're got a helluva career ahead of you. It certainly wouldn't hurt her to hitch her already successful wagon to your rising star."

"Even if I were a reincarnation of Truman Capote, why would she be willing to give up such a large portion of potential earnings?"

"That's simple." Mary Lou folded her hands on the top

of her glossy desk. Her smile reminded Chelsea of a Chesh-
ire cat. "She has this idea—and by the way, I agree—that
the book, like her consultant agreement with the Mega-Mart
stores, will serve as a marketing tool for all her other projects."

Eventually making her far more profit than royalties from
her autobiography would ever earn, Chelsea considered.

"That makes sense."

"Although she's extremely talented, Roxanne's true genius has always been marketing," Mary Lou agreed.

In spite of herself, Chelsea was tempted. It certainly
would gain her a great deal of international exposure, since
Roxanne Scarbrough was a household name all over the
world. But still, the idea of working with the unpleasant
woman was less than appealing.

On the other hand, eighty percent of a guaranteed bestseller was nothing to sneeze at.

"Her last three books stayed at the top of the *Times* list
for six months," Mary Lou said.

"The offer is tempting," Chelsea admitted reluctantly.

"It could catapult you into superstar ranks. Then, of
course, there would be the additional audience you'd pick
up. An audience that would provide a built-in market for
your novel. When you get it finished."

"Hopefully in this lifetime," Chelsea muttered. Heaven
help her, she could feel herself being drawn to the bait.
Which wasn't all that surprising, since she could probably
name five writers off the top of her head who'd push a rival
beneath a crosstown bus for the opportunity she was being
offered. But still…working with Roxanne Scarbrough?

As much as she liked and respected Mary Lou, Chelsea
reminded herself that the agent could be devious. Especially
when working to clinch a deal. Refusing to be steamrollered
into anything, she lifted her chin in a stubborn angle.

"I'll have to think about it."

"Of course." Mary Lou sat back in her chair and gave Chelsea a pleased, satisfied smile. "And while you're thinking, why don't you get out of this terrible weather?"

"Good idea. Why don't you call my editor and have her assign me an article about snorkeling in the Bahamas."

"Actually, I had somewhere closer in mind. Roxanne thought you might want an opportunity to speak with her personally, at her home in Georgia, before coming to a decision. I agreed it was a good idea. She would, of course, pay all your travel expenses."

Promising to give Mary Lou an answer by the end of the week, Chelsea left the office. As she dashed through the cold rain toward the battered yellow cab the doorman had hailed for her, Chelsea couldn't deny that the idea of a few days spent lying poolside in a warm southern sun sounded more than a little appealing.

It would also allow her a breather from her recent nonstop schedule. It would force a time-out in her ongoing argument with Nelson. Just the memory of how she'd spent the weekend had her digging in her bag for her roll of antacids.

Despite the French toast—which unsurprisingly, hadn't turned out nearly as well as when Roxanne had prepared it for Joan Lundon—despite the fact that she'd told him time and time again that she was a print journalist, he'd spent the entire two days pushing the idea of her "branching out" into television.

As she chewed the chalky tablets she seemed to be living on these days, it crossed Chelsea's mind that the concentration required by ghostwriting Roxanne Scarbrough's biography could take her mind off her problems.

While giving her a whole set of new ones, Chelsea considered as Roxanne's furious eyes and pursed lips came to mind.

* * *

Raintree

It was the house that cotton built. Constructed in 1837, prior to the Civil War, it was the same Greek Revival style made familiar the world over by the most famous movie ever made about the South. Twenty-two Doric columns—three feet in circumference and forty feet high, Cash estimated—surrounded the two-story house, eight in front, and seven on either side.

"The walls are eighteen inches thick." Roxanne ran her hand over the exterior facing. "And the bricks were made right here on the property."

"By slave labor."

She shot him a surprised, faintly censorious look. "That wasn't unusual for the time."

"Unfortunately, you're right." Deciding that if he was going to allow political correctness to enter into his business decisions—especially in this part of the country—he'd be broke before the end of the year, Cash put aside his discomfort with how the house had been constructed.

"Your porch is crumbling." He put a booted foot on one of the boards, crushing it like an eggshell. "It's about to cave in."

"So we'll replace it. Surely that shouldn't be so difficult."

"No. But it's the first thing that will have to be done, or workers won't be able to get into the place safely."

"I hadn't thought of that." She rewarded him with an admiring look. "How clever of you."

"Not clever. I'm just not wild about the idea of having some plasterer break his neck."

Before risking the porch, he spent a long time examining the foundation. It appeared to be solid. And the cracks could be easily fixed.

"I realize you've already had an engineering report," he said, looking up at the massive columns. "And the foundation certainly looks secure. But since these are supporting the roof, I'll want them professionally inspected, as well."

"I certainly don't want the roof caving in during my gala open house ball," she agreed.

He had to give her credit for having a vivid imagination. The place, which was even more a challenge than he'd expected, reminded him of the house the Addams family might live in were they to decide to relocate to the old South. But she was already planning balls. Which figured. Balls were a traditional southern event—like high school Friday night football—planned with all the attention that the Joint Chiefs of Staff gave to planning an invasion. And with as much hoopla and pageantry as a New Orleans Mardi Gras.

"The house has a marvelous history," she told him as she followed him through the rooms. Lacy spider webs hung in all the corners, draped over fireplace mantels. "It was built by a young man, Edwin Blount, a distant cousin to Eugenia Blount Lamar."

The name had been dropped as if he were expected to know it. He didn't.

"Eugenia was a president-general of the Daughters of the Confederacy," she explained at his politely blank look.

"Ah." He nodded. "That Blount."

Her eyes narrowed momentarily, as if suspecting she'd heard a tinge of sarcasm in his mild tone. Obviously deciding she'd imagined it, she went on with her story.

"They were to be married in the gardens out back. But the bride ran off with her daddy's cotton broker on the day of the wedding. Poor Edwin." She sighed dramatically. "It was a terrible scandal."

"I can imagine." Cash's mutinous mind conjured up another image of Chelsea, seated behind him on his Harley, escaping from her cousin's wedding.

It had been their last night together. And their hottest. He could remember every single detail except how many times she'd come. They'd both lost track long before dawn. Before he'd taken her back to her safe, traditional, old-money life. And her stiff-necked boyfriend.

What would have happened, Cash wondered, if she'd agreed to go to San Francisco with him that night? Would they have gotten married? Would he have become successful—and in turn, rich enough—to turn his back on the career he'd sought with such single-minded determination, to return home to his roots?

Hell. Reminding himself that Sunday morning quarterbacking was an amateur sport, and that thinking about might have beens was for losers, Cash returned his thoughts back to Roxanne's running monologue.

"Of course the poor man couldn't possibly live in the house," she was saying. "Not after having received such a crushing emotional blow. Not to mention such a public humiliation."

As he ran his fingers through the dust coating a nearby window, Cash murmured something that could have been an agreement.

"So he sold it to Ezekial Berry. Who was, of course, a descendant of the Virginia Berrys of Atlanta. His wife, Jane, was one of the Chattahoochee Valley Fitzgeralds. She was pregnant with their first child at the time."

There was simply no escaping it. *Who are your people?* Cash decided that the old European aristocracy had nothing on southerners when it came to tracking ancestral bloodlines.

He wondered how anxious Roxanne Scarbrough would be to work with him if she knew his background. "The window glass has lost a lot of glazing,'' he said. "But the majority of it, at least on this floor, seems in good shape.''

"Well, that's good news.''

"It could be all you're going to get.'' He crossed the room. "The plaster's a mess.'' He picked at the cracked and broken wall. "See this?'' He plucked out some black fibers and handed them to her.

"They feel a bit like paint brush bristles.''

"Close. It's hair. Curried from the backs of horses or hogs undoubtedly raised on the plantation. Builders used it to help hold the plaster together.''

"How ingenious.''

"It's also expensive to replace.''

"Surely they don't use hog hair any longer?''

"No. Although, the technique's the same, with plaster or strands of Fiberglas in place of the hair. But a good plaster man is hard to find these days. And when you can find one, he doesn't come cheap.''

She tossed the black hairs onto the scarred wooden floor. "I told you, Mr. Beaudine, money is no object.''

Her words reminded Cash that he'd definitely come home to a new South. A booming South. A South on the rise. And riding that tide of economic prosperity were new people, creating new jobs, making new money. And spending it with an enthusiasm that made the old southern aristocracy sit up and take notice.

"Now where have I heard that, before?'' he murmured as he squatted down and frowned at the ominous trail of sawdust running along the baseboard.

"In this case it's the truth,'' she snapped, abandoning her spun sugar demeanor. "This home is my pièce de résistance. It's the culmination of my life's work. Everything I've done, everything I've struggled for, ends here. There will be,'' she

repeated firmly, her eyes as hard as stones, her lips pulled
into a thin line, "no expense spared to do this correctly."

Cash couldn't help being impressed with her resolve. But
he was still not entirely convinced. As they finished the tour
of the house, risking the treacherous stairs to examine the
second floor, he wondered if she realized that this project
was a helluva long way from creating the ultimate Easter
basket.

"That's another thing." He leaned against the crumbling
wall of the grand entry hall, folded his arms across his chest
and looked down at her. "You're going to have·to decide
whether you want to renovate Belle Terre. Or restore it."

"Renovate, restore, what's the difference?" She was
clearly growing impatient at his unwillingness to embrace
her latest enterprise.

"There's a big difference." As her tone grew more harsh,
he purposely kept his mild. "A restoration is a pure as possible replication of a home to its original state. While a
renovation is exactly that—rebuilding to update the home
with modern conveniences, to make it new again. And if
authenticity has to fall by the wayside, too bad."

Her frown revealed that she'd not exactly thought this
little dilemma through. Cash wasn't surprised. He'd discovered that most people had a rather serendipitous view of
turning some crumbling ruin into an exact replica of its former glory, while also wanting to toss in a few Jacuzzi tubs,
microwave ovens and media walls for comfort and conve-
nience.

"As a purist, I believe I'd favor restoration." Her gaze
slowly circled the high ceilings and hand-carved moldings.
"However, having seen the bathrooms, I have to admit that
there's a great deal to be said for renovation."

Her eyes, which revealed intelligence and resolve along
with the first sign of concern Cash had witnessed, met his.

"I don't suppose we could combine the two?" she asked hopefully.

"That's usually the way it's done."

Her relief was palpable. "Then that's what we'll do. This project is incredibly important to me, Mr. Beaudine. I have a film crew on hand to document the reconstruction. I'm also in the process of negotiating with a writer, Chelsea Cassidy, to collaborate on my autobiography, which, will, of course, include the restoration of Belle Terre."

"Chelsea Cassidy is your biographer?" Having grown up having to fight for everything he'd accomplished, Cash had never been a big believer in fate. The idea of Chelsea coming to Raintree to ghostwrite Roxanne Scarbrough's life story had him reconsidering.

"You know Ms. Cassidy?"

"I read her article in this month's *Vanity Fair*."

It had managed to be interesting, amusing and insightful. All at the same time. Which had been a surprise. He'd known that Chelsea was intelligent. And ambitious. But since their relationship hadn't included much conversation, he'd failed to realize she was extremely talented outside the bedroom.

"Considering her lightweight subject matter, the article was quite entertaining," Roxanne sniffed. "She does, however, happen to be the most sought after writer in her field. It's quite a coup that she's agreed to write my life story."

Roxanne failed to even consider the possibility that Chelsea might refuse the assignment.

"Won't it be difficult to collaborate?" Cash asked. "With her living in New York and you here in Raintree?"

One thing he didn't want to do was to agree to take on such a Herculean restoration project only to discover that the owner of the house was spending most of her time in the

Big Apple instead of where she belonged—on the job site making decisions.

"I'm sure it would be, if that's the way we were working," Roxanne agreed. "However, I intend for Ms. Cassidy to move into my house with me. That way, I can continue to oversee the restoration of Belle Terre and she can get a true feel for who I am. And how I work."

It was the truth, so far as it went. The one part of her answer that was an out-and-out lie was the idea that anyone would learn the truth about who she really was.

That idea brought back George Waggoner's letter. And caused another bubble of icy panic.

"We should discuss my fees," Cash said. "I'm not inexpensive."

"I didn't expect you to be. I demand the best, Mr. Beaudine. And am willing to pay for it. I was also told by your other clients that you usually work on an hourly basis, rather than a flat fee."

So she'd checked him out. That wasn't so surprising, Cash decided. It also revealed that she had a sensible head on those silk-clad shoulders. Since his return to Georgia, he'd had more than one prospective customer want to hire him simply because of his illustrious reputation.

And then there were always those lonely wives who were more than willing to have their husbands pay to knock down walls and change roof lines while they received a little personal fix up in the bedroom.

Those jobs Cash had steadfastly refused.

"Flat fees are easier to calculate with new construction because there aren't so many surprises. With renovations, hourly fees seem to work best. Another way we can do it, since we're probably going to exceed whatever schedule we come up with by several weeks in a project this big, is for me to bill you twenty percent of the total construction costs.''

"I believe I prefer that last option," she mused. "However, we'd have to negotiate the payment schedule."

"Of course."

"And what extras you intend to bill for. Such as which of us pays for inspections, blueprints, telephone calls, fax charges and such."

"You've done your homework."

"Of course. I didn't reach the heights I've reached by being foolish about money, Mr. Beaudine."

Cash nodded. "I'm beginning to understand that, Miz Scarbrough."

"Then do we have an agreement?"

He glanced around the house, thought about the challenge it represented and knew that it could be a pile of crumbling bricks covered with Spanish moss and kudzu vines and he'd have no choice but to take it on, now that Chelsea was part of the picture.

"If we can work out the details," he said, not wanting to let Roxanne think she could win the upper hand that easily.

She waved off his qualification. The diamonds adorning her fingers and wrists glistened like ice in the late afternoon sun streaming through windows in need of reglazing. "I'm sure there'll be no problem." She held out her hand. "Shall we shake on agreeing to come to an agreement, at least?"

Cash took her outstretched hand. "Looks like you've just hired yourself an architect."

Arizona

George Waggoner sat in the seat of the Greyhound bus speeding across the Sonoran Desert, stared blearily out the window and decided that this had to be the shit ugliest country he'd ever seen. It was all dirt. And rocks. Hell, it reminded him of somethin' a tom cat would crap in.

"And on the eighth day, God looked down, slapped his forehead and said, hot damn, I finally found the place to put the world's litter box."

Enjoying his little joke, he chuckled, which in turn drew a nervous smile from the young woman sitting across the aisle from him. George glared back.

Another goddamn slant-eye. Just like the one behind him. And the wrinkled up, yellow-skinned old bitch in front of him. Christ, the entire country was being overrun with the chinks, wetbacks and rag heads. Pretty soon there wouldn't be any room left for the real Americans. He took a slug from the bottle of rotgut whiskey he had wrapped in a paper bag and waited for the kick.

They weren't like the niggers back home, either. Back in Georgia, blacks with any brains at all could take one look at him and know that it was better just to stay the hell out of his way.

But these assholes were different. They were pushy. All the time crowding in where they didn't belong, talkin' their gibberish about Christ knew what.

Hell. It was bad enough that the government didn't do anything about keeping them out. Personally, if he was the president, he'd go on television and declare a national hunting day on immigrants. Make a bundle off sellin' the hunting tags that would pay off the national debt, and let good old boys like George Waggoner take care of the problem.

And not just a day, he decided. Hell, just pass a constitutional amendment making it open season on everyone who wasn't a red-blooded American. That'd be a guaran-goddam-teed way to solve the problem.

He took another pull from the bottle. Then pointed his

index finger at the woman across the aisle, aimed and pulled the trigger. In his mind's eye, he received a certain satisfaction from imagining that sloped head explode like an overripe crenshaw melon dropped onto the sidewalk from the top of the prison tower.

She gasped, her gaze locked on his, like a scared mouse hypnotized by a swaying cobra. Enjoying the fantasy, and her fear, he winked.

Visibly trembling, she jumped to her feet and hurried back up the aisle to the rest room. George barked a cigarette-roughened laugh that degenerated into a rattling cough. Then he settled back in the seat, returned to his bottle and contemplated the look on little ole Cora Mae Padgett's face when he showed up on the doorstep of Roxanne Scarbrough's fancy mansion.

Chapter Four

New York

Although Chelsea's suit was comparatively restrained, the emerald color proved a stunning foil for her brilliant hair. As she dashed into the Plaza's Palm Court, heads swiveled, watching her make a beeline for a table across the way.

"I'm sorry I'm late." She bent down and kissed her mother's cheek. "I didn't think I'd ever get out of that interview with Bruce Willis."

Deidre Lowell managed a brittle smile. "You could have simply informed the man that you had a luncheon date with your mother."

Chelsea grinned, still riding the high of her successful morning. "I suppose I could have tried that," she agreed. "But then I would have missed the neatest story about the day he and Demi took the kids to the zoo, and—"

"I'm sure it's a delightful tale," Deidre cut her off. "However, I have an appointment for a facial at two, and since I don't dare keep Rodica waiting, I suggest you sit down and order.''

The cool, perfectly rounded tones were all it took to puncture the little bubble of happiness Chelsea had been riding due to her successful morning. She'd discovered at an early age that unless she tried very hard to avoid it, conversations with her mother usually resulted in her apologizing. A bit resentful at feeling like a chastised six year old, she did as instructed.

They managed to exchange a bit of small talk about her mother's book club group and numerous charitable activities while they waited for their orders to be delivered. By the time their salads and cups of Earl Grey tea were delivered, Chelsea had actually begun to relax. Which was, of course, always a mistake.

Deidre's gaze swept over her. "You know, dear," she said, "you really need to get your hair trimmed. You're starting to look like the Longworths' sheepdog, what was his name? Mercedes?''

"Bentley. And I've been busy.'' Hating herself for falling into old patterns, Chelsea brushed her bangs out of her eyes.

"So Nelson has been telling me. He says your career has been taking up a great deal of time recently.''

Chelsea would have had to have been deaf not to hear the scorn her mother had heaped on the word *career*. She told herself that one of these days she was going to get used to the unwavering disapproval.

After all, her mother had made her feelings known from the beginning. In fact, frustrated by a teenage Chelsea's total lack of interest in proper pastimes such as dancing school at the Colony Club, tennis at the Meadow Club, and regattas at Newport, Deidre Lowell had shipped her off to Switzerland to be schooled in womanly graces.

Those four years in exile, which were, thus far, the worst

experience of her life. Even worse than her mother's bitter divorce from Chelsea's father when she was six. Or the death of Dylan Cassidy when she was ten.

Rather than deter her daughter from her chosen goal, all Deidre Lowell (she'd long since dropped the *Cassidy* acquired upon her ill-fated marriage to Chelsea's father) managed to do was make the flame burn hotter. Brighter. It was during those years when she'd been banished abroad that writing became the only fixed star in Chelsea's firmament.

"It's been hectic," Chelsea allowed. "But I'd rather be too busy, than have no work at all."

Her mother didn't answer. But the way her lips drew into a tight disapproving line spoke volumes.

"Nelson said you're going to write a book about Roxanne Scarbrough."

"I'm considering it."

"Who on earth would buy such a book?"

"Perhaps all those millions of people who buy her lifestyle books," Chelsea said mildly. She refused to be drawn into a position of defending a woman she didn't even like.

"She's nouveau riche."

"I don't know about the nouveau. But you've got the rich part right."

"Honestly, Chelsea." Deidre frowned and took a sip of tea from the gilt-rimmed cup. "Must you joke about everything?"

"I'm sorry. It's just that I'm not sure people care about things like that anymore, mother."

"I believe you're right."

"You do?" Chelsea took a sip of her own tea and contemplated ordering champagne instead. After all, any occasion when she and her mother actually found something to agree about should be celebrated.

"Of course. And that," Deidre said stiffly, "is precisely

what's wrong with this country. People have lost all sense of values.''

''I don't believe gilding a few pomegranates will lead to the downfall of western civilization,'' Chelsea argued lightly.

''Laugh if you want to, but the woman is a menace. Would you believe that I found Tillie in the kitchen, watching her television program and practicing folding napkins into the shapes of swans?''

''That is hard to believe.'' Chelsea decided that if the longtime Lowell housekeeper, a woman infamous for having things her own way had actually become a fan, it was no wonder Roxanne topped the *NYT* bestseller list week after week.

''I nearly had a heart attack,'' Deidre, who'd never been known for overstatement, said grimly. ''I really don't believe you should encourage such things, Chelsea.''

''I haven't made up my mind whether I'm going to take the offer, Mother.''

''An interview with some self-appointed style maven is not exactly on a par with achieving world peace,'' Deidre stated in the superior tone Chelsea knew well.

''True enough. But it could be important to me. It could mean a lot of national publicity.''

''That's precisely what disturbs me,'' Deidre complained. ''All this striving to get your name in the magazines. And newspapers. Good grief, Chelsea, you sound just like your father.''

Despite her frustration, that icy remark drew a quick grin. ''I'm going to take that as a compliment.''

''You would.'' Deidre shook her blond head. ''I don't understand you.''

''I know.'' And never had, Chelsea tacked on silently. ''And as much as I'd love to try to explain it to you again, you have a facial to get to. And I have to try to track down John Kennedy Jr. I heard the most amazing story this morning—''

''You know I refuse to listen to Kennedy gossip, Chelsea,'' Deidre cut her off.

''I know, but—''

''Joe Kennedy was nothing but a shanty Irish bootlegger who married above himself. Even though Rose was Catholic, she could have done much better.''

''I know you believe that—''

''It's the truth. However, speaking of marriage, when are you and Nelson going to start planning your wedding?''

''How about the year 2002?''

''I do so hate it when you're flippant, Chelsea.''

Chelsea sighed. All her life she'd been inexorably maneuvered into an alliance between the Lowell and Waring families. Recalling all too well the acrimonious fights that had shattered her parents' marriage, Chelsea had feared repeating their mistakes. But whenever she tried to explain her concerns, Nelson would calmly point out that since Warings never fought, she had nothing to worry about. Even knowing that was true, Chelsea was still not ready to take the risk of making their relationship permanent.

''Nelson agrees we should wait. If nothing else, there's my trust fund to consider.''

''I don't know what was in your great-grandmother's mind when she came up with that ridiculous restriction. However, it's not as if you really need the money since Nelson is certainly well off in his own right. And the longer you wait to start your family, the more difficult it will be to bear children.''

Chelsea decided this was no time to point out that Rose Kennedy was forty-two when the youngest of her eight children had been born.

"I'm not ready to have children, mother," she repeated what she'd already said so many times before. Although her mother didn't appear to have a maternal bone in her body, lately she'd begun to display a very strong sense of dynasty. "Right now it's all I can do to juggle my career."

"Well, of course you'd hire a nanny," Deidre said. "If you insist on continuing your work, a child needn't interfere with your writing. Or your life."

"I have no intention of handing my child, when I do have one, over to some stranger."

Having grown up in the rarified world of nannies and housekeepers and private schools, Chelsea had vowed to create a better, warmer world for her own children. She was looking forward to baking cookies, volunteering at school carnivals and attending Little League games. Just not now.

Deidre arched a perfectly shaped blond brow. "I suppose that criticism is directed at me?"

"No." Chelsea took a deep breath. Why was it that conversations with her mother always turned out like this, she wondered miserably. "Of course not. I only meant that I wanted to be a more hands-on kind of mom."

"That's what you say now." Deidre gave her daughter a knowing look across the table. "The first time you change a diaper or go hours without sleep because of a teething baby, you may change your mind."

The idea of Deidre Lowell dirtying her manicured hands by changing a diaper made Chelsea smile. "I guess that's a risk I'm going to have to take."

"Again, I'm not surprised. You always have been a risk-taker, Chelsea." She put her napkin down onto the table and stood up, prepared to leave. "Just like your father."

As before, she did not make it sound like a compliment. Having apologized enough for one day, Chelsea took it as one.

After a week of uncharacteristic vacillation—during which time she changed her mind at least a dozen times, although she still had misgivings about the proposal—Chelsea decided to take Roxanne Scarbrough up on her offer to visit Raintree, Georgia.

Since Raintree was too small for its own airfield, Chelsea was required to land in Savannah. From the air, the riverside city looked like an island, surrounded by pine forests and salt marshes. As the plane touched down on the runway, Chelsea, who'd never considered herself at all psychic, started to shake inside, like a tuning fork trembling at a discordant chord.

As promised, Roxanne's assistant was waiting for her as she exited the jetway.

"Hello, Ms. Cassidy," Dorothy Landis greeted her with a welcoming smile. "It's good to see you again."

"Hi. It's good to be here." That wasn't exactly the truth, but Chelsea was trying to keep an open mind.

"Ms. Scarbrough is so pleased you decided to take her up on her offer to visit us. She's personally prepared the guest suite for your arrival."

Being forced into meeting with the doyenne of decorating was one thing. Spending even one night under the same roof with the unpleasant woman was decidedly less than appealing.

"I'd planned to check into a hotel," Chelsea hedged as they made their way through the passengers crowding the terminal.

When Mary Lou had assured her all the arrangements had been made, she'd conveniently withheld this vital bit of information. Chelsea decided she and her agent were going to have to have a little chat when she returned to New York.

The friendliness momentarily disappeared from the assistant's eyes, leaving behind the hard edge Chelsea had witnessed in the greenroom. "That's certainly not necessary. Besides, Ms. Scarbrough insists you stay with her."

"Then I'm afraid Ms. Scarbrough's going to be disappointed."

Dorothy gave her a long, thoughtful look. Then, apparently recognizing tenacity when she saw it, shrugged her acquiescence.

"Raintree has a lovely old inn. We'll stop there on the way to the house." That matter settled, Roxanne's assistant turned to more practical concerns. "Let's retrieve your luggage, then we can be on our way."

"We can skip the baggage claim."

"Surely you brought more than this single bag. And your—uh—purse."

Chelsea almost laughed at the disparaging look Dorothy gave her well-worn leather duffel bag. The same bag her mother had once declared to resemble a pregnant sow. "It's all I need. Since I'm not going to be here all that long." Chelsea figured it would probably take twenty-four hours, tops, to confirm that there was no way she would be able to work with Roxanne Scarbrough.

"Oh, dear." Dorothy's pale hazel eyes held little seeds of worry. "Ms. Scarbrough was expecting you to stay at least the week."

"It appears this is Ms. Scarbrough's day for disappointments."

Dorothy gave her a judicial sideways glance. "Do you know, I believe we may have misjudged you," she murmured. "I'm getting the impression that you're a great deal tougher than you appeared the morning we met in New York."

"Unlike your employer, appearing on national television isn't exactly a normal, everyday occurrence for me."

"Ms. Scarbrough certainly has a great deal of media experience," Dorothy agreed mildly. "In fact, a television crew is in Raintree, taping a documentary on her career."

An autobiography and a documentary. Chelsea couldn't decide whether to be appalled or impressed that the woman whose sole claim to fame was arranging flowers and setting luxurious life-style standards no mortal woman could possibly hope to achieve could have been put on such a lofty pop culture pedestal.

The setting sun stained the sky over Savannah the hue of a ripe plum. The air was perfumed with the scent of flowers and a hint of salt drifting in from the marshes surrounding the city, and the sea, which was twelve miles down the winding Savannah River. The lovely old houses with their great verandas and lacy railings and fences reminded her of New Orleans.

"This is truly lovely," Chelsea said as they drove through the city.

"It is, isn't it?" Dorothy said. "There's a local saying that Savannah is a lady who keeps her treasures polished for the pleasure of her guests.

"The city was originally established in 1733, by James Oglethorpe, to practice agrarian equality. The idea was that the goods the settlers produced would be sent back to enrich the British Empire.

"He laid the city out in squares, on the Renaissance ideal of balance and proportion. It was the loveliest city in the South. And one of the few that managed to save its grand old homes from General Sherman.

"You know, of course, that Sherman virtually destroyed Atlanta on that sixty-mile wide path of destruction to the sea."

"Even we native New Yorkers have seen *Gone With the Wind,*" Chelsea said with a smile.

"Hollywood couldn't even begin to describe the horror

that no-account Yankee wrought on our people," Dorothy muttered bitterly, as if the Civil War had just ended yesterday. "By the time he reached Savannah, it was obvious diplomacy was in order. A delegation of businessmen rode out to meet him and offered him one of the finest houses in the city as his headquarters.

"Fortunately, the general accepted the offer and moved in. Which saved Savannah from the fate of Atlanta.

"During the 1950s the city fell into decay," Dorothy continued her travel guide spiel. "Wrecking crews were demolishing the mansions for their handmade Savannah gray bricks to build suburban homes, destroying what Sherman had left standing a hundred years earlier.

"Finally, civic pride rose to the rescue. And now Savannah's inner city is one of the largest national historic districts in the nation. The people repolished the lady's jewels and tourism is booming."

They left the city, driving past the mysterious marshlands, along the Savannah River through a backcountry bursting with tropical lushness. Dorothy pointed out fields of tobacco, rice, soybeans and peanuts.

They'd been driving for about thirty minutes when they came to a small community of unhurried, shady streets. The green-and-white sign at the town limits welcomed visitors to Raintree, Georgia, est. 1758. Population 368. Gateway to the Gold Coast.

Although Chelsea thought that the slogan might be overstating the town's importance, she could not fault its beauty.

The buildings lining the main street were draped in a dreamy embrace of oak and moss, surrounded by an explosion of fiery pink azaleas. White-pillared gas lamps with round white glass globes were beginning to flicker on.

They passed the commercial center, two blocks of stucco-covered brick buildings with wide awnings that made the town look as if time had stopped there. A pair of old men in bib overalls played checkers in front of a store, as Chelsea suspected old men had been doing in that location since the town was established in the 1750s. In the window, signs advertising a sale on six-packs of Dr Pepper and a new three-day checkout period for the latest videocassettes provided a faintly jarring note to the languorous scene.

In the heart of the town—surrounded by a wide square of diagonal parking spaces—a courthouse glistened as white as new snow. A carillon of chimes pealed out the hour on the towering clock. It was, Chelsea noted with a glance down at her watch, ten minutes late.

"That's Colonel Bedford Mallory," Dorothy said, pointing out a marble statue of a confederate soldier astride a horse. "He's a local boy who distinguished himself under General Johnston at the Battle of Kennesaw Mountain. Every Confederate Memorial Day, the ladies of the Raintree Garden Club decorate the statue. They also decorate the graves of both confederate and union soldiers in the cemetery."

Once again, Chelsea had the strangest feeling she'd stepped back in time. "Do you have any industry in Raintree?"

"Industry? Like a carpet mill? Or furniture factory?" When Chelsea nodded, Dorothy shook her head. "No. Although we're on the river, we never really became an industrial center. It's still mostly agricultural, although more and more of the farmland is being sold off to build homes for people who work in Savannah, but want to escape the hustle and bustle of the city for the small-town life."

Chelsea decided not to mention that being accustomed to Manhattan, Savannah had seemed far from bustling. "Well, Raintree certainly looks like a tranquil town."

So tranquil, Chelsea mused, that if she did decide to stay,

it might be difficult to get into the proper mood to work on her novel. If she'd ever seen a place less likely to harbor thoughts of murder and mayhem, it was this one.

"It's quiet," Dorothy agreed, "but like all small towns, it does have its hidden depths. And its secrets."

"I love secrets," Chelsea confessed cheerfully as Dorothy pulled the car up in front of a lovely two-story building. The red bricks had faded over the years to a soft pink, but the shutters framing the windows were a bright fresh white. The windows glistened, brilliant red azaleas and creamy magnolias overflowed clay pots on the wide and inviting front porch.

"Oh, this is wonderful!" Chelsea said as she entered the cozy lobby that reminded her more of a private home than a hotel. The scent of fresh-cut flowers perfumed the air.

"Welcome to the Magnolia House," the man behind the hand-hewn counter greeted her. He looked around thirty, with friendly blue eyes and tousled blond hair. His soft drawl gave evidence of local roots.

After introducing himself as Jeb Townely, her host, he filled out the paperwork quickly, then carried her bags up to her second-floor room.

"I hope you'll be comfortable here," he said as he opened the door. More flowers bloomed in vases on a small cherry writing desk and atop the dresser. There was a tray with two glasses, a bottle of mineral water and a tin of cookies on the table. The bed was canopied, and like the rest of the furniture, appeared to be a genuine antique.

"I think I may just stay forever." Chelsea could feel the tensions of her day melt away as she drank in the cozy ambiance of the room.

"I know the feeling." His smile deepened to reveal the dimples on either cheek. "Magnolia House has been in my family for nearly two hundred years. After three failed peanut crops in a row, I decided the green thumb possessed by all the other Townelys just passed me by. So, I opened the house up as an inn, and—'' he rapped his knuckles on the desk ''—so far, so good.''

''I don't know a thing about the hotel business, except for having stayed in too many over the past few years. But I think you've done a marvelous job.''

''That's real nice of you to say, Miz Cassidy.'' He handed her the key. ''If you need anything else, I'll do my best to oblige. Just dial the operator. Anytime day or night.''

''Don't tell me you operate the switchboard, too?''

''No. I hired a nice widow lady who likes a chance to talk to people,'' he said. ''But, since I live here, I'm usually around.''

''Doesn't that make for a twenty-four-hour day?''

''Sometimes. But I like making people comfortable. Besides, although my daddy couldn't teach me farming, he did manage to drive home the lesson that no southern gentleman worth his salt shirks his responsibility.''

''Didn't the Tarleton twins say much the same thing? At the barbecue at Twelve Oaks? Right before they went rushing off to get themselves killed in the war?''

''Chivalry is not always as easy as handing out battle site maps and delivering ice to rooms,'' he allowed with another friendly grin that had Chelsea thinking he might have been a bust at growing peanuts, but Jeb Townely was a natural-born innkeeper. ''You all take care now,'' he said as he left. ''And Dorothy, tell your mama *hey* for me.''

''I'll do that.''

Chelsea thought she detected a lack of enthusiasm in Dorothy's tone at the mention of her mother, but knowing that she was expected at Roxanne's for dinner, she didn't dwell on it.

Chelsea took less than five minutes to hang up tomorrow's suit and freshen up. Then they were on their way again.

Roxanne's Tudor house was set in the center of a rolling green lawn that could have doubled as a putting green. Pear trees sported fluffy spring blossoms, daffodils lined the sidewalks in a blaze of saffron and gold and the dogwoods were beginning to bloom. Chelsea remembered Roxanne saying something to Joan Lundon about a new house she'd bought.

"I'm amazed anyone would be willing to give this up," she murmured.

"Ms. Scarbrough has always enjoyed a challenge. And Belle Terre certainly is that. Personally, I think she'd be better off taking a page out of Sherman's book, torching the place and starting over."

"But that wouldn't play well in a documentary."

Chelsea's dry tone earned a faint smile. "I suspected I was going to like you," Dorothy said.

As she got out of the car, instead of the traffic and siren sounds she was accustomed to, Chelsea heard mockingbirds and wrens flitting from branch to branch in the maples flanking the driveway.

The muscle that had formed a steel band around her forehead loosened. Perhaps Mary Lou was right. Perhaps a change was just what she needed. And where else better to recharge her internal batteries than in a friendly southern town that defined serene?

Chapter Five

If the outside of Roxanne Scarbrough's home reminded Chelsea of an English manor house, the foyer was reminiscent of Monet's gardens at Giverny. Flowers bloomed everywhere, on the floor, the walls, and along the molding at the top of the high foyer ceilings.

Although she hated to give the unpleasant life-style expert credit for anything, Chelsea had to admit that she was very, very good at creating a picturesque and inviting stage for herself.

"Ms. Scarbrough always has drinks in the front parlor before dining with guests," Dorothy informed her as she led the way across the sea of pink marble scattered with antique Aubusson rugs.

The room was small. And decidedly feminine, more boudoir than parlor, which was why the man standing beside the fireplace seemed so rivetingly male. He was turned toward Roxanne, engaged in conversation, allowing Chelsea to view only a rugged profile. He held a glass of amber liquor; the cut crystal looked dangerously fragile in his long dark fingers.

When Roxanne murmured something that made him throw back his head and laugh, the rich dark sound stirred deeply hidden, but strikingly familiar chords inside Chelsea.

"Well, we finally made it," Dorothy announced their presence, her matter-of-fact tone sounding like a strident, off-key note in the lush intimacy of the scene.

Both Roxanne and the man turned toward the door. As his too familiar, darkly mocking eyes locked with her wide, disbelieving ones, Chelsea drew in a sharp, unwilling breath.

For an unmeasurable time—it could have been seconds, or an eternity—they just looked at one another across the lushly romantic room. He lifted his glass in a mock salute.

"Hello, Irish." His smile was more challenge than greeting.

The name was one he'd sometimes called her on those rare light, almost comfortable moments, after the hunger had been temporarily satiated. But there was nothing comfortable or light about her feelings as she heard it now.

He knew! The words ricocheted in her head as she glared back at him. From the wicked gleam in his eyes, she guessed he'd known she was going to be here, and was enjoying this moment considerably.

Her temper rose. Although it took Herculean effort, she managed to force it down, turning her anger from heat to ice. "Hello, Cash."

The voice she heard coming out of her mouth could have belonged to her mother. Although Deidre Whitney Lowell would eat her quilted Chanel handbag before ever permitting herself to be openly rude, she could, with a brief, dismissing glance or a murmured statement, make her target all too aware of her extreme displeasure.

Having been on the receiving end of that chilly disapproval more times than she could count, Chelsea knew it well. Well enough to have no difficulty imitating it now.

Roxanne's suddenly sharp gaze swung from Cash to
Chelsea, then back to Cash again. "I had no idea that you
two were acquainted." She did not sound overly thrilled by
the discovery.

"Chelsea and I are old college friends," Cash revealed.
Although he was talking to Roxanne, his gaze stayed on
Chelsea's face. "From Yale."

"Why didn't you say anything?" There was a challenging, almost petulant edge to the older woman's voice.
"When I first mentioned that Ms. Cassidy was my biographer?"

"We were discussing Belle Terre at the time." His gaze,
as it moved to Roxanne, was as mild and unruffled as his
tone. "I didn't see any point in getting sidetracked with
inconsequential issues."

So now she was an inconsequential issue? Even though
she told herself that he wasn't important enough to be able
to hurt her, Chelsea's chin came up. "I thought you were
living in California."

"I was." He began moving toward her, striding across
the tulips blooming on the needlepoint carpet underfoot.
She'd forgotten how tall he was. How strong. And how his
body possessed a lethal sort of grace that had always reminded her of a panther.

Accustomed to his former uniform of jeans and a T-shirt,
she'd thought it had been his clothes that had given him the
look of a rebel. But now, taking in the sight of him, clad in
a casual, loosely constructed, yet obviously expensive cream
linen jacket, ivory cotton shirt and oatmeal-hued slacks, she
could still feel a dangerous energy radiating from him. Like
the hum of the ground beneath your feet right before lightning strikes.

Her quick glance took note of a gold Rolex watch he
certainly hadn't been able to afford when she'd known him.

He'd traded his scuffed leather boots in on a soft gleaming pair of silvery lizard cowboy boots that managed to scream wealth and independence all at the same time.

He stopped inches away from her, the tips of his boots nearly touching the toes of her hot pink high heels. When she didn't offer the hand that was hanging stiffly at her side, he reached down, unclenched her fist, and laced their fingers together with a casual air that seemed as natural to him as breathing.

Cash Beaudine had always been an intensely physical man. And not just in bed. Whenever he spoke, he'd gesture, using those strong dark hands so capable of causing havoc to every nerve ending in her body, to emphasize his words. During their few conversations, she could recall, all too well, how he constantly ran his fingers across her shoulder, down her arms, played with the ends of her hair, stroked the back of his hand up her face.

"I've spent the years since graduation in San Francisco." His thumb stroked intimate circles of heat against the sensitive flesh of her palm. "Now I've come back home."

Chelsea's stomach clenched at the unwelcome news. They'd be having snowball fights in Raintree's town square before she'd take on a project that would have her staying in the same town with this man.

"I hadn't realized this *was* your home."

"I thought you were old friends." Roxanne was watching them carefully, as if aware of the undercurrents humming between them.

"We were acquaintances," Chelsea retorted, retrieving her hand with a jerk. She didn't know which of them she was more furious with: Cash for toying with her emotions, or herself for letting him get under her skin.

He flashed the sexy, wicked smile she remembered all too well. "*Friendly* acquaintances."

His voice deepened on the correction, causing another significant pause to settle over the room.

Just when she thought she was going to explode from the tension building up inside her, a petite young woman came dashing into the parlor on a whirl of filmy black-and-brown gauze skirts.

"I'm sorry I'm late! I've been on the phone with my money people, Roxanne. They love the stuff we've shot so far...." Her voice drifted off as she viewed Chelsea.

"Oh, hi. You must be Chelsea Cassidy." Her light brown eyes, barely visible beneath bangs longer than the rest of her short-cropped sable hair were sparked with intelligence. Her smile was friendly and open. "I'm a fan. I love your writing. It's so energetic. And fresh."

She held out her hand. Her nails, Chelsea noticed irrelevantly, had been chewed to the quick. "Jo McGovern. I'm filming a documentary on Roxanne's restoration of Belle Terre."

"I've heard about it. It's nice to meet you." Chelsea managed a sincere smile. "And thanks for the kind words about my work."

"I meant them. Roxanne says you're going to be writing her autobiography, so I guess that means we'll be working together. Sort of."

Before Chelsea could answer that she hadn't yet come to any decision, Roxanne deftly broke into the conversation.

"Would you care for a drink, Chelsea?"

"No, thank you," Chelsea said quickly. Cash had already upset her equilibrium. The one thing she didn't need was any alcohol.

"Well then, since we've all been introduced to one another, and been brought up to date on where we're living, I suppose it's time we go in to dinner." Roxanne placed her hand on Cash's arm, obviously expecting him to escort her into the dining room.

With a slow smile, he accepted. Dorothy followed behind the pair.

"Isn't Cash Beaudine the most magnificent man you've ever seen?" Jo murmured to Chelsea as they brought up the rear of the little parade. "If I'd known Roxanne was going to hire him to restore her home, I would've paid *her* for the chance to do this documentary."

"I suppose he's good-looking." Chelsea shrugged. "In a rather rough-hewn sort of way."

"Just the way I like my men," Jo said with a quick bold grin that, with her short, perky hairstyle, made her resemble a pixie. "I already spend too much of my time working with the artsy-fartsy Village types. When it's time to let loose, I want my men rough and tough and basic. A good ole boy with an edge. Like this one."

Not knowing exactly what to say to that, Chelsea merely murmured a vague response. It did cross her mind, however, as she observed Roxanne's red nails glistening like fresh blood on the sleeve of Cash's cream linen jacket, that Roxanne Scarbrough and Jo McGovern shared the same taste in dark, dangerous men.

As she once had.

But those days were nothing more than a youthful, rebellious fling. If there was one thing the loss of her beloved, larger-than-life father had taught Chelsea, it was to invest no more in a relationship than she could afford to lose. Cash Beaudine didn't mean anything to her now, because he hadn't meant anything to her then. The only thing they'd had in common was sex. Pure and simple. But it was over.

They'd made a clean break. And never looked back.

It had been better that way, Chelsea assured herself as she found her name on the dining room table, written in a

flowing calligraphy on an ivory card held between the petals
of a red porcelain rose.

As she sat down in the needlepoint chair seated across
from the object of all her internal distress, Chelsea found
him watching her, with that mocking, knowing way he'd
always had, and couldn't help remembering that night,
standing in the window, watching him ride out of her life.

At the time, she'd thought it would be forever.

Unfortunately, she'd been wrong.

The dining room was decorated in the same floral style
as the rest of the house. Somehow, it managed to be both
rich and light at the same time. Like lemon meringue pie.
Or an airy puff pastry filled with rich, sweetened cream.

The curved legs of the Queen Anne table and spiderweb-
backed chairs were distinctly feminine and vaguely sensual.
The carpet was a monumental achievement of Persian wo-
ven art portraying a graceful pattern of curling vinery resting
on a butter-toned field. Scattered across the luminous, thick-
piled rug were colorful, fanciful birds and prancing dogs.
Water lilies, reminiscent of those hanging in the Metro-
politan Museum, floated serenely on the mural painted on
the far wall. Lighted glass cabinets lined the other walls,
filled with floral-patterned china.

"I'm a hopeless flower addict," Roxanne said over the
soft, melodious strains of Chopin piped into the room
through concealed speakers as she noticed Chelsea's study
of her collection. "Like Monet, or Renoir, I must be surrounded by flowers."

"I would imagine that makes you very popular with the
local florists." Chelsea's gaze was drawn to a lush display
of two dozen full-blown pink roses that had been casually,
yet artfully arranged in a sterling champagne cooler atop an
antique green marble-topped hunt board.

Roxanne laughed, seemingly delighted at the suggestion. "All the best florists in the state know my name."

"Which isn't surprising," Jo said with a burst of youthful admiring enthusiasm. "Since I doubt if there's anyone in America who isn't familiar with the name Roxanne Scarbrough."

"Aren't you sweet? But I fear that's an exaggeration, dear." As a silent servant arrived with their salad plates, Roxanne rewarded the filmmaker with a smile that was a twin of the one she'd flashed so easily at Joan Lundon. "Hopefully, by the time we finish restoring Belle Terre, that will be true."

The Caesar salad had been dressed in the flavors of the South with peanut oil, country ham and corn bread croutons. It was unusual and delicious.

"I can't wait for you to see Belle Terre, Chelsea," Roxanne said as the servant whisked away their empty plates. "It's such an exciting challenge. And Cash has promised to restore the grand old house to its former glory, haven't you?"

Chelsea, watching closely, couldn't help noticing that the bright smile warmed and turned decidedly more intimate as it was turned on the only male in the room. Her first thought was that there was a lot more going on here than just a professional collaboration. Her second thought—and the one that truly concerned her—was why she should even care.

"I'll give it the old college try." He returned the smile with a friendly one of his own. And although he wasn't addressing Chelsea directly, she had no doubt that the *college* reference was for her benefit. Reminding her of a time she thought she'd put safely behind her. A time when she'd realized she was coming too close to surrendering her heart along with her body. A time when her self-protective instincts had kicked in, making her refuse to look any further than their next clandestine meeting.

"I'm not certain I'll be staying long enough to see the house," she said, wanting to put her cards all on the table right now so she wouldn't end up feeling obligated.

"You never know," Roxanne said agreeably, surprising Chelsea with her sanguine attitude. Her only sign of discomfort was a faint toying with the ruby-and-diamond ring adorning her right hand. "You wouldn't be the first northerner to fall in love with Raintree and decide to stay."

"As lovely as the town is, I sincerely doubt that will happen." Growing up in Manhattan, Chelsea had always thrived on the pulsating, hectic beat of the city. What New York's critics called gritty and exhausting, she found energizing.

Ignoring Chelsea's polite yet firm insistence, Roxanne's gaze circled the table, including the others. "Ms. Cassidy is a vital link in the chain of our success." Although her bright smile didn't fade in wattage, her eyes were two sapphire blades. "We must all do our best to convince her to join us in our little enterprise."

Once again Chelsea was surprised. She'd expected another tantrum, like the one she'd witnessed in New York. But instead, the woman was being unrelentingly cordial. Even friendly. Obviously, this overt southern hospitality was another carefully staged performance.

Before she could respond, the maid returned with crystal custard bowls of icy lemon sorbet to clear the palate for the next course.

"Tell me, Chelsea," Roxanne said, "did you always want to be a writer?"

"For as long as I can remember. I've been accused of having ink in my veins." Her father had told her that, Chelsea remembered with a little hitch in her heart. The day after her sixth birthday party. It had been the last thing he'd said to her. Right before he walked out the door of their Park Avenue apartment. Never to return.

"I wrote my first story when I was five years old." And had illustrated it with crayons on a roll of butcher paper Tillie had brought home one day with an order of lamb chops.

"Imagine." Roxanne was eyeing Chelsea with the interest an anthropologist might observe a member of a newly discovered Stone Age tribe. "Knowing your own mind at such a young age. I'm quite impressed. But of course, I suppose that had something to do with your father's influence. Dylan Cassidy must have been quite a role model."

It was certainly no secret that the Associated Press Pulitzer prize-winning reporter turned Emmy-winning war correspondent was her father. Neither was it common knowledge. Chelsea wondered if Mary Lou had mentioned it, or if Roxanne had done a little investigating on her own.

Her fingers tightened around the sterling handle of her fork. "My father was quite an act to follow."

"Which is undoubtedly why you chose the type of work you do," Roxanne decided. "Instead of concentrating on hard news." Her tone was so smooth, her expression so pleasantly bland, Chelsea couldn't quite decide whether or not she'd just been insulted.

"Celebrity journalism is safe," she agreed. "At least most of the time."

That earned a faint chuckle from Cash. Glancing over at him, he gave her a quick grin of approval she tried not to enjoy.

"It must be exciting," Jo said, seemingly unaware of the little drama taking place, "going to all those parties with movie stars and famous athletes."

"Reporting on parties isn't the same as being invited to them," Chelsea said.

"Still, I'd imagine it's a good way to get close to people."

"It's one way." Although glitzy parties did provide Chelsea the access she needed to her subjects, she'd overheard more than one celebrity complain that inviting the press to social events was like giving them a length of rope and inviting them to a hanging party.

"You know, I've never met a celebrity journalist before," Cash said, entering into the conversation. "I have to admit I'm not sure what, exactly, it is you do. Although I suspect it's not quite the same thing as Hedda Hopper gushing about Joan Crawford's new fur coat or Elizabeth Taylor's diamond earrings."

Chelsea bristled. Then tamped down her knee-jerk response to what she suspected might be sarcasm and decided to take the opportunity to enlighten him, and even more importantly Roxanne, about how she worked.

"Things have definitely changed since the job was created to lionize stars and to enable them to be worshiped by the masses, without being envied. The old movie magazines, of course, were mostly just promotional vehicles for the studios," she allowed.

"There seem to be four schools of thought in celebrity journalism these days. Unfortunately the type that gets the most press, is the one who seems to admire any famous person who manages to get through a day without committing rape or murder."

"And that's not you," Cash guessed.

"Hardly. Others approach a story with their own prejudices, and if the facts don't fit their view of the situation, or the person, they ignore them."

"I *do* hope that's not you," Roxanne said.

"Not at all. Others have a reporting style more suited to "60 Minutes." Sort of a 'gotcha,' where they take shots at famous people and try to make their subject look foolish. Or guilty of something."

"I know *that's* not you," Jo said.

"I try to remain fair to my subjects and myself by reporting the truth," Chelsea said. "Without any personal bias, and not worrying about whether or not it demeans or flatters the subject."

"I remember reading a bio line about you in *Vanity Fair*," Jo said. "It mentioned you beginning your own newspaper when you were still a girl."

Despite her earlier discomfort with the situation in general, and Cash in particular, Chelsea laughed.

"I talked my great-grandmother into buying me a junior printing press when I was ten. The type was rubber, instead of metal, and each piece of paper had to be individually hand stamped, but I loved it."

"How innovative of you," Roxanne said. "I'm quite impressed with your ambition."

"I'm not sure I had any choice in the matter. As I said, I was born a writer." Chelsea decided the time had come to turn the attention back to their hostess. "So, what made you decide to beautify the world, Roxanne?"

"Like you, I had no choice."

The tiny pinched lines that suddenly appeared above Roxanne's top lip hinted at hidden depths. Perhaps even secrets. Everyone had secrets, Chelsea reminded herself. One of hers was currently sitting across the table from her. Her curiosity stimulated, she wondered what secrets she might discover behind Roxanne's attractive, carefully constructed facade.

"I have always had a deep visceral need to be surrounded by beautiful things."

"Well, you've certainly managed to do that," Jo piped

up enthusiastically in a way that had Chelsea thinking that she seemed more cheerleader than documentary filmmaker. "Your home is absolutely stunning."

Roxanne's gaze swept around the room with obvious satisfaction. "Yes," she agreed. "It is."

The dinner of glazed carrots and snow peas, sweet potato soufflé, roast quail that had been boned, stuffed, then cunningly reassembled to look like its former self, was perfect. Roxanne, Chelsea suspected, would accept nothing short of excellence.

"This sure beats the hell out of the buckshot quail I grew up eating," Cash drawled as he cut into the tender bird.

Roxanne shook her head in mock resignation. "What is it about southern gentlemen and their addiction to hunting?" She took a sip of wine and eyed Chelsea over the rim of the stemmed glass. "Tell me, Chelsea, dear, is your Nelson a hunter?"

Chelsea didn't know which she found more surprising: that Roxanne knew about Nelson, or the way Cash seemed to stiffen at the mention of the man he'd always insisted was so wrong for her.

"Actually, Nelson prefers golf."

"A tedious pastime," Roxanne scoffed. "All those men dressed in horridly garish clothing chasing a little ball around for hours and hours. I will never understand the appeal." She turned toward Cash. "I assume you're a golfer."

"Never had time to take it up," he said, not mentioning that in the early years, he couldn't afford the balls, let alone the clubs. He turned the conversation to Roxanne's beloved Belle Terre, which she was more than happy to talk about for the rest of the evening.

Dessert was a rich bread pudding drenched in a caramel whiskey sauce that left Chelsea feeling soporific. Even the caffeine in the French roast coffee blend couldn't overcome her sudden exhaustion.

She turned down the offer of brandy in the parlor. "As much as I've enjoyed this evening, I think I'd better take a rain check. It's been a long day."

"I do wish you were staying in one of the guest rooms," Roxanne complained. "Then you'd only have to go upstairs to bed."

"It's so convenient," Jo said, revealing that she was ensconced somewhere upstairs. "And far nicer than any hotel."

"The offer is always open," Roxanne said. "If you decide to change your mind." She rose from the table to see her guest to the door. Dorothy, who hadn't yet finished her dessert, instantly jumped to her feet.

When Cash stood up as well, Chelsea first thought he was merely being polite. A minute later, she was reminded that manners—southern or otherwise—had never been his style.

"I'll drive Chelsea to the inn."

The declaration affected Chelsea like a jolt of adrenaline.

"That's not necessary," she and Roxanne said together.

"Really, Cash," Roxanne continued, "it's Dorothy's job. For which, I might add, she's very well paid to do."

"I need to see Jeb about some work he wanted done to his gazebo, anyway," Cash said. "No point in Dorothy having to go out of her way." Somehow, without using any outward force, he was deftly herding them all toward the front door.

"Roxanne, I can't remember ever having a better meal. It was a true masterpiece of culinary achievement." He took hold of her hand and in a gesture that left Chelsea openmouthed, lifted it to his lips. "Though spending time with you is downright hazardous to a man's waistline."

"Don't worry, Cash." Her voice was a sultry purr. "With

all the work you'll be doing at Belle Terre, you'll burn off any extra calories.''

Chelsea was uncomfortable watching Roxanne's avid, greedy eyes moving over Cash's face, eating him up as if he were a piece of rich, whiskey-soaked pudding. She cleared her throat, drawing Roxanne's attention back to her.

''Dinner was wonderful,'' she seconded Cash's review of the meal. ''What time would you like to get together tomorrow to discuss the book?''

''First you need to see Belle Terre. Why don't I have Dorothy pick you up at ten? We can drive out to look at the house, then discuss our little project after that.''

She was, of course, being steamrollered again. But as exhausted as she was, Chelsea decided not to argue. ''I'd like to see the house.'' She turned to Jo. ''But I have to ask that you don't videotape me at the site. Unless I agree to the collaboration.''

''Until,'' Roxanne said coyly.

She may be tired. But she wasn't a fool. Chelsea tilted her chin. ''Unless,'' she repeated.

A significant little silence settled over the foyer as the war of wills was waged.

Roxanne was the first to back down. ''Unless,'' she agreed with a smile that didn't begin to reach her eyes. Chelsea knew the woman was not surrendering. Rather, she'd wisely chosen to retreat from the battlefield and fight another day.

Roxanne Scarbrough was outrageously egotistical. And, Chelsea suspected, ruthless. But she was also talented, intelligent and fast becoming an American phenomenon. Chelsea knew she'd never like the woman. But then again, when you earned your living as a celebrity journalist, it was probably best not to write about people you admired.

Once, when profiling Diane Keaton, Dominick Dunne had

revealed missing the actress the moment he'd dropped her off at her hotel. Chelsea could not imagine ever feeling that way about Roxanne.

"Well," Cash said, seemingly determined to move things along, "we'd better get going."

Chelsea said polite goodbyes to Roxanne, Dorothy and Jo. She did not say anything to Cash. Not on the way down the long brick sidewalk to the driveway, although she couldn't resist arching a brow at the black Ferrari.

As soon as she settled into the black leather seat, she leaned her head back, closed her eyes, and promptly fell asleep.

Chapter Six

The unseasonably warm spring night was drenched with the sultry scent of sun-ripened flowers. The fact that he was too tall to drive the Ferrari with the top up had never proven that much of a problem for Cash. He simply kept an eye on the barometer, avoided getting caught in rainstorms if possible, and enjoyed the feel of the wind as he raced through the dark and nearly deserted streets of Raintree.

Achieving success in California had allowed him to return to Georgia in style. He'd come a helluva long way from that kid who'd been born in a sharecropper's shack and had spent his teenage years sneaking peeks through keyholes in the whorehouse. He was no longer the rough, angry young man who'd seduced a passionate, old-money WASP princess at Yale.

He'd come to terms with his past. Was pleased with his present. And definitely looking forward to the future, including the restoration of Roxanne Scarbrough's beloved Belle Terre.

So why was it, he wondered, slanting a sideways glance at the sleeping Chelsea while paused at the town's single stoplight, that this redhead from his past could walk into a room and suddenly make him feel sixteen years old again? A hot, horny teenager who knew too much about sex and nothing about love.

He studied her profile and told himself that he'd certainly seen more perfect women. Her nose was not the classical slender style favored by girls of her New York set, but slightly pug. It was also familiar.

When Roxanne revealed that Chelsea's father had been Dylan Cassidy, he'd realized her illustrious family tree boasted an appealing crooked branch. Although he'd only been thirteen when the reporter had been killed in a civil war in some forgotten third world country, Cash remembered the man's death well.

Not only had he delivered the newspapers that carried the news in a half-page obituary, all the girls in the whorehouse practically declared a day of mourning. Dylan Cassidy— looking like Indiana Jones in his khaki shirt with the epaulets, along with that hint of brogue he'd brought to America with him from his Irish homeland—had apparently provided a dash of much needed fantasy for a group of women who'd given up fantasizing.

The light turned green. Cash stepped on the gas while doing some quick, mental arithmetic. Chelsea would have been ten when her father's bullet-riddled body being dragged through those dusty streets had been repeated in newscast after newscast.

Pity stirred. Cash tamped it down as he pulled up in front of the inn. As soon as he cut the engine, Chelsea woke up.

"I suppose I should apologize." She shifted in the seat and ran her hands through the long slide of hair.

"For what?"

"For falling asleep. It wasn't very polite."

"I don't recall either of us being all that concerned with

politeness.'' He plucked the key from the ignition. ''Not when we were spending every chance we got fucking our brains out.''

Ignoring her sharp intake of breath, he opened his door and unfolded his long length from the car. Before he could come around and open her door, she was standing on the sidewalk.

''You're still as rude and hateful as ever, I see,'' Chelsea snapped as they walked into the cozy lobby.

''And you're still as drop-dead gorgeous as ever. Even if you are too damn thin.''

His hand was on her back in a possessive, masculine way that annoyed her. But not wanting him to think he held the power to affect her in any way, she did not insist he take it away.

''A woman can never be too thin,'' she quoted her mother's axiom as she strode briskly across the pine plank floor.

''That's a crock. Men like a woman to have some meat on her bones. Something to hold on to while they're tangling the sheets.''

''Some men aren't fixated on sex.''

''Some men need to learn to prioritize.'' His hand slid beneath her hair. His fingers cupped the back of her neck.

Chelsea tossed her head and inched away. ''You've done your duty, Cash. You can leave now.''

''Without escorting you up to your room? Honey, I don't know how your Yankee fellas do things in New York City, but no southern gentleman worth his salt would let a woman wander around all by her lonesome late at night. Even in a friendly town like Raintree.''

''Good try. But we both know that you're no gentleman. You're just trying to talk your way into my room. And my bed.''

A couple approached. From their surreptitious, suddenly interested glances, Chelsea realized that they'd heard her gritty accusation.

"Actually, now that you mention it, though I've admittedly spent the evening thinking about what I was going to do when I finally got you alone, believe me, sugar, talking wasn't one of the options.

"Besides, if I wanted to jump your bones, I sure as hell wouldn't need to wait until we got to your room to do it. I'll bet the keys to that shiny black Ferrari parked outside that there's a janitor's closet around here somewhere."

The couple was pretending interest in a revolving rack of bright postcards. At Cash's provocative suggestion, the woman gasped and out of the corner of her eye, Chelsea saw the man grin. Refusing even to acknowledge that reminder of her outrageous behavior on that last night they'd spent together, Chelsea balled her hands into fists at her sides and managed, just barely, not to slug him.

She was no longer the young dream-driven girl who'd been fixated on this man. She'd worked hard and achieved a measure of success. In fact, her celebrity profile of Tom Wolfe had even earned a begrudging, "Nice work, dear," from her mother.

She'd changed over the intervening years since her time with this man. But the one thing that seemed the same, dammit, was the way Cash Beaudine could still get beneath her skin.

She began marching up the stairs, Cash right beside her. Openly fascinated, the couple followed at a discreet distance.

"You really haven't changed a bit." Chelsea gritted her teeth.

"Not in any of the ways that count," Cash agreed cheerfully. His arm looped around her waist. "I still like my whiskey neat, my cars fast, and my women hot."

He really was disgusting. And wicked. Wickedly handsome with a wicked tongue and, she remembered to her regret, wonderfully wicked hands. Refusing to dignify his remark with an answer, Chelsea refused to look at him.

But she was not unaware of him. The lazy sexual energy radiating from Cash was palpable. She thought of how, when he'd first walked toward her on that loose-limb stride, looking so darkly masculine that he literally overwhelmed the floral romanticism of Roxanne's parlor, he'd brought to mind a sleek black panther.

Now, he reminded her of a thick-maned lion, sprawled beneath a tree in the blazing Serengeti sun, lazily biding his time until he felt moved to pounce.

When she stopped in front of her door, the man and woman passed. But not without casting one last fascinated look back over their shoulders at Chelsea and Cash.

"Y'all have a nice night now," Cash said affably.

Their faces flushed a matching scarlet as they hurried away.

"Alone at last." Cash turned toward Chelsea, with that melting sexuality in his eyes she'd once found impossible to resist. She could suddenly feel the heat and steam of the South as he cupped her rigid chin in his fingers and without hesitation, took her mouth.

The explosion was instantaneous. At the first feel of his firm hard lips on hers, Chelsea felt a jolt that shook her all the way to her toes, like lightning shocking its way across a midnight dark sky. Before she could recover, molten heat began to flow thickly through her veins.

Her heart was pounding in her chest and in her ears like thunder. Chelsea couldn't think. Then, as he fisted his hand in the wealth of hair at the nape of her neck and yanked her head back, holding her to the relentless kiss, she didn't want to think.

Unwilling to consider the rashness of her behavior while his ravenous mouth was creating havoc to every atom of her body, she twined her arms around his neck and clung.

Sensing her surrender, tasting her fiery need, Cash changed the angle of the kiss, lessening the pressure, but none of the power. The need to take raged through him; he'd been going nuts, sitting across the table from her, managing to keep up his end of the dinner conversation, while his mind was obsessed with wondering what she was wearing beneath that sassy hot pink suit.

He'd remained polite while Roxanne tried to stake her claim, but he'd watched Chelsea watching Roxanne's performance and knew she believed he was sleeping with his famous client. Which wasn't all that surprising, considering that he certainly hadn't been a monk when they'd met all those years ago.

Realizing that this wasn't the way to prove to her that she was wrong, Cash slowly, reluctantly released her mouth.

"You're still a helluva good kisser, sweetheart." He released her hair, sliding his fingers the entire length through the bright strands.

"For a Yankee," she repeated what he'd told her that first time he'd stolen a kiss.

It had been on a cold gray January day, beneath a leafless tree glistening with winter ice. Before his mouth had touched hers, she'd been freezing. When it ended, she'd been surprised that they hadn't melted all the snow in New Haven.

He smiled, sharing the memory. "For a Yankee."

The warm smile threatened to be her undoing. Her hands were damp and that distressed her. She was trembling and that infuriated her.

"You realize, of course, that you had no right to do that."

Temper suited her. Haughter didn't. She was a woman born for passion. Which once again made him wonder what the hell had made her think she could be happy with that tight-assed Yankee.

Cash nearly shook his head at the waste, then reminded himself that if Waring was keeping her satisfied, she wouldn't have responded so quickly, and with such unrestrained hunger to him.

"No right to do what? Kiss you?" He continued to play with the ends of her hair. "Or make you so hot you practically swallowed me up whole?"

She tossed her head, freeing herself, and moved away from him. "You know, it really is depressingly true. Despite the Ferrari and the Rolex, you really haven't changed, Cash."

She tried to insert the key in the lock, but her hands were not steady and it took two tries before she managed to open the door. "Good night."

"Not yet."

Frustrating her further, he followed her into the suite. The moment she caught a glimpse of herself in the gold-framed mirror that was hanging over the antique Hepplewhite desk, Chelsea nearly groaned. There was no point in trying to pretend she'd remained unaffected by the power of Cash's kiss. Not when the evidence was written in bold script all over her face. Her pupils were still too dilated, her cheeks too flushed, her lips too swollen.

Cash came up behind her. "If I live to be a hundred, I'll probably never figure it out."

Reluctantly, she met his puzzled gaze in the mirror. "Figure what out?"

"What it is about you that somehow makes you the most beautiful woman I've ever seen. You shouldn't be," he mused out loud. His eyes took a slow tour of her face. "In the first place, your eyes are too damn wide for your face. They always used to remind me of those paintings of waifs that were all the rage in Mega-Mart stores back when I was a kid."

He flicked a casual finger down her nose. "Your nose is too pug, and if you look at it just the right way, it's a tad crooked. And your mouth is too big."

The unflattering description stung. It shouldn't, dammit. But it did. "If this is the way you usually compliment a woman you're trying to coax into bed, Cash, it's no wonder you had to pounce on the first female you managed to get alone in a hotel."

"I've never been one to turn my back on opportunity." He put his hands on her shoulders as they continued to face the mirror together. He decided, for discretion's sake not to mention that he'd never felt the need to coax. Not when the women came so willingly, in such numbers, all by themselves.

He knew what they liked. In bed and out, which tended to make the affection mutual. Women came. Then they went. And since Cash had always had a rule about being up front about the fact he had no intention of settling down into a long-term, 'til death do you part relationship, usually they parted friends.

Although he wasn't a man who enjoyed emotional entanglements, Cash could appreciate the irony of being reunited with the one woman who'd once, in another place and another time, had him actually considering marriage.

"It really is the damndest thing," he said, shaking his head as he returned his thoughts to Chelsea's cockeyed, but appealing face. "One by one, your features are all wrong. But put them together and they make one helluva irresistible whole."

Her hair still smelled like an Irish meadow of wildflowers after a summer rain. Drawn to the scent, he pressed his lips against the top of her head. "And that's why I kissed you, Chelsea. Because although it doesn't make a lick of sense, you're a drop-dead gorgeous woman that no man in his right mind could resist."

"I suppose that explains it. You said it yourself, Cash. It doesn't make a lick of sense. Which can only mean that you're obviously out of your mind."

"True enough." He grinned. "I suppose, if you wanted to get real technical about it, you could say I'm still crazy after all these years.... Crazy about you."

This wasn't going to work. There'd been a few instances during dinner when Chelsea had thought she might be able to pull this challenge off. But collaborating with a woman who gave new meaning to the word *temperamental* would be difficult enough. Throw in a former lover who knew how to push all her hot buttons, and the challenge suddenly become untenable.

"What do you want, Cash? Really?"

Good question. And one that other than getting Chelsea Cassidy naked, Cash realized he didn't really have an answer for. Not yet, anyway.

"Why don't I get back to you on that?"

"Why don't you just stay away? And let me do my work?"

He slipped his hands into the pockets of his slacks and rocked back on his heels. "Does that mean you're going to write Roxanne's book for her?"

"I haven't made up my mind."

"And now I'm making your decision more difficult by muddying the waters."

There was no point in denying it. "Yes."

Although he managed to restrain the smile, Cash couldn't

stop the glint of satisfaction in his eyes. "Roxanne can be a very persuasive woman."

"As you no doubt have discovered for yourself. Since you've agreed to work with her on her beloved Belle Terre."

"It was a beautiful home once. It could be again. And do I detect just a hint of jealousy in your modulated eastern seaboard tones, Irish?"

"Not at all. Why should I care who you're sleeping with these days? And stop calling me Irish."

"Whatever you say."

"Good night, Cash." She literally pushed him out the door. "I'll suppose I'll have no choice but to see you tomorrow."

She was unsurprised when her rudeness slid off him like rain off a mallard's back. "I'll be looking forward to it."

That made one of them. Grateful to have this unsettling evening finally come to an end, she shut the door behind him, turned the latch and fastened the chain. Then she leaned back against the door and closed her eyes.

Which was a mistake. She could still see him, looking down at her with that cocky grin on his lips and devilment in his eyes. It just wasn't fair, she thought on a renewed burst of temper, that any one man could be so sexy.

She shook her head as she bit into an antacid and assured herself that the only reason she'd responded so strongly to Cash was that she'd been caught off guard. Forewarned was definitely forearmed. Now that she knew what she was up against, tomorrow she'd be prepared.

Feeling better, she went into the adjoining bathroom. After she'd washed her face and brushed her teeth, Chelsea gave herself a long unflinching look in the mirror.

"You're going to be strong. You're going to resist him," she instructed her reflection. "You will remind yourself, whenever your damn juices start flowing, that you managed to spend an entire evening with Mel Gibson and only once wished he'd shown up for the interview wearing a kilt.''

Her little pep talk concluded, Chelsea felt much better. She marched out of the bathroom, and was about to climb into bed when a white envelope lying on the table caught her attention.

The envelope was sealed; her name had been typed on the front. Deciding it must be a phone message that had come while she'd been at Roxanne's, Chelsea opened it.

A single line had been typed onto a plain white piece of paper. ''She who sups with the devil needs a spoon with a very long handle.''

Chelsea stared down at the typewritten proverb, chilled at the idea of someone being in her room. She could not imagine who it might have been.

Her next thought, as she remembered Cash's wicked kiss, was to wonder which devilish dinner companion the note, which seemed like a warning, was referring to: Roxanne Scarbrough? Or Cash Beaudine?

Unfortunately, a call to Jeb failed to solve the mystery, although she was immensely relieved to learn he was the person who'd put the envelope in her room. Apparently he'd found it on the downstairs desk when he'd come in from watering the back garden.

Although she couldn't believe she was in any real physical danger, the warning, along with Cash's greedy kiss, left Chelsea feeling edgy. Finally, when she seemed destined to spend the long lonely night tossing and turning, she flicked on the bedside lamp, booted up her laptop computer and went to work on her novel.

Suddenly, the idea of murder in Raintree didn't seem so far-fetched after all.

* * *

George climbed stiffly down from the bus, ran his tongue against his fuzzy teeth and decided fuckin' Joe Camel must've died in his mouth while he'd been sleeping. And whenever he blinked, it felt as if half that damn Arizona desert grit was glued to the back of his eyelids.

He knew a little hair of the dog would take the edge off. But that one drink could, as it so often did, lead to another. And another. And pretty soon, if history was anything to go by, he'd land his ass in jail and be headed right back to the joint. Which would blow his genius plan to kingdom come.

No, George decided. He wasn't going to make any mistakes this time. This scheme was surefire. So long as he managed to keep focused. And when he was finally finished with Roxanne Scarbrough, he'd be standin' in high cotton.

"Guaran-goddamn-teed," he said to himself as he studied the map of Raintree he'd bought when the bus stopped in Atlanta. Slinging his duffel bag over his shoulder, he began whistling an out of tune rendition of George Strait's "Ace in The Hole" as he headed off toward his wife's house.

Chapter Seven

Although the crumbling antebellum mansion was in a terrible state of disrepair, and the exterior of the house was in the process of being sandblasted, Chelsea had no trouble seeing the marble-pillared structure as it could be, with a lot of hard work and money.

It would also take an architect with vision and a sense of history. Was Cash that man? Chelsea wondered, having never thought of him in such terms.

Apparently, Roxanne believed that he was. Although it was obvious Roxanne found Cash sexually appealing, Chelsea doubted she'd be willing to spend such a vast amount of money just to get the man into her bed.

Of course, any woman who'd experienced the incomparable sex Chelsea had shared with Cash could be excused for considering the idea, she thought as he came out of the house to greet them. "'Morning, Roxanne. Jo. Miz Landis,'" he called out as he crossed what had once been a lawn and was now matted brown turf. "Lovely day, isn't it?" He turned toward Chelsea. "Good morning, Irish. I hope you slept well."

"Like a baby," she assured him in a wintry voice that didn't fool Cash for a moment.

She was lying. The strain of a sleepless night—the increased pallor of her complexion along with telltale circles beneath her eyes—showed on her fascinating, one-of-a-kind face. Deciding not to call her on it, he turned to Roxanne.

"I've got some good news for you."

"You know how I love good news."

"We found a stone cellar beneath the kitchen floor that wasn't on the plans."

"It must have been used to hide the family silver from the Yankee invaders."

"That's what I figured. It's cool down there. And the stone walls are as solid as, well, rocks. I thought you might like to turn it into a wine cellar."

"Oh, what a wonderful idea!" She placed her hand on his arm and turned to Chelsea. "Do you see why I absolutely adore this man?"

"Any architect who can conjure up a wine cellar is worth hiring," Chelsea said mildly.

"Oh, I've come to expect miracles from Cash." Roxanne turned back to him. "Speaking of which, I have some ideas about the master bathroom."

They walked toward the house, Roxanne sharing her latest "brainstorm." She might have arrived at the house carrying a Gucci briefcase instead of a pair of white gloves, but like any good southern belle worth her salt, when it appeared she might be losing ground about taking out what Cash insisted was a supporting wall, she fluttered her eyelashes and pulled out all her feminine wiles to try to win her point.

Roxanne possessed Scarlett O'Hara's beauty, brains and tenacity. Chelsea could easily imagine her running a lumber company or eating turnips, prepared in a nice champagne sauce of course, or wearing drapes to the jailhouse, if that's what it took to save Belle Terre. But there was nothing fiddle-dee-dee about this woman who obviously knew her own mind so well.

"Federal troops occupied Raintree during the march to the sea," Roxanne informed Chelsea as they made their way gingerly through the downstairs rooms, stepping over the holes where rotten pieces of flooring had been torn out.

"The occupation saved it from being burned. Unfortunately, Sherman's scoundrels did torch all outbuildings." Roxanne waved toward the windows and from the scowl on her face, Chelsea guessed she was picturing those long-ago fires. "And then they had the unmitigated gall to turn the front parlor into a stable."

"The soldiers brought horses into the house?" Chelsea asked disbelievingly.

"To protect them from rebel sharpshooters," Cash explained. "It was common practice at the time."

"And a distasteful practice it was, too," Roxanne snarled. It was obvious that she considered this high sacrilege. "Do you have any idea what hooves can do to a good marble floor?"

"I can imagine," Chelsea murmured, drawing a quick grin from Cash, who realized that his Yankee lover was just as out of her element here in the deep South, as he had been freezing his ass off in Connecticut.

"They even made blankets for their horses out of the oriental rugs. And turned the piano into a watering trough," Roxanne continued. "And, of course they looted the place—all the chandeliers, the furniture, the crystal and china, why even the silver that had been in the family for generations!"

Her scowl deepened. "I'm certain, if you were to go to some of the so-called finest homes in New England today, you'd find Yankees dining with pieces of Berry silver service.''

''Not that Ms. Scarbrough has anything against her northern fans,'' Dorothy said quickly. Chelsea immediately recognized the statement as a veiled warning to her employer.

A warning that hit home. As if suddenly remembering Chelsea was one of those damn Yankees, Roxanne pulled her features back into a smooth, calm mask and smiled. ''Well, of course I don't.''

Chelsea smiled back. ''I can see how living among such constant reminders of the Civil War—''

''The War Between the States,'' Roxanne corrected sharply. ''I've never understood why northerners insist on calling it the Civil War. Since there was absolutely nothing civil about it.''

Chelsea had no intention of getting embroiled in old battles. ''I can certainly understand how a person could be affected by the ghosts of all who have lived here.''

''Speaking of ghosts, dear, I must show you the bedroom. Where the Berry's poor daughter Rose Ann passed on from a broken heart when her dear James—that's James Boddie, from the Troup County Boddies—was killed at the Battle of Chickamauga.''

''I don't know if it's such a good idea for you all to go upstairs,'' Cash said.

''Really, Cash,'' Roxanne complained, ''there are construction workers tramping all over the place—''

''That's the definitive term. They're workers, Roxanne. They belong here.''

Roxanne proved immovable. ''I want Chelsea to see the room. And besides, Jo hasn't taken her *before* shots yet.''

Frustrated, but deciding that this was not exactly a hill to die on—he'd determined the stairs reasonably solid weeks ago—Cash decided to give in. "I'm going first. To make sure it's safe."

"Thank you, Cash," Roxanne said demurely.

"Next time you come out here you're wearing a hard hat," he instructed her over his shoulder as they climbed up the right wing of the double floating staircase.

"You're the boss," she agreed without missing a beat.

Walking right behind Cash, Chelsea heard him mutter something that could have been agreement. Or a curse.

The bedroom had a marble-framed fireplace, more crown molding, and little niches set into the plaster walls. The windows were opaque; the faint amount of sunshine managing to make its way through the glass made the dust motes swirling in the air look like dancing yellow fireflies.

"This is where it happened," Roxanne said. "In bed. After receiving the news, Rose Ann didn't speak to anyone for two months. Then one day the poor girl just closed her eyes and departed this life. Her mother later wrote in her journal that she believed her daughter had been united with her beloved James."

Chelsea rubbed her arms. Although she knew it had to be her overactive imagination, she could have sworn that the temperature in the room had dropped at least twenty degrees.

"That's so romantic." Jo sighed as she turned her camera on the four-poster bed that was draped in dusty curtains.

"It would be, if it was true," Roxanne agreed. "Unfortunately, for some reason, Rose Ann's spirit has remained here. Right in this very room."

Chelsea exchanged a quick, surprised look with Cash, who shrugged in return. "Are you claiming the house is haunted?"

"Of course." Seeming not at all disturbed by how her would-be autobiographer might take this little news flash,

Roxanne said, "Let's go downstairs again. You haven't seen the ballroom. It's truly magnificent. I'm planning the most wonderful party there, as soon as Cash and I finish the restoration."

Perhaps it came from seeing too many movies, but Chelsea had no difficulty at all picturing the immense, high-ceilinged room with its double hung windows, elaborate scrolled plaster detailing, and ceiling frescoes depicting southern life as it had once been. She could practically hear the music and see the men in frock coats and women in satin and lace, the women's hoop skirts looking like colorful hollyhock blossoms as they twirled gaily around the gleaming parquet floor.

"It's magnificent."

"Isn't it?" Roxanne's eyes gleamed as her gaze roamed the room. "Ezekial brought the floor back from one of his trips to Italy before the war. It's no wonder Margaret Mitchell got her inspiration for Tara after visiting here."

"Really?" Jo asked. The unmasked excitement in her voice made Chelsea think she was already considering ways to insert scenes from the movie into her documentary.

"Of course," Roxanne insisted. "Why, everyone around these parts knows that Tara was patterned after Belle Terre. Which is what's going to make this restoration so much more meaningful."

Not to mention lucrative, Chelsea thought, deciding that if this story was even remotely true, Roxanne truly had stumbled on a gold mine.

A sudden, tinny trill had Roxanne reaching into her handbag for her cellular phone. "Hello?" She covered the mouthpiece with her hand. "I'm sorry. It's my housekeeper." She gave them a look that said, servants, what can you do with them? "What is it LaDonna? I happen to be busy at the moment."

As she listened to the near hysterical housekeeper begin to stutter out the problem, Roxanne felt a cold fist of fear tightening around her heart. She forced a stiff, frozen smile toward the others.

"If you'll excuse me a moment."

Her heels tapping briskly on the scarred marble foyer, Roxanne went back outside, across the lawn, stopping behind the huge construction Dumpster the contractor had delivered the first day on the job. Although the sun was rising high in the sky and the temperatures were slated to hit another record high today, she felt as if she'd suddenly found herself buck naked in the middle of a blizzard.

"What do you mean he won't go away," she rasped. "Just tell him to leave. Then shut the door."

"But you don't understand," the usually composed housekeeper said on something close to a wail. "I tried that. And he just went around to the side door. He insists on talking with you, Miz Scarbrough." The next words confirmed Roxanne's worst fears. "He says he has a business proposition for you."

As frightened as she was, Roxanne couldn't resist a rich, ripe curse at that. Business? Blackmail was more like it.

"Shall I call the police, Miz Scarbrough?" LaDonna Greene asked.

"No!" She could deal with George, Roxanne assured herself. The same way she'd dealt with everything else in her past. She was right on the verge of achieving everything she'd struggled for. Everything she'd sacrificed for. She'd come too far to allow one miserable alcoholic wreck of a mistake to stop her now.

"Tell him he'll have to wait in the garden. I do not want that man in my house. I'm at Belle Terre. I'll leave immediately."

"Yes, Miz Scarbrough." There was a slight, hesitant

pause. "It's nearly lunchtime. Shall I serve him some iced tea and sandwiches? I was preparing the cold pesto chicken breasts for your guests, as you'd instructed this morning, but—"

"No!" She may have to speak with the bastard, but Roxanne was damned if she was going to play hostess. "Don't feed that man a fucking goddamn thing. Do you hear me?"

"Yes, ma'am."

Feed him? Roxanne asked herself furiously as she lowered the antenna on the phone. Only if she could prepare an arsenic salad with cyanide dressing. And serve it to him herself.

She indulged herself with the momentary fantasy of George writhing on the floor in poison-induced agony, then pasted a smile on her face and went back into the house.

"I'm so sorry. But a pesky little problem that needs my personal attention has come up."

Her smile was as brittle as glass. As were her eyes. Chelsea, observing her closely, noticed the bright spots of pink riding high on her cheekbones. But beneath that flush, she thought Roxanne's complexion looked oddly pale. Almost ashen. And her voice held a faint edge that was not quite anger.

Contrasts. Chelsea had witnessed Roxanne holding court at her dining room table with charm and grace. On one of her bestselling videotapes she'd seen Roxanne down on her knees in the garden, planting daffodil and tulip bulbs.

And if the business statistics cited in a recent *Wall Street Journal* were even partly true, Roxanne Scarbrough the CEO was on track to someday equal Lee Ioccoca or Ross Perot in financial clout. And then, of course, Chelsea couldn't forget the rude, arrogant prima dona who'd terrorized the staff of "Good Morning America."

Roxanne possessed more facets than the diamonds that

had glittered icily at her lobes in the candlelight during last night's dinner. Once again, despite last night's mysterious warning, or perhaps because of it, Chelsea was reluctantly intrigued. Discovering the core woman beneath all the glamour and hype could be a stimulating challenge.

"I've certainly seen enough to get a flavor of what you have in mind, Roxanne. Perhaps, once we get back to your house and you take care of your business, we can discuss our individual views on ghostwritten autobiographies. To see how compatible we are," she explained, when Roxanne shot her a startled look.

"You want to come back to my house? To discuss the book?"

Chelsea sensed something was definitely wrong here. Why did the woman think she'd gotten on that plane yesterday and flown all the way down here from Manhattan? To discuss stabling procedures during the Civil War? War Between the States, Chelsea reminded herself.

"We could discuss it at the inn, if you'd rather."

"Of course I'd prefer meeting at my home, Chelsea, where we could get to know one another in a more intimate setting," Roxanne insisted. "It's just that I have no idea how long this little matter will take, and I hate the thought of you having to wait."

"I don't mind. Really."

"But I do." Roxanne turned the full power of her smile on Cash. "I do so hate to impose on you this way, but do you think you could take Chelsea back to the inn?" She returned her gaze to Chelsea. "Then we could get together around eight? I'm having some friends in that I'd truly love for you to meet."

Her rich and famous friends, Chelsea decided as she turned toward Cash. "If you have something else to do—"

"I think it sounds like a great plan. We can have lunch. And catch up on old times."

"What a good idea!" Roxanne actually clapped her hands together at the suggestion, surprising Chelsea, who'd thought she'd detected No Trespassing signs posted all over Cash last night.

"You don't have to buy me lunch."

"We both have to eat. And this will give me a chance to try to impress you so you might want to write a book about me someday."

"I can't see that happening," she said mildly.

He grinned, a fatal woman-killing grin she doubted many women would be able to resist. "Never say never."

Their eyes met. And held.

And in that suspended moment, Chelsea knew that staying in Raintree, working in close proximity to this man would be the most reckless thing she'd ever done. Even more rash than leaving the country club with him the night of her cousin Susan's wedding.

What was worse, as his wicked gaze moved down to her lips, Chelsea feared she might actually do it.

Damn. As he met the green fire in her eyes—a flame that triggered something primal inside him—Cash cursed himself for allowing this woman to get under his skin so damn easily. Not that it had been any different seven years ago. The moment he'd seen her he'd wanted her with a desperation like nothing he'd ever experienced before or since. Until now.

He imagined stripping Chelsea naked, carrying her upstairs to that dusty draped bed. He visualized Chelsea lying beneath him, her legs entwined around his waist, her body glistening with a damp sheen as he reclaimed her once and for all. He could hear the breathless little sounds she made as he took her higher and higher, he could see the startled wonder in her eyes as she climaxed, crying out just the way she had that first time, when he'd taught her exactly how high she could fly.

He was so caught up in the sexual fantasy, it took him nearly a full minute to realize that Roxanne was speaking to him.

"I'm sorry." He dragged his mind and his eyes back to her. "My mind was wandering. I was thinking about extending the portico. What did you say, Roxanne?"

"I said I found Chelsea first," Roxanne protested lightly. "And a true southern gentleman would never steal away a lady's biographer."

"Ah, but I've never claimed to be a gentleman."

"That's for sure," Chelsea muttered beneath her breath. But it was loud enough for Cash to hear.

"Don't worry, Roxanne," he said. "I'm not going to steal Chelsea. I'm just going to feed her."

As soon as he heard the words coming out of his mouth, Cash knew he was lying. He was going to steal Chelsea Cassidy.

Not from Roxanne.

But from that blue-blooded Yankee, Nelson Webster Waring.

The idea, as the group departed the mansion in separate cars, Chelsea now in the Ferrari, rather than Roxanne's Mercedes, proved inordinately appealing.

"I suppose you think you're clever," Chelsea muttered.

"That thought does occur to me from time to time."

"I was talking about the way you managed to get me alone with you again."

"I didn't do a thing. It was Roxanne who suggested it," he reminded her.

"Sure. After you probably paid one of her minions to put a dead fly in the champagne punch she's planned for tonight's little gathering, thus forcing her to race back to the city and leave us alone."

"Damn." He shook his head with good-natured humor. "I should have known better than to try to put anything by you, Irish. Especially since you have an exceedingly bright head on those slender shoulders."

It was the first compliment she could ever recall hearing from this man that didn't involve something sexual. "I never was all that wild about you calling me Irish." That was a lie. The truth was that her blood had warmed a little whenever he drawled the intimate nickname. It still did. Which was why she wished he'd stop using it. "If you even dare try for Red—"

"I wasn't referring to the color, Chelsea. I was talking about what's inside." He slid her an approving sideways glance. "Although I have to admit that your hair color was the second thing I noticed about you."

"What was the first?"

"Your ass."

Chelsea shook her head, crossed her arms, and struggled with the smile that was trying to break free on her lips. "I should have known better than to ask," she grated, pretending a sudden interest in the scenery streaking by the window as the big black car roared down the country two-lane road.

"You did—still do, for that matter—have a right fine ass, Chelsea darlin'," he assured her with the easy manner of a man who considered himself a connoisseur of such things. "Then you turned around and I got a look at your face. Your crazy, crooked, wonderful face. And it was like getting a sucker punch, right in the gut."

Actually, Cash recalled with painful clarity, the punch had hit lower. "I told myself, Cash, ole boy, you're a goner. Better take a deep breath because you're about to go under for the third time."

"Liar."

She'd been the one who felt that way. She'd been the one who'd felt the power of his gaze, experienced that silent overwhelming urge to turn around, and when she'd finally surrendered, had gazed across the winter dead lawn and known that from this moment on, her life would never be the same again. The idea had been both terrifying and thrilling.

"Why would I lie about that? Surely you felt it, too?"

Her reaction to him had been instantaneous, intense, and totally out of proportion. Not to mention irresistible. "I was terrified."

"That makes two of us. I felt as if I'd been poleaxed. I'd already had more than my share of women by the time I'd met you, Chelsea. But none of them ever got beneath my skin—and in my head—like you."

He said it so casually, Chelsea could almost believe him. *Almost.* "Why didn't you ever tell me?"

"And give you the upper hand?"

"Control was always important to you."

"In some ways. Like in the sack. But believe me, darlin', the power Lee surrendered to Grant when he handed his sword over on the steps of the Appomattox courthouse was nothing compared to what I gave up the first time I kissed you."

His voice was unusually gravelly, his words tinged with an intriguing combination of humor and frustration. And, she thought, a bit of leftover anger.

"I didn't know."

"That was the point."

They remained silent the rest of the way into Raintree, each lost in their own thoughts. Their own version of that reckless time.

Outwardly, at least, Cash had changed. Oh, no one would

ever mistake him for a lawyer or Wall Street banker, but the expensive linen suit he'd worn last night with such natural panache was a very long way from the faded jeans and black T-shirts he'd favored back in their days together at Yale.

His hands, while not professionally manicured like Nelson's, were no longer oil stained from hours spent repairing his motorcycle. Becoming momentarily distracted as she looked at them resting lightly on the steering wheel, Chelsea wondered if his fingertips were still callused. That thought took her wandering mind down another more perilous path, as she recalled, all too vividly, the feel of those roughened hands on her eager body.

Although the air conditioner was blowing cool air through the dashboard vents, memories of all the things he'd done to her, all the things they'd done together, caused an unbidden heat to invade her veins.

Caught up in old memories, Chelsea didn't notice that he'd pulled off the road until he was parking the car. She eyed the ramshackle white building with the name, The Original Catfish Charlie's, hand lettered in bright blue paint.

"Is this where we're going to have lunch?"

He laughed at the reluctance she couldn't quite hide. "Don't worry, Irish. You've had enough culture shock for one day. I thought I'd get takeout and we'd have a picnic. It's too nice a day to sit inside some stuffy fake southern mansion dining room. And this way we can have a chance to talk."

"Do you think that's such a good idea?"

"Eating? Or talking?"

She thought about the note left in her room last night and decided doing either with this man could prove dangerous. "Talking."

He took off the bayonet-style sunglasses with his left

hand and leaned toward her, slipping the right beneath her long hair. "You can tell me I'm all wet here, but I'm getting the impression that you're probably going to accept Roxanne's offer."

"I'm leaning that way," she admitted.

"So, if I'm restoring her beloved Tara—"

"Belle Terre."

"Tara." Cash's smile was slow and easygoing and, she admitted, very appealing. "Down here in *Gone With the Wind* country, there are more antebellum homes that supposedly served as the inspiration for Mitchell's fictional Tara than you can shake a hickory stick at. And in far too many of them, you'll find belles named Lady or Sister or Fancy, who dress up just like Scarlett and give tours."

"Although I truly hate to admit it, that kind of sounds like fun."

It took no effort at all to imagine carrying Chelsea up a wide staircase to bed. "You'd make a dynamite belle."

"For a Yankee," they both said together. Then laughed. The mood lightened again. For now.

Cash had not yet taken his hand way. His fingers began massaging her neck. "The point is that we're both going to be collaborating with Roxanne on projects that are important to her. And this is obviously a lady who believes in a hands-on management style."

That much was true. When Chelsea thought about the way Roxanne was constantly putting her hands on Cash, she experienced a jolt of jealousy. "Agreed."

"So, that being the case, we're bound to end up spending a lot of time together. Whether you like it or not."

"What about you?"

"What about me, what?"

"You said, whether *I* liked it or not. What about you?"

"Oh." He smiled, trailed a finger down her throat and

imagined touching his tongue to the soft fragrant flesh. "I like the idea just fine."

She shouldn't. She couldn't. But, of course she did, too.

He read the ambivalence in her eyes and knew he'd been responsible for putting it there. Cash felt a rush of purely male satisfaction.

He'd woken up in a rotten mood this morning after spending the night dreaming of Chelsea. Hot, intensely vivid dreams that had left him rock-hard and horny as a three-peckered billy goat.

He'd dragged himself into the bathroom, where he'd stood beneath a cold shower, refusing to flinch as the icy water pounded against his chest and ran down his stomach and legs. When the drastic recovery measures learned from Bobby Ray Mullins, coach of his high school Bulldogs football team, did little to help, Cash had not been all that surprised.

There were certain inarguable axioms of life: like the way it always rained right after you washed your car, or how the catfish finally began serious biting—instead of nibbling away at the edges and stealing bait—just when you ran out of worms. Or how, whenever he got within puckering range of Chelsea Cassidy, all his carefully conceived plans to keep his distance went flying straight out the window. The good Lord had given him brains and a penis; unfortunately, where this woman was concerned, he'd only given him enough blood to run one at a time.

Last night Chelsea had been attracted, but angry. Today she was tempted, but wary. Cash figured it would take no time at all to knock down those final parapets that would allow her to come to him. Willing and eager.

"We'll have a nice lunch. Talk about old times, maybe even have a few laughs. And when we're finished, we'll have gotten rid of the tension that could screw up our individual projects.

"It's going to be tricky enough working with the country's most famous Steel Magnolia," he told Chelsea. "No point in making things more difficult for ourselves."

He had, she knew, a very good point. His coaxing smile was as innocent as an angel's. But devilment danced in his eyes. "I have one question."

"Shoot."

"Are you responsible for the note left in my room last night?"

"What note?"

"The note warning me about the dangers of supping with the devil."

"You're kidding."

Watching him carefully, Chelsea decided his surprise was honest. "It's not exactly something I'd kid about."

He rubbed his jaw thoughtfully. "Roxanne's not the easiest person to get along with. Perhaps some well-meaning person just wanted to make sure you knew what you were getting into."

"I suppose so." It was, after all, the logical answer. Especially since she'd seen Roxanne in full form in New York. "Of course, it also crossed my mind that the note could be referring to you."

He laughed at that. "I always did admire your imagination, darlin'. I may be a little rough around the edges, but you're safe enough with me."

Liar. "Have lunch with me, Chelsea," he coaxed yet again with that deep drawl that conjured up images of magnolias and moonlight and made her feel warm all over. "I promise to be on my very best behavior."

"All right." She caved in, as she suspected he'd known all along she would. "It sounds like a sensible plan."

"Oh, I'm just full of plans, darlin'." He dipped his head and kissed her. A brief flare of heat that ended nearly as soon as it had begun, but still left her lips tingling.

"Now, why doesn't that surprise me?" she murmured, watching him disappear into the building.

Chelsea decided to trust him. This could work out, she decided as she watched the sea gulls circling over the Dumpster out back of the fish shanty. It could work out very well.

It couldn't have gone better. As he waited for his order of beer-fried catfish, hush puppies, cole slaw and corn muffins, Cash remembered the soft look in Chelsea's eyes just before he kissed her, and assured himself that it wouldn't be long before he had this woman right back where he wanted her.

In his bed.

And his life.

Oh, not permanently. He was, he reminded himself firmly as he dug into his wallet and pulled out one of the crisp new twenty-dollar bills he'd gotten this morning from the automatic teller, not a forever kind of guy.

But this time around, he wasn't going to let her get away until he'd finally satisfied his hunger for a woman who no longer seemed impossibly out of reach.

Chapter Eight

Heaven help her, Roxanne thought with a sinking heart as she walked up the front sidewalk and found George Waggoner sitting on her veranda, he looked even worse than she'd feared. She was vastly relieved that she'd sent Dorothy and Jo off on a tour of the area, suggesting Jo could film some local color. She had no idea how she could have explained this.

He stood up when he saw her coming, and jammed his hands into the back pockets of his green-and-brown camouflage pants. The first thing she noticed was that he'd put on a lot of muscle since their days together. Back then he'd been skinny as a post rail with the beginning of a beer gut. A black T-shirt fit snug over a hard, rippled body. Blue tattoos snaked up his arms.

He obviously spent a lot of time working out. But beneath the coppery tan his skin looked oddly sallow. And the red veins crisscrossing the whites of his eyes like lines on a Georgia Department of Transportation map revealed that he hadn't yet won the battle of the bottle.

She stopped a few feet in front of him, which allowed

her to read the words written beneath the white skull gracing the front of the T-shirt. *Kill them all.* The words were written in what was meant to appear to be dripping blood. *And let God sort them out.*

Lovely sentiment, she thought acidly. And one he personally knew something about.

"Hey, sugar," he greeted her with a grin that revealed two tobacco-yellow chipped front teeth. He'd gotten the injury in a fight over her. At the time she'd believed he was defending her honor. Later, she'd decided George Waggoner didn't know the meaning of the word. "Aren't you just looking damn fine?"

"You look like hell." She spat the words at him like bullets. Her hands fisted at her sides. "How did you find me?"

"Now that wasn't all that difficult, honey bun. Since you do seem to be just 'bout the most famous woman in the South. Even more famous than Margaret Mitchell, is what some folks are sayin'."

His bloodshot eyes took a wicked tour of her, from the top of her blond head down to her Italian-leather-clad feet. Then back up again, lingering on her breasts before returning to meet her blistering glare.

"Damned if you aren't a sight for these sore tired ole eyes, Cora Mae."

"The name's Roxanne Scarbrough," she said acidly. "Ms. Scarbrough, to you."

"I don't know if I think much of that," he mused, rubbing his jaw. He'd splashed on some Old Spice. Either she hadn't noticed it, or she'd moved on to likin' something else. Which was, of course, what his little bride always did.

Hell, her very own stepdaddy had warned him that he was taking on more trouble than the girl was worth. That she should've been drowned at birth, like a sack of mongrel pups. But at the time, she'd been the most beautiful girl George had ever slept with. And she'd seemed so damn grateful to him for gettin' her away from the man who'd popped her cherry after her mama had passed on the summer she was twelve.

She'd been sixteen years old when they'd gotten hitched. He'd been a month shy of a year older. He had dreams of goin' to Nashville and pickin' his Fender guitar on the stage of the Grand Ole Opry with George Jones and Johnny Cash. She had dreams of becoming rich and famous and livin' in a mansion just like Graceland.

After they were married and living in the trailer at the auto-wrecking yard where he worked, he promised someday, when he made the big time, he'd buy her the fanciest damn house in the South. She told him she'd rather just buy it for herself.

And then she was gone.

But not before he'd killed a man for her.

Of course, that old goat Jubal Lott deserved what he'd got, George reminded himself. And a helluva lot more. But dammit, Cora Mae should've been more appreciative!

"The problem is, if you're Miz Scarbrough, seems like that'd make me Mr. Scarbrough. And I've kinda grown used to my own name after all these years." This time his grin was oily and sly. "Not that you'd understand 'bout that, I guess."

Roxanne almost countered that she was surprised he wasn't accustomed to answering by a number than a name, then shut her mouth just in time. She was not going to get into any kind of discussion with this man. She was going to hear him out. Pay him off. Then send him on his way. That was the decision she'd come to in the car on the way into town from Belle Terre. And that was the decision she intended to stick to.

"What are you doing here, George?"

"Can't a man pay a little social call on his wife without havin' to explain himself?"

"We're divorced. And have been for years."

"Mebee." He pulled a Marlboro down from behind his ear, broke off the filter, and tossed it aside. "Mebee not."

Inwardly, she reeled, as if struck by a body blow. Outwardly, she didn't so much as blink. "What the hell does that mean?"

"It means I don't recall ever gettin' any divorce papers."

"They were sent to you." Her icy eyes met his and held, denying him to call the lie. "And you signed them."

"Funny, but I don't recollect doin' that." He rubbed his jaw again. Then shook his head. "No. Seems to me if a man signed papers that important, it'd stick in his mind."

"It was obviously stored in a part of the brain killed off by alcohol."

He lit the cigarette with a turquoise-and-silver Zippo lighter, rocked back on his heels, and began puffing away as he looked up at the sky. As if pondering on the matter.

When she realized exactly how much the slimy no-account bastard was enjoying this, Roxanne could have killed him.

"Nope," he decided finally. "Now, I don't want to call you a liar, Cora Mae—"

"Roxanne."

He smirked. Then continued right where he'd left off. "But I know damn well I didn't sign any divorce papers. So, the way I see it, Cora Mae Waggoner—and, I imagine, the state of Georgia sees it—your husband's just come home."

Roxanne was nothing if not tenacious. "You signed them."

"Well, now, sugar—" he glanced down at his watch

"—most of the clerks at the courthouse are probably on their lunch break. But I bet if we went there together, and talked real nice, some sweet little gal might be willing to locate a copy of our decree. So we can settle this right now."

They both knew exactly what they'd find.

They both knew she'd forged his name.

Hell, Roxanne thought darkly.

"Looks as if we've got ourselves a Mexican standoff." He didn't even try to conceal the enjoyment he was receiving from her discomfort.

She gritted her teeth and marched past him, nearly radiating with pent-up rage. "You may as well come in. I refuse to discuss this out on the street like common people."

"Never been anything common about you, Cora Mae," George said obligingly.

As he followed her into the flowered foyer, George's rough laugh sent icy chills up Roxanne's spine.

The Ferrari's radio was tuned to a country station. When Chelsea began humming along with Alan Jackson, Cash slid her a sideways glance.

"I wouldn't have taken you for a country music fan."

"Oh, I tune in from time to time," she said, lifting her uncomfortably hot and heavy hair off the back of her neck. "Between the opera and the opening night at the symphony."

Her voice was as dry as one of the dusters that he'd had the misfortune to spend a summer drilling in the oil fields of west Texas. He'd been told that there was a lot of money to be made in black gold. And truthfully, even the roustabout pay he'd earned wasn't bad. But falling into bed bone weary every night with that dirt imbedded into every pore just hadn't seemed worth it. So, he'd returned to Georgia and spent the rest of his college vacations shrimping out in the Gulf Coast.

The work was just as hard. And shrimp was just as bad smelling—perhaps worse—than Texas crude. But at least he wasn't in danger of baking to death in the dust.

When he didn't respond to her sarcasm, Chelsea glanced his way. "Did it ever occur to you that you have a habit of putting people into neat, tidy little pigeonholes?"

He didn't deny it. As an architect, he continually took infinite pieces of minutiae, and successfully put it all together. It was mandatory that every line, every curve, every angle, all come together into a coherent, workable whole. Any deviation from the plan was asking for trouble.

"You may have a point." He turned off onto a winding narrow road. "But you do the same thing."

"I do not."

"Are you telling me you didn't view me as some black-leather-jacket-wearing, motorcycle-riding rebel?"

"You did wear a leather jacket. And ride a motorcycle."

"Gotta give you that one," he said agreeably. "But contrary to the old adage, clothes don't make the man. Putting my old jacket on your Yankee boyfriend sure as hell wouldn't have heated up his thin blue blood.

"Face it, darlin', he was safe. I was dangerous. Two opposites who you kept in separate little boxes, pulling us out according to your whim. Or your need. When you wanted to feel grounded, you stayed with him. When you wanted to fly, you came to me."

Even discounting his arrogant claim that he could make her fly—which, dammit, he could—the description was horribly unflattering. "Surely you don't believe that's true?"

"Got a better explanation?"

Of course she did. As they drove past acres of rice fields,

she tried to come up with a single argument and came up distressingly blank.

"I thought so."

His smug, knowing tone made her temper flare and caused her to dig in her bag again for more antacids. If she did decide to stay in Raintree, she'd undoubtedly have to begin buying Rolaids by the case.

"And what about you? Are you telling me that you didn't get off on screwing the Deb of the Year?"

"It had its moments." Ignoring her glare, he grinned. "Like that late-night excursion to the library stacks, when you managed to disrupt western civilization from Athens to Florence."

The memory flooded back. His clever, wicked hands unzipping her jeans, slipping between her damp panties and her hot skin, stroking her moist flesh, bringing her to a mind-blinding orgasm within seconds.

In an attempt to keep her knees from buckling, she'd grabbed blindly at the shelf he'd pushed her up against, sending books alphabetized from *A* to *F* tumbling to the floor.

"Lord, I can't believe we did that." But they had, she remembered. And more. "What if we'd been caught?"

"I suppose someone would have gotten an up-close and personal lesson on research techniques."

"It was stupid. And reckless." And *wonderful*.

"That was the point," he said again. "It was also dangerous, which makes my other point, since I doubt if you've ever behaved with such lack of decorum with your Yankee."

Despite the passing of years, despite how far Cash had come, it did not escape her attention that one of the things that had not changed was his utter lack of regard for the other man in her life.

"What I had...have," she corrected, "with Nelson is different."

"Safe. Predictable."

She couldn't deny it. She also refused to admit it.

"Comfortable," she corrected not quite truthfully. She and Nelson hadn't been entirely comfortable in each other's space for months. "Fulfilling." Now that *was* a lie. "And why do you even care about my relationship with Nelson, anyway?"

Cash knew he was in big, big trouble when even hearing the creep's name could cause his gut to clench. "Because we're going to be lovers. And although I suppose it really doesn't matter in the whole scheme of things, I'd kind of like to know if you're sleeping with me because of what I can give you. Or what your blue-blooded lover boy can't."

Well, she certainly couldn't accuse him of beating around the bush. For a southerner, Cash had always been as unflinchingly direct as the New England Yankees that had provided the sturdy rootstock of her Lowell and Whitney family trees. But if he thought they could merely pick up where they'd left off, he had another think coming.

"We're not going to be lovers."

"Of course we are."

His easy arrogance fueled her irritation yet again, effectively expunging an unbidden image of her and Cash rolling around in his unmade bed in his rented room that had always smelled of wood smoke, gasoline from the garage below and sex.

"Pretty sure of yourself, aren't you?" Another thing that seemed not to have changed in the least during their time apart.

"No." The single word, honestly spoken, drew her gaze back to him. "I'm that sure of us."

Her irritation dissolved. Her mouth went as dry as the

roast turkey her mother's cook served every Thanksgiving. She was trying to think of something, anything, to say, when the road ended and he stopped the Ferrari in front of a house. Chelsea focused her attention in its direction as they got out of the car.

It was two stories high, but rested on a raised basement, which essentially made it three stories. A bark-shingled, sweeping roof with three gabled windows took up the top half of the house; a screened porch with dual stairs going down to the ground took up the bottom half. Both ends were flanked with chimneys.

"It's darling." The horizontal plank siding had been painted a soft white that gleamed like a pearl in the shimmering sun.

"The wood is hand-hewn heart pine timbers from here on the property. They were pegged, instead of nailed. The basement is made of tabby—equal parts oyster shells, lime made from the shells, sand and water. It was pretty much standard around this part of the state because it's durable and the components were more easily accessible than brick."

"It's such a different style from so many of the houses I've seen."

"That's because when most people think of the South, they tend to picture Greek Revival homes, like Belle Terre. This is a West India cottage. The original owner had owned a tobacco plantation in the islands and moved here when he was given a land grant in the 1750s from King George II. I guess he liked the house he left behind, so he duplicated it here."

"Has it been occupied all that time?"

"Off and on. The previous owner passed on about ten years ago and the place has been sitting empty. I rescued it from the kudzu, and started restoring it."

He glanced around. "The original plantation was fifteen hundred acres." He looked out over the lush green landscape that had grown wild during its years of abandonment. "It's down to about a hundred. When I get the place cleared off, I'm thinking about planting peanuts. Or, maybe pecans. I'm working on a crop plan with the county extension agent."

"You own a hundred acres of riverfront property? As well as this house?"

"It's not all riverfront. It's also mortgaged up to the rafters. Which is why I agreed to work with the dragon lady. Would you like a grand tour?"

"I'd love to see the inside."

Chelsea stopped in front of the door and couldn't help smiling at the small metal plaque. "Rebel's Ridge?"

"I didn't name it," he said, somewhat defensively.

Chelsea laughed. "It's perfect."

He'd been a rebel when she'd known him at Yale, and although anyone would have to consider him respectable now, the fact that he'd turned his back on a prestigious career to return home to this small southern town proved Cash still marched to his own drum.

"It was named during the war," Cash said. "Confederate soldiers were garrisoned here to keep a lookout for Union troops coming down the river."

She grinned up at him, enjoying his seeming embarrassment. "It still suits you."

Cash shrugged. But secretly, he guessed he agreed. Which was why, although he'd always considered naming houses pretentious, he'd replaced the plaque after sanding and repainting the siding.

"Oh!" She stared in delight as she walked into a cool cream-walled entry hall. "It's so much larger than I expected."

"The house itself is about eighteen hundred square feet. The fifteen-foot ceilings help give a feeling of spaciousness and all the windows make the veranda seem part of the interior."

Although the outside of the house was deceptively simple, the inside boasted exquisite plaster work. Chelsea admired the plaster cornices and medallions along the edge of the ceiling and framing the doorways.

She expressed appreciation for the hand planing on the walls and ceilings, and the pine woodwork that he told her had once been painted a bright robin's egg blue.

"The only thing on it now is a clear sealant," Cash said. "I wanted the beauty of the wood to show through."

"Well, you certainly succeeded there." She ran her hand across the double doors to the parlor and found them as smooth as a baby's bottom. "It's truly lovely, Cash. You should be so proud. I understand now why Roxanne's thrilled you agreed to restore Belle Terre."

Her obvious admiration should not make him feel so damn good. Like some rooster strutting around the barnyard showing off for a bunch of hens. No. Cash scowled at that image, thinking it fit her Yankee lover more than him.

How about a stallion galloping around the paddock, showing off for a mare? Better, Cash decided. But he still didn't enjoy realizing exactly how much her approval meant to him.

"I must've peeled off twenty layers of wallpaper before I could replaster," he said as he led the way upstairs to the bedrooms. "These holes are from minié balls."

Chelsea ran her fingertips wonderingly over the indentations. "From the war?"

"One of the final skirmishes of Sherman's campaign took place right here. Two days before those businessmen surrendered Savannah to him. Five Confederate infantrymen and a dozen Union solders were killed. There's a stone marker outside.''

Chelsea glanced out the window. The house, as its name implied, had been built on a ridge overlooking the river in one direction, the abandoned farmland in the other. ''What are those?''

Cash followed her gaze to the cluster of buildings in the distance. ''Old plantation outbuildings. That one to the left is the barn. Then the blacksmith shop. And the smokehouse.

''And those three white tabby buildings used to be slave quarters. After the war, when the slaves were freed, they become sharecropper cottages.''

Something had changed in his voice. It had become rougher. And possessed an edge she was not accustomed to hearing in his deep tone. ''Cash?''

He shook his head. ''Sorry. My mind was wandering again.''

He wondered what she'd say if he'd told her that he was picturing a young boy, playing marbles in the dirt in front of one of those spartan cabins, while his mother rolled out dough for peach pies in the tiny, ill-equipped kitchen.

He continued showing her the upstairs, which was in more disarray than downstairs. ''I'm taking things a room at a time. I figure I should finally have the place finished just about when I'm ready to collect Social Security.''

''They say everyone needs a project,'' she teased.

''At least I know what mine is through the next millennium.''

They went back downstairs. Then he took her out to the backyard. The marker for the fallen soldiers was located in the shade of an old willow tree.

As she stood beside the simple gray stone, the bygone era seemed very real to Chelsea for the first time.

''This is so sad.'' She sighed as she looked down at the

stone. There were no names. Just the date of the battle. And a single line dedicated to the bravery of the Yankees and Rebels who'd fought and died there that day.

"War always is unfortunate. But civil wars are more tragic than most, because neither side is fighting for territory or domination. But for opposing ideals." He shook his head. "There's no real winning a war like that."

"I'd never thought of it that way," she admitted. "But I suppose you're right."

The tour concluded, they walked down the steps to the boat dock. When he'd mentioned taking her out on a fishing boat, she'd pictured an old wooden or aluminum rowboat with an outboard motor. This boat was a sleek, low Fiberglas craft that reminded her of a fighter jet. She stared in amazement as he pointed out the electronic gadgetry: hydraulic pedestal seats, the water temperature gauges, the aerated fish wells, the flickering orange lights of the depth finders and electric trolling motors.

"Surely you don't need all this to fish?"

"Of course you don't. But it makes it more fun."

"Like your Batmobile makes driving more fun?"

This time his grin was more sheepish than cocky. "The Ferrari was an impulse, one I don't regret. But I'm about ready to trade it in on a car I can drive in the rain." When she glanced over at him curiously, he elaborated. "I'm too tall to drive with the top up."

"Maybe you should consider moving to the desert. Phoenix, Tucson, Las Vegas."

"I suppose I could do that. But I've decided that I'm just a southern boy at heart, so I'm stuck here. It'd probably be easier just to get the Jag I was looking at last week."

Once again, Chelsea was amazed by how much Cash's situation had changed. Although she'd suspected he was talented—they didn't let just anyone into the Yale school of architecture—never could she have imagined her rebel lover living so comfortably in a world of expensive cars, sleek boats, and two-hundred-year-old plantation homes.

Unwilling to admit how that thought confirmed his earlier accusation, that perhaps his appeal had initially been his lack of wealth, which made him so different from the boys she'd grown up with, she decided the time had come to at least give him credit for accomplishing so much.

"I'm impressed."

"By a Jag? This from a girl who was probably handed the keys to a sporty Mercedes convertible on her sixteenth birthday?"

"It wasn't a Mercedes." It was a BMW. Her mother drove the Mercedes.

"A Beemer, then."

She couldn't help laughing at how accurately he'd hit that target. "Ah, we're back to the pigeonholing problem," she accused lightly. "And no, Jags don't impress me. Nor do Ferraris, fancy homes, or speedboats."

"So, since it isn't my conspicuous consumption of consumer goods, what is it about me that impresses you? Other than my devastating good looks and animal magnetism?"

Even though the last two had to count for something, Chelsea understood he was joking. "I'm impressed by how hard you must have worked to achieve all this." She waved her hand, encompassing the little corner of paradise he'd carved out for himself. "I had no idea architecture paid so well."

"It does in the Bay Area."

"Yet you left."

"I told you. I'm a southern boy at heart."

He did not tell Chelsea *that* had proven the biggest surprise of his life. For years he'd plotted and schemed and saved to escape the stultifying rigidity of southern society.

Where a man was judged by who his family was, and not for who *he* was. Where the content of the social register was more important than the content of a man's character.

"So you came home."

He threw back his head and laughed at that. "In a way."

He didn't elaborate on his reaction. And Chelsea didn't ask. But as he headed the boat downriver, Cash wondered what she'd say if she knew that he'd been born in one of those little tabby slave cottages and had lived there until that rainy spring day his father had died under a John Deere tractor.

The day of the funeral his mother had gotten evicted by the landlord and they'd moved into town, where she managed to find work doing laundry and cleaning other people's houses while he delivered papers, swept out the pool hall, did odd jobs for Fancy and ran errands for her girls.

The first place he'd gone, after returning to Raintree, had been the whorehouse. He'd been disappointed, but not surprised to discover it had been condemned in his absence. And razed to make room for a Piggly Wiggly supermarket.

Cash still couldn't decide if that was progress or not.

"Whooee," George whistled appreciatively as he stared at the opulent surroundings. "I gotta tell you, Cora Mae, you done yourself proud. Hot damn if this place isn't nearly as fancy as Graceland."

He picked up a Lalique rabbit, one of her prized zoo collection; the crystal split the afternoon sun streaming in through the windows into rainbows that danced on the floral papered walls.

"And it's a helluva long way from that tar paper shack you and your mama and stepdaddy lived in." He exchanged the rabbit for an elephant.

As he ran a finger down the crystal trunk, Roxanne stared

at his torn and ragged cuticles, his grease-encrusted hands with the dusting of black hair on the back and felt a surge of revulsion so strong it made her shudder. How could she have ever allowed this man to touch her?

"Keep your voice down," she instructed him. "I don't want my housekeeper hearing our conversation."

"Then perhaps you better give her the rest of the day off," he suggested. "Because you and I have a lot of unfinished business to take care of. And believe me, sugar, after ridin' that bus all the way across the country, I'm damn well not going to leave until we get things settled."

Although his yellow smile appeared harmless enough, Roxanne saw the seeds of violence lurking in his red-veined eyes and knew he meant it. "Wait here. I'll be right back." She plucked the crystal from his hands and replaced it to the shelf. "And don't touch anything."

It took some doing, but she managed to convince her housekeeper that she'd be safe. Now, if only she could convince herself, Roxanne considered grimly as she returned to the library and found him sprawled in her Queen Anne wing chair, drinking whiskey from one of her Waterford tumblers.

"That happens to be an iced tea glass."

"Always hated iced tea." He took a drink and breathed out a long satisfied sigh. "Even if it is the goddamn national drink of the South. But the glass is just about the right size. Saves refilling."

"I'm so pleased you're pleased." Although Roxanne did not usually drink—she hated risking any loss of control—these were not usual circumstances. She tossed some Irish whiskey into one of the shorter old-fashioned glasses, then sat down in the chair across from him.

"Since I have no desire to rehash old memories with you, George, let's just knock off the bullshit and get down to the bottom line. How much will it take to make you go away?"

"Now, sweetie pie," he complained, "you're taking all the fun out of this. This here's the South, Cora Mae. Just because you're making money hand over fist like some Wall Street banker don't mean that you gotta start acting like a damn tight-assed Yankee.

"I may not know as much 'bout bidness as you do, but ain't you supposed to start softening me up a little before we get down to the nitty-gritty?"

"I'd rather suck mud from the Okefenokee Swamp."

"That could be arranged."

"Are you threatening me?"

"Just makin' conversation, sugar." He stood up, tossed back the liquor and headed toward the door. "But if you don't want to hear me out, mebee I can find someone who will."

Although sweat was beginning to puddle between her breasts, a lifetime of acting allowed Roxanne to keep her tone cool. "You're forgetting one thing. You can't tell people about me without risking being brought up on murder charges yourself."

"You know, I've had plenty of time to consider that possibility," he agreed. "But the thing is, honey bun, if there *is* any evidence around about your stepdaddy's unfortunate and untimely demise, it's gonna point straight at you."

"That's not true! You killed Jubal."

"There's not a lick of proof of that," he reminded her. "In fact, now that I think on it, the only thing that might just suggest Jubal Lott's death wasn't from that mugging the night he got drunk down at the Dewdrop Inn, is that letter you wrote me beggin' me to kill him. And saying that if I didn't, you'd have to do it yourself."

"But you did kill him." She'd never forget that day. Never forget how terrified she'd been. And how happy.

"I've got an alibi sayin' different. In case it ever comes up." He rubbed his jaw. "I also still got that letter."

"I don't believe you." Her crisp tone belied her pounding heart.

"You can believe what you want. But it's the truth."

"Let me see it."

"You don't think I'd carry it 'round with me? All these years?" He shook his head. "Hell, Cora Mae, you know me, I'd lose my head if it weren't screwed on real tight. That's why I tucked it away somewhere nice and safe. Never know when something like that's gonna come in handy."

She'd suffered nightmares about this moment. More times than she'd cared to count. The fears that she managed to keep at bay during the day crept back at night, invading her sleep, torturing her dreams, leaving her sitting bolt upright in bead, drenched in sweat.

She closed her eyes, took a long breath meant to calm and made her decision. "Name your price."

He did. And it was, as she would have suspected, ridiculously low, considering the circumstances. "Fine. I'll need some time to get to the bank. I will, of course, want this to be a cash transaction."

"Cash works for me," George said agreeably. This was turning out to even easier than he'd hoped. "There's one more little thing."

Caught up in the logistics of how she was going to explain the need to transfer fifty thousand dollars in cash from her corporate account to her personal account, it took a minute for his words to sink in. "What now?"

"Well, you see, I got myself in a bit of trouble a while back—"

"Now why doesn't that surprise me?" she muttered.

"Now, honey bun, there's no need to get nasty. The thing

is, I ended up doin' a little time for what was mostly a misunderstanding.''

That explained his pasty complexion, she decided. It was obviously prison pallor. "I don't see why your legal difficulties should have anything to do with me." A horrible thought occurred to her. What if he'd broken out of prison? What if the authorities were searching for him right now? What if they tracked him here?

"The thing is, I've got this probation officer who thinks I oughta be workin'."

"What a novel concept."

He did not seem to take offense at her remark. "You always did have a smart mouth on you, Cora Mae. 'Course these days your words are more the fifty-cent kind, 'stead of the nickel ones you used to toss at me. But they still hit the mark."

"You were telling me about your probation officer."

"Yeah. Well, the way I figger it, I need a job or I'm gonna have to go back to Arizona. And you're fixing up that old house, so you're bound to need guys handy with a hammer."

He paused, not bothering to add how Jubal had died after having his head bashed in with a sixteen-ounce claw hammer. There was no need. Not when they both remembered that night so vividly.

"I figure this is another one of those cases of us being able to help each other out."

"There is no way in hell I would hire you. Which is a moot point, because I'm not even involved in such petty details."

"Now it may be a petty detail to you, Cora Mae. But it's goddamn important to me. I need this job. And you're gonna get it for me."

His eyes had turned to hard black stones. For the first

time since he'd arrived, she was looking at the cold-blooded killer she knew him to be.

"I can't."

"Of course you can. And you will."

"Who will I say you are?"

"How about your husband?" When that earned a glare, he laughed. "Now, honey bun, you're underestimating yourself again. Like that lady on "Good Morning America" said, you've got one helluva imagination. So, think something up. But think fast. Because the clock's tickin' on this one."

"Why can't you just take the money and go away?"

"And end up on "America's Most Wanted" for jumping parole? Nope. That wasn't one of your better ideas. Guess you'll have to try again."

"I suppose I could say you were a cousin of one of my office employees."

"There you go." He grinned. "So, how about we have a drink to celebrate? You got any champagne?"

Chapter Nine

Although Chelsea felt guilty about playing hooky when she still hadn't made a decision about writing Roxanne's book, as Cash steered the boat away from the dock, she realized this was exactly what she needed. She'd been working so hard for so long, she couldn't remember the last time she took some time out to enjoy herself. The last few years of her life had swept like a speeding runaway locomotive down the career track she'd so purposefully chosen.

Five minutes passed. Then ten. And still neither Cash nor Chelsea spoke. She didn't ask where they were going; she wouldn't have known the location if he'd told her. Instead, for once, she was content to simply relax.

She watched the scenery for a while. Then, lulled by the movement of the boat churning through the water, and the warmth of the sun, she unbuttoned the top three buttons of her blouse, rolled up the sleeves, leaned back, closed her eyes, trailed her hand idly in the water and allowed her mind to wander.

Watching her, Cash wondered if she knew how gorgeous she was, with her rich copper hair fluttering in the wind, her exquisite face tilted up toward the sun, her lashes bright spikes on her porcelain cheeks. Her scent drifted toward him, faint, slightly spicy, distinctly sexy, creating a tug that was no longer unexpected, but frustrating just the same.

His gaze slid to her left hand. Her fingers were long, her nails short and unpainted. She wasn't wearing a ring, something that had been intriguing him from the beginning. Meredith had suggested she'd married. But if that was the case, considering how much dough her Yankee had, Cash would have expected her to be sporting a diamond the size of the Georgia Dome.

Of course, huge flashy rocks were more Roxanne Scarbrough's style. But at least, if she'd finally taken the plunge, Waring would have insisted she wear a gold band. If for no other reason than to stake his claim.

Dreams Cash thought he'd forgotten, memories he thought he'd buried deep inside him, came flooding back. And with them all the painful desires and frustrations he'd suffered during that crazed time when just looking at Chelsea Cassidy had made him ache with a need that went all the way to the bone.

Angry that she could still affect him so intensely, without even trying, he said, "It's getting hot. I think it's time we cooled off before lunch."

He thrust the throttle forward, causing the sleek boat to streak forward like a thoroughbred breaking out of the starting gate. Chelsea was pushed back against her seat, the wind began whipping her hair into a fiery froth, the deep vibrating thrum of the engines stirring her blood.

The scenery on the banks of the river became a dark green blur, the boat bucked as it cut a swatch down the center of the river, sending up a spuming rooster tail.

She laughed. "This reminds me of riding your Harley," she shouted over the roar of the engines. The water churned wildly in the wide wake behind them. "You always drove too fast."

"I don't remember you complaining."

"I wasn't now." Her hair flew into her face, and she pushed it back with both hands. "I was just remembering how much you always liked speed."

"Not all the time," he shouted back. "Some things I liked to do very, very slowly."

"What we had was over a long time ago," she insisted, leaning forward so she could be heard.

"You sure about that?"

"Positive," she lied without compunction.

"I don't suppose you'd be willing to let me kiss you again? And see if you still feel the same way afterward?"

"That's not necessary."

"It might be easier just to get it out of our systems. Once and for all."

"Why don't you worry about your own system? Because mine's just dandy, thank you."

He flashed her a wicked grin that came just short of calling her a liar. "Whatever you say."

They raced down the river in silence, each aware of the other. Finally, after about twenty minutes, he cut the engines.

"You're getting too much color." Her cheeks were pink and a sprinkling of freckles were scattered over the bridge of her nose.

"If I'd known I was going to spend the afternoon on a river, I would have brought along some sunscreen."

"No problem." He reached into a cabinet and pulled out a white tube of sunblock and handed it to her. His gaze settled on that rosy V of flesh framed by her unbuttoned blouse. "Want some help spreading it on?"

"No, thanks."

He sighed and decided that it was probably for the best. "Whatever you want. I'll put up the canopy."

While she spread the creamy white lotion over her face and arms, he busied himself setting up an awning to shade them.

The fried catfish and hush puppies were drenched in grease. They were also delicious. "I can't believe I ate all that," Chelsea said, staring in amazement at the empty box.

"You always were a woman of strong appetites," Cash reminded her wickedly.

Only with you, she could have answered, but didn't. "I'd weigh a thousand pounds if I lived down here."

"A few pounds couldn't hurt." She'd always been slender. But now she was thin. And her face, while still stunning, appeared almost gaunt. "If you're not careful, you're going to end up looking like one of Tom Wolfe's New York X-ray women."

She paused in the act of wiping her greasy hands on the white paper napkins. "You read *Bonfire of the Vanities?*"

Her surprise was so transparent he could have throttled her. "Sure. Between issues of *Guns and Ammo* and *Redneck Journal.*"

She flushed, knowing she'd been guilty of stereotyping again. It also made her uncomfortable to realize how much like her mother—or Nelson—she must have sounded.

"I'm sorry. I didn't mean it that way. I just don't think of men as reading that much fiction. Unless it's Tom Clancy, or Michael Crichton, or some macho male fantasy story."

"Are you questioning my manhood now?" His easy smile assured her he was teasing.

"Of course not. It's just that…" She dragged a hand through her hair. "I suppose the truth is, we don't really know all that much about each other."

"Now's as good a time as any to resolve that. We never spent much time talking."

They'd had better things to do back then. Over the years he'd tried to tell himself that his uptown girl was just another lay. Better than most, but nothing to get all twisted up in knots over. So why did he still get that aching pain in his heart whenever he remembered the night she'd turned down his proposal?

"Except for that last night," she murmured.

"My mouth sure as hell ran away with me that night."

"I liked listening. Your plans were so exciting. I remember thinking at the time…" Her voice drifted off.

"What?" This time he caught her hand on its way through her hair. "What were you thinking?"

The way he was looking at her—hard and deep—made her mouth go dry. She dragged her gaze to the lush green riverbank. "That you were the only person I'd ever met who could possibly understand how driven I was."

"Is that all?"

"I don't remember." She shrugged, still refusing to meet his probing dark eyes. "It was a long time ago."

"Chelsea." He captured her chin in his free hand and turned her head toward him. "What else were you thinking?"

She swallowed and decided that after all this time there was no point in not telling him the truth. "I envied you your ability to start fresh somewhere, where no one knew you. I admired your courage to take off all on your own. And—" she took a deep breath "—I wished I could go with you."

"I asked you to."

All these years she'd wondered. And now she knew. Chelsea wondered why the answer left her feeling so strangely sad. She closed her eyes briefly, allowed herself a momentary regret for lost opportunities, then reminded herself yet again, that those days, and that strange and wonderful night, was in the past.

"I wondered about that. But I wasn't sure. And I was afraid that if I said yes, you'd laugh at me and tell me I'd misunderstood."

"I wouldn't have laughed. Not at you." His fingers trailed down her throat. "Never at you." He'd told himself that he'd left Chelsea Cassidy behind that night. But he'd lied. Because seven years and countless women hadn't managed to dilute the emotions she could instill.

Because he realized that he was suddenly standing on the brink of a precipice and a wrong step could send them both tumbling over the edge, he backed away. Both physically and figuratively.

"That last night, you let me do all the talking. I think this time it's your turn."

She shrugged and tried not to be disappointed when he stopped touching her. "There's not that much to tell."

"It's a long road from summer in the Hamptons to eating greasy fried catfish on the Savannah River. I'd like to hear the story."

"This may take a while," she warned.

He leaned back, stretching his legs out in front of him. "I'm not going anywhere."

To Chelsea's amazement, once she started, the words poured forth, like floodwaters surging through a broken dam.

He already knew, from the dinner at Roxanne's about her famous father. And the fact that she'd written her first story when she was five.

"But it was the newspaper that changed my life," she recalled now.

"The one you printed with the press you got for your tenth birthday."

"It was the best present I'd ever received." Her mother had bought her another Madame Alexander doll—which was immediately locked away with the others in the glass display case in her fairy-tale princess bedroom.

"Six months after the premiere edition of the *East Side Weekly Tribune* hit the streets, I had one hundred and fifty subscribers. Four years later, the *Tribune* was being professionally printed on an offset press in Queens, I'd hired six classmates as stringers and my subscription list had more than tripled."

"I'm impressed."

"Thank you." She grinned. "You're supposed to be. Of course, there wasn't much hard news. Mostly it was just gossip."

Although the old-money WASPs who resided in the privileged environs of Manhattan's East Side would have denied enjoying anything so common as gossip, each Saturday morning an amazing number of them would sit on their terraces with cups of coffee and discover what their neighbors had been up to all week.

"Gossip makes the world go 'round," Cash said. "And it sounds as if since there weren't any clotheslines on Park Avenue for people to chat over, you were clever enough to spot the need and fill it."

She liked the idea that instead of belittling her youthful efforts, Cash immediately understood.

"Your folks must have been proud."

"I like to think my dad would have been. Unfortunately, he was killed before he was able to read an issue."

"I'm sorry."

She shrugged and fought against the unbidden and unexpected sting of tears. "I've gotten used to it."

"Getting used to it and getting over it are two different things." He ran his palm down the slide of her hair. "My dad died when I was just a kid, too.

"I didn't know."

"No reason for you to," he said simply. "He died in a farm accident. A tractor fell on him. I found him when I went out to call him in to dinner."

"How terrible!"

"It wasn't one of my better days." When he felt the pall settling over what he'd hoped would be an enjoyable afternoon, Cash decided it was time to change the subject. "So, I'll bet your mother was proud of having a budding journalistic star in the family."

"Hardly. She'd like nothing more than for me to get married and provide a Lowell heir."

So Melanie had been mistaken. Chelsea wasn't married, after all. Cash knew he was in deep, deep trouble when he experienced a cooling rush of relief.

"How about Waring?" He congratulated himself on managing to say his rival's name. "What does he think of the idea?"

"He's very proud of me," Chelsea hedged.

"That wasn't what I asked. Are you and the Yankee still planning to get married?"

"Eventually." Her tone lacked conviction, even to her own ears.

"How about kids?"

"Of course we'll have children. Eventually." And when they did, she intended to give them roots, Chelsea thought. A sense of belonging she'd never experienced in her own family.

"Seems to me if you really loved the guy, you'd have married him by now. Career or no career."

''Not that it's any of your business, but there happen to be extenuating circumstances.''

''That's bullshit.'' He leaned forward, until his lips were inches away from her tightly drawn, unpainted ones. ''If you were my woman, Chelsea, I wouldn't let anything stand in the way of getting you to the altar.

''And I can sure as hell tell you that if we'd been together as long as you and that blue-blooded creep have been playing house, we'd already have a couple of rug rats. In fact, if I took you home and did what I want to do to you right now, before the sun came up tomorrow morning, you'd have my baby growing beneath that fine smooth belly.''

His hand splayed over her stomach, causing her nerves to tangle. ''Dammit, Cash, if you don't quit touching me—''

''I like touching you.'' He also planned to do a lot more of it. But for now, not wanting to scare her away, he retrieved his hand. ''You realize, of course, this would be a lot easier if you'd gotten fat and ugly these past few years.''

That earned a faint smile. ''I'm sorry.''

He laughed at that. ''I'm not. You're as gorgeous as ever. More so with that aura of success around you.'' He took her hand in his and laced their fingers together again. ''Answer me one question.'' His expression sobered. ''Are you happy?''

''Of course. I told you, Cash, although it might not be the kind of journalism that made my father famous, I truly love my work, and although things have admittedly been hectic this past year, my career has really begun to take off lately, and this opportunity to work with Roxanne, if I accept the offer, is bound to garner me a lot of attention. Especially since I'm also working on a novel that my agent assures me should sell and—''

''I'm not talking about work. I'm talking about your life.''

"But my work is my life." She thought of his lovely riverfront home, complete with acreage. The boat, the car, the expensive jacket he'd worn to dinner last night. "You, of all people, should be able to understand that."

"I do. To a point. But I guess I really wanted to know if you and the yuppie prince are happy together."

"Of course we are." Once again, her voice lacked conviction.

"He's the wrong man for you, Chelsea. Always was. Always will be."

"And I suppose you're claiming to be the right man for me?"

"Hell, no." This time his rough laugh held not a trace of humor. "But that hasn't stopped me from wanting you all these years. From thinking about the might have beens. And waking up from some hot dream and being forced to think of you clear across the country, lying in some other man's arms. In some other man's bed."

"Actually, the bed is mine," she corrected nonsensically. "I inherited it from my grandmother Lowell."

"Quit splitting hairs. You know what I mean."

"Yes." Her voice was little more than a whisper. "Because I've felt the same way about you so many times."

There was a little hitch in her voice that ripped at his heart. "Dammit, Chelsea." He lowered his forehead to hers and closed his eyes. "You're not making this any easier."

"I know." She closed her own eyes and sighed. "I don't know what you want from me."

"That makes two of us." He tamped down his frustration. And his need. "Maybe we ought to think on it."

Chelsea could tell it was not his first choice. If she were to be perfectly honest, she'd have to admit that it wasn't exactly hers, either. But it was the wisest course.

"That's probably a good idea."

"Probably." He felt every bit as unenthusiastic as she sounded. "It's undoubtedly the grown-up thing to do."

"The mature thing," she agreed. "The sensible thing."

"Right." The corner of his mouth tilted. "We'll take things slow. Get to know one another. Consider all the options, where we've been and where we're going. And then—" he bent his head and gave her a quick hard kiss that left her head spinning "—we can get naked and drive each other crazy."

He was as outrageous as ever. Amused at the words she knew were not really a joke, Chelsea tried to remember the last time anything or anyone had made her laugh.

The late afternoon sun, riding low on the horizon, slipped beneath the awning to shine in her eyes, making her realize how long they'd been out on the river.

"We should probably be getting back," she said.

Before starting the engines again, he paused, gave her another long look, then unable to resist touching her just one more time, ran a finger down her cheek. Her skin was warm and slightly flushed in a way that made him want to taste it.

"It's too late for going back, Chelsea. For either of us."

Knowing in her heart that he was right, but not knowing what on earth she was going to do about these unruly feelings he'd triggered, Chelsea didn't answer.

After sending George on his way with $250 in cash, a bottle of Dom Pérignon and a promise to have the fifty thousand dollars for him tomorrow, Roxanne went upstairs, sat down at her dressing table and began rubbing moisturizer into her hands, which, appearances to the contrary, suddenly felt cracked and dry. She plucked a cotton boll from a Waterford vase, and brushed a fingertip over the hardened spikes sticking out of the fluffy white cotton.

Her mind drifted back, to those long hot miserable days of her childhood. While other children would be splashing down at the swimming pool, or watching movies in the air-conditioned splendor of the Fox theater, she'd been out in the fields behind their ramshackle tar paper sharecropper's cabin, chopping cotton. Although it had been hotter than blazes, the spikes on the cotton bolls could rip the skin, forcing her to wear long pants and oversize cast-off flannel shirts belonging to her brutal stepdaddy.

The work had been so backbreaking that by the end of the day, she'd be on her hands and knees, crawling down the endless cotton rows, carrying the sack on her back, earning a mere two dollars for every pound she managed to pick. Most of that two dollars, of course, Jubal would manage to drink away. And then he'd come home.

Remembering all those nights he'd come into her room, into her bed, forcing his disgusting, smelly bulk on her, she closed her eyes and moaned. A headache pounded behind her eyes.

Then she took a deep breath and told herself sternly that Cora Mae Padgett no longer existed. Roxanne Scarbrough had taken her place, and Roxanne was a force to be reckoned with. She tossed the cotton boll back into the vase and began massaging a ridiculously expensive, sweet-scented lotion into hands that had once, since you couldn't pick cotton while wearing gloves, been rough and cracked and raw.

Now they were as smooth as an infant's bottom, and her nails, which she had done every Thursday afternoon, were manicured to perfection. She'd put the torn and bleeding cuticles and pus-filled wounds behind her. At least she thought she had.

But then again, she'd thought she'd left George Waggoner in her past, too.

Unfortunately, she'd been wrong.

Dead wrong.

The afternoon on the river taught Chelsea two things. The first was that she still had unresolved feelings for Cash.

The second was that she needed to cut her hair. It clung hot and heavy to her neck and felt like a rug on her back. Acting on impulse, as she so often did, after Cash dropped her off at the inn, she turned around and walked two blocks to the Curl Up and Dye beauty salon across the street from the courthouse.

Forty-five minutes later, she was staring at her reflection in the mirror.

"Well?" the stylist, a young woman about Chelsea's age, asked nervously. "What do you think?"

Good question. And one Chelsea was struggling to answer herself. She ran her fingers through her boyishly short hair. "I look like Little Orphan Annie." Once the heavy tresses had been cut to chin-length, her coppery hair revealed a soft, natural curl.

"It shows off your incredible eyes," the owner of the salon, who'd watched the transformation, ventured encouragingly. Everyone had gathered around to view Chelsea's reaction, including the young man whose job it was to sweep up the long bright lengths of hair lying all over the black-and-white tile floor.

It certainly did do that, Chelsea considered, remembering what Cash had said about her eyes being too big. Now, they seemed to take up her entire face. She turned around, using a hand mirror to examine the curls at the nape of her neck. As she spun back toward the bright wall of mirrors, her new image caught her by surprise.

What she looked like, Chelsea decided, was a grown-up.

Until now, she'd never realized how childlike her long straight schoolgirl hair had appeared.

She grinned at this adult woman who'd been living inside her and ruffled the bright curls with her fingers again. "I love it."

There was a collective sigh of relief.

Chelsea paid the bill with her American Express card, overtipping everyone from the owner to the shampoo girl. Forced to wait while the receptionist called for credit card's approval, she couldn't stop staring at her reflection.

A brave, strong woman was looking back at her. A woman capable of handling all storms that might blow her way. A woman who could handle Roxanne Scarbrough *and* Cash Beaudine without blinking an eye.

"I'm sorry." The receptionist's quiet voice captured Chelsea's attention. To her horror, she watched as the young woman pulled out a pair of scissors and cut the gold card in half.

"What are you doing?"

"I'm sorry." The receptionist repeated. Her expression and her voice confirmed her honest reluctance. "But I was told to confiscate your card."

"Confiscate?"

That was ridiculous. She made a good living. She always paid her bills on time. She was a Lowell. A Whitney. Her family *never* had credit cards confiscated. Well, perhaps her father may have, she allowed reluctantly, if her mother's accusations about Dylan Cassidy's free-spending life-style were even remotely true.

"There's obviously a mistake."

"I'm afraid you'll have to discuss that with American Express," the receptionist said.

The owner, having noticed the problem, appeared beside Chelsea. "Perhaps another card?" he suggested easily.

It seemed a good idea. Until two MasterCards and a Visa

were also rejected. Horribly embarrassed and confused, Chelsea paid the bill in cash.

Embarrassed and angry as she marched back to the inn to call Nelson, she didn't notice the lone individual, standing beside the statue of Colonel Bedford Mallory, watching her with unblinking concentration.

"Don't worry about a thing," Nelson assured her after she'd related her less than stellar experience. "It's merely a little mix-up with an electronic fund transfer. Melvin's getting it all straightened out. I was going to call you, but it slipped my mind."

"Slipped your mind? Nelson, I'm down here all alone in a strange town, with useless credit cards, and it slipped my mind?"

"I've been a little busy myself, darling," he said stiffly, revealing that she'd wounded his ego. *Tough.* "The stock market has been all over the place the past few days. I've been having to shift accounts like crazy just to stay even."

Still smarting from having been so embarrassed, Chelsea managed to keep from responding. She knew that if she got started, she'd start shouting at him. And as difficult as Nelson was to argue with in person, trying to hash this out long distance would be futile.

"I'm coming back tomorrow evening," she said in her coolest voice. The departure time on the tickets Roxanne had booked for her were not her first choice. When she'd called the airline to change to an earlier flight, she'd been told there were no available seats. "We'll discuss it then."

"I told you, Chelsea, the problem is being taken care of. There's absolutely nothing to discuss."

"That's what you think." Before he could answer, she slammed the receiver back onto its cradle with more force than necessary.

She'd no sooner hung up when the phone rang. She

scooped it up. "I thought you didn't want to discuss it," she snapped.

"Ms. Cassidy?" an unfamiliar voice responded hesitantly.

Hell. "Yes?"

"This is Ms. Kinney. From American Airlines. I wanted to inform you that a seat has opened up in first class on tomorrow's 8:00 a.m. flight to La Guardia. If you'd like it."

"Yes. Please, reserve it for me," Chelsea said quickly, relieved that at least something was going her way. "Thank you. And I'm sorry for my rudeness. I thought you were someone else."

"That's all right, Ms. Cassidy," the smooth voice assured her. "It seems to have been that kind of day for everyone. I'm glad I could help."

With that taken care of, Chelsea began to dial Nelson again, then decided against it. What he'd done was horrendously inconsiderate. Why give him time to think up more excuses? Arriving early would give her the element of surprise.

She went into the bathroom to take a shower to get ready for Roxanne's party. At first the sight of the unfamiliar woman in the mirror took her by surprise. Then she felt her irritation melt away.

All right, perhaps the people at the Curl Up and Dye thought she was a deadbeat. But at least, she thought with a quick grin, she looked damn good. For a deadbeat.

Chapter Ten

The party was everything Chelsea would have expected it to be. The food, prepared with recipes from Roxanne's book, *Entertaining for Special Occasions* was delicious, the wine flowed freely and the conversation was interesting and stimulating.

The life-style expert had pulled out the local big guns, introducing Chelsea to not only the mayor of Raintree, but the entire city council, two state legislators, and a Georgia Supreme Court Judge. Several members of the World Series Champion Atlanta Braves were in attendance, as was the South's most famous power couple, Ted Turner and Jane Fonda.

Besides herself, the other guest of honor appeared to be Vernon Gibbons, founder and CEO of the nationwide Mega-Mart discounting chain. Chelsea knew the multimillionaire to be a self-made man. She also determined, during their brief conversation, that he was more than pleased with his creation.

"So you're the little gal who's gonna write Roxanne's life story," he said, looking her up and down as if she were a piece of horseflesh he was considering buying for his famed thoroughbred stables.

"Nothing's been finalized yet." She managed a distant smile as she tried, with scant success to retrieve her hand, which was still being held prisoner between both of his.

"You know," he said, "I've been thinkin' about writing a book."

What a surprise. If Chelsea had a dollar for every time someone told her that, she could probably outbid Vernon Gibbons for that New England department store chain he was rumored to be trying to take over.

"I'm sure it would make fascinating reading," she said politely.

"Of course it would," Roxanne enthused. "Vernon's the quintessential American success story."

"I've always been known for gettin' what I want," he agreed. Although his tone was conversational, the rough lust in his gaze as it settled on Chelsea's breasts made her uncomfortable. "Maybe you and I could get together and discuss a collaboration of our own." His eyes crawled downward in a way that made her feel as if he were stripping off her red silk suit. "After you finish workin' with Roxanne, that is," he tacked on when Roxanne stiffened.

Unbelievingly, he was blatantly staring at the juncture of her thighs. Chelsea would rather collaborate with Charles Manson than spend five minutes alone with this man. She tugged her hand free.

"My agent handles all my business affairs." Unfortunately, manners drilled into her from the cradle, and her unwillingness to create a public scene, kept her from slapping his face. But her tone turned Deidre Lowell cool. "And I'm afraid my schedule is already quite full." She feigned a smile. "But I certainly wish you luck."

Chelsea could feel his eyes on her as she walked away.

Although she was accustomed to men's glances, she couldn't remember ever feeling so violated.

In desperate need of fresh air, Chelsea slipped out onto the veranda. She was leaning against the balustrade, enjoying the sweet scent of Roxanne's spring garden, when she was aware of someone walking up behind her.

She turned around, afraid Gibbons might have followed her out and was surprised when she viewed the familiar face instead. "Well, hello."

"Hello, to you, too." Jeb Townely smiled down at her. "I like your hair."

"Thanks. I think I like it, too."

"So, do you want to mention something about small worlds? Or shall I?"

She smiled back and felt her earlier discomfort fading. "I suppose, considering how small Raintree is, I should have realized you knew Roxanne."

"Oh, everyone knows Roxanne. If I had half the PR operation she has, the Magnolia House would be booked through the turn of the century."

She laughed at that. "I think I'm supposed to become part of the machine."

"So I hear. I guess that means you'll be staying in Raintree a while?"

"If I accept the offer." She couldn't keep her personal doubts from her tone.

"Roxanne isn't the easiest person to work with."

"Does that observation come from personal experience?"

"She redecorated Magnolia House for me. After Cash managed to turn it from a one-family house into an inn. I'm assuming, since he's working on Belle Terre, that you two have met."

"Yes."

"Cash is a good friend. Even if he did break my nose when we were kids."

"He broke your nose?" Chelsea was appalled. But not particularly surprised, knowing Cash as she did.

"He didn't have any other choice," Jeb said with a nonchalant shrug. "I was a smart-mouthed fourteen-year-old kid with more sass than brains. I called his mamma a name." He frowned as he thought back on that day. "So, naturally, he beat the living daylights out of me."

"Naturally," Chelsea said dryly.

"Along with the broken nose, he knocked out my front tooth, blackened both eyes, and gave me a cut that took five stitches to close up." He touched his finger to a thin white line beside his right eye. "See?"

Although she told herself that she was surely imagining it, Chelsea thought she detected a faint hint of pride in his tone.

"I've never considered violence any way to solve a problem." The minute she heard the words leave her mouth, Chelsea wished she could take them back. She hadn't meant to sound so stiff-necked and preachy.

"That's because you're a woman," Jeb said with a slow easy grin that assured her he hadn't taken offense. "Now, the way us guys see it, if anyone insults your mamma, or your sister, or your woman, well, you just don't have any choice but to defend their honor."

She laughed at that. "Ah, we're back to the code of the Tarleton twins."

"There you go." His grin widened. "But it worked out just fine, because after I left the hospital emergency room, my daddy made me go find Cash and apologize."

"You had to apologize to Cash? After he beat you up?"

"I told you—"

"I know. You insulted his mother." Chelsea shook her

head, deciding that if she lived to be a hundred, she'd never entirely understand the male thought process. Then she tried to imagine Nelson behaving the way Cash had if anyone insulted her, and knew it would never happen in a million years.

"Now you're catchin' on," Jeb said approvingly. "We've been best friends ever since."

"Nothing like a broken nose to establish a little male bonding."

"You still tellin' that old story, son?" An all too familiar voice came from a dark corner of the veranda. "Lord, I'm amazed you're still able to find someone who hasn't heard it."

"Chelsea's new in town," Jeb reminded Cash. "I figured she hasn't had a chance to hear what a hellion you were."

"Were?" Chelsea couldn't resist asking as she studied him backlit by the discreet landscape lighting. Dressed in a dark gray shirt with a band collar and a pair of black linen slacks, he looked disgustingly sexy.

Jeb laughed at her accusation and even Cash chuckled.

"That's cold, honey," Cash complained. "Even for a Yankee. But you know, it's the strangest thing."

She waited for him to continue, but he just stood there, grinning down at her, with that wicked, good old boy glint in his eyes.

"All right," she huffed finally. "What's the strangest thing?"

"The meaner you are to me, the more I like you." He rubbed his chin and turned toward Jeb, who was looking at them with blatant interest. "You've known me, how long, Jeb? Twenty years?"

"About that."

"So, in twenty years, have I ever revealed any tendencies toward masochism?"

"None that I could see."

"I was afraid of that." Cash sighed. "I must be a sick person. Sick or perverse."

Chelsea made a face. "I'd guess the second."

He shot Jeb a wounded, hound dog gaze. "I gotta tell you son, I'm definitely in a world of hurt when it feels so good to have a lady stomping all over my heart with her skinny spiked heels." He turned back toward Chelsea who was enjoying herself too much for her own good. "I don't suppose you have any of those black leather thigh-high boots?"

She almost grinned but recovered. Why was it that Vernon Gibbons had made her feel so uncomfortable with a mere glance, yet Cash's outrageously sexual suggestion made her want to laugh? "I'm afraid I left them in Manhattan. With my whip and leather handcuffs."

"Leather handcuffs." He groaned. "I tell you, Jeb," he said with another slow shake of his head, "I think I'm in danger of falling head over heels in love with this sharp-tongued, mean-spirited Yankee female."

Love. He meant it as a joke. But the word still ran through Chelsea like an electric shock. "I'd better be getting back," she said. "I want to thank Roxanne for arranging this party on such short notice."

"Roxanne has a genius for getting things done when she puts her mind to it," Jeb replied.

"That's because she rolls over obstacles like a Sherman tank," Cash added. "Not that she'd be real pleased with that analogy," he decided. "Bein' that Sherman tends to be a four-letter word down here. After the war."

"Between the States," Jeb explained to Chelsea, who nodded. She'd already learned that lesson.

Glancing at her watch she decided it was time to leave. Before she made a mistake and enjoyed Cash's company too much. "Although I'd love to stay here and listen to your war stories all night, I have an early flight in the morning."

Cash hated himself for needing to ask. "Does that mean you're not taking the job?"

"No. It means I need to discuss the logistics of a possible commuter relationship with Nelson."

Although she knew it was perverse of her, she enjoyed seeing the irritation move across his face. She did not mention that she and Nelson were going to discuss a great deal more than her possible collaboration.

"Need a ride to the inn?" Jeb asked, earning an even darker look from Cash.

"Actually, Jo has already volunteered. I think it's her turn to try to talk me into writing the book." She held out her hand. "Good night, Jeb."

"'Nite, Chelsea." He enclosed both her hands in his in an interested, but unpushy way. "I sure do hope you decide to stay. And not just because you pretty up my house."

"Lordie, how you southern gentlemen do go on." She laughed at his light flirtation. When he released her hand, she bestowed a warm, sincere smile on him before arranging her expression into a polite mask as she turned toward Cash. "Good night."

"Night, Irish. Sweet dreams."

Both men watched her walk away. "Now that," Jeb said, obviously enjoying the sway of her hips in the same red silk suit Nelson had vetoed for the "Good Morning America" appearance, "is one lusciously put together female."

"She's also taken."

"I heard Roxanne telling someone she's involved with some guy in New York. Is that the Nelson she mentioned needing to talk things over with?"

"That's the guy. And I notice her supposedly belonging to someone else didn't stop you from bird-dogging her."

"Well, hell, Cash, the guy's just a Yankee. The way I see it, I'd be doing the little gal a favor to help her see the error of her ways."

"It's not the damn Yankee who's got dibs on her."

"Dibs?" Jeb gave him a blank look. Comprehension dawned. "Sweet Jesus, you're a fast worker."

"Nothin' fast about it. Tell you what… Let's you and me go out and get drunk. And I'll tell you a story about Cash Beaudine's long-ago adventure in Yankeeland."

Jeb's gaze went from Cash to inside the French doors, where Chelsea was saying goodbye to Roxanne. "I take it this tale involves a certain gorgeous redheaded writer."

"You always were a quick study." He put his arm around his longtime friend's shoulder. "And you look at Chelsea that way again—"

"What way?"

"Like a starving man staring through the diner window at a piece of hot peach pie with vanilla ice cream meltin' on top. Now, I'm not saying I can't understand the attraction, because I can," Cash allowed. "But keep it up, and I'll have no choice but to kick out your lung. After I break your nose again."

Jeb unconsciously rubbed the widened bridge of his nose. "As fond as I am of breathing, I gotta tell you, Cash, when you're talking about a woman that fine on the eyes, lookin' kinda comes natural."

Cash had to give him that one. A man would have to be blind not to notice Chelsea Cassidy. And even then, her scent would get to him.

"You can look," he decided magnanimously. "But that's all. Touch and you're a dead man."

Jeb chuckled. "And to think people have accused you of bein' unreasonable." He gave Chelsea one long last look, then sighed, knowing when he was licked. "Since the best-looking female in Georgia's just been put off-limits, I may as well get drunk to soothe my wounded heart.''

"May as well," Cash agreed, none too pleased with the idea that Chelsea was on her way back to his rival in the morning. "How about dropping into The Swamp Fox and shooting some pool?''

"I'd say that's a plan." Jeb's natural good spirits returned. "Lilah Sue Jackson's had her eye on me for some time. Last time I was in there, she even gave me a free draft on the house."

"Lilah Sue always has known how to squeeze a penny 'til old Abe cries uncle," Cash said. "If she's giving away the profits, I'd say that's a right positive sign."

"We had good times back in high school, all those nights down at the river watchin' the submarine races, before she married John Henry."

"They've been divorced, what, six months now?"

"Seven." Jeb grinned. "Maybe tonight's the night sweet little Lilah Sue's gonna get lucky."

Cash laughed. "I do admire your powers of recovery, son."

Unlike many other self-made men, Vernon Gibbons made no secret of his humble beginnings. Instead, he flaunted his plebeian roots.

Born in a hollow in rural Tennessee, Gibbons had dropped out of school when he was sixteen to support his ailing mama and five younger brothers and sisters. He did not see having to leave school as any great loss. All a high school diploma would have gotten him would be a job in the mines, like his daddy before him who'd died of black lung disease.

Having no intention of spending his life below ground, only to die wheezing his guts out in some charity ward,

Vern got a job in the local five-and-dime store, unloading stock in the back room, polishing the front windows and sweeping the floors.

One hot steamy August afternoon, on the day before his seventeenth birthday, he was unloading some drums of cleaning supplies when he caught the manager, an overweight bottle-blond divorcée in her thirties, with a doughy face and a frizzy perm, looking at him the way he intended to look at the ice-cold Dr Pepper waiting for him when he finished the job. Janey Porter's pale eyes, magnified behind the thick lenses of her glasses, were riveted on his bare chest.

He slowly ran a hand down the sweaty flesh. Her avid gaze followed. All the way to the metal button at the waistband of his faded, patched jeans. Then lower, still, to where the worn denim hugged his sex.

Although she was no beauty queen, the blatant desire that flamed in those wide blue eyes, and the way she unconsciously licked her lips, sent heat flooding into his groin.

He'd grinned, a bold knowing grin that caused color to flood into her cheeks and sent her scurrying back to the safety of her cramped and windowless office. But later, after the store had closed and the other clerks had gone home for the night, he'd taken her, right on top of her scarred wooden desk, driving into her like a jackhammer until she'd screamed with the force of her orgasm.

They fell into a comfortable pattern. During the day, Janey taught him everything she knew about the discount retail business. A smart boy, and an ambitious one, Vern had learned quickly. At night, he kept her sexually satisfied and though it curtailed his social life, he considered it a small price to pay for such a valuable business education.

Her glowing monthly reports to the home office won him a series of promotions, from loading dock, to clerk, to assistant manager, to weekend manager. She was his most avid supporter and although the term had not been in use in those days, she was his mentor. A role she realized, too late, that she'd played too well. Eighteen months after having sex on top of her desk, Vern arrived at the store to find her bawling her eyes out.

She was being transferred to the home office, she'd told him between sobs. To work as a bookkeeper in shipping. His heart pounding in his ears like cannon fire, he'd had to ask. Who was the company planning to move into her spot as manager?

Vern had tried like hell not to display his pleasure at her answer. But hot damn, not only was he now the top dog, with a corresponding raise in pay, he was also going to be free to return to catting around with the local lovelies. Life didn't get much better than this!

Pasting a regretful frown on his face, he allowed Janey to take him out for a combination congratulations-farewell rib eye steak dinner with all the trimmings at the Chat and Chew. For the first time since their affair had begun, he spent the entire night with her, treating her alternately with passion and gentleness that brought her to drunken tears more than once.

Although it wasn't his nature to be tender, Vern understood the concept of debt. His success was due to this woman; he figured he owed her a night to remember.

And it wouldn't hurt, he'd reminded himself as he'd helped her pack her few shoddy belongings into her battered old Pontiac Bonneville the next morning, to have a friend in the home office.

Utilizing what his lover had taught him, along with his instincts for knowing what customers wanted even before they knew themselves, he began making changes that nearly doubled the profits of the store in the first year. Two years later, he was netting out more profit than most of the big-city Nashville stores.

He'd been manager for five years when the chain was sold to a New York retailer who had no interest in keeping the rural stores running. Getting a loan from the bank was a snap; he'd met the bank owner at a Chamber of Commerce mixer and routinely went hunting with him. Using the borrowed funds, he'd bought the building, expanded the floor space to double the capacity and renamed it Mega-Mart. Then he hired his old lover away from their former employer and made her his comptroller.

At the gala grand opening celebration, he'd boldly announced that this was only the first store in a chain that would set the world of retailing on its ear.

Although some of the locals scoffed at his high-and-mighty attitude, Vern had the last laugh. By his twenty-fifth birthday, he'd expanded to twenty-five stores throughout Tennessee, Arkansas and West Virginia. By age thirty he was a millionaire. And that was just the beginning.

Now, at age sixty, Forbes ranked him the third richest man in America. Never one to be satisfied with being less than the best, he figured he still had plenty of time to make that number one slot before he was eligible for social security.

Which was why he'd signed the multimillion dollar deal with Roxanne Scarbrough. He was already the king of mass-market discounts. What he needed, was the touch of style she'd provide.

"Class for the masses," he'd dubbed it.

At the same time, he'd make her a household word, even with people who considered a picture of Elvis on black velvet to be the height of decorating chic.

After her other guests departed, Roxanne invited Vern into her office to show him the working drawings of the plantation house. She poured them both a glass of Rémy Martin and offered him a cigar. Vernon Gibbon's appreciation of food, aged cognac and illegal Cuban cigars were legion. As were tales of his sexual liaisons.

For a man who seldom made a bad business decision, his personal life had proven less successful. He'd been married eight times at last count, fathered sixteen children. Never one to dwell on the negative, he actually joked that his annual alimony and child support payments cost him more than most men made in a lifetime.

"Well," Roxanne said, after they'd gone through the spec sheets and Cash's preliminary drawings, "what do you think?"

He chewed thoughtfully on his cigar. "You're taking on quite a challenge. You know, you could end up feeling like a dog who's just caught himself an eighteen-wheeler and doesn't know what the hell to do with it."

"It's quite a challenge," she agreed. "But I believe I'm up to it."

"Hell, I don't doubt that for a minute, honey bun," he said. "But what about this Beaudine fella?"

"He comes highly recommended."

"I had my people do a background check on him," Vern revealed. "The word around San Francisco is that he's a maverick."

"Most highly successful men are." Her smile suggested the description could certainly be applied to him. "But I can handle him."

His dark eyes swept over her. "I'll just bet you can."

Vern took a long puff on the cigar, sending a noxious cloud of smoke up to the ceiling, then stabbed it out into a Lalique ashtray. He patted his lap. "So, now that we've got business out of the way, sweetie pie, why don't you come to daddy?''

She smiled as she rose slowly from the chair. Her eyes glittered with raw, lascivious intent. ''I thought you'd never ask.''

Chapter Eleven

Roxanne had dressed carefully for the evening, choosing a simply elegant Yves Saint Laurent black crepe dress with a high neckline, long sleeves, white cuffs and collar. She'd kept her makeup simple. With the exception of the four-inch high heels and sheer black hose, she looked as demure as a nun.

She slowly unbuttoned the snowy cuffs at her wrists, then reached around to unzip the dress. When it fell to the floor, she stepped out of it and walked across the room, clad in a black lace bustier, matching garter belt, jet stockings and hooker heels. She'd bleached the hair framed by the belt this morning; the pale blond curls contrasted vividly with the ebony lace.

"You are a sight for sore eyes, sugar," he said, expelling a long deep breath.

Those were the same words George had used. Roxanne suffered a momentary panic, then reminded herself that the only thing George Waggoner and Vernon Gibbons had in common was that they'd both started out poor.

George was the quintessential loser, while Vern was a

winner all the way. Which was why she hadn't protested when he'd explained in an offhand way that sex would be part of their deal.

As hard as she'd tried to exorcise the ghosts of her past, deep down inside in the furthest reaches of Roxanne's mind, a bit of the barefoot girl with the Salvation Army hand-me-down clothes still lingered. And that girl found it exciting as sin to be screwing the third richest man in America.

He'd been sexually attracted to her from the beginning. And during these past months, she'd appealed to that attraction, making her most tried and true cast to net him and keep him.

Kneeling beside the flowered chair, Roxanne brushed her lips lightly against his. When he didn't respond, she traced a sensual circle around his mouth with her tongue, coaxing a response. Again, nothing. She tilted her head back and gave him a knowing smile.

"You're being purposefully difficult tonight," she accused lightly.

"I'm an old man. Guess I need a little more convincing." He might be sixty but sexually he was far from over the hill. Roxanne knew from personal experience he had the stamina of a stallion.

She sighed, causing her breasts to rise above the lace cups of the bustier. "I suppose I'll just have to try harder."

His dark eyes held a wicked glint. "There you go."

She gave him a teasing love bite on his chin, then covered his mouth with hers, treating him to a long, deep kiss and was rewarded when his tongue tangled momentarily with hers in a slow, sinuous dance. Leaning closer, she placed a palm against his snowy shirtfront and felt the increased beat of his heart.

She stood up and backed away again, inviting him to take a long look at her. Which he did. She watched the bulge

JoAnn Ross

straining against his trousers and knew he was not as un-affected as he liked to pretend.

Teasing him with the flair of a skilled concubine, she spread her legs wide apart. The provocative stance caused a flame to leap in his dark, unblinking eyes.

Knowing she had his undivided attention, reveling in the role of exhibitionist, she began caressing her breasts, squeezing them, stroking them, cupping them in her palms, lifting them toward him as if offering the most succulent of ripe fruits. He was breathing harder now and his face was growing flush. A thrilling feeling of power surged through her veins. Improvising, she slipped the index finger of her right hand between her vermillion lips and began sucking on it, while her left hand did not cease its sensual caresses.

Vern stood up. ''Come here,'' he ordered roughly.

When she did as instructed, he put a hand on the top of her head, urging her back down to her knees. Knowing what he wanted, she unzipped his suit pants; his straining penis jutted up from the wiry nest of pewter hair like a tree branch.

She stroked it. Ran a carmine-tipped nail from the root up to the huge purple-pink knob, then repeated the fiery path with her tongue. When she pointed the tip of her tongue and stuck it as deeply as she could into the slit, moving it around and around, he groaned.

''You keep doing that, and I'm gonna fucking explode.'' He grabbed hold of her hair and lifted her head, taking advantage of her still-parted lips as he shoved his engorged penis into her mouth, holding the top of her head in order to force her to accept every throbbing inch as he thrust it harder and deeper.

Just when Roxanne thought he was going to come in her mouth, he pulled out, dragging her to the floor. He ripped off the rest of his clothes and began driving into her with rough animal ruttishness, his thrusts so deep, so powerful, that she came again and again, gasping as she brokenly spurred him on with sexual obscenities.

Finally, he let go, flooding her with his seed in a climax that went on and on. His shout echoed around the room like the victorious mating bugle of a bull elk. Then he collapsed on top of her, his passion spent.

The room was dark, illuminated only by the soft glow of the television monitor. The lone viewer sat in the shadows, watching the couple's raunchy mating. The unblinking eye of the lens took in the long white thighs wrapped around the man's thickened waist, focused on the thick cock as it disappeared into the slit hidden by those swollen pink folds and glistening pale pubic hair.

If there was one thing this tape proved, other than the fact that Vernon Gibbons was even butt uglier without clothes than he was when dressed, it was that Roxanne Scarbrough was a whore. Oh, she didn't sell her body on the street corners for twenty-five bucks a blow job, the way Cora Mae Padgett might have done. But whether you fucked for pocket change or millions didn't change what you were.

The watcher picked up a pistol, stroked the blue steel and imagined replacing that thick penis with the gun barrel. Pain and pleasure were so often interchangeable; it was difficult to know where one ended and the other began.

But Roxanne would discover the difference. And soon.

The watcher pointed the pistol and pulled the trigger.

"Bang, bang, bitch. You're dead."

The idea was, as always, immensely pleasing.

Chelsea was not all that surprised to arrive at the Savannah airport the following morning and find Cash waiting at the gate.

What worried her was the unbidden fluttering in her stomach created by the sight of him, looking sexier than any man had a right to in something as simple as jeans and a blue chambray shirt.

"What are you doing here? And don't tell me you have a sudden urge to visit the Big Apple."

He flashed his killer grin. "Now that you mention it, that's not such a bad idea. I don't suppose you know anyone who'd be willing to give a country boy a tour of the big city?"

"I'm afraid not."

He sighed. "I was afraid that's what you'd say." Without asking, he joined her in the line of passengers waiting to check in. When he reached for her bag, she mutinously switched it to the other hand.

In front of her a woman was complaining that she'd been promised a window seat. The unwaveringly friendly woman behind the counter kept tapping obligingly on her computer keys, searching out an available substitution.

"What *are* you doing here, Cash?" she asked again.

"Seeing you off."

"Why?"

"Because we didn't get a chance to talk last night."

"Yes, we did." The other passenger walked away, seemingly mollified. Chelsea moved up.

"Not alone," Cash said.

"There wasn't any need for that." Chelsea handed over her ticket.

The reservations clerk, whose name tag actually read Scarlett O'Hara began tapping the keyboard. "I have you in seat 3-A, Ms. Cassidy." Her smile warmed considerably as she turned the wattage toward Cash. "Will you be flying with us today, sir?" Her drawl was as smooth as honey, as rich as the pralines Chelsea had bought in the hotel gift shop to take back to Mary Lou.

"Now, if I were going to fly anywhere, you can bet it'd be on your fine airline," Cash assured her. "But I'm afraid I'm just seein' my lady off."

"Oh." Glossy red lips turned downward in a pout. The disappointed clerk stuck Chelsea's ticket into a red-white-and-blue jacket and handed it back to her. "Have a nice flight."

"Thank you." Chelsea took the ticket and walked toward a nearby row of molded plastic chairs. "Well, you certainly made an impression. She's probably hoping the plane will crash, putting me out of the picture."

"Bein' friendly is her job."

"Since when does being friendly involve practically stripping a man naked with her eyes? Which, by the way, had too much blue eye shadow."

Cash was enjoying her obvious irritation. A jealous woman was definitely not an indifferent one. "I didn't notice. I was too busy looking at you." He ran his fingers lightly through her hair, ruffling the waves. "Did I mention how much I like your new hairdo?"

It was a casual, unthreatening touch. It was also, in this busy terminal teeming with travelers, unnervingly intimate. "I don't believe it came up."

"I was afraid of that. Damn. I think my only excuse is that I was too pixilated by the sight of you in that snazzy red silk suit to think straight."

"Pixilated?" She could feel her lips curving despite her best effort to stop them.

"A nine-letter word meaning enchanted." His fingers continued down her cheek. His head lowered, sensual intent gleaming in his eyes. "Enthralled." His hand cupped her chin. "Or, if you want to get down to the nitty-gritty, hot and bothered. Did I mention that I had to threaten to kick out Jeb's lung because of the way that sassy skirt hugged your cute little ass?"

"You didn't!"

"Of course I did. But Jeb understood. After all, there's an unspoken code about leering at your best friend's lady."

"I'm not your lady."

"Sure you are," Cash said patiently. "Believe me, darlin', I've always been a firm believer in southern hospitality. But I don't cancel an appointment with the governor to show up at the airport to wave goodbye to *every* good-lookin' woman who visits Georgia."

"You had an appointment with the governor? Dressed like that?"

"It was at his mamma's house here in Savannah. She's looking to remodel and it's a little hard to crawl around in the attic in a suit and tie. The governor thought I was the man for the job. He also mentioned needing a little work on the executive mansion."

"And you canceled an opportunity like that? For me?"

"Actually, if you want to get technical, I postponed it." She shook her head in disbelief. "Why?"

"I told you. You're my woman."

He made it sound so simple. "You really are crazy."

"Pixilated," he reminded her. He gave her a long look, then shook his head.

"What's wrong?"

"Damned if I'm not gonna miss you, Chelsea. Maybe I oughta see about buying a seat off one of the other passengers."

"No!" She drew in a deep breath. "I don't want you coming to New York with me."

"Afraid I'll break Nelson's nose?"

"Of course not." The very idea was ridiculous.

"I would, you know. If he tried to keep you."

"I'm not any man's possession."

"Good. Then you can go home, say goodbye to Nelson and come back to me. That's probably the best way to handle it," he decided, rubbing his jaw. "Quick and neat, and it'll save me having to kick out his lung. Or cut off his—"

"Don't you dare say another word!" She glanced around, afraid some of the passengers awaiting boarding might have overheard his ridiculously male comment. "You really have to stop talking to me this way in public."

"I'd be happy to oblige. But the thing is, Chelsea, you don't give me much chance to have these little chats in private." He slid a fingertip down the slope of her imperfect nose. "So, I don't see as how I have any choice but to take advantage of whatever opportunity I can get. Wherever I can get it."

Wanting—needing—to get this settled once and for all, she grabbed his hand and dragged him over to the neighboring gate, which was nearly empty.

"Look, I'm not going to deny that I'm attracted to you—"

"That's a start. Because I sure as hell am attracted to you."

She ignored his interruption. "And I have no doubt that sex with you would be as potent as ever."

"That's pretty much what I've been thinking."

"Would you please stop agreeing with me? And let me continue?"

He gave her a be-my-guest gesture.

"Thank you." She took a deep breath and was about to continue when he broke into her already scattered chain of thought.

"Chelsea?"

"What now?"

"If you want me to keep my mind on what you're saying, I'd be much obliged if you wouldn't do that."

"Do what?"

"Breathe like that. Watching that silk come up and down makes a man think about what's underneath. And although I like to think that I've come a long way from the days when I did *all* my thinking with my glands, I've got to admit, darlin', that the sight is more than a little distracting."

She closed her eyes, began to take another deep, frustrated breath, then cut it off in the middle of inhaling. "You really are incorrigible."

"And you really are lovely."

When she opened her eyes, they were filled with confusion. "You don't understand."

"Sure as God made little green apples, I'm trying to. But it's a little difficult, when you won't open up and tell me the truth about what you're really thinking. And feeling."

"It's complicated."

"Life usually is. The thing is, I never would have taken you for a coward."

"I'm not a coward!" Dylan Cassidy's little girl, a coward? The very idea was inconceivable.

"You're running away."

"I'm going home."

"Same thing. You thought you'd safely locked away all your feelings for me—and about us—seven years ago. But then you came to Raintree, and Pandora's box got opened, and all those unruly feelings have broken loose. And you're scared.

"So you're running back to Nelson. Where you'll be safe. And secure. And bored to tears. Because your blue-blooded

Yankee wouldn't have a clue as to how to satisfy a woman of your fiery passions.''

There was too much truth in the statement to deny it. Chelsea wondered when Cash had gotten so insightful. Or perhaps it was merely that she'd become transparent. Neither idea gave her a great deal of comfort.

The row of seats was empty. Chelsea sat down in one. Cash took the one beside her. When he captured her hand in his, she didn't pull away.

''You don't understand.''

''I'm trying to,'' he reminded her mildly.

''It's just that the past few months have been a bit of a strain. Okay,'' she admitted to him—and to herself—''more than a bit. As much as I love my work, it seems I've been spending half my life on planes and in hotels.''

''Can't be easy, keeping up with the jet set.''

''It's not. Which is why I'm considering writing this book.''

''Not that I want to bad-mouth the lady, but I can't see how working with Roxanne would lower anyone's stress level,'' Cash observed.

''Granted. But it would also give me the economic freedom to slow down. And to finish the novel I've been trying to write for the past two years.''

The same novel her mother refused to discuss. The novel Nelson jokingly called her own personal *War and Peace*.

''I'll bet it'll be a crackerjack book, when you get it done.''

Like so much else about Cash, his easy words caught her by surprise. ''You're just saying that.''

''I may have acquired some polish over the years, but I still speak my mind. And I don't say anything I don't mean. You're a talented writer, Chelsea. You've got a real knack of knowin' what makes people tick that should make you able to create some powerful characters. And I know first-hand how imaginative you can be.''

A sexy glint flashed in his eyes, come and gone so fast that if she hadn't been watching him so closely, Chelsea would have missed it. "Put all that together in a novel and you can't miss.''

His instant, unqualified support caused a strange lump to form in her throat. "We're getting off the point again,'' she said finally. "I came down here to Raintree for a new start.''

"And instead you discovered some loose ends you never knew you'd left untied.''

"Yes.'' Her gaze met his. "What I was trying to explain was that you're a complication, Cash. At a time when I honestly can't handle any more complications.''

It certainly wasn't the most flattering thing he'd ever been called. Cash tamped down the prick to his ego and concentrated instead on the stress radiating from her too tense body.

"Seven years ago, you let me ride out of your life, Chelsea. Now, maybe that's what you had to do. What you should have done. Or maybe you made a mistake. I don't know and I don't care, because second-guessing the situation isn't going to get us anywhere.

"I know I should say I'm sorry I'm complicating your life, Irish. But I'm not sorry. And, to tell the truth, you're not the only one surprised by all this. Because I thought I'd moved on.

"I told myself I'd gotten over you and I'd almost—on the good days—made myself believe that. Then you walked into Roxanne's flowery parlor and I realized I couldn't breathe—''

"Cash—''

"Shut up.'' His tone was mild; his eyes were not. "I'm going to get this out once and for all so you have something to think about while you're on that plane. I'm through lying to myself. And I'm plum out of regrets. So, the thing is, whatever happens with you and Roxanne's damn book, I'm not going to lose you again.

"Whether you come back to Raintree, or I have to go to New York, I'm going to have you, Chelsea Cassidy. And you're going to love it."

She blinked at his rough, almost threatening tone. "That's all this is about, isn't it? Sex."

She smelled like sunshine and spring rains. And temptation. With a capital *T*. He could have strangled her for it. When he realized that fury was closer to the surface than he'd suspected, and fear right on its heels, he ruthlessly checked both emotions and reminded himself of exactly what he wanted to achieve.

"You're the one who keeps talking about sex," he reminded her. "I'm not going to deny that I want your body. But as attractive and appealing as it admittedly is, that's just packaging. I want a lot more than that."

She shook her head. "I can't give you what you want. Not now."

"Now, there you go again, underestimating yourself." He bent his head and brushed a light kiss against her furrowed brow. "I'd also like to say that I'm willin' to give you time to sort things out. But I can't promise that. Because there are always going to be choices to make, Chelsea. And there are always going to be problems. That's life. I'm not going to back off. Not this time."

This time he kissed her lips. A hard kiss that tasted of hunger, frustration and resolve. A kiss that made her head spin even as it left her wanting more.

"This wasn't supposed to happen."

"Too late." He kissed her again, this time letting his lips linger, nibbling at hers, creating a golden glow that shimmered through her like liquid sunshine. Forgetting that they were in a public place, she lifted her hands to his shoulders and allowed herself to sink into the tantalizing warmth.

"Damn," he muttered against Chelsea's mouth as the public address system announced the preboarding of her flight. "I guess you'd better get on board."

"Yes."

He tilted his head back and traced her still tingling lips with a roughened fingertip. "But you'll be back."

"Yes." Her entire vocabulary, which had always been her strength, seemed to have narrowed down to that single word.

Her mind still fogged, she was barely aware of standing up and making her way toward the departure door. Right before she handed over her boarding pass, Cash pulled her into his arms and gave her another brief hard kiss that left her breathless.

"Hurry back."

"Yes."

Her equilibrium shaken by Cash's mind-blinding kiss, Chelsea couldn't remember walking down the jetway and was only vaguely aware of the flight attendant welcoming her onto the plane.

As she fastened her seat belt buckle and looked out at the terminal, she could see Cash standing beside the wide window wall. When he realized he'd caught her eye, he flashed her another of his woman-killing grins and gave her a thumbs-up sign. Then walked away.

Chapter Twelve

She'd planned to work on her novel during the flight to New York. But the words, which had always flowed so easily for her, refused to come. And her characters had suddenly turned as stubborn and silent as stone.

It was all Cash's fault, she thought furiously. He'd filled her mind, shoving aside all the other things she should have been thinking about—her novel, Roxanne's offer, Nelson.

She hated the way she'd felt that little burst of pleasure when she'd seen him standing at the departure gate, hated the panic she'd felt when his deep, drugging kiss made her feel as if she were sinking into quicksand.

What she had—what she'd always had—with Cash was hot and exciting. Chelsea couldn't imagine ever not wanting him. She didn't believe there'd ever be a time when just looking at the man couldn't cause that painful-pleasurable little hitch in her heart.

But there had to be more to life than sex. Like mutual respect. Commitment. Love.

Seven years ago, when she'd tried to picture a life with Cash, she couldn't do it. They were strangers who'd come together in darkened rooms like thunder. And lightning. And when the storm had passed, she'd return to her own world. Her own safe, secure, familiar world, she admitted, thinking back on Cash's unflattering accusation.

Last year, when her schedule had begun to get more and more hectic and her life had seemed in danger of spinning out of control, she'd dragged herself to what had been billed as a quiet family dinner only to discover that Nelson had also been invited. While under normal circumstance Chelsea would have been more than a little irritated by her mother's blatant matchmaking ploy, on that evening, she had to admit that she found Nelson pleasantly familiar.

The on-again, off-again relationship they'd had since childhood had been in its off phase, after Nelson had become increasingly irritated at being stood up because Chelsea had hopped a quick jet to California to interview Sharon Stone, or flown to the Dominican Republic to track down rumors of a possible Madonna-Dave Letterman secret wedding. Understanding his pique, but unwilling to change her life, Chelsea had assured him she understood his need for a woman who'd live up to his expectation and wished him well.

That night, as they'd talked during dinner, she'd been surprised by the 180 degree shift in his feelings. Amazingly, he'd listened to her stories of celebrity gossip, which he'd always scoffed at as tabloid trash before.

She had just spent two of the most hectic weeks in her life at the part circus, part zoo that was the Cannes Film Festival, so when he invited her to spend a restful weekend with him at a quaint little bed-and-breakfast in Vermont, Chelsea had accepted.

And when, six weeks after that, he'd suggested living together, she'd agreed to that, as well. It was, Chelsea thought now, one of the few things she'd ever done that had earned her mother's immediate approval.

"Everyone knows you've always loved Nelson," Deidre had said over hearts of palm salad at her summer cottage at Newport. "Just as we all know you're going to marry him. And finally unite our two families."

At the time, although she'd hated the way her mother had made her potential marriage sound like an old-fashioned dynastic merger, Chelsea had not disagreed. Especially since, now that Nelson was so much more supportive of her career, she suspected her mother was right. She probably would marry Nelson. Someday. When she was thirty.

Chelsea was looking out the window at the endless sea of puffy white clouds when she realized that she'd been lying. Not so much to her mother, but to herself. Chelsea had always prided herself on the journalistic detachment that made her an expert at reading others so clearly. But she was not at all accustomed to looking into herself. Now that Cash had triggered this unwelcome introspection, forcing her to face the niggling little suspicions she'd tried to ignore, Chelsea was discovering a few home truths.

She wasn't going to marry Nelson. Not someday. Not in two years. Not ever. Despite his seeming turnaround concerning her work, she'd not quite been able to shake that niggling little worry that after marriage, he'd revert to type and want her to become a malleable, decorative society wife. If that turned out to be the case, she knew she'd never be able to give him what he needed.

Now, for the first time, she realized that she'd had it all wrong. The truth was that Nelson would never be able to give *her* what *she* needed. He wasn't the kind of husband she wanted.

Which didn't mean, Chelsea reminded herself firmly, that Cash was.

* * *

The apartment was hushed. The only sound was the steady ticktock of the Seth Thomas mantel clock in the foyer. Hearing muted voices coming from the bedroom, Chelsea decided that Nelson must be watching television. Which was a little strange, since at this hour of the day he could usually be found in the study, tracking his trust fund portfolio on the personal computer linked to a Wall Street brokerage firm.

For someone who had no real responsibilities, Nelson's schedule had always been as rigidly set as a fly in amber. Mornings were spent with the *Times*. After that came a game of squash with friends, which helped him keep the trim, lean figure that looked equally attractive in custom-tailored suits, a tuxedo, or casual chinos and Ralph Lauren Polo shirts.

Lunch was at the august Knickerbocker Club, where he'd spend the early afternoon reading the *Wall Street Journal*. Then he'd return home to work on their investments. Dinner was usually eaten out. Then invariably, he'd be in bed before the end of the news. Alone, more often than not, Chelsea admitted, since she'd usually have to stay up to meet an article deadline.

The door to the vast master bedroom suite was ajar. The room was dark. But not so dark that Chelsea couldn't see Nelson pumping away at some woman, who was urging him on with an amazingly inventive stream of four-letter words, a running commentary of exactly what he was doing to her. What she wanted him to do.

They shifted positions, allowing the woman to look over his shoulder. As their gazes met, Chelsea recognized Heather Van Pelt.

Even as the truth of what she was seeing ricocheted around her mind, Chelsea told herself that she shouldn't be surprised. And, since she'd already made the decision that she couldn't marry this man, she shouldn't be hurt.

But she was. Surprised and hurt and angry. Without a word, she turned away and headed back down the long hall.

"Nelson!" Heather tried to wiggle free, but he kept pounding into her. His grunts were coming faster now, and louder, signaling his approaching climax. "Goddammit, Nelson." She slammed her hand against his shoulder. "Chelsea's home!"

He let loose a shout as he spilled into her, even as he was trying to pull out.

"What the hell did you say?" His face was red, his blue eyes huge and unbelieving.

She pushed him off her and scrambled free, searching around in the tangled paisley Pratesi sheets for her underpants. "I said Chelsea's home. She saw us, Nelson. She saw everything."

"Christ." He jumped from the bed and scooped up his discarded clothing.

"Chelsea." Nelson was struggling into his pants as he chased after her. "Sweetheart. Wait. We need to talk."

Sweetheart? Chelsea stopped in her tracks. "There's nothing to talk about." She felt the hot moisture filling her eyes and hated letting the son of a bitch witness her humiliation. "As they say, a picture's worth a thousand words."

Nelson thrust his long aristocratic fingers through his blond hair. "I can explain."

"I'm sure you can." Tears threatened. She stubbornly blinked them away. "But it won't make any difference. Not anymore."

His handsome face crumpled in distraught lines. He grabbed her arm. "Chelsea, be reasonable."

She looked down at the male hand on her sleeve as if unable to recognize who it belonged to, wondering how it had gotten there. On the verge of humiliating herself by bursting into tears, she welcomed the anger that steamrollered over the pain.

"You want me to be reasonable?" she screamed, momentarily forgetting the lessons learned at her mother's knee. Ladies always matched the fingertips of their gloves before putting them away, they always crossed their legs at the ankles, and they never, ever raised their voices.

"I think I'm being extremely reasonable, Nelson!" Her green eyes raked over him, stopping just below the belt. "Most women would be in the kitchen, getting a butcher knife to cut your fucking prick off!"

Another rule broken. Ladies never cursed. As for the F-word, her mother had never felt the need to even mention such a taboo.

He cringed at both her tone and her words. Desperate, he handed her a piece of blue-and-white pottery. The Chinese bowl had been a Christmas present from his Aunt Marian, Chelsea remembered.

"Perhaps you should throw something," he suggested helpfully. "It might make you feel better."

It might. If she threw it at his cheating head. "The only thing that would make me feel better would be shooting you through your miserable black heart."

Despite the circumstances, Chelsea found herself momentarily enjoying the image of Nelson with an enormous smoking hole in the center of his chest.

"But since you're definitely not worth going to prison for, I'm sure you'll understand if I choose not to stick around and have a civil chat with you and your bimbo."

Plucking his hand off her sleeve, she turned and continued toward the front door, managing, somehow, to walk as sedately as a woman on the way to one of her mother's book circle meetings.

"You wouldn't leave for good? Not over a single indiscretion?"

Stopping again, she turned around. "Are you telling me that this is the first time you've slept with another woman?"

Relief swept over his features. "Yes. Of course. Heather just came by to drop off some papers from your office. Research for that Val Kilmer piece.

"Wanting to be polite, I offered her some coffee. Then one thing led to another and pretty soon she started coming on to me and, well, hell, Chelsea, I'm only human. But I promise, darling, it will never happen again."

First *sweetheart* and now *darling*. Chelsea decided that he must be going for some sort of record. She also knew that he was lying.

There'd been so many hints of infidelity, beginning when he'd disappeared for hours during their vacation trip to London three months ago, she realized now. But unwilling to believe she could have made the mistake of agreeing to marry a man who was so horribly wrong for her, Chelsea had purposefully overlooked them.

"If you actually expect me to believe that this is the first time you've gone to bed with another woman, you must think I'm either incredibly naive or stupid." Her voice cracked. Chelsea drew in a painful breath. "And while I'll reluctantly admit to being the first, Nelson, I am *not* stupid."

"It's the truth," he insisted, not at all convincingly. When she gave him a long hard stare that told him she wasn't buying his pitiful story for a minute, he said, "Besides, if you'd only be honest with yourself, Chelsea, you'd have to admit that what happened was your fault."

"My fault?" So much for remaining calm. Her voice went up several octaves, nearly high enough to shatter the Baccarat crystal vase filled with American Beauty roses on a Chippendale table beside the door. "How the hell was you sleeping with my editorial assistant my fault?"

"If you'd been home more, if you hadn't gone running off to Georgia—"

"*You* were the one who insisted I go to Raintree. *You* were the one who was pressuring me into the collaboration with Roxanne Scarbrough in the first place. *You* were the one who kept telling me that I'd regret passing up such a potentially profitable career opportunity."

"That's true," he admitted reluctantly. "But if you'd paid more attention to my needs when you *were* at home, I wouldn't have been forced to turn to another woman. The only reason I was vulnerable to Heather's seductive wiles was because I wasn't being satisfied at home."

He nodded to himself, obviously pleased with his analysis of the situation. "You know what they say, Chelsea."

She folded her arms across the front of her silk blouse. "What do they say?"

Her tone—as cold and dangerous as melting ice on a glacier—flew right over his handsome blond head. "That another woman can't break up a happy home."

It was, Chelsea realized, probably the first true thing he'd said thus far. It was also the single statement she agreed with.

"You're right." Although she knew she still had a great deal of pain and anger to deal with, at the moment, Chelsea felt a soothing calm settle over her. "Neither one of us has been happy for a long time.

"Goodbye, Nelson." She turned away again and resumed walking toward the door.

"Where the hell do you think you're going?"

"On a treasure hunt."

"A treasure hunt?" He stared at her. "Where?"

"That's none of your business."

Finally, unable to resist, she swept the vase off the table, causing a dozen red roses to hit Nelson smack in the chest. With the satisfying sound of crystal shattering on the marble floor, she left the apartment, literally slamming a door on this sorry chapter of her life.

Since she was, as she'd told Nelson, no fool, Chelsea went straight to the bank to close out their accounts. Less than thirty minutes after discovering her fiancé in bed with another woman Chelsea learned that Nelson was guilty of a great deal more than being a common, garden-variety philanderer.

He was a crook. Having depleted his own trust fund, he had continued to run up credit card charges while hiding the bills from her. In addition, he'd raided their savings and overdrafted their joint checking account.

She was, a stunned Chelsea discovered, flat broke. Fortunately, she was able to borrow the money for plane fare against her advance from Mary Lou, who was delighted she was agreeing to write Roxanne's book.

"I don't have any choice," Chelsea muttered. Having always taken money for granted, it was coming as a shock to discover that she suddenly didn't have any.

"This book will make a bundle," Mary Lou assured her. "And meanwhile, you can live rent-free with Roxanne."

"I'd rather not. It seems to me, if I'm as hot a writer as you and Roxanne keep saying I am, she should be willing to pay my living expenses at the Magnolia House while I'm working on the first draft of her book."

"I'm sure that won't be a problem."

That little item of business settled, three hours later, Chelsea was on her way back to Georgia.

And despite her lingering anger and shock, she found it more than a little ironic that fate had her beginning a new life in a state that had literally risen from the ashes.

Chapter Thirteen

Later, Chelsea would decide that her first mistake was allowing Mary Lou to talk her into flying back to Savannah first class.

Her second mistake was accepting the glass of champagne the flight attendant had offered the moment she'd settled into her seat.

Her third, and fatal mistake, was to continue to drink the entire flight. Upon landing, a cheerful skycap helped with her luggage and managed to pour her into the back seat of a taxi.

For this act of kindness, she tipped him nearly all the cash in her billfold. To his credit, he returned most of it, reminding her she'd need money for cab fare.

"That is so sweet of you," she said, nearly moved to tears by this act of pure generosity. "I never thought I'd become so dependent upon the kindness of strangers." A tear slipped down her cheek.

The skycap exchanged a look with the cab driver, who, accustomed to seeing the human condition in all its frailties, merely shrugged.

"So, miss," he said, "where would you like to go?"

"Magnolia House." She sniffled as she began digging around in her purse for a tissue. "In Raintree."

"Raintree? That's quite a drive."

"Oh. Of course, you're right." She held out the bills the skycap had just returned to her. "Is this enough?"

"Sure. But wouldn't you rather call someone to come fetch you?"

Chelsea thought about that. Roxanne would send her assistant in a New York minute. But she didn't want to disturb Dorothy's evening. And she definitely wasn't up to seeing Roxanne right now. Jeb might come. If for no other reason than to live up to his idealistic role of the southern gentleman. But she had no business disrupting his life, either.

And then, of course, there was Cash.

Chelsea sighed. "No," she decided. "I don't think so."

"Okay. Raintree it is."

As he pulled away from the curb, Chelsea settled back, relieved to have that little problem taken care of. Soon they were on the road leading outside of town. She put her head against the back of the seat, watched the lush green scenery passing by the window and idly listened to the broadcast of the Atlanta-Giants game on the taxi radio. When the Braves went down to defeat in the 10th inning, the driver cursed beneath his breath and switched off the radio.

"I'm sorry the Braves lost," Chelsea said.

He shot her a glance in the rearview mirror. "That's okay. Can't win 'em all."

"Tell me about it. After the way the Yankees broke my heart last season, I'm trying not to get my hopes up this year."

"You must be a New Yorker."

"I was born in Manhattan. How about you?"

"Born and bred in Savannah. My wife, by the way, is

from Raintree. It's a real nice little town. We've thought about raising our kids in the country, but there's not a lot of work out there."

"No. There doesn't seem to be," she agreed. "But, Savannah seems lovely, too."

"It's a real pretty place," he agreed. "And friendly. We get a lot of tourist business."

"So I was told." A little silence settled over them. "So you're married?"

"Yes, ma'am. Fifteen years last month."

"Fifteen years." She tried to imagine that. "Are you happy?"

"Sure." He shrugged.

"Do you love your wife?"

This time the look he gave her in the rearview mirror was decidedly uncomfortable. "I suppose so. Oh, we have our fights, like every other couple—"

"Warings never fight," she informed him.

"Every couple fights."

"Not the Warings. It's unseemly." She shook her head emphatically. "They have disagreements."

"You a Waring?"

"No." She shook her head again. "I almost was," she added as an afterthought. "But I escaped."

"Are we glad about that?"

This time she nodded. "Very glad. Extremely glad. Ecstatically glad."

"If you're happy, I'm happy," he said.

"I am." Her voice trembled. "R-really." She was appalled to feel the moisture trailing down her cheeks. "In fact, I've never been happier."

Chelsea stared blindly out the window again. "Wait," she said, as she viewed the river. Suddenly, although she'd always prided herself on her independence, always insisted that she didn't need anyone, Chelsea couldn't bear the idea of being alone. "I've decided I don't want to go to the Magnolia House, after all. Can you take me someplace else?"

"It's your nickel. I'll take you wherever you want to go. So long as it isn't out of state," he tacked on. "I'd have to stop and call my wife and let her know I was going to be gone a while first."

"That is so, so sweet." More tears. Lord, Chelsea thought on some distant level, who'd have thought she'd be a sappy drunk?

Since she didn't know Cash's address, Chelsea had no idea how to find his house. She could remember its name—Rebel's Ridge—but that proved scant help.

Fortunately, the driver thought to call his dispatcher. Discovering that the private number was unlisted, the dispatcher looked up the number for the architectural offices of Cash Beaudine in the phone book. Since the office was closed for the weekend, the call was picked up by Cash's answering service, who patched it through to his home after being told it was an emergency.

"We got it," the driver told Chelsea when the dispatcher radioed back with the address.

"You're so clever." Her eyes began filling up again. "And sweet. Your wife is a very fortunate woman."

"I'll tell her you said so."

Having been forewarned by the dispatcher, Cash was waiting when the taxi pulled up in front of his house. He opened the door, paid the driver and added a substantial tip. "Thanks for bringing her here safely."

"No problem." He grinned, his teeth flashing in his dark face. "I think you've got some guy named Waring to thank."

"Waring the weasel," Chelsea muttered, stumbling a little as she stepped out of the cab. "No. A worm. Waring the worm. That's more like it."

Wondering what the hell had happened in New York, Cash steadied her, then deciding that there was no way she was going to be able to walk up the sloping sidewalk under her own steam, hefted her up, flung her over his shoulder and carried her into the house.

"This is a sweet, sweet house," she said, staring down at the gleaming pine floors. "But I wonder why I didn't notice when I was here before that you built it upside down."

"It's not upside down. You are." He strode into the living room and plopped her down onto the couch.

"Oh." She glanced around. "You're right. It's not upside down." She blinked. Once, twice, and then a third time. "But I think it's spinning. Like the revolving lounge at the top of all those Hyatt hotels. But faster."

Despite the mascara streaks on her cheeks, Cash decided she was one of the only women he'd ever seen who could somehow manage to be gorgeous when drunk. "You're smashed, lady."

"Am I?" She considered that for a moment. "I don't think so," she decided. "Not yet." She flashed him a smile designed to bring a man to his knees. "I don't suppose you have any champagne in the house?"

He did. In fact, he'd bought it specifically with her in mind. But Cash decided not to reveal that little fact. "Sorry."

"So am I." She sighed. "I've never been much of a drinker, but I have decided today that champagne just may be my favorite drink in the entire world."

"I'll order a case first thing tomorrow."

"Thank you." She stood up, weaving like a willow in a hurricane. "You know, Cash," she said, holding on to the arm of the sofa, "I have a great deal of admiration for your architectural talents."

"Thank you."

"But I feel I must inform you that your floor is slanting."

"I'll check it out."

"Good. Because it makes it very difficult to walk."

"Perhaps you ought to sit down, then."

"Actually, I was thinking about lying down."

"There you go. That'd probably be even better."

"With you." As Cash watched, she began unbuttoning her blouse.

"What are you doing, Chelsea?"

"What does it look like I'm doing?" When she got to one particularly stubborn button, she simply yanked on the silk, sending the small pearl skittering across the floor. She tugged the blouse free of her waistband and tossed it in the direction of an overstuffed chair. It hit the seat cushion, then fluttered to the floor like a wounded bird.

"It looks as if you're taking off your clothes." He wondered exactly how far she intended to go with this little striptease. And more importantly, how far a gentleman should allow her to go.

Reminding himself that he'd never been known to be much of a gentleman, Cash decided there was no point in interfering with her performance. Not yet, anyway.

"That's very smart of you, Cash. But then, I've always known you were intelligent. Even when we were at Yale."

She moved on to the skirt, unfastening the back hook. Cash decided that the sound of the zipper slowly lowering was the sexiest thing he'd ever heard.

He also realized he'd better at least make an effort to stop her from doing anything she'd regret in the morning.

"Chelsea—"

"I mean, sometimes, I'd wonder about it," she mused,

cutting him off in midwarning. "How someone like you—
a bad boy rebel from below the Mason-Dixie line—actually
managed to slip past the guardians of eastern seaboard gen-
tility. But then I decided that you must be very very smart.
And gifted."

The skirt slid down her hips, landing around her feet. She
stepped out of it. When she looked as if she were about to
fall on her face, Cash reached out and caught her arm.

"And I was right," she said. "Although you do seem to
have trouble with sloping floors." She glanced out the windows at the river. "It must be because you built your house
on a hill." She nodded. "That's undoubtedly it."

She was now down to a skimpy little lace-and-silk camisole adorned with flowers that looked as if they'd washed
off an impressionist painting, matching panties and a pair
of lace-topped nylons. Beneath his fingers her skin was as
smooth as the silk now decorating his heart pine floor.

When she slipped a strap off her shoulder, a streak of
chivalry he'd never known he possessed steamrollered over
his desire to watch the floral camisole join the rest of her
clothes.

"Irish, do you have any idea what you're doing?"

"Of course." She took in a deep breath that caused the
camisole to slip enticingly. "I told you, Cash. I am taking
off my clothes." She slipped the other strap down. "And
then I'm going to let you make love to me."

"That's very generous of you."

His dry tone managed to infiltrate itself into the alcohol-
induced fog surrounding her brain. "You certainly don't
sound very pleased about the proshpect." She stumbled over
the last word.

He viewed the hurt rise in her eyes and was sorry he'd
been the one to put it there. But, dammit, if he took advantage of what she was offering, if he allowed himself to do

An Important Message from the Editors

Dear Reader,

Because you've chosen to read one of our fine books, we'd like to say "thank you"! And, as a special way to thank you, we're offering you a choice of two more of the books you love so well, and a surprise gift to send you — absolutely FREE!

Please enjoy them with our compliments...

Pam Powers

Peel off Seal and Place Inside...

EDITOR'S
FREE GIFT
SEAL
THANK YOU

What's Your Reading Pleasure...
ROMANCE? _OR_ SUSPENSE?

Do you prefer spine-tingling page turners OR heart-stirring stories about love and relationships? Tell us which books you enjoy – and you'll get **2 FREE "ROMANCE" BOOKS or 2 FREE "SUSPENSE" BOOKS with no obligation to purchase anything.**

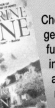

Choose **"ROMANCE"** and get **2 FREE BOOKS** that will fuel your imagination with intensely moving stories about life, love and relationships.

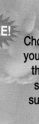

FREE!

Choose **"SUSPENSE"** and you'll get **2 FREE BOOKS** that will thrill you with a spine-tingling blend of suspense and mystery.

FREE!

Whichever category you select, your 2 free books have a combined cover price of $11.98 or more in the U.S. and $13.98 or more in Canada.

And remember... just for accepting the Editor's Free Gift Offer, we'll send you 2 books and a gift, ABSOLUTELY FREE!

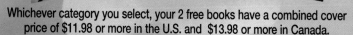

YOURS FREE! We'll send you a fabulous surprise gift absolutely FREE, just for trying "Romance" or "Suspense"!

® and TM are registered trademarks of Harlequin Enterprises Limited.

Visit us online at
www.FreeBooksandGift.com

THE EDITOR'S "THANK YOU" FREE GIFTS INCLUDE:

▶ 2 Romance OR 2 Suspense books

▶ An exciting surprise gift

YES! I have placed my Editor's "thank you" Free Gifts seal in the space provided above. Please send me the 2 FREE books which I have selected, and my FREE Mystery Gift. I understand that I am under no obligation to purchase anything further, as explained on the back and opposite page.

PLACE
FREE GIFTS
SEAL
HERE

Check one:

ROMANCE
193 MDL DVFJ 393 MDL DVFL

SUSPENSE
192 MDL DVFH 392 MDL DVFK

FIRST NAME

LAST NAME

ADDRESS

APT.#

CITY

STATE/PROV.

ZIP/POSTAL CODE

▶ DETACH AND MAIL CARD TODAY! ▶

(BB1-04) © 1998 MIRA BOOKS

The Reader Service — Here's How It Works:

Accepting your 2 free books and gift places you under no obligation to buy anything. You may keep the books and gift and return the shipping statement marked "cancel." If you do not cancel, about a month later we'll send you 3 additional books and bill you just $4.74 each in the U.S., or $5.24 each in Canada, plus 25¢ shipping & handling per book and applicable taxes if any.* That's the complete price and — compared to cover prices starting from $5.99 each in the U.S. and $6.99 each in Canada — it's quite a bargain! You may cancel at any time, but if you choose to continue, every month we'll send you 3 more books, which you may either purchase at the discount price or return to us and cancel your subscription.

*Terms and prices subject to change without notice. Sales tax applicable in N.Y. Canadian residents will be charged applicable provincial taxes and GST.

If offer card is missing write to: The Reader Service, 3010 Walden Ave., P.O. Box 1867, Buffalo, NY 14240-1867

BUSINESS REPLY MAIL

FIRST-CLASS MAIL   PERMIT NO. 717-003   BUFFALO, NY

POSTAGE WILL BE PAID BY ADDRESSEE

THE READER SERVICE
3010 WALDEN AVE
PO BOX 1341
BUFFALO NY 14240-8571

NO POSTAGE
NECESSARY
IF MAILED
IN THE
UNITED STATES

what he'd been wanting to do for days, for weeks, ever since seeing her on that damn television program, he suspected she'd be a lot more upset when she woke up tomorrow morning.

"I want you, Chelsea. But not this way."

"What way is that?" It took a special woman to even attempt haughter while drunk, clad solely in her underwear, but Cash had to give Chelsea credit for pulling it off. Almost.

"Drunk. And obviously upset. When we do make love, I want to be sure you'll remember it. And, more to the point, I want you to know who it is you're in bed with. I won't settle for being a substitute for any man. Especially some Yankee weasel."

"Worm," she corrected.

"Worm."

She took a deep breath that sent the camisole slipping down the slope of her breasts, to cling tenuously at the tips. The slightest movement, the merest touch, would send it the rest of the way to her feet.

"And for the record, you wouldn't be a substitute, Cash." Her thickened tongue got all wrapped around the words, but she managed to make herself understood. "In fact, since a certain recent incident in my life has made me decide that honesty is the best policy—the only policy—I must admit that the worm was always a substitute—and a poor one— for you."

Damn. Cash could have throttled her. It was bad enough that she showed up at his door just when he'd been fantasizing about all the things he should have done to her yesterday afternoon on his boat.

Hell no, that wasn't enough for her. She had to do a goddamn impromptu striptease in his living room, then, just when he was trying his damndest to keep his itchy hands off her creamy flesh, she had to announce that all the time she'd been with the weasel—the worm, he corrected—she'd been thinking of him.

He could have her, Cash knew. Right now. Right here. He could drag her down onto the sofa, rip those silky panties off and get her out of his system. Once and for all.

He ran his hands down her arms, linking their fingers together. In an inordinate test of willpower, he drew her to him, until they were touching, thigh to thigh.

"We seem to have a little problem here, Chelsea, darlin'."

He was so close. So wonderfully close. She could feel the heat coming from his body, seeping into her bloodstream, her bones. She tilted her head back and looked up at him. "The only problem I can see is that you're wearing too many clothes."

"Lord, lady." He laughed, but there was no humor in the rough sound. Only pain. "You sure make it hard for a guy to do the right thing."

"What if I don't want you to do the right thing?" She slipped her hand from his and pressed it between them. "And speaking of hard…"

"Dammit, Chelsea." He jerked her hand away before her stroking touch had him exploding. "I'm trying to be a gentleman."

"I don't want you to be a gentleman!" It was her turn to flare. "I want you to make love to me! I *need* you to make love to me! It's only fair, after…"

Even as drunk as she was, she realized what she'd been about to say and quickly shut her mouth. So fast and so hard, her teeth slammed together, sending cymbals crashing through her head.

It wasn't fast enough that Cash didn't immediately catch on. "Ah, sugar." He sighed, bent down and touched his forehead to hers. "If it's a revenge fuck you're looking for, you've come to the wrong place."

He sounded as disappointed as she felt. She wrapped her arms around his waist and pressed her cheek against his chest. "I was going to break it off with him anyway," she muttered into his shirt. "So why does it hurt so badly?"

Cash knew he was sunk when his need to comfort over-rode his need to take. Although she hadn't told him what had happened, he had a pretty good idea what she'd walked into when she'd shown up in New York hours before her scheduled arrival time.

"Sometimes wounded pride can sting worse than a broken heart." His hands stroked her back. His lips brushed over her temple. "But the good news is that it heals a lot faster."

"Really?"

She was looking up at him, hope and trust shining in her wet eyes. She was an emotional woman, Cash reminded himself. Even though she tried not to be. She was a romantic woman, even though he suspected she'd deny it with her last dying breath. And she was far more vulnerable than she allowed anyone to know.

He grinned. "Scout's honor."

She managed a smile at that. A wobbly smile that wrapped satin cords around his heart. "I don't believe you were ever a Boy Scout."

"You're right." He couldn't have afforded the uniform, even if those stalwart leaders of young men had been willing to allow him into their ranks. Which Cash suspected they undoubtedly wouldn't have.

He lifted both camisole straps, settling them back onto her shoulders. "The worm's an idiot. You're well rid of him."

"Yes." Of this she was absolutely certain. "I am."

The room was spinning faster than ever. Chelsea felt as if she were on a runaway carousel. "I think I also may be very very drunk."

"I noticed that."

"Of course you did." She gave him a blurry smile. "We've already determined that you're an intelligent, clever man." The mercurial mood swings she'd been demonstrating since arriving at his door had her full, unpainted lips turning down in a pout. "Even if you won't let me seduce you."

"Later," he promised.

"How do you know I'll feel like seducing you later?" Her tone suggested she just might refuse him for spite.

Cash grinned. At her. At himself. At this ridiculous situation. "I'll take my chances." He scooped her up in his arms and began carrying her down the hallway.

"Where are we going?"

"I'm putting you to bed."

"Oh, goodie." She leaned her cheek against his chest and sighed with feminine satisfaction.

"Alone."

She looked up at him, surprised and more than a little disappointed. "I never would have expected this from you, Cash Beaudine."

"Believe me, sweetheart, it's coming as one helluva surprise to me, too." He entered the bedroom, pulled back the spread and slid her between the sheets.

"I was supposed to check back into the Magnolia House," she remembered suddenly. "Jeb may worry if I don't show up."

"I'll call him and tell him you've been detained."

"Thank you." Every muscle in her body began to succumb to the blissful comfort of the wide bed. She could feel them going lax, one by one. Her brain was on the verge of shutdown. She closed her eyes. "For everything."

There was no point in answering. She was already asleep. Her breathing was slow and deep. The lines in her forehead and the deep brackets beside her mouth softened.

Cash stood there, looking down at her, thinking how inviting, how right, she looked in his bed.

He sat down in the chair beside the bed and simply watched her.

Soon, Cash promised himself.

"I don't understand," Mildred Landis whined. "Didn't you tell Miz Scarbrough that your mother was ill?"

"Yes, Mama," Dorothy lied deftly as she cut the fryer into pieces.

"Then she should have let you come home early. So you could take me to the doctor."

"Mrs. Wickersham already agreed to take you to the doctor, Mama."

"But Mrs. Wickersham isn't kin." Mildred poured another two fingers of Johnnie Walker Red into her glass. Then, on reconsideration, added another splash. For medicinal purposes.

The glass was one of a set of crystal she'd inherited from her mother. The gold rims had been worn off over the years from heavy use. Mildred was not the first generation of Palmer women partial to spirits.

"It's a daughter's duty to take care of her mother." She took a drink and enjoyed the warm feeling that flowed through her. She hadn't gotten to the click yet. But it would come.

"Keeping my job *is* taking care of you, Mama," Dorothy said. "Without it, we wouldn't have the insurance that pays for all your doctor's visits. And your pills."

And the money for all the damn booze you guzzle down like tap water, she felt like adding, but having had to put up with Roxanne's tantrums all day, Dorothy wasn't up to arguing with her mother.

Ignoring the litany of complaints she'd been hearing all her life, Dorothy skinned the chicken, cutting away the pebbly flesh and fat. If she allowed herself to actually listen to her mama, she'd probably start to scream. And the problem with that was, she wasn't sure if once started, she'd be able to stop.

She began dipping the chicken pieces in the milk. With her mother's voice droning in her ear, she let her mind to wander to New York. And to Chelsea Cassidy.

The writer's refusal to immediately succumb to Roxanne's will was making Dorothy's life a living hell. Roxanne was not easy to get along with at the best of times. When she wasn't getting her way, she could make the Wicked Witch of the West look like unrelentingly pleasant Melanie Wilkes by comparison.

Even as she wished Chelsea would agree, so they could all get on with their lives, Dorothy secretly admired her gumption. It took a lot of nerve to stand up to Roxanne. Lord knows, she'd never been able to manage it.

Of course, if she didn't have Mama...

"Are you listening to me, Dorothy Rose?"

"Yes, Mama," Dorothy murmured obediently. The air seemed to be growing thinner by the minute. There were times when she found it difficult to breathe around her mother.

"Then why didn't you answer my question?"

"I'm sorry." She dipped the chicken into the bread crumbs. "I guess I was thinking about work."

"That's all you think about," Mildred complained, her false teeth clacking. "Your precious work. If you thought half as much about your poor ailing mother as you do that fancy career of yours, all the time jet-setting up to New York City—''

''I'm Ms. Scarbrough's personal assistant. I have to go where she wants me to go.''

''Even if it means abandoning me?''

''I'd never abandon you, Mama.''

That was, heaven help her, the unfortunate truth. Dorothy frowned as she thought about her sister, happily living in Minneapolis with her husband and two children. And her brother, a police captain in Albuquerque. They'd both escaped, leaving her here in the house they'd all unhappily grown up in, trying to please a woman who steadfastly refused to be pleased.

''That's what they all say,'' Mildred muttered.

She'd heard this before, more times than she could count. How everyone had run off, allowing her mother to play the role of the martyr. A role Dorothy suspected she relished because it gave her an excuse to drink. It never occurred to Mildred that her drinking was what had run all the other members of her family off in the first place.

''What was your question, Mama?''

''What question are you talking about?''

''You asked me a question,'' Dorothy reminded her.

''Oh. That's right. I wanted to make sure you're not using whole milk on that chicken.''

''It's Pet evaporated skim milk, Mama.''

''Good. Because I gotta watch my cholesterol. The doctor says my heart could go at any time. Just stop. Like an eight-day windup clock on the ninth day.''

Doc Roberts, who'd taken care of the Landis family for years, had assured Dorothy that her mother's heart was as strong as a mule. And it wasn't as if she did anything to put a strain on it. Days were spent lying on the sofa, devouring the *National Enquirer* and the *UFO Newsletter* and watching television.

To make matters even worse, this past year, as her drinking had increased, she'd started confusing old movies with reality. *The Exorcist* had her convinced Satan was living in the attic and it had been nearly impossible to get her to take a bath after she'd seen the dead woman in the tub in *The Shining*.

Just last week Sheriff Burke had called Dorothy at work with the unwelcome news that her mama had taken a potshot at the mailman with the 12-gauge Ithica shotgun Irwin Landis had left behind when he'd escaped his alcoholic wife and their nightmare of a marriage fifteen years ago.

"I don't know what's wrong with the police nowadays," Mildred had complained bitterly as Dorothy had driven her home. Unfortunately, the mailman had insisted on pressing charges. "Joe Burke oughta be goin' after that serial killer, instead of arresting a potential victim."

"There isn't any killer, Mama."

"Then you want to tell me why that man came to the house, if not to kill me? A person is most usually dead before skinning."

"No one was going to kill you. Or skin you, Mama. Mr. Littleton has been our postman for years. He's come to the house nearly every day since I was a little girl."

"He was going to skin me. Then he was going to eat me," Mildred insisted. "With a fine Chianti."

"Oh, Lord." Comprehension came crashing down. Stopping at the sign at the intersection a few blocks away from the house, Dorothy lowered her forehead to the steering wheel and prayed for strength. "You've been watching *Silence of the Lambs,* haven't you?"

"Always hated Chianti," Mildred muttered. "It's too

damn sweet for my taste. I don't know how those eye-talians can stand to drink it. But then again, what can you expect from damn wop foreigners?''

The next morning Dorothy had called the cable company, and cut off access to The Movie Channel.

''Don't worry, Mama,'' she said now as she put the chicken in the oven. ''I got this recipe right out of Oprah's cookbook. It's about as healthy as you can get.''

''I'll bet Oprah would take care of her mother,'' Mildred muttered, returning her focus to herself, as always. ''Specially if her mama were on the brink of death.''

That said, she tossed back the drink, then held her glass out for a refill.

Chapter Fourteen

Chelsea woke with a splitting headache and a tongue that felt as if it had mysteriously grown a coat of fur while she'd been sleeping. Without opening her eyes, she reached out for her alarm clock. When she realized it wasn't there, that she wasn't at home where she belonged, her first thought was that she was back in the bedroom at Magnolia House.

No, that couldn't be right. She remembered checking out of the inn. And going to the airport.

And flying back to New York.

New York.

The memory came crashing back. Nelson in bed with Heather. Nelson asking her to stay. Nelson having the nerve to accuse her of driving him into another woman's arms with her own selfish neglect.

She remembered walking out of the apartment. And going...where? Although it was difficult to concentrate, she struggled to recall what she'd done next.

The bank. Where she'd learned that the man she'd tried so hard to love had robbed her blind.

She'd been in a state of shock, she remembered, as she'd

left the bank and taken a taxi uptown to Mary Lou's office. From there to the airport, where she caught the next plane to Savannah, then a cab to Raintree. Where she'd planned to check back into Jeb's cozy inn.

So, that's obviously where she was, after all.

Pleased to have solved that little puzzle, she forced her eyelids open. The drapes were closed, cloaking the room in a comforting darkness that while easy on her aching eyes, did nothing to help her figure out what time it was. She looked around, hoping to find a clock, when her gaze collided with Cash's. He was sprawled in a chair not far from the bed.

"What are you doing here?"

He lifted a dark brow. "Where would you expect me to be? It is my bedroom."

"*Your* bedroom?"

She sat up and looked around again, seeking some proof that he was lying. But the pillow case her head had been resting on all night told the truth. It carried his scent, revealing that somehow, she had ended up in Cash's bed.

"I'm not at Magnolia House?"

"Since you weren't in any condition to leave last night, I called Jeb and told him you'd be checking back in this afternoon. Unless you'd rather just stay where you are." Cash liked the idea of keeping her in his house. And in his bed.

"No." She shook her head then wished she hadn't. "No," she repeated, flinching. She tentatively lifted the sheet and noticed with some relief that she was still wearing her underwear. "Did we...? I mean, we didn't...?"

"Did we, what?"

"Dammit, Cash, you know very well what I mean. Did we make love or not?"

"You can relax. Nothing happened, Chelsea."

Oddly, she was vaguely disappointed. "You wouldn't lie. Not about that."

"No." His answer was curt. Harsh. And although softly spoken, it made her head ache even worse. She began massaging her temples in a vain attempt to soothe the throbbing as she tried to recall how she'd ended up here, in Cash's bed.

"I have my faults, Chelsea. But taking advantage of a woman in the condition you were in when you showed up at my door last night isn't one of them."

His smile was a grim slash completely lacking in humor. "Although, I'll have to admit, you put what little character I have to the test when you started that striptease routine."

"Oh, God." Her memory flooded back, bringing with it a rush of humiliation. She suddenly remembered taking off her clothes. Remembered daring—then, heaven help her, begging!—him to make love to her.

She flopped back against the pillow, closed her eyes again and covered them with her arm. "I'm so embarrassed."

"There's no need to be. You're not the first woman to drink too much champagne."

"I'll bet I'm not the first woman to come on to you, either," she mumbled.

"No."

"Well, that's certainly honest."

"I've never lied to you, Chelsea. So, there's no reason to start now. Of course there have been other women in my life. Too many, at times, when I was younger and less discriminating. But none of them have anything to do with you and me."

"It would if we were together."

"If we were together, sweetheart, there'd be no reason for me to ever want any other woman."

"That's probably what all men say."

With that single statement, she filled in the blanks of the questions he'd been asking himself all night long. "I told you, I don't lie. If the reason you got drunk yesterday was because you'd found out your Yankee worm is a liar—''

"Not only a liar, but a cheat." She sighed. "I caught him in bed with an editorial assistant from the magazine."

"That's got to hurt," he allowed.

"You don't seem all that surprised by the revelation."

"Actually, I'm not. Since the guy was screwing around on you back at Yale."

"He was?" She couldn't believe that. "Why didn't you say anything?"

"I figured you had an open relationship. Since you weren't exactly faithful at the time, either," he reminded her.

"That was different," Chelsea muttered, unwilling to concede that she wasn't exactly on firm ground here. "Nelson and I weren't living together back then. We weren't seriously discussing marriage."

"What you had with Nelson—" he heaped an extra helping of scorn on his rival's name "—doesn't concern me. It didn't back then, and it doesn't now. The point is that you're not the first woman, or man, for that matter, to have an unfaithful lover.

"So now that you've discovered that your blue-blooded fiancé is a two-timing bastard, you move on. And forget it."

"Move on with you?"

"I have a few things in my favor," he said mildly. "I don't snore, I don't steal the covers, I don't lie. And my male ego's strong enough that I don't have to pump it up by screwing around on a woman I'm supposed to be committed to."

"Next you'll be assuring me that you can make the earth move."

"That goes without saying."

His smile was too appealing. Too enticing. "I think I could have accepted Nelson being unfaithful," she admitted quietly. "In fact, I honestly wasn't all that surprised. It was the other thing that set me off."

"The other thing?" He ran through a list of possibilities. "This assistant," he said carefully, "it *was* a female?"

"What?" Deciding the alcohol must have killed off a great many brain cells, Chelsea didn't immediately get his meaning. "Oh, yes." She laughed. "Nelson isn't gay. Not that there's anything wrong with being gay," she said quickly.

"Nothing at all," he agreed. "And now that we've both proven ourselves to be properly politically correct people of the 90s, you want to tell me what, exactly it was, that decided to make you try to drown the guy in champagne?"

"He mugged me." She remembered, as she'd left the bank, thinking he'd been no different than those street criminals who came up behind you at the automatic teller, held a gun to your head and demanded your money or your life.

"Mugged?" He was out of the chair like a shot, his hands curled into fists at his sides. Chelsea stared up at him, stunned. He looked like a man about to commit mayhem. Or murder. "If he so much as laid a finger on you—"

"No!" She reached out ineffectually. "I was speaking metaphorically, Cash. What I meant was that he stole all my money."

It was the one thing he never would have considered. Cash would have been no more surprised if she'd told him that her Yankee worm had taken up with aliens from another planet.

"You're kidding."

"Believe me, being broke is nothing to kid about. He cleaned me out. Lock, stock and mutual funds." She sighed.

"I kept telling myself on the flight back down here that money isn't everything. But it's embarrassing to have to borrow lunch money from your agent."

It occurred to him that seven years ago he may have actually enjoyed this little reversal in roles. Now, hearing the news, he could only feel a cold fury at Waring. And sympathy for Chelsea.

Although perhaps, he considered, there was a silver lining to this. "How are you planning to afford the inn?" Even as he called himself a bastard for enjoying the idea, it crossed Cash's mind that perhaps she'd have to stay here with him.

"That shouldn't be a problem. My agent is working something out with Roxanne."

"So you've decided to take the job."

"It's not as if I have any choice. I told you, Cash. I'm flat broke. I need the money."

"There's always your job on the magazine."

"Journalism doesn't pay very much," she admitted. "I never could have afforded to live the way Nelson and I did if I hadn't had family money."

The inheritance from her father, which consisted mostly of two life insurance policies, had gone into interest bearing bonds that had provided a small, but steady income. Then there were various bequests from grandparents and other assorted Whitneys and Lowells that had allowed her to live comfortably.

"And now it's all gone?"

"All but my trust fund." Fortunately, her great-grandmother's attorneys had drawn up an ironclad trust that, even with all his slimy, sneaky tricks, Nelson hadn't been able to get around.

"Of course. The trust fund." Cash nodded. Obviously among the wealthy, broke meant something different than it did to the rest of the world's mere mortals. "Since you brought it up, may I ask how much we're talking about?"

"Two million dollars. Give or take a few hundred thousand."

"Two million?" He shook his head in self-disgust. And he'd been feeling sorry for her? *Hell, suckered again, Beaudine.*

"But I can't touch it for another two years. So, for the time being, I'm still broke."

"Can't you borrow on the funds? Use it for collateral for a loan?"

"No." It was her turn to shake her head. "My great-grandmother was very specific about that. Since she wanted her heirs to understand the value of work, she arranged it so we couldn't come into wealth at too young an age. She was also an early feminist, which is why, I suppose, she put in that other clause."

"What clause?"

"That if any female heir marries before her thirtieth birthday, the trust reverts to charity."

Suddenly, he understood everything. "That's why you always said you were going to marry the worm when you were thirty."

"Yes."

"So you could get the money."

"It's quite a lot of money," she felt obliged to point out.

"I'm not arguing that. I'm just finding it interesting that love comes with such a convenient price tag among the upper classes." He folded his arms and looked down at her. "So, what's the cutoff point?"

"Cutoff point?" Her head was throbbing, her eyes felt as if they were bleeding, her mouth was as parched as Death Valley, and her stomach was anything but steady. She really was not in the mood for an in-depth discussion of her distressing financial situation.

"There's an old joke," he said, not answering her directly. "About a man who asks a woman if she'll go to bed with him for a million dollars. When she immediately agrees, he asks her if she'll go to bed with him for five dollars. Well, of course she's insulted. So she asks him what he thinks she is."

"'We've already determined that,' the man tells her. 'Now we're just establishing price.'" Cash's lips curled in an unappealing smirk.

"If your great-grandmother's trust fund was five dollars, you'd have married the worm and not given it a second thought. But two million was enough to wait for. There's a pretty big range in between. I was just wondering what *your* price is, Irish."

"I don't want to discuss this with you right now, Cash," she said, hedging the issue until her head stopped pounding enough to let her come up with an answer. "The fact is that right now, I don't have a penny to my name.

"And yes, I could stay on at the magazine, but my editor was one of the people advising me to take a leave of absence to collaborate with Roxanne. She's already made a substantial offer for first serial rights."

"So, looks like you're going to be sticking around for a while." His tone was casual, but she could tell he liked the idea. The funny thing was, as irritated as she was at him for his attitude concerning her trust fund, she liked the idea, too.

"Yes," she said. "I guess I am."

After a shower and a light breakfast of cinnamon toast, tea and fruit, which Cash prepared and her stomach, amazingly, accepted, Chelsea began, just barely, to feel like a new woman.

Cash drove her to the inn, carrying her bags into the cozy lobby.

"Thank you," she said. "For everything."

"You don't need to thank me, Chelsea."

"Yes, I do." She nodded. Then cringed as the movement sent boulders tumbling around in her head. "Perhaps I can buy you lunch. Or dinner."

"Are you asking me out on a date?"

"Of course not," she said a bit too quickly. "I was simply trying to repay your hospitality."

"Darlin', any time you want to come sleep in my bed, you're welcome. And you damn sure won't have to buy me lunch afterward. Besides, a woman in your situation should watch her pennies."

"Oh." Amazingly, she'd put her financial fix out of her mind. Even more amazing, and depressing, was the knowledge that he was right. She couldn't believe that she couldn't freely buy a man a damn cheeseburger.

He ran a finger down her nose in an affectionate gesture that carried no sexual overtones. "I'd offer to spring for lunch, but I'm afraid I've made other plans."

"With Roxanne?" The words were out of her mouth before she could stop them. Damn. It wasn't any of her business who he spent his free time with.

"No, not Roxanne."

"Oh."

He knew she was dying to ask, understood pride was standing in her way, and decided to help her out. "I promised a friend we'd go out and drown some worms."

"You're going to drown worms?"

She looked so appalled by that idea, Cash laughed. "Fishing, city girl. We're going fishing on the river. See if we can hook a few catfish."

"That sounds nice." She wondered if the friend was tall, blond and buxom.

"You don't have to clean them. But Jamie likes getting out on the boat."

"Who wouldn't." Obviously blond. Platinum, no doubt. With big southern hair tailor-made for a beauty queen tiara. And she'd undoubtedly have a perfect figure, the kind made for swimsuit competitions and Playboy auditions. Chelsea envisioned a Miss April clone lounging on the deck of Cash's boat in an itsy-bitsy bikini. "It's a lovely boat."

He'd lost her. Cash could feel her retreating mentally from the conversation and wondered what he'd said wrong.

"How about I take a rain check," he suggested. "Tell you what, if we catch enough fish, I'll treat you to my own recipe for fried catfish. I hate to brag, but even Jamie swears it's the second best in Georgia."

"I suppose Jamie makes the first best?" she asked acidly as her rebellious mind conjured up the blonde wearing high heels, a towering chef hat perched atop her platinum bouffant, and a frilly apron over her swimsuit while cooking up a mess of fried catfish for her talent competition.

"Actually, his mom owns Catfish Charlie's. She holds the title for the best catfish in the state."

"*His* mom?" Chelsea stared up at him. "Jamie's a man?"

"An eleven-year-old boy."

"A boy."

Cash grinned when he heard the obvious relief mixed in with her surprise. "You were jealous."

"Don't be silly." She tossed her head and lied through her teeth. "I was not."

"You were." Rocking forward on the balls of his feet, he placed a quick light kiss against her tightly set lips. "And

I gotta tell you, Irish, it makes me feel damn good. Since I've been jealous of the worm for years.''

"You were? Why?"

"Because he had you, of course."

She'd half expected him to mention Nelson's wealth, or family ties. His admission came as a surprise and a pleasure. "That's a sweet thing to say."

"It's the truth. As for Jamie, his dad Charlie and I were fishing buddies back when we were in high school. He died a couple years ago, and Sharleen's been working her tail off, like a retriever during quail season, struggling to keep the business afloat by herself and trying to keep an eye on a growing boy.

"When Jamie got caught shooting out windows with his BB gun on a bunch of tract houses under construction last fall, I stepped in and took him under my wing."

"That's very nice of you."

Cash shrugged. "To tell the truth, it started out as a favor to an old friend. Then I realized that I'm the one getting the benefits from the deal. Jamie's one terrific kid." He smiled. "Maybe one of these days you can come over and the three of us can go out on the boat. Make a day of it."

"I'd like that."

It was the truth. And although she didn't realize it now, later Chelsea would look back on this conversation and realize this was the moment when she'd fallen in love with Cash.

Chapter Fifteen

Although her head was splitting and her stomach felt as if giant condors had taken up residence in it, as she rode out to Belle Terre with Roxanne, Dorothy and Jo, Chelsea decided that was a small price to pay for yesterday's indulgence.

Workmen crawled all over the plantation house, like industrious worker ants on a hill. Painters were sandblasting years and layers of paint from the brick exterior; at one end of the house, a scaffolding was being erected in order to repair the chimneys.

"Fortunately, the inspection didn't reveal any major structural flaws," Roxanne said. "My contractor, Mr. McBride, assured me that all we need is a little mortar mix."

She went on to describe, in more detail than Chelsea could have possibly wanted to know, the upcoming chimney repairs.

"And voilà," Roxanne waved her hand toward the chimney stacks as she finished up the lengthy explanation, "the chimney is as good as new.

"Better, even, since Cash suggested raising the height of

all the chimneys another eighteen inches to improve the draw. He assures me that will prevent a recurrence of all those dark smoke stains on the ceilings.''

"You certainly know a lot about construction, Roxanne,'' Jo chirped.

"I didn't when I started this project,'' Roxanne said as she bestowed her patented public smile on the camera lens. "In fact, I always thought flashing was something dirty old men wearing raincoats did to shock people. Then Cash explained it's the metal seam connecting the roof of the house to the walls and chimneys. He's been a wonderful teacher,'' she enthused. "And so incredibly patient.''

Her gaze drifted across the dead lawn to the porch, where Cash appeared to be engaged in a technical discussion over a set of blueprints with a large man Roxanne had introduced as the contractor, Mac McBride. Both men were wearing work clothes and blue hard hats.

"I don't believe I could manage all this without him.''

"You certainly seem to be taking a hands-on approach to all this,'' Jo prompted.

"If you're going to go to all the trouble to restore a wonderful old home like Belle Terre,'' Roxanne said, playing to the camera again, "it's important to be on-site every day. Because no matter how carefully you plan, there are always surprises. Unfortunately, more bad than good.

"But Cash called yesterday with news about another wonderful find. They discovered that the plaster wall between the parlor and the library had originally been made of brick. Cash suggested using the brick on the oven wall in the kitchen. Isn't that a wonderful idea?''

"Wonderful,'' Jo and Chelsea agreed together. Dorothy, Chelsea noticed, remained grimly silent. As she'd been all morning. Since Roxanne's assistant could never be described as loquacious, Chelsea hadn't paid any attention to the fact that she was even more quiet than usual this morning.

"Can we see it?" Jo asked.

"Of course." Roxanne was leading the way up the front porch when Cash stepped in front of them.

"Good morning, ladies. Can I help you with something?"

"I was just going to check out the brick you called me about," Roxanne said. "I'm so excited."

"I think you'll find it worth getting excited about," Cash said. "That's one of the pleasures of working on these old houses. You never know what you're going to find." He handed them each a hard hat, putting Chelsea's on top of her head himself. The gesture drew a sharp, questioning look from Roxanne, but she refrained from saying anything.

The brick was, as promised, wonderful: red and pink and aged. Chelsea could easily imagine it adding an ambiance of warmth and comfort to the kitchen.

While Roxanne led Chelsea out back to show her where she had plans for an herb garden, Cash's attention drifted to one of the laborers who'd paused on his way to wheeling a load of debris to the huge Dumpster. He'd noticed that same man eyeing Chelsea when she'd climbed out of Roxanne's Mercedes. And although construction workers were infamous for ogling good-looking women, there was something about the man—even discounting his greasy hair that had been tied back into a ponytail with a leather thong and the tattoos decorating his beefy arms—that made Cash uneasy.

"Who is that guy, anyway?" he asked McBride.

The contractor's gaze followed Cash's. "Some ex-con. He's apparently just out of the pen, but I talked with his parole officer before I hired him, and he said the guy's done his time and wants a chance to rejoin society."

So the tattoos were prison art. This knowledge did not make Cash feel a helluva lot better. "Do you believe that?"

McBride shrugged. "Don't much matter if I do or not. Since it wasn't my choice to hire him in the first place."

Cash was surprised. Mac McBride was a fifth-generation contractor, whose family had gotten its business start rebuilding the South during Reconstruction. The McBrides had a reputation for being hardworking, honest, and unrelentingly independent. He couldn't imagine anyone forcing this man to do anything.

"Whose choice was it?"

"Miz Scarbrough's."

"What?"

"The lady called me up, told me that there was this guy, kin of some old secretary, who needed a job. Said he knew his away around a construction site, so she thought mebee I could hire him. When I told her my carpentry crew was pretty much filled, she suggested I take him on as a laborer. And she'd pay his salary."

"*Roxanne's* paying him?"

"He's no kin of mine," McBride pointed out. "I sure as hell wasn't gonna have his pay comin' out of my profits. If the lady wants to carry him on her books, it's no skin off my nose. So long as he does what he's told and keeps out of trouble."

"From the looks of him, that might be asking a lot."

Another shrug. "Then he'll land his ass back in jail and I won't have to worry about him."

It made sense. So far as it went. But as he watched the man continuing to watch Chelsea, Cash wished he could feel as unworried as Mac sounded.

As Chelsea followed Roxanne out to the garden site, she felt the man she'd first seen looking at her when she'd gotten out of the car staring at her again. There was something about him that made her distinctly uneasy. Although she tried to ignore him, she couldn't quite resist sneaking a glance. When her gaze collided with his openly lascivious one, she quickly looked away. But not before she saw him lick his lips in a purposely obscene way that sent a frisson of icy fear up her spine.

After the inspection of Belle Terre, the women returned to Roxanne's house, where Chelsea watched Roxanne work. Chelsea had always considered herself a high-energy person. But Roxanne proved to be a whirlwind.

She began every day at five-thirty, working out in the gym she'd installed on the second floor of her home. By seven she'd showered, dressed and dictated a host of letters that would be typed into word processors and sent out by a staff of twelve secretaries working in Savannah. Then she'd make her morning inspection of the ongoing restoration.

Not that the drive out to the construction site was wasted. It seemed a constant stream of ideas would flow into her mind, at which time she'd stop her dictation to Dorothy in midsentence, instruct her assistant to make a note of the idea, then continue on as if the interruption had never occurred.

Back at the house, she ate lunch—a cup of nonfat cottage cheese and half an apple—at her desk, while she worked on more projects and kept in seeming constant touch with her publishers and the seventy-five employees in New York who kept the Roxanne Scarbrough machine running smoothly.

Midway through the afternoon, she took a thirty-minute swim. "The water relaxes me and helps me think," she'd told an incredulous Chelsea. During the swim, Dorothy ran back and forth along the side of the pool, dutifully making more notes and fielding telephone calls on a cordless phone.

Although Chelsea was invited to stay for dinner, during

which Roxanne planned to go over the day's work with Cash, she begged off. With the unrelenting pace Roxanne had set all day, Chelsea hadn't had time to think about Cash. And what his reappearance in her life would mean.

After returning to Magnolia House, she ordered a glass of wine from the bartender in the small restaurant-lounge and took it to the sunroom, where she sat in a wicker chair and watched the purple shadows spreading over the formally designed garden that was in glorious full bloom.

"Good evening," a familiar voice said behind her.

Chelsea turned and saw Jeb standing in the doorway. "Hi. I was just enjoying the sunset. And the garden. It's so peaceful." And exactly what she needed after the last two days.

"There's a story about that garden."

"Now why aren't I surprised at that?"

He chuckled. "We southerners do tend to like our stories, I suppose," he agreed. "I wouldn't want to bore you."

"On the contrary, I'd love to talk about something that didn't have to do with work."

"I warned you Roxanne keeps a pretty fast pace."

"A world-class marathoner couldn't keep up. So," Chelsea continued putting her feet up on the wicker hassock and taking a sip of the crisp gold chardonnay, "tell me the garden story."

He sat down in a wicker loveseat across from her. "When the South seceded from the Union, we Townelys owned Twin Oaks, a house in Savannah, and a second, larger plantation outside Atlanta. You can imagine what happened to that."

"Sherman burned it."

"The man sure was a mite careless with matches," Jeb said good-naturedly. "In a way, we were lucky. Most of the family money was safe in English banks when the war broke out, so it didn't end up bein' tied up in Confederate funds, like so many other people's.

"But the war went on a lot longer than anyone expected, and the expenses continued to grow, without any profits coming in, so we still fell on hard times when it ended.

"Although the Atlanta plantation house had been burned to the foundation, we sold off the land it had been sitting on, along with the Savannah house, to pay our debts. But that didn't leave us enough acreage to grow a decent crop. So, my great-great-granddaddy Townely leveled my great-great grandmother Emily's garden and planted cotton in the fields surrounding this house.

"Every spring, whenever he'd travel to England to do business with his bankers, Miz Emily would plant her flowers. Then, when he'd get back to Raintree, he'd till them under and replant his cotton. That battle of wills, I'm told, went on for nearly fifty years until he finally died of consumption during a particularly cold winter."

"That's too bad."

"He was an old man," Jeb said with a shrug. "Nigh onto ninety when he passed. Well, everyone figured my great-great grandmother would have one heckuva garden, now that she didn't have him around to ruin things, but she surprised everyone by planting cotton."

"Why?"

"Because cotton paid the bills," he said simply.

"A practical woman, your great-great-grandmother," Chelsea murmured.

"Most southern women are."

"Ah yes, the steel magnolia stereotype."

"I suppose most stereotypes possess a grain of truth, which is how they become stereotypes in the first place."

"My family has always been proud of its roots," she murmured, thinking of all the Lowells and Whitneys who'd distinguished themselves over the generations. And, of course, she couldn't leave out Dylan Cassidy, who'd added his own successful branch to her already illustrious family tree. "But we certainly don't live our history like you all seem to do in Raintree."

"We're big on tradition down here," he admitted. "Take this house, for example. There have been Townelys living on this piece of land for more than 150 years. The house has been standing for nearly that long, and there haven't been all that many changes, although each generation has added the modern conveniences of the day—electricity, modern bathrooms, central heat."

"And what did you add?"

"Air-conditioning and the media room. And, as you can see, I restored my great-great-grandmother's garden. Rox-anne helped me, and working with old diaries, I think we were able to get it pretty much the way Emily would have wanted it."

"That's a lovely idea."

"It makes a nice retreat for guests, which keeps the inn full most of the time, which pays the taxes," he said, proving that it was not just southern woman who could be practical. "I think Miz Emily would be proud to see it in all its glory." He flashed her a sheepish grin. "But I'm not sure she'd be real wild about the big-screen TV that's takin' up her company parlor."

He suddenly slapped his forehead. "I just remembered why I came looking for you in the first place," he said in response to her questioning look. "I'll be right back."

He left the sunroom, returning as promised within the minute with a bouquet of daffodils.

"That's so sweet of you. How did you know I love daf-fodils?" She dipped her head into the sunny gold blooms.

"Actually, the flowers aren't from me, though now I wish

I'd thought of it. They were delivered this afternoon. There's a card,'' he said helpfully.

Vowing that no matter how much the bright yellow blooms lifted her spirits, if they were from Nelson, she was going to throw them away, Chelsea plucked the small white envelope from amidst the blooms.

"I remember you telling me they reminded you of sunshine," someone had written in a bold masculine scrawl. "I thought you might need a ray or two today." He'd signed it simply, Cash.

Chelsea had forgotten the day they'd seen the brave little yellow flowers poking their heads through the snow and marveled that Cash could have recalled her enthusiasm over the bright harbingers of spring.

"That's better," Jeb said.

"What's that?"

"Your smile. You looked awfully sober when you arrived this morning."

"If I'd managed to stay sober last night, I wouldn't have the mother of all headaches today."

"Ah." His eyes twinkled. "I'm sorry."

"You're not the only one." She sighed. "My father was alleged to have been a two-fisted drinker. Obviously I didn't inherit his capacity for alcohol."

"I had an uncle who was mighty fond of sour mash bourbon," Jeb revealed. "One time, when I was home from college on a semester break, I made the mistake of going fishing with him. I don't remember crawling home, but I do remember hoping to die the next day. But he showed up at first light with a box of nightcrawlers, fit as a fiddle, looking forward to another day on the river. I think that ability comes with time. And practice."

She returned his friendly grin with a grimace. "You're

probably right. Which is why I've decided to leave getting drunk to the experts from now on.''

The single glass of wine, along with Jeb's easygoing companionship, relaxed Chelsea. She remained in the garden for a long time, enjoying the sweet fragrance of the flowers, the soft spring air, the dazzling sunset that tinted the clouds to crimson and gold.

When she felt something brush against her leg, she jumped. Then she looked down and realized it was only a fat old orange cat.

''Well, hello.''

Although overweight, the cat proved light on its feet as it jumped agilely onto her lap and promptly settled down as if planning to spend the night. Its rumbling purrs sounded like a small motor in the still of the garden. As she stroked the marmalade-colored fur, Chelsea felt herself relaxing even more.

When her thoughts drifted to New York, to yesterday's scene with Nelson, to the eye-opening visit to the bank, she scowled. Her fingers tightened on the fur, earning a sharp feline complaint.

''You're right,'' she told the cat, ''it's too nice an evening to ruin it thinking about the past.'' And although only a little more than twenty-four hours had gone by, Chelsea knew she'd already moved beyond the pain. And the hurt. Now, the trick was to keep from succumbing to resentment.

She resumed stroking the cat and willed herself to relax. Her wandering mind unsurprisingly returned to Cash.

He was a difficult man to understand. Far more complex than she'd given him credit for during their time together at Yale. Back then she'd taken him at face value: the leather-jacket-clad rebel who redefined passion. It had been simpler to think of their relationship as purely sexual. Easier.

''There you are!''

The voice jerked Chelsea out of her reverie, causing a physical start that made the cat dig its claws into her thigh. She looked up and saw an elderly woman moving toward her like a schooner at full sail.

"Honestly Cicero, if you don't stop straying off, I'm going to take you to Doc Martin and have your nuts cut off. That should put a halt to your carousing."

She plucked the cat from Chelsea's lap. "You shouldn't encourage him," she scolded. The scent of gin on her breath explained the slurred drawl.

"I'm sorry. He was just visiting."

Chelsea bestowed her most conciliatory smile on the woman whose hair had been dyed the same bright orange color as the cat's fur.

"He had no business gettin' out." She lifted the huge ball of fur to eye level. "Bad boy!" Cicero, Chelsea noticed, remained unfazed by her owner's irritation. "Males are all tomcats," the woman huffed. "Whatever their species. There's no keepin' them home where they belong."

Thinking of Nelson, Chelsea was inclined to agree. But before she could say anything, the woman had switched gears. "You're that New York writer."

"Yes." Chelsea was not surprised the word had gotten out. There wasn't much that stayed secret or personal in Raintree. "I'm working with Roxanne Scarbrough."

"So I heard. And for the life of me, I can't figure out why anyone would think a Yankee writer could do justice to a southern woman."

Irritation flashed, but Chelsea reminded herself that it wouldn't do her any good to get into a confrontation with a drunk. Even one decades older than herself.

"I'm going to try my best to live up to Ms. Scarbrough's expectations."

"Good luck," the woman muttered. "She's a bitch. But you've already probably figured that out for yourself."

"I don't think—"

"Yeah, yeah. I understand. You don't wanta screw up the job. But let me tell you, that class act is exactly that. An act. The woman may act like Princess Di, but she's trailer trash. As for that tall tale about growing up in Switzerland, it's my opinion she read *Heidi* one too many times."

That stated, she turned on her heel and marched away, none too steadily, down the garden path. Bemused, Chelsea went back inside where she found Jeb in the lobby.

"I just had the strangest encounter," she said. "Do you know an older woman with orange hair?"

He looked up from sorting the mail. "Sounds like Mildred Landis. Was she tipsy?"

"I think she'd been drinking."

Jeb nodded. "That's Mildred, all right. I hope she didn't bother you."

"No." She thought about telling him what the woman had said about Roxanne, then decided the negative accusation was probably just a case of small-town envy. "She was just looking for her cat."

"Poor Cicero. He manages to escape every so often, but she always tracks him down. Makes you understand why old Irving Landis didn't leave a forwarding address when he skipped town."

"Landis. Is she—"

"Dorothy's mamma," Jeb revealed. "And believe me, between working all day with Roxanne, and having to go home to Mildred, I don't envy the lady's life even a little bit."

Chelsea murmured an agreement. And tried to put the disagreeable woman out of her mind. But as she tried to work on her novel, Mildred's accusation kept going around and around in her thoughts, like a leaf in a whirlpool.

Mildred Landis was obviously an alcoholic. And, like so many people with drinking problems, she appeared to have a very large chip on her shoulder.

But, Chelsea reminded herself as she turned off the light and tried to go to sleep, just because she was a bitter, resentful drunk didn't mean that she wasn't right about Roxanne.

Damn. George cursed as the room was thrown into darkness. He'd installed the hidden cameras in the bedroom while the owner had gone into Savannah yesterday. Unfortunately, he wasn't able to see a fucking thing, since the girl dressed and undressed in the bathroom like some kinda damn nun. He knew he should have installed some cameras in there while he'd been at it, but Townely had come home early and he sure as hell hadn't wanted to get caught. That would have ended up gettin' him a one-way ticket back to the pen.

He might not be a video expert like that New York bimbo who was makin' the film about Cora Mae, George allowed, thinking of all the fancy equipment she was lugging around all the time. But during a year stint in the country jail for drunk driving, he'd met a guy who did surveillance work for the mob who'd taught him enough about cameras to go into business for himself.

At first the women playing the starring role in his low-budget porno flicks had been willing participants. But unfortunately, the kind of cunts who'd get off on being filmed having sex were lousy actresses. It had been then George had come up with the idea of hiding the cameras in the closet.

The tapes had been good. At least better than when the

bimbos kept playing to the camera lens like they thought they were Marilyn Chambers. But porno films featuring consenting adults fuckin' were a dime a dozen these days. It seemed every Tom, Dick and Mary with a video camera was selling their home movies.

It was then George had come up with the great idea to add a twist to the plot.

Memories of the women who'd unknowingly starred in the rape and bondage videos made him stone hard. Wrapping his fingers around his penis, he watched the writer sleep. Her tossing and turning caused her to kick off the sheet and made the red silk nightshirt hitch high up on her hip. When her hand unconsciously slipped between her legs, his throbbing sex convulsed feverishly.

It was obvious the little gal needed a real man. And hot damn, he had just the one in mind.

The anticipation was all it took to make him come.

After a restless night spent dreaming of Cash, Chelsea woke up tired and cranky. But as she stood under the shower, willing the water to wake her up, her mind drifted back to that strange encounter with Mildred Landis in the garden. Even as Chelsea reminded herself that her job was to tell Roxanne's story—in Roxanne's words—the woman's assertions had piqued her natural curiosity. So much so, that while Roxanne was taking her daily swim, Chelsea decided to seek out Jo.

The filmmaker was in her room, her attention glued to a portable television.

"I hope I'm not disturbing your work," Chelsea said.

"Of course not." Jo waved her into the room. "I was just watching the tape of yesterday's visit to Belle Terre.

Chelsea looked at the screen just in time to catch a close-up of the laborer who'd been leering at her.

"God, that guy is creepy," Jo muttered, unknowingly echoing Chelsea's thoughts. "I'll definitely have to edit him out." She pointed the remote control toward the television, darkening the screen. "What can I do for you?"

"I was wondering how much research you did on Roxanne before you arrived here in Raintree to begin taping."

"I located some early interviews. And her agent gave me some tapes of television appearances."

"But nothing else? Nothing about her years before she became famous?"

"Since there was no reason for her to be interviewed before she was famous, all I know about her early years is what she's told me," Jo said. "And most of that is already public knowledge."

"The story about her parents dying in that car crash in Switzerland? And her being raised by doting servants in some rural alpine village until she returned to the States to go to college?"

"That's about it."

"Didn't you think it was strange? That none of her parents' family took her in?"

"I thought it was a little unusual at first," Jo allowed. "But Roxanne explained that the Swiss woman had been her nurse for years. And her husband was their chauffeur. Apparently her parents' will provided for them to have a comfortable living so long as they continued to care for her. Which was a pretty good deal."

"It might have been a good deal for the servants," Chelsea argued with a frown. All morning she'd been thinking of what Jeb had told her about southerners' strong feelings concerning their roots. And families. "But Roxanne is a southerner. And I've gotten the impression that down here south of the Mason-Dixon line, family takes care of family.

"A little girl is orphaned and no one comes forward to

claim her. Not even some maiden aunt she never knew she had. Don't you think that's a little odd?''

"Odd, perhaps," Jo admitted. "But not impossible."

"So, you're just going to buy the story—hook, line and sinker? You're not going to investigate her past?"

Jo's normally perky expression turned puzzled. "I'm not taping "60 Minutes," Chelsea. I'm merely filming a documentary on Roxanne's inimitable style. On how she achieved success and why millions of women strive to emulate her."

"Even if she's a fraud?"

"Are you implying she lied about her past?"

"Not lying," Chelsea hedged. "Perhaps embellishing is a better word."

"Everyone embellishes." Jo shrugged. "We're talking about a woman who teaches other women how to gild pine cones," she stated matter-of-factly. "It's not as if Roxanne is running for president. If she does have some skeletons rattling around in her past, I suppose it's her right to keep the closet door shut."

"There you are!" Roxanne's appearance in the open door forestalled Chelsea from answering. "I've been looking everywhere for you girls." Her patented smile did not reach her eyes, making Chelsea wonder just how long she'd been standing there. And what, if anything, she'd overheard. "I'm ready for my interview."

Chelsea knew that her father would not have let the matter drop. Dylan Cassidy would have locked onto the story like a pit bull on a particularly juicy bone and not let go.

But as she went back downstairs with Jo and Roxanne, Chelsea reminded herself that she'd gone out of her way not to fall into the trap of trying to follow in her father's too large footsteps. She was inclined to agree with Jo. If it wasn't for that strange anonymous note she'd received her first night in Raintree. And Mildred Landis's admittedly unreliable accusation.

Chapter Sixteen

The rest of the week continued in the same pattern, with Chelsea following Roxanne from her house to Belle Terre, back to the house, trying to fit in interviews whenever possible.

"Of course I realize I have critics," Roxanne told Chelsea late Friday afternoon. The fabric swatches and wallpaper samples Dorothy had spent the day acquiring from various Savannah wholesalers covered the conference table. "But I don't pay any attention to them."

"Aren't you at least hurt—or irritated—by what they say about you?" Chelsea asked carefully. Although she hadn't seen any indication of Roxanne's temper, she continued to remain on guard.

"Of course not." Roxanne turned toward Jo, who was busy adjusting the lighting at the other side of the room.

"Is your camera on, Jo, dear?" Roxanne asked.

"Of course, Roxanne."

When wasn't it on? Chelsea wondered. The documentary filmmaker, who always seemed to be hovering somewhere nearby, had already taped enough footage to rival the length of *Gone With the Wind*.

"Good." Roxanne nodded, satisfied. "Because I want to make certain this gets into our little film." She folded her hands in her lap and looked directly at the lens. "My critics don't understand the power of dreams. Fortunately, my readers do.

"Those people who have described me as the hostess from hell, or the Diva of Domesticity, are those same people who've bought into the myth that modern 90s women aren't interested in beauty or comfort."

She leaned forward in her chair. "I'll be the first to admit that life is far more complex for women today. I certainly don't spend my days lounging around on a satin chaise, eating Godiva truffles and drinking Dom Pérignon. I work hard.

"But I'm not alone. I often think about the woman who spends all day on her feet, ringing up people's groceries, who goes home to a family who doesn't care that her arches are aching and her head is splitting. They're hungry. They want dinner.

"The nurse who's running an emergency room, juggling child care and taking care of her aged parents puts in more hours in a day than the average Fortune 500 company CEO. And she's still expected to help with homework.

"All over America, women are working harder and achieving less satisfaction. Free time has almost disappeared from their lexicon."

"Isn't that one of the issues your critics raise?" Chelsea interjected carefully. "That the nurse who's trying to cook hamburgers while coaching her kid for the upcoming spelling bee and trying to find someone to take her mother a hot meal every day doesn't have time to bake homemade Christmas cookies. Let alone wrap them in gold leaf."

"Lord, I am beginning to wish I'd never suggested that gold leaf," Roxanne flared. Out of the corner of her eye Chelsea viewed Jo preparing to stop filming. But Roxanne managed, with a visible effort, to compose herself.

"Of course I don't expect everyone to follow my suggestions exactly. That particular project was designed to force my publishers to use all color photos."

"I don't understand."

"Of course you don't, dear," Roxanne said patiently. "Which is why I'm going to explain it to you. When I first came up with the concept of marketing my style suggestions in coffee table book form, my publishers—who were incredibly shortsighted number crunchers, by the way—could not believe that modern, career-oriented women cared about creating a nice environment.

"Which, of course, is ridiculous, because years ago, women were taught to create a peaceful, appealing home for their husbands to escape to after a long hard day at the office. My question is, why shouldn't women deserve the same retreatlike atmosphere when they return home?"

"Perhaps they deserve it," Chelsea agreed. "But there are a lot of women out there who'd tell you that what they need is a wife to take care of all those niceties they don't have time for."

"You have to set the table," Roxanne argued. "Why not use attractive china and cutlery? And how long does it take to pick up a bouquet of daisies at the supermarket on the way home, and put them in a nice little depression glass tumbler in the center of the table?"

"But you go beyond that."

"Well, of course. If I didn't, I would have been a one-book author." She gave Chelsea a placid, self-satisfied smile. "My fifteen books have sold millions of copies, and every single one is still in print. *Southern Comforts* magazine sells nearly two million copies each issue, and the advertising revenues are up ninety-four percent from when the magazine launched last year.

"My arrangement with Mega-Mart stores ensures that all those middle-class working women who can't afford sterling, or who weren't fortunate to inherit it, are still able to set a lovely table with Roxanne Scarbrough's signature flatware.

"And for less money than it costs to take a family of five to the movies, they can also buy a tablecloth and matching napkins for those special Sunday afternoon dinners at home. The designed to mix-and-match stoneware is also quite affordable."

She crossed her legs and sat back in the chair again. "There will always be those provincial New Yorkers who dress as if they're going to a funeral every day of their lives, who live in their miserable little rabbit warrens in filthy canyons where the sun never shines, who somehow feel superior because they live in Manhattan.

"And each morning, they trudge their way through the filthy streets, stepping over those poor unfortunate homeless people who they no longer even see, to ride the subway to some miserable job working on a newspaper or magazine, where they attempt to eke out some personal satisfaction by trashing others who choose not to buy into the eastern seaboard mentality.

"There is nothing I can do to make these people appreciate my efforts. Although I must say, that if they incorporated just a little bit of the Roxanne Scarbrough style into their lives, they'd undoubtedly feel cheerier. But of course, that could result in their losing their jobs. Jobs that require them to look down their noses at anything they can't understand."

"You make it sound so depressing," Chelsea murmured,

thinking that although her own life in Manhattan was not so unrelentingly bleak, Roxanne had hit pretty close to home.

"It is. And that's exactly my point. Women don't have to live such bleak existences. Not if they'd listen to me. And let me help them."

"Surely you don't believe that all it takes for a woman to achieve domestic bliss is imagination and a glue gun?"

Roxanne surprised her by laughing at that. "That's precisely what I'm saying. You'll see, Chelsea," she said. "We'll make a southern belle out of you yet."

That idea was so preposterous, Chelsea laughed.

But later that night, as she soaked in the special herbal bath salts Roxanne had insisted she take back to the hotel with her, and ate her way through the little gilt-wrapped box of white chocolate brownies that had also been pressed upon her as she'd left the house for the day, she had to admit there was something to be said for pampering.

It was nearly midnight. After going over the plans for hours, Cash decided it was time to call it a day.

"I think we've done about all we can for tonight, Roxanne," he said, rolling up the set of working drawings.

"Do you have to leave? We haven't finished with the kitchen cabinets."

That was true. They had, however, managed to add a pantry, eliminate the narrow hallway, as he'd suggested doing in the first place, and added a mudroom that prevented having to walk directly into the expanded kitchen from outdoors. Personally, Cash didn't feel that was such a bad night's work.

"I think I've got the idea of the new changes you want," he assured her. "It won't take that long to finish the specs."

"Fine. You can show them to me tomorrow evening."

She pulled a long slender cigarette from the gold mesh case on the table between them. Cash leaned forward to light it for her.

Roxanne inhaled. "Vernon Gibbons is jetting in from Nashville for an afternoon meeting and I've invited him to dinner," she said on a blue cloud of smoke. "Since his store will be carrying knockoffs of many of the furnishings and accessories, naturally he's interested in our progress."

"I'm afraid I'm going to have to pass on dinner."

"Oh?" Her perfectly shaped brow arched. Her red lips drew into a tight line as she inhaled more deeply on the cigarette.

"I'm going to New York to check out a house on Long Island that's being demolished. The millwork is from the same time period as Belle Terre. I thought I might be able to pick up some interior doors. And, if we're lucky, get enough crown molding to replace what's rotted in the library and dining room."

"Oh." Appeased, she relaxed her expression. She put the cigarette out in an ashtray, stood up with a lazy grace, then, as if tired from a long day of work, began rubbing at the small of her back. Cash suspected the gesture, which caused her full breasts to press against her royal blue silk blouse, was done for his benefit.

"The house used to be owned by a Vanderbilt," he said. "Wish me luck, I'm hoping for wonderful things."

"So am I." Before he could perceive her intentions, she twined her arms around his neck and lifted her lips to his.

Her mouth was lush and wet. As she pressed her voluptuous body against him, her scent, dark and sexy, surrounded him. When her tongue trailed a circle of sparks around his mouth, Cash had no doubt that this was a game Roxanne played often. And well.

"Roxanne." After removing her arms from around his

neck, he put his hands on her waist and broke the contact of their bodies. "You're an incredibly sexy woman—"

"And you're an incredibly sexy man." She smiled and pressed a pampered hand against his chest. Her nails gleamed like rubies beneath the sparkling glitter of the chandelier.

"And it's not that I don't find you appealing. Hell, any man would—"

"Why do I hear a *but* in there?" Her eyes turned as cool as frost.

"I don't believe in mixing work and pleasure."

"That's not what I hear." Her finger slipped between two shirt buttons. Her bright nail teased across his skin. "Marian Fuller told me that as good as you were designing corporate boardrooms, you were even better in the bedroom."

He sighed, telling himself that he should not be all that surprised by her revelation. She'd told him she'd checked him out. That being the case, it was inevitable she'd run into a few women from his less than sterling past in San Francisco.

"That was a long time ago. And since then I've decided that getting emotionally involved with a client—"

"Or a client's wife," she interjected, drawing a bit of blood by pointing out exactly what an unprincipled bastard he'd been in his younger years.

"Or a client's wife," he agreed gruffly. The admission had him comparing his own behavior with that of Chelsea's worm of a fiancé. Although he hated to admit it, he didn't come off all that well himself. When Roxanne turned her attention to another button, he caught her wrist, retrieved her hand and held it between both of his to keep it out of trouble.

"The thing is, I came to the conclusion that mixing sex and work only complicates things."

"Not if the parties involved take it for what it is," Roxanne argued. "No strings. No commitments." Her eyes were liquid pools of enticement as she looked up at him. When she touched the tip of her tongue to her top lip, the move so blatantly sexual as to be almost a caricature, Cash had to restrain himself from laughing. "I'm not that bad in bed, myself, Cash."

He had no doubt of that. He also suddenly realized how a male black widow must feel on his wedding night.

"I believe that's probably one huge understatement, Roxanne. But I'm still afraid I'm going to have to pass."

"I could get a new architect."

"You could." He decided there was no point in reminding her that they had a contract. "But you're not going to find one who'll do as good a job on your house. Not to mention the fact that all those hours of tape your little filmmaker has taken of us working together would have to be tossed out."

She looked up at him, studying him thoughtfully. "Marian also said you were extremely intelligent. She failed to mention you were principled."

"That's probably because she never saw all that much evidence of any principles. As I said, that was a long time ago."

The dry humor in Cash's tone soothed her irritation and embarrassment and proved contagious, causing Roxanne to laugh.

"You've no idea how much that makes me wish I'd met you when you were younger." Proving that she was nothing if not tenacious, Roxanne placed a hand against his cheek. "You realize, that after Belle Terre is renovated, I'll no longer be your client."

Sherman's ghost would be invited to afternoon tea at Belle Terre before he allowed himself to get personally involved with this woman. Before Cash could think of something to say that would let her down gently, the library door opened.

"I'm sorry." Embarrassed color, like a fever, flooded from the collar of Jo's flowing black blouse up to her short, spiky brunette hair. "I didn't mean to interrupt."

"That's all right, dear," Roxanne said on a sigh that underlined her surrender. "Cash was just leaving." Switching gears once again, she said, "Which will give me the opportunity to view the tape of my interview with Chelsea that you shot this afternoon."

As he escaped the house, Cash found himself tempted to drive over to the inn. Although Chelsea would undoubtedly be in bed at this late hour, the idea of her warm and sleep tousled was unreasonably appealing. And her defenses would undoubtedly be down.

Thinking back on what he'd told Roxanne, that he'd become a man of principles when it came to the women that he took to bed, he reluctantly reminded himself that they had the entire weekend ahead of them. There was plenty of time.

Patience was, after all, reputed to be a virtue. The problem was, Cash considered as he drove through the dark and deserted streets, he'd never considered himself an even remotely virtuous person.

Chelsea was crossing the lobby on her way out of the inn the next morning when the front door opened and Cash walked in.

"Good morning, Irish," he greeted her cheerfully. "All set to go?"

"Go where?"

"To the airport, for starters. Then The Big Apple."

"How did you know I was going to New York?"

"A little birdie told me." He'd cut out his tongue before he implicated Jeb.

"It was Roxanne, wasn't it?"

"Nope." He glanced around. "Where's your luggage?"

"I don't have any. That's what this trip is all about. I'm retrieving the rest of my clothes. I'm tired of washing my underwear out in the sink every night."

"That could get to be tiresome," he agreed easily. "You should have said something. You would have been welcome to use my washer and dryer." The idea of her panties tumbling around with his Jockey briefs was undeniably appealing.

"That's very kind of you. But you've been busy."

"As a beaver. Of course, so have you. Whatever else you want to say about Roxanne, the lady does work at warp speed.

"Perhaps when all this is over, we can take a vacation. Down to the Caribbean. Or Cozumel. We can lie in the sun, drink Mai Tais with those cute little paper umbrellas, I'll rub suntan lotion all over your body.... To keep you from getting burned," he said when she shot him a quick warning look.

Then, rushing in where even the most stalwart angel would fear to tread, he tacked on, "And, of course, since it's too hot to be outside during the afternoon, we could spend all those hours waiting for dinner making love."

The scenario was too enticing for comfort. Her nerves tangled, as they always did when he was around. "It's very nice of you to offer to take me to the airport, but Dorothy already promised—"

"I assured Dorothy that since I was already booked on the morning flight to New York, there wasn't any point in ruining her Saturday."

"If you're making this trip because of me—"

"I need to check out some millwork for Roxanne."

"Millwork?"

"Doors, molding, sconces. Woodwork."

"Oh." She shouldn't be so disappointed, Chelsea told herself. She shouldn't. But she was.

He ruffled her hair in a friendly, unthreatening gesture. "So, you see, the trip really is business. But I can't deny that the fact that you were already planning to go to New York proved quite an incentive. And I refuse to be responsible for whatever naughty ideas you come up with after I finish my work."

"You really are impossible."

"And you really are lovely." He bent his head and brushed his lips against hers. "Even this early in the morning."

The kiss was barely more than a whisper. But it made her feel as if he'd touched sparklers to her skin. Before her heart settled down again, he flashed her that inimitable grin. "Ready to go?"

She should not be surprised, Chelsea decided, upon learning that he'd called ahead and changed her seat assignment. Cash was a man accustomed to getting what he wanted. And he'd made no secret of wanting her.

And even as she told herself that she should object to his high-handed behavior on general principles, she thought of the crowded coach seat she'd frugally booked for herself and decided there was no point in causing a scene at the gate by arguing.

Cash was surprised and relieved when she accepted the change of seats with nothing more than a raised eyebrow.

"I have to admit," he said as the plane took off, "I was expecting fireworks."

"Oh?" Liking the idea that she had him a little off guard, Chelsea gave him the mildest of looks. "About what?"

"I figured you'd consider my behavior high-handed."

"I do."

"That's it?"

"I'm sorry." She crossed her legs, enjoying the extra room more than ever before. "I suppose I should thank you. It was a very generous gesture on your part." She smiled up at him. "Apparently architecture pays very well."

"It's not a bad way to earn a living." He frowned as he thought how his hourly rate was more than his sharecropper daddy had made in a week. "Especially if you make partner in a large international firm."

"Which you did." She'd gone to the small Raintree library to look him up, surprised to find a lengthy write-up in *Who's Who.* "Your second year at Mathison, Tang, Kendall and Peters."

"You've been doing your homework." Cash liked the idea she'd been interested enough to check him out.

"I was curious. Just as I'm curious why you left San Francisco and a job that obviously paid very well. Not that restoring old houses doesn't sound challenging, but—"

He chuckled at her obvious worry he'd think she was demeaning his present work. "It's extremely challenging. And immensely rewarding. I told you, I've discovered that down deep, where it really counts, I'm just a good ole southern redneck."

"Not a redneck. But I have to admit, I always had trouble seeing you fitting into the corporate world."

This earned a full-blown laugh. "You're not the only one. By the time I left San Francisco, I felt as if I were in danger of suffocating every time I had to walk into those hushed, mahogany-paneled, Montgomery Street offices.

"It wasn't that I wasn't given a great deal of indepen-

dence, because I was. But there were so many management
levels, so many clerks and draftsmen and associates to do
all the grunt work, I never really felt connected with any of
my projects.''

"Yet the civic center you designed in Milan won several
international awards.''

"True. And I'm damn proud of that. Not the awards, but
how well the complex blended in with the surrounding architecture. The problem is, I can count on one hand the
times I managed to get away from the office to actually visit
the job site myself. I was too busy wining and dining prospective clients, convincing them that our firm was the only
one that could possibly design their projects.

"Then there were all the meetings, which were more often than not about how to keep the money flowing in, rather
than the work itself. We were amazingly successful at what
we did. The problem was, that I didn't like what I was
doing. And I discovered that it's true what they say. That
money can't buy happiness.''

"I could have told you that,'' she murmured.

He picked up her hand from her lap, uncurled her fingers,
which she'd unconsciously tightened into fists, and laced
them with his. "I doubt if I would have listened, back then.
Some of us have to learn our lessons the hard way.''

"Of course, it's not exactly as if you're poor now.''

"Got a point there,'' he agreed. "And I won't deny that
I like all the toys the money pays for. But if it were a choice
between being happy and being rich, I'd take happy any old
day.

"And if I wanted to spend the rest of my life with a
woman, you can damn well bet I wouldn't let a measly two
million dollars stand in the way.''

There had been a time, not too long ago, when Chelsea
would have found that declaration impossible to believe.

Now, she realized that he was telling her the truth. Which had her wondering, yet again, what would have happened if she'd simply run away with him that night.

"It probably wouldn't have worked," he said quietly.

"What?"

"You and me. Back then."

She tilted her chin and arched a brow, uneasy that he could read her so well. "You didn't tell me you were a mind reader."

Cash shrugged. "You can call me a chauvinist, but the way I see it, the first man who figures out how to read any woman's mind will be able to make a fortune marketing his secret. But with you it isn't necessary. Because your exquisite, funny face gives you away, every time." He brushed his knuckles down her cheek and watched the color bloom. "Besides, I've been wondering the same thing lately. A lot."

"And?"

"And I've come to the reluctant conclusion that we both had too much to prove. To ourselves. And to the world."

Chelsea didn't immediately answer. Instead she thought about that for a long time as the plane continued toward New York. And by the time they'd landed, she'd come to the conclusion that he was right.

"I can't believe this!" Chelsea stared down at the key that was proving useless.

"The worm must have changed the locks," Cash said. "We'll have to have the doorman call a locksmith."

"That could take forever." She glanced down at her watch. "I know where he is." She turned and marched back down the hallway. "I don't need you to come with me," she said as they waited for the elevator.

It was the same thing she'd told him when he'd insisted

52 JoAnn Ross

on accompanying her to the Park Avenue apartment. He hadn't listened then, just as he wasn't going to listen now.

"Of course you don't. But I'm coming, just the same."

Chelsea shook her head. "You're going to make me crazy."

He grinned down at her. "Count on it."

And as furious as she was, the wicked gleam in Cash's dark eyes had her almost smiling on the way down to the street floor.

Of all the clubs in New York City, the august Knickerbocker Club was the most devoted to guarding its members' privacy. Indeed, a visitor to Manhattan would never suspect that the four-story, redbrick house with white marble trim located at the corner of Fifth Avenue and 62nd Street was a social gathering spot for the city's most influential citizens.

Chelsea and Cash had no sooner entered the marble foyer when one of the blue-jacketed attendants who stood sentry at the front desk rose and greeted her politely. "Good morning, Ms. Cassidy." A faint frown carved furrows in his forehead as his glance slid obliquely over Cash. "May I help you?"

"Good morning, Jerry. I'm here to see my former worm of a fiancé."

"I'm not sure—"

"I am." Ignoring his sputtered protest, she marched up the marble stairs into the club's spacious reading room. The room was broad and long, a place of heavy leather furniture, green-shaded lamps and comfortable male tradition.

"I want to handle this," she told Cash. "So please do me a favor and not say anything."

"Does that mean I can't knock him on his ass?"

"Although I'm tempted, I think it might be better if you don't."

"Damn. I was rather looking forward to a nice little brawl before lunch."

Chelsea located Nelson immediately. He was seated in an enormous brown leather wing chair, engrossed in the business pages of the *New York Times*.

A disgruntled male murmur followed her across the room, causing the object of all her consternation to glance up from his paper.

"Hello, Chelsea," he greeted her with a remarkable lack of surprise. He looked through Cash as if he were invisible.

"You've changed the locks on my apartment."

"I believe, technically speaking, that the apartment belongs to me."

"My money paid the rent."

"Ah, but my name is on the lease." He gave her a calm smile that made her want to slap him. "Remember? You were out of town at the time. I believe you were shooting pool with Tom Cruise and Nicole Kidman in Australia."

"Your signing the lease was only a technicality."

He waved her protest away as if it were an errant fly that had somehow managed to gain entrance to these hallowed halls. "Why don't we let our attorneys settle the technicalities?"

Her cheeks flushed a brilliant red, but she managed, with effort, to restrain herself from picking up a nearby vase of lilies and bashing it over his smug blond head.

"I don't think you quite understand the way this is going to work," Cash said, breaking his promise to remain silent. He put both arms on the chair and leaned down so his face was threateningly close to the worm's. "You're going to give Chelsea a key so she can get her things out. *Right now.* Or I will break every bone in your body."

Nelson blanched, but held his ground. "Who the hell are you?"

"Cash Beaudine. The man who would love nothing more than to throw you through that window if you don't start cooperating."

Nelson turned back toward Chelsea. "Your friend is incredibly rude."

"I'm also capable of incredible violence." Cash's voice was calm, his eyes were ice. "Which you are about ten seconds from discovering firsthand."

Nelson gave him a long look. Then shrugged, as if deciding this was neither the time nor the place to fight back. As it was, every man in the place was surreptitiously studying the little drama from behind his newspaper.

"Fine." He returned his gaze to Chelsea, who was deriving enormous pleasure from Nelson's obvious discomfort. "But I'll trust you to take only your personal items from my apartment."

"There's nothing you have that I'd be the slightest bit interested in," she assured him. She smiled up at Cash, who'd straightened and was standing beside her, his fingers on her waist in a possessive, male way. "Are you ready to leave?"

"I was ready five minutes ago."

"Fine." She held out her hand.

Nelson reached into his pocket, retrieved the gold key ring she'd bought him at Tiffany's last year for Christmas, removed the brass key and put it into her palm. "You can leave it with the doorman."

"That's precisely what I was thinking." Actually, she'd considered tossing it down the nearest sewer grate.

"I'd better come back with you," Cash said when they were outside the club again. "In case the worm decides to show up and harass you."

"He won't. If there's one thing Nelson will do anything to avoid, it's a scene," Chelsea assured him. "Besides, don't you have to get to your meeting with the contractor who's demolishing that old house?''

"I can call and change it.''

"But what if someone else gets the millwork you're interested in?'' Cash had explained to her how sought-after such handcrafted woodwork was on the flight from Savannah.

"There are other houses. Other millwork.''

Knowing how much this particular one meant to him, Chelsea was moved he'd be willing to make such a sacrifice for her.

"I'll be fine.'' She reached up, placed both hands on his shoulders, went up on her toes and gave him a brief, soft kiss.

Her lips were soft and sweet and only made him want more. Resisting the urge to crush her to him, Cash asked, "What was that for?''

"To thank you.''

"For threatening to beat the guy up? Hell, darlin', you don't have to thank me for that. That was the fun part.''

Once again he had her smiling at a time when she should have been furious. Or in tears. "I enjoyed that part immensely. But I was talking about everything. Thank you for being you.''

Cash was momentarily stunned at how much those simple words meant. "You make it easy.''

They stood there, toe to toe, in the middle of the sidewalk, oblivious to the pedestrian traffic swirling around them. "I booked a two-bedroom suite at the Paramount, thinking you might need a place to stay,'' he said. "Unless you'd planned to stay at your mother's—''

"No.'' She cut him off quickly. If there was one person she didn't feel up to right now, it was her mother. "The suite sounds wonderful. Except for one thing.''

"What's that? If you don't like the Paramount, we can try the Plaza, or the Four Seasons, or—"

"No." She pressed her fingers against his mouth, once again stopping him in midsentence. "The Paramount is fine." Although she'd never actually been in the hotel known for its artistic, cutting edge celebrity clientele, anywhere Cash was would be more than fine with her. "It's just that you won't be needing that second bedroom."

He gave her a long look. "If it's because of the worm—"

"It's you." Her eyes revealed what her heart had already accepted. "It's always been you."

Cash let out a huge breath he'd been unaware of holding. "Lord, do you know what it does to me, to have you say something like that, right before I have to leave you?"

She laughed, amazed and pleased that it was proving so easy to be honest with him. Honest with herself. "About the same thing it does to me to say it." Her warm, loving smile lingered in her eyes, tilted the corners of her generous lips upward. "Go to your meeting, Cash. I'll be waiting for you."

She could not have said anything that would have given him more pleasure. "I like that idea. Meanwhile..."

He drew her against him and crushed his mouth to hers, kissing her with passion. With promise. With a power that had explosions going off inside her.

Mindless of the fact that she was on a public street, only blocks away from the apartment where she'd grown up, forgetting that Nelson, or any one of their friends could come out that door at any moment, she clung to Cash, her avid lips responding with equal fervor as the air around them grew thick and hot.

"Lord," Cash said on a ragged breath, as the staggering kiss finally ended, "I thought Manhattan didn't have earthquakes."

"It doesn't." Unsure her trembling legs would support her on their own, Chelsea continued to cling to him.

"Are you saying that was us?"

"I think so."

"Lord," he repeated with a slow shake of his head. "I think we may be in trouble."

"I think you may be right." She'd forgotten how enjoyable trouble could be, under the right circumstances. "You know that suite you've booked?"

"Yeah?"

Chelsea detected a slight tensing of his body that revealed he still didn't quite trust how easy this was turning out to be. "It *does* have a broom closet, doesn't it?"

He laughed at that. A deep, hearty sound that managed to exorcise the last of his tension. "We can do better than that," he promised her as he trailed a circle of fire around her lips with his fingertip. "Much, much better."

Chapter Seventeen

Dorothy was relieved at how much easier life was when Chelsea was around. Although she'd ostensibly been hired to write a complimentary biography, Roxanne was media savvy enough to realize that less flattering bits and pieces of her life could ultimately appear in an exposé article for *Vanity Fair*.

Which was why, whenever Chelsea was in the vicinity, Roxanne somehow managed to keep a tight rein on her flash-fire temper. The same way she did whenever Cash was present. Indeed, her public behavior remained so unrelentingly charming, Dorothy decided that it was too bad they didn't give Academy Awards for Best Performance by a Diva of Domesticity.

Unfortunately, with both Chelsea and Cash in New York, *together?* Dorothy wondered, all Roxanne's pent-up fury burst out, like acrid pus from a boil.

"That is *not* the color I chose," Roxanne screamed at the painter after he showed her a sample piece of wallboard.

"You said you wanted the exterior to be the color of

buttermilk.'' He stood back, crossed his arms and studied the painted board. ''That looks like buttermilk to me.''

''It's not buttermilk, you blind idiot! It's milkweed!''

''Milkweed?'' He shot a disbelieving glance as if to say, *Can you believe this broad?* to Dorothy.

''Milkweed,'' Roxanne affirmed viciously. ''Having developed the shade for my decorating line for Mega-Mart, I'm more than a little familiar with it. Buttermilk has more yellow in it.''

He shrugged. ''You want more yellow? You got it. All you had to do was ask.''

''And all you had to do was follow my instructions and get it right the first time.'' She jabbed a finger in his direction. ''You're fired.''

''Excuse me?''

Her eyes were crystal lasers as they bored into him. ''Are you deaf as well as stupid? I refuse to work with someone so obviously lacking in artistic vision. That being the case, you're fired.''

It was the painter's turn to get hot. ''You can't fire me! I have a contract to paint your damn house, signed by the general contractor. And last time I looked, lady, you sure as hell weren't him.''

She drew in a harsh breath, as if stunned that any mere workman could dare question her authority. ''Then I'll fire the fucking general contractor!''

Before he could respond, the phone rang. Dorothy scooped it up.

''Hey, sweetheart, give me the boss lady,'' George Waggoner said.

''I'm afraid she's busy at the moment. She's meeting with the painter.''

''I don't care if she's meeting with the fucking president of the Confederacy,'' he shot back. ''Put her on the line.''

When she'd first met George Waggoner, Dorothy's flesh had crawled. He was evil. And dangerous. Which was why she'd been stunned when Roxanne insisted Mac McBride place him on the construction crew at her own expense.

Even more appalling was the way this man, who was, after all, only a distant cousin of a former secretary, had been granted seemingly unlimited access to Roxanne.

He'd already dropped by the house twice. Once more than was necessary to thank her for her intervention on his behalf. He drank Roxanne's whiskey. And he called several times a day.

"I'm sorry Mr. Waggoner—"

"Is that George?" Roxanne dropped her diatribe in mid-sentence.

"I'm sorry, Roxanne," Dorothy said. "I tried telling him that you're too busy to take any calls, but—"

"That's all right. Tell him I'll be with him momentarily." Her gaze raked over the painter one final time. "You have one more chance to get this right. Don't fuck it up."

He flushed, a bright, angry red from the collar of his work shirt to his forehead beneath the white painter's cap. But obviously realizing what a publicity plum it would be for his own business to remain part of this project, he held his tongue.

"Yes ma'am." He left her office, closing the door on something just this side of a slam.

"Stupid incompetent man," Roxanne muttered after he was gone. "It's becoming more and more impossible to find decent help." Her scowl deepened as she glanced at the floor samples on her desk. "Dorothy, I want you to return these to Savannah and tell the man that they are not the Carrara marble I requested."

"He assured me they were Carrara when I picked them up," Dorothy said without thinking. Nearly biting off her tongue, she realized she'd allowed herself to become lax since Chelsea's arrival.

Roxanne lifted a brow. "So now you're an expert on stone?" Sarcasm dripped from every tightly enunciated word.

"No, Roxanne, of course not. I was only telling you what the store owner told me."

"Well, he obviously lied. Which is not all that surprising, considering the profit he stood to make if I hadn't caught him. This is obviously domestic marble." She picked up a piece and glared at it with such disdain Dorothy almost expected it to crumble to dust in Roxanne's hands. "If I wanted domestic marble, I could go to Tennessee." Her scathing tone suggested that she'd just as soon visit Bangladesh. "I want the Carrara marble samples in my office first thing tomorrow morning."

"It's getting late." Dorothy didn't need to look at her watch. She'd been counting the hours until she could escape all day.

"So?"

"The store will be closed before I can get to the city."

"Then you'll have to call the owner and instruct him to stay open, won't you?"

Damn. She was going to be late getting home to make dinner again. Which was going to make her evening as upsetting as her day. Heaven forbid that her mother microwave one of the meals Dorothy had prepared and put in the freezer last Sunday.

Dorothy wondered, as she so often did these days, how it was that her life could have come to this. She was only thirty-three years old, dammit. No longer young, but far from old. Not even middle-aged. It was Saturday. She should be home getting ready to go on a date.

A fantasy billowed in her mind. She pictured herself,

dressed in a lovely flowered silk dress slow dancing with Cash Beaudine. His lips were brushing over her temple. Her cheek. Her mouth. His body was strong and hard and aroused.

You are, he murmured while nibbling on the stunningly tender flesh of her earlobe, *the most beautiful, desirable woman I've ever met. I want you. Dorothy. In my bed. All night long.*

It had been a very long time since she'd had sex. Ages. She tried to remember the face of the man—a butcher down at the Piggly Wiggly—and couldn't. But she could remember his hands. Rough textured and rough handling.

In her fantasy, she was looking up into the face of this man who'd been starring in so many of her dreams lately. *Oh yes. Cash,* she said on a soft, shimmering sigh.

"Dorothy! Are you listening to me?"

The strident voice caused her sensual fantasy to burst like a soap bubble. "I'm sorry, Roxanne, what did you say?"

Roxanne gave her a long, hard, warning look. "I swear, Dorothy, I don't know where your mind is these days."

"I'm sorry. I'm just having a few problems at home."

"Well, see that you don't bring them to work," Roxanne responded with a decided lack of interest.

"Yes, ma'am." Scooping up her handbag and the floor samples, she escaped, like the painter before her.

One of these days, Dorothy Rose, she promised herself as she dialed the number of the tile warehouse on her cellular phone from the car, *it'll be your turn.*

As soon as she was alone, Roxanne scooped up the receiver. "What the hell do you think you're doing?"

"Now, Cora Mae," George drawled sapiently, "is that any way to greet your husband?"

"We had a deal, George. I did my part. Now why don't you leave me the fuck alone?"

"Tsk, tsk. What would all your fans say, if they could hear you? That's not exactly how a properly brought up southern lady is supposed to talk." Then he chuckled. "Oh, that's right. I keep forgettin'. Your upbringing wasn't exactly proper, was it, sugar?"

Roxanne ground her teeth, reminding herself that this was the trouble with blackmailers. Once they got their claws into you, they just wouldn't let go.

"I'm not going to give you any more money, George."

"Now, Cora Mae, did you hear me asking for money?"

No. But that would come. "I'm extremely busy at the moment. Do you think we could just cut to the chase, for once?"

"You know, honey pie, if I didn't know better, I'd think that along with changing your name you'd become a Yankee, the way you're always cutting to the chase, and gettin' to the bottom line. Didn't anyone ever tell you that stress can kill you?"

"Blackmail's not exactly an occupation for someone hoping to be long lived, either," she snapped back.

There was a long pause on the other end of the line. "Are you threatening me, Cora Mae?"

There it was again. That rough low tone that brought to mind a diamondback's deadly rattle. George Waggoner was a loser and a drunk. But he could also be dangerous. Jubal Lott lying six feet underground in the paupers' cemetery was proof of that.

"Of course not." She tried to mask her impatience, and her sudden fear. "It's just been a bad day."

"Mebee you need to get out," he suggested. "How about you and me finding some out-of-the-way honky-tonk and doin' a little two-step?"

She'd be dancing with the devil before she two-stepped with this man. "I think I'll pass on that, George." She caught a glimpse of herself in the gilt-framed mirror across the room. Her face was the color of ash, her brow was deeply furrowed.

Smoothing the lines with a fingertip, she tried again. "Would you please just tell me why you called?"

"It's about the job."

"What about it? If you don't like it, too bad. Because—"

"Oh, I liked it okay. Used some muscles I haven't for a few years, but it felt good to be sore at the end of the day. Even if it did remind me of our old days cuttin' cotton."

She flinched. Damn him! She didn't want to be reminded of those days. Something else he'd said filtered into her consciousness.

"You said *liked.*"

"Well, see that's the problem, Cora Mae. I got myself in a little trouble this afternoon, and that bastard McBride fired me."

She closed her eyes and sank down into her chair. "I'm sorry, George. But what does this have to do with me?"

"You gotta get me back on that crew."

"I can't. I've already pulled too many strings as it is."

"I guess you didn't hear me, Cora Mae. I said you have to get my job back for me. Or it's back to the pen. And believe me, sugar, this time I won't be going alone."

When she'd first left Georgia—and her husband—not a day had gone by that she hadn't expected to hear those words. As time went on, she'd started feeling safer. Until she'd finally managed to convince herself that she'd gotten away scot-free.

After all, the sheriff had ruled her stepdaddy's death a homicide by unknown assailant or assailants. Jubal Lott had been a rough-talking, hard-drinking, brawling bully. He'd also been a pain in the behind of the rural community thirty miles outside Athens, where Cora Mae Padgett and George Waggoner had grown up. That being the case, there hadn't been all that much incentive for the law to go looking very hard for Lott's killer.

"What, exactly, did you do?" she asked, hoping that it stopped short of mayhem. Or murder.

"Nothin' that bad. I took a few nips at lunch. Which I got a right to do," he complained. "Bein' off the clock. But that asshole caught me and said he's got a no alcohol on the job policy."

"That makes perfect sense to me."

"Mebee to you. But the way I see it, it's none of his goddamn business what I do on my own time. So, I popped him one."

"Popped him? You hit him?"

"Knocked him flat on his ass," George agreed with a self-satisfied chuckle. "He landed in a wheelbarrow of concrete mix. You should have seen it, Cora Mae. It was, as they say, one of them Kodak moments."

"Dammit, George, how do you expect me to smooth something like that over?"

"Are you kidding? Look at you, Cora Mae. Look at the con job you managed to pull off with that Roxanne Scarbrough act. You're not gonna convince me you can't sweet-talk that man into taking me back."

She'd begun to tremble. Sinking into the chair, Roxanne fought for control. And won. "I'll do my best." Her voice was not as strong as she would have liked.

"You'd better, sugar. Because it's your tight little butt that's on the line here. Not mine."

The dial tone buzzed in her ear, sounding like a hive of angry bees.

Seeing her atypically terrified face reflected in the mirror reminded Roxanne of the last time she'd been so frightened.

The night Jubal died. And all the years before that, when he'd come home drunk and force himself into her room, onto her bed, and between her legs.

"Dammit!"

Shaken to the core with new fears and old pain, she yanked the phone out of the wall and sent it flying across the room. It hit the target dead on, shattering the glass.

The crooked shards of glass remaining in the gilded frame made her face look like something Picasso might have painted.

She made her way on unsteady legs to the bar, where she poured a generous amount of whiskey into a glass. As she tossed it back, downing it in long thirsty swallows that both burned and calmed, Roxanne failed to see Jo, standing silently in the shadows just beyond the slightly open office door.

It wasn't easy clearing her things out of the apartment. Chelsea tried to stick to basics: clothes, a handful of personal belongings that held significant sentimental meaning, like the scrapbook of newspaper clippings written by Dylan Cassidy and the stuffed panda bear her father had sent her for her birthday after accompanying Richard Nixon on his historic trip to China.

She also retrieved all the pieces of jewelry from the wall safe, except those Nelson had given her. She was vaguely surprised her jewelry was there and wondered if pawning the diamond earrings and matching necklace she'd inherited from her Aunt Julia Lowell was too tacky even for Nelson; or, since she so seldom wore them, if he'd simply forgotten they existed.

She'd give them to her mother, she decided. Or, on second thought, she'd save them for her own daughter.

Surprisingly, packing her clothes proved the hardest task.

Because it forced her to go into the bedroom, and face the bed—her grandmother's bed!—where Nelson had betrayed her.

Reminding herself that her nearly lifelong relationship with him had been over before she'd caught him tangling the sheets with Heather Van Pelt, Chelsea threw the contents of her closet and dresser into suitcases. Then left the apartment.

The Paramount was located in trashy, but always vibrant, Times Square. The moment Chelsea walked into the eerily quiet Philippe Starck designed lobby, she felt as if she'd suddenly stumbled onto the set of a film noir. Or *Barton Fink*. The vast interior, with its art deco styling and cool gray stone was part 1930s ocean liner, part Bat Cave. The architect responsible for the overhaul of the formerly SRO hotel had obviously been a man of unique vision. Chelsea immediately understood why Cash had selected it.

The people lounging around the lobby, uniformally dressed in black, possessed the air of the punk-international fashion and rock scenes.

The reservations clerk, a young man sporting a ponytail and wearing an ashram smock over his baggy black linen slacks, was surprisingly helpful, despite his exceedingly hip appearance. He welcomed her to the Paramount and summoned the bellman, who could have been his twin, to take her luggage upstairs to the suite.

His dark eyes scanned over the assortment of Louis Vuitton cases. Then he looked back down at his computer screen. "Mr. Beaudine booked the room for the weekend. Were you planning a longer stay with us?"

"Oh, no." She managed a faint smile as she realized that even Elizabeth Taylor undoubtedly didn't travel with so much luggage for a mere weekend visit. Especially to a hotel where a pair of black leggings and a black T-shirt would prove quite sufficient. "It's a long story."

"Most of the good ones are," he said agreeably as he handed her the key.

The suite was decorated in black, white and gray, which could have seemed sterile, but was anything but. In fact, it was decidedly sensual, which she attributed to the curving lines of the furniture and softly glowing art deco lamps. She had the bellman put her luggage in the second, smaller bedroom.

After he'd left, she went into the main bedroom, where her attention was immediately captured by the oversize headboard depicting Vermeer's *The Lacemaker*. An American Beauty rose lay on one of the white pillows, a hot scarlet note punctuating the cool tones of the room like the crash of cymbals in the middle of a slow, sexy alto sax jazz riff.

Comparing this almost spare decor with the gilt-and-marble opulence of the Plaza or the Four Seasons—which Nelson would undoubtedly choose, were he to recommend a hotel—Chelsea decided Cash could not have selected a more romantic location. Somehow it managed to be both exciting and soothing at the same time. Which, now that she thought about it, was exactly the way he always made her feel.

Feeling the need to wash Nelson—and the lingering depression that had attached itself to her while she'd been cleaning out the apartment—off her, Chelsea went into the black-and-white tiled bathroom and started the water running in the tub.

As she threw a handful of sparkling bath crystals into the tub, she felt like a high school girl preparing for her senior prom. Which was, of course, ridiculous.

But as she lay back in the silky, fragrant water, her mind on the evening ahead, Chelsea decided that wasn't such a bad way to feel.

It should be illegal for any woman to look so damn sexy, Cash thought as he entered the suite and found her waiting. It should be illegal for any woman to possess such power over a man.

Over the years he'd managed to convince himself that he'd put her out of his mind, but now he knew that was a lie. The truth was, that like it or not, he'd thought of her innumerable times during their time apart: whenever fat, fluffy snowflakes had drifted down from pewter clouds, when spring flowers opened to a benevolent sun, whenever stars sparkled diamond bright in an indigo sky. She was in his head, and in his blood. Whatever happened between them, Cash knew that he was doomed to spend his life thinking of this woman.

"You look damn good for someone who spent the afternoon sweeping up the cold ashes of a lifelong relationship," he said. It was the truth. She was wearing a brilliant red off-the-shoulder dress that ended high on the thigh and fit her slender curves like a tomato casing. A trio of thin glittery gold chains dangled from each earlobe.

She shrugged, drawing his eyes from her legs back to the creamy flesh of her shoulders. "As you said, they were cold ashes."

Cash had to ask. "Any regrets?"

"Not a one." When she shook her head for added emphasis, her hair bounced enticingly, making his fingers practically itch with the need to run through those silk copper curls. "I told you, I'd already decided to break it off. In a way, I suppose Nelson actually did me a favor. After his little afternoon delight with Heather, I don't have to feel guilty."

"You haven't done anything to feel guilty about."

"Not yet, perhaps." Her green eyes were giving him a gilt-edged feminine invitation. "But the night's still young."

Cash let out a long breath he'd been unaware of holding. "Let me shower and change and I'll take you out to dinner. Somewhere special. Like Lutece. Or the Rainbow Room. I remember you liked to dance."

Not that they ever had. They would have had to have gone out in public for that to have happened.

"You don't have to change." Chelsea thought he looked wonderfully sexy in the jeans and denim shirt.

"Yes, I do." He'd gotten a sniff of himself in the elevator coming up from the lobby. Although he was not ashamed of good honest labor-induced sweat, neither was its aroma all that conducive to romance. "I won't be long. If you're hungry, I can order some cheese and crackers from room service."

"No. I'm not that hungry." Not for food, anyway, she amended silently as her eyes fell on that intriguing dark triangle of flesh framed by the open neck of his shirt.

He watched the desire rise in those incredibly expressive eyes and felt the familiar stirring deep in his groin. "Do you have any idea what it's always done to me when you look at me that way?"

His voice was rough. And pained. And thrilling. "Yes." She met his gaze with a level, absolutely honest one of her own. "Because I always feel the same way whenever you look at me."

Cash had been anticipating this moment since learning that Chelsea was coming to Raintree. He'd planned to seduce her, to bed her as many times as it took to get her out of his mind. But now, looking down into her face, he realized that somehow, when he wasn't looking, he'd gotten caught in a snare of his own making.

"I won't be long," he repeated. Soft, warm feminine desire radiated off her in waves. If he didn't move now, it would be too late.

It was not her first choice. But, Chelsea reminded herself, they had all night. "I'll be waiting."

Exhaling another long deep breath, Cash continued to look at her for a long, silent time. Then reluctantly left the room.

He turned the shower on cold, and stood beneath the icy spray, willing it to temporarily sate his hunger. He'd waited too long for this not to do it right. He'd decided a night on the town was in order. Belatedly remembering they were right in the middle of the Broadway theater district, he wondered if he should have the concierge call around for tickets to a show.

Damn. He should have thought this through more carefully. The problem was, he considered as he ducked his head beneath the shower head, causing the glacial water to stream down his face, his plans for the trip had centered around ensuring that Chelsea didn't return to her Yankee worm, checking out Roxanne's millwork, then making love to the woman who'd been driving him nuts for weeks.

Over the years, as part of the sophisticated veneer he sometimes donned as camouflage for the poor sharecropper's kid he'd once been, Cash had developed a polished, highly effective courtship ritual. Which had uncharacteristically flown out the window the moment Chelsea had walked into Roxanne's parlor.

He was going to do better, Cash decided. Beginning now.

He was as good as his word, taking less than ten minutes to shower and change, emerging from the bedroom, clad in a charcoal Armani suit, white silk shirt and Confederate red silk tie.

"Gracious."

"Something wrong?" He felt like a fool for needing her approval. But, dammit, he did.

"No." She continued to stare at him in a way that wasn't entirely flattering. "That suit's just very…New York." He would not have looked out of place on Wall Street. Or Madison Avenue. Indeed, she considered, he looked exactly like the type of man her mother would be thrilled to have her bring home.

"I would have brought my blue-and-white striped seersucker, but last time I wore it in Manhattan, everyone kept mistaking me for Matlock."

The smile took the bite out of his words, allowing her to smile in return. "I'm doing it again, aren't I? Stereotyping you."

"A bit."

"I'm sorry."

"Don't worry about it." He crossed the room to her. When he put his hand on the side of her face, his touch proved both soothing and enticing. "I didn't want you to be embarrassed. In case we run into anyone you know."

Once again he reminded her that not only had they never gone dancing in public, they'd never even gone to a restaurant together. Chelsea's eyes misted.

"I could never be embarrassed by you." She covered his hand with hers. "Not even back then."

"That's funny. I don't recall being asked to be your date for your sorority graduation dance. Or the winter carnival, or your cousin Susan's wedding at the country club, or—"

"All right. I get the point." Thinking back on her behavior, which was far more suited to her pretentious mother, Chelsea felt a rush of embarrassed heat, the bane of all redheads, flush into her face. "I guess I was a snotty brat. So why did you put up with me?"

"I told you, you had a great ass. Besides," he touched his lips to hers, letting her feel his smile, "you were a terrific lay."

Her laugh expelled her tension. "Well, that's certainly honest."

"I told you I'd never lie to you." He tilted his head back, looking down at her as he ran his hands over her shoulders, down her arms and linked their fingers together. "So, are you saying you were attracted to my brilliant, incisive mind?"

"We were young," she hedged. "We had sex on the brain."

"We may have been young." With only the slightest tug, he drew her closer, until their bodies were a mere whisper apart. "But the thing is, Chelsea, I always have sex on the brain whenever I'm around you." He lifted her hand to his lips and touched the tip of his tongue to the center of her palm, causing a flare of heat. "Which is why we'd better get out of here before I give in to temptation and find out if you're wearing anything beneath that dress."

"I wouldn't mind staying in." His eyes, his touch, the sensual kiss, all conspired to make the blood thicken, then simmer in her veins. "And sending out for room service later."

This time the invitation was unmistakable. Once more Cash managed, just barely, to resist. "I've waited too long not to do this right. We're going out to dinner. And maybe the theater, if the concierge can round up some tickets, then dancing."

"As lovely as that sounds, I don't really feel like spending most of the evening in a theater with a bunch of strangers. How about a compromise? We can eat dinner here, in

the hotel restaurant, and afterward, come back to the suite
and dance to the radio. Alone.''

She was a siren. A witch. Cash doubted he'd ever be able
to deny her anything. ''Sounds like a plan.''

Surrendering to the lure of her softly parted lips, he lowered his head and kissed her, his passion laced with the edgy
frustration of a hunger too long denied. Chelsea responded
freely, her emotions flowing from her to pour over him.

''Lord, you feel good.'' He released her hands and drew
her against him, pleased to feel her body warming as the
heat rushed to the surface of her smooth, perfumed and powdered flesh.

His teeth nipped and nibbled, his tongue stroked the
wounded flesh before plunging, deep and greedy, causing a
soft moan to escape her ravished lips.

Her head was spinning. Sensation after sensation tore
through her. Her hands dived beneath his suit jacket to explore the ridges of muscle at his back. Hunger met hunger,
need fueled need. Embers she'd once believed cooled
sparked and burned like wildfire through the blood.

He dragged his mouth from hers and began planting
kisses up the side of her face, her temples, her eyes, along
her jaw. With a soft, shuddering sigh, she tilted her head
back, offering him access to the creamy column of her neck.

Her skin was as hot as molten lava, her heart was beating
wildly in her throat. Cash touched his tongue to the pounding bloodbeat and imagined he could taste her desire. He
felt the vibration of her moan as he returned his mouth to
hers, cupped her hips in his hands and pressed her tight
against his aching erection.

The kiss went on and on, pulling them both deeper and
deeper into a smoky, tumultuous world. When he realized
he was on the brink of dragging her to the floor and peeling

that skintight, scarlet-as-sin dress off her, Cash forced himself to pull back. Just a little.

"I promised you dinner."

The long hot kiss had left Chelsea feeling unnaturally dizzy, as if she'd just taken a ride on an out-of-control carousel. "I don't need dinner."

"Ah, but I do." He trailed the back of his hand up her throat, her cheek. "I skipped lunch today and I'm starved. And you should eat something, too." His slow, wicked smile promised untold delights yet to come. "You're going to need to keep your strength up."

She tossed her head at that, causing the tousled curls to bounce like springs. "I've always been known for my stamina."

He remembered. Which had always been part of his problem, Cash considered. He'd remembered too many things about Chelsea. Too well. And for too long.

He folded his arms and grinned down at her. "So have I."

Chelsea had never been one to back down from a challenge. Either spoken, or unspoken. "Well, we'll just have to see who the better man—or woman—turns out to be."

"I think I've just felt the sting of a velvet gauntlet across my cheek." Laughter danced in his dark eyes.

"That's very perceptive of you."

"Thank you." He played idly with a gold earring. "Did I also mention that I'm not accustomed to losing?"

"What a coincidence," she said sweetly. "Since I'm not, either."

"That could make for an interesting night."

"My thoughts, exactly." She scooped up her satin evening bag and linked her hand through his arm. "Ready to go? I'm suddenly very hungry."

As they entered the elevator, which was already crowded

with a trio of six-foot-tall teenage girls made up to look like
featured players in a rock video, and a clutch of silver-haired
ladies clutching Fifth Avenue shopping bags, she looked up
at Cash and murmured, so only he would hear, "And by
the way, in answer to your earlier question, I'm not wearing
anything under this dress."

He gave her a long look. "Nothing?"

"Nothing at all. Except—"

"I knew it," he leaped in, vastly relieved. The thought
of sitting across a dinner table, knowing that she was naked
beneath the snug red material would have definitely proven
distracting.

"I did dust on a little scented powder."

The sexually provocative image inspired by her words
was all it took to send the blood roaring back into his groin.
He bent his head and brushed his lips against her earlobe.

"That's hittin' below the belt, darlin'."

She smiled up at him, smug in her little victory. "Precisely."

It was going to be, Cash thought with a blend of frustration, anticipation and humor, a very long evening.

And an even longer night.

Chapter Eighteen

Roxanne lay back in the tub, soaking out Vern's latest ravishment. Since he was in the process of getting a divorce from wife number nine, who, premarital agreement notwithstanding, was trying her best to get her hooks into his fortune, he'd insisted on keeping their affair a secret. Which suited her just fine. For now.

He'd left a half hour earlier, but not before leaving her bathed in his orgasms. For a man in his sixties he was hung like a stallion and had the stamina of a man half his age.

He was remarkable. And, of course, the fact that he was filthy rich certainly made him even more appealing. Appealing enough, she thought now, as she lifted a long leg out of the bubbles and ran a sponge from ankle to thigh, to marry. She wouldn't mind being Mrs. Vernon Gibbons. Even if she was forced to sign one of those nasty prenuptial agreements, just having his name tacked onto hers would give her enormous financial clout.

After all, how far would Ivana have gotten if she hadn't been Mrs. Donald Trump? Without the high-profile, jet-set existence that had put the couple on the cover of *People* time after time, she would have been just another blond has-been foreign skier with an accent.

But even after the divorce, she'd come out smelling like a rose, with enough money to keep her comfortable, a high-profile image that resulted in ghostwritten novels, talk show appearances, and an advice column, of all things.

Oh yes, there would definitely be some advantages to marrying Vernon Gibbons. Of course, Roxanne decided, as she switched to the other leg, like so many other business decisions, there would also be a downside. Vern was not a sophisticated man. In fact, she'd heard rumors of him using a Louisville slugger to break the legs of wife number four's karate instructor when the man had made the mistake of taking the concept of private lessons from the gymnasium into the bedroom.

Her planned seduction of Cash Beaudine would have to be abandoned. Which was a shame, since every erotic instinct Roxanne possessed told her that the sexy architect would be a masterful, passionate lover.

As was Vernon, of course, she reminded herself. Lowering her leg to the water, she squeezed the sponge, causing the cooling perfumed water to stream over her breasts.

He was a perfect match for her. Sexually and financially. The King of Discount and the Diva of Domesticity. It had a nice ring. Together they could rule the merchandising world. If there was one thing Roxanne enjoyed even more than hot sex, it was money. And Vernon definitely had enough of that to keep her happy for a very long time.

She was smiling as she left the tub and wrapped a thick fluffy towel around her slightly sore body.

Her smile faded as she walked into the adjoining bedroom and viewed the man sprawled in the flowered wing chair.

"What the fuck are you doing here?"

George lifted the Waterford iced tea glass filled with

bourbon in a salute. "Is that any way to greet your husband?"

Hell. How could she have forgotten about George? He
was the one obstacle to her cleverly conceived plan. She
had no doubt that the moment she announced her engagement to Vern, George would challenge their divorce, em-
broiling her in a decades-old murder.

Equally unpalatable was the idea he might remain quiet
until after the wedding, then demand a share of her new
husband's fortune to keep her secret. That, she decided, was
more likely.

Bile rose in her throat. She pushed it back down and
forced her whirling mind to calm. She could handle this,
she assured herself. There was too much at stake to let a
loser like George Waggoner screw up her life.

"What do you want, George?" she repeated in a voice
far calmer than she felt.

He gave her a long look that caused goose bumps to rise
on her arms. He'd obviously been drinking all day. He
smelled like a distillery and looked like a skid row bum.

"Actually, sugar, I've been thinking that since you seem
to be bumpin' uglies with old man Gibbons—"

"I am not—"

"Shut up." His voice was quiet. But his order was backed
up by the knife he pulled out of his boot. "Like I said, since
you've been giving it away to that old buck, and probably
to Beaudine—"

"That's not true. I haven't—"

"I said, shut the fuck up!" He was on his feet, the deadly
knife in his hand. There was a murderous gleam in his feral
eyes, reminding her all too well of another time he'd looked
this same way. But then his weapon of choice had been a
carpenter's claw hammer.

He nodded when she did as instructed. "That's better." When he ran the flat end of the blade up her cheek, Roxanne could literally feel the blood flow from her face. "You know, it's the damndest thing," he mused.

His breath reeked of whiskey, almost making her gag. Roxanne drew in a deep breath. "What?"

"Most women get uglier when they get older. You're better looking than you were when you were a girl." He trailed the knife blade around her jaw, and down her throat. When it experimentally touched the tip at the hollow where her blood was pounding wildly, she struggled against swallowing.

"Yes, indeed." He took hold of the top of the towel in his left hand and with one vicious downward swipe, yanked it away. "I figger it's time I took my husbandly rights."

He drew the knife across the crest of her breast, allowing the razor-sharp edge of the blade to touch just deeply enough to draw blood. Little beads of red dotted her flesh.

She thought her knees were going to cave out from under her. If he wanted her to beg, she would. After all she'd done in the past, begging was a small price to pay to stay alive.

"Please, George."

"Please, what, sugar?" he asked absently, as he turned the knife back to the flat edge and drew it slowly, tauntingly down her torso, over her rib cage, beyond her navel, and lower still. "Are you asking me to fuck you? Like you ask that hairy old gorilla?"

She'd *rather* go to bed with a gorilla. But, she didn't want to die, either.

"Yes." The surrender came on a long, ragged note. "Please, George. I want you."

"You want me to fuck you."

"Yes." She'd forgotten how, toward the end, when he'd begun to drink heavily, he'd been unable to get an erection unless she talked dirty. And finally, even that hadn't been enough, she remembered, her hand unconsciously going to her cheek, where she could still feel the faint edge of the bone he'd broken with his fists. "I want you to fuck me, George."

"Hard."

"Hard."

"In the ass," he prompted.

"Yes." She briefly closed her eyes. She'd survived worse. She *would* get through this, she vowed. "In the ass."

She opened her eyes just in time to witness an evil yellow grin that sent a frisson of shivers up her spine. "Sugar, I thought you'd never ask."

They had dinner on the mezzanine. Unusual for the city, the lighting was subdued, the noise level almost hushed. It was, Cash and Chelsea both agreed, perfect.

"You never told me," she remembered, "how things turned out at the house."

"Not too bad." He'd been excited about his afternoon earlier. His success had paled compared to his plans for this evening. "There was some hand-carved ceiling molding that should look great in the parlor. And I got a front door that's got to be seen to be believed. It was carved in France for some winery. It's solid oak, twelve inches thick, covered with vines and bas-relief clusters of grapes."

"Roxanne should be pleased. It sounds exquisite."

"It is. But not half as exquisite as you."

For some reason the compliment, and the masculine admiration gleaming in his eyes made Chelsea strangely nervous. She dragged her gaze away, garnering her scattered composure. Down on the lobby floor, she watched a famous British rock star arrive with his sizable entourage.

"That really is one dynamite dress." Surrounded by the

sea of black favored by the other diners, she stood out like a defiant flame.

"I know redheads aren't supposed to wear red," she murmured, parroting what her mother and Nelson had been telling her for years. "But it's always given me confidence."

"Did you feel you needed confidence tonight?"

In the old days, they wouldn't have been having this discussion. She realized she'd have to get used to the idea of him being so forthright. She also realized that she'd never be able to hide anything from those knowing dark eyes that seemed capable of looking all the way into her soul.

"I suppose so." She began fiddling nervously with the cutlery. "After all, it's been a very long time, and although the chemistry between us is still as strong as ever, stronger, actually—"

"Chelsea." He reached across the table and covered her hand with his. "Relax. It's okay."

"What is it about you that makes me stutter and stammer? And babble. Lord, I never babble. Not ever, not even when I was a teenager. Why, anyone can tell you that..." Her voice drifted off and she managed a faint, sheepish grin. "See what I mean?"

"I think it's probably the same thing about you—about us together—that makes me feel like a fourteen-year-old virgin again."

"Really?" Her initial response was relief that she was not alone in these tumultuous feelings. Her second thought, and the one that came crashing on the heels of the first, was that he was far more sexually experienced. "You lost your virginity at fourteen?"

"Fifteen. It was sort of a birthday present." Despite the circumstances of his upbringing, the memory earned a reluctant smile.

"And so much more original than a baseball glove," she

said dryly. No wonder he'd been so skillful when she'd known him. He'd already had years and years of practice. "I suppose you're going to tell me that your father, in some sort of southern male rite of bonding, took you down to the local whorehouse for a boy's night out?"

"Actually, you're half right. It *was* at a whorehouse on the outskirts of town. But my father didn't have to take me. I was already there."

"You went there on your own? At fifteen? Surely you had some friends along for support?" She could imagine, with some effort, a group of teenage boys pooling their paper boy money and getting the grand idea to hire a prostitute. Especially in Raintree, where inhibitions seemed to melt away in the steamy southern climate.

He decided to be straight with her now. Her reaction, whatever it turned out to be, wouldn't change how tonight would end. But it would definitely set the tone for their future.

"I worked there, Chelsea. From the time I was thirteen until I went to college. And sometimes, during vacations after that."

She was momentarily speechless.

"I told you how my dad died when I was a kid."

She nodded and covered his hand with hers.

"We were sharecroppers. The owner of the farm came to the burial and told my mom he was real sorry about the accident, but she was going to have to leave, because there was no way a widow and a skinny kid would be able to keep the farm going."

"That's hateful!"

"It was the way things were back then. And he was right about us not being able to run the place by ourselves. Even when my dad was alive, we lived hand to mouth. I remember one really bad winter, after that summer's crop had gotten destroyed in a tropical storm, we were reduced to eating robins.''

His eyes turned reminiscent; his smile was grim. ''There were these gall berries growing wild by the house. When they fermented, the robins ate them and got dead drunk. We could almost pick them off the branches. Dad and I gathered up all those drunk birds, crushed their heads, and mama fried the breasts in lard, mixed them with some rice and baked them into robin jambalaya.

''Mama was Scots-Irish, from the Blue Ridge country in the hills. The country that was in the movie, *Deliverance?*''

Chelsea nodded her familiarity with the movie and the lush green, wild scenery.

''She was used to the hardscrabble life, so it never seemed to bother her that we didn't have two plug nickels to rub together.

''She took in washing and ironing, which didn't help her reputation in town, since that was work normally only done by black women. I used to take the wicker baskets of clothes back to those big houses in Raintree for her. At first I couldn't believe people lived like that. Then, I went through a stage when I was angry at what I considered the injustice of it all.''

''That's not surprising,'' she murmured, thinking of how he'd carried that anger with him to Yale.

''I suppose not. But it sure wasn't very constructive, either. I got in a lot of fights in those days.'' He stared out at some middle ground, giving Chelsea the feeling he was seeing himself as he'd once been.

''Anyway, after we were evicted, we moved to a boarding house in town and she got some work as a maid, but then she got sick, so I did what I could to help out. I had the usual kid jobs, paper route, mowed lawns, that sort of stuff, but it didn't even make enough to pay for her prescriptions.

"So one day, I was stealing some aspirin from the Rexall Drugstore—we couldn't afford the pain pills the doctor had prescribed—when the owner of the whorehouse, who'd come in for some hair dye, saw me put the bottle in my jacket pocket. She waited until I got outside, gave me a lecture, then offered me a job sweeping up and running errands after school and on weekends.

"Then, once a month, I'd hitchhike up to the mountains, where my mama's people were from, and use the money I'd earned to buy whiskey."

"I don't understand."

"One of the things folks brought with them from the old country was the recipe for making Scotch whiskey. It was one of the few ways a poor mountain farmer could raise cash. And, of course, his wife used it in the home remedies she made and sold. One summer I spent a couple of weeks working on one of those stills and discovered that not only is it illegal and dangerous, moonshining's just about the hardest work a man or woman can do.

"But since Raintree county was dry in those days, my mama's family's recipe sold better than ice-cold watermelon on the Fourth of July."

Chelsea thought about the life Cash had described. "I think I'm beginning to guess what it was that Jeb said that made you break his nose."

Cash's smile was slow and reminiscent. "He called Mama a bootlegger. Just like Al Capone. That would've been bad enough by itself. But coming from a kid from one of those big houses, well, I just had to pop him."

"That's quite a start to a friendship."

"The Townelys weren't like some of the other rich folk in Raintree," Cash conceded. "After Jeb and I became friends, they'd invite me to dinner, then send me home with the leftovers. It was years before I figured out Mrs. Townely always had her cook make extra on the nights I came over.''

"That's nice."

"They were nice people. And they helped me realize that there was a life beyond Raintree, if I was willing to work hard enough for it. Becoming rich became an obsession. I promised my mama I'd buy her one of those fancy houses like Roxanne's Belle Terre. And make her queen of Tara. But she died before I could make good.''

"It was the thought that counted." She turned their hands, linking her fingers with his in the center of the small black table. "Besides, she knows what a success you've made of your life, Cash. And is proud of you.''

"You sound awfully sure about that."

"I am." Her gaze was earnest, her green eyes sober. "If I couldn't believe that my father somehow knew that I was a successful writer—although admittedly not in his class— I'd feel horribly let down.''

"Good point. And one I'll think about."

"I'm glad."

He lifted their joined hands to his lips and kissed her fingertips, one by one. "And, if you're right, I'll bet your dad thinks you've done just fine. Following your own star, which doesn't shine any less brightly than his.''

The touch of his lips on her skin sent tiny flames, like sparklers, skipping through her blood, warming her from the inside out. "How badly did you want that cheesecake for dessert?" she asked.

He read the desire in her eyes. "Why don't I order a couple of pieces to go?''

Her smile was nothing less that beatific. "I knew you were an intelligent man.''

They returned to the room with two orders of raspberry

cheesecake in a foam box and a bottle of champagne Cash immediately put on ice.

"Would you like a glass now?" The waiter, obviously recognizing the opportunity for a generous tip, had also sent along a pair of flutes.

"No." She shook her head as anticipation and nerves warred within her. "I don't need any champagne when I'm with you, Cash."

"Believe me, darlin', I know the feeling." He drew her into his arms.

An unseen maid had left the radio tuned to an oldies jazz station after turning down the beds. As if on cue, Billie Holiday began singing about her man.

For a long, silent time, punctuated only by the occasional scream of a siren or taxi horns outside the window, they merely swayed to the music, to several more songs until Quincy Jones's "One Hundred Ways" began to play.

"That's not enough," he murmured against her hair.

"What's not enough?"

"One hundred ways." He pressed his lips against her temple, rewarded when he felt her pulse leap in response. "Do you have any idea how much I want you?"

He pulled her closer to him, moving in time to the slow, lonely sound of an alto sax that brought to mind steamy southern nights, and the sweetly seductive scent of night-blooming flowers. "I want you, Chelsea. In more ways than I could count. And not just for tonight."

One hand tightened on her waist while another fisted in her hair, tilting her head back again, holding her wary gaze to his. "Not just for tomorrow night. A thousand nights won't be enough."

A flicker of fire leaped beneath her skin when he slid his wicked, clever hands between their bodies and his fingers began tracing slow, aching circles on her breasts.

She was trembling. It stunned her. When his thumbs stroked over her nipples, a liquid, shimmering pleasure drifted through her, warming her body and clouding her mind. She slipped her own unsteady hands beneath his jacket to his back, and held on.

Chelsea thought she'd known desire before. She'd thought, during her long ago time with Cash, she'd known need. But those emotions hadn't come close to the intense hunger she was suffering now. She moved closer, exalting in the feel of his hard male body. Reveling in the heat that threatened to have her melting like a candle beneath a hot southern sun.

"If you don't kiss me…really kiss me…I think I'm going to scream."

"Can't have that." Banking the fire for now, he brushed a tingling kiss against her lips that only left her wanting more. "I'd hate for us to get thrown out for disturbing the peace."

His mouth rubbed over hers, lingering, then drawing away. Once. Twice. A third time. His lips remained cool while hers warmed. But instead of the instant flash fire she'd once experienced with this man, the heat was a golden glow, infused with tenderness.

He reached behind her to unzip her dress. It slid down her body like a silken waterfall, creating a scarlet puddle at her feet.

"Good lord." He stared at the erotic sight of her standing in front of him, wearing only a pair of high heels and those long gold earrings. "You weren't kidding about not wearing anything beneath that dress."

Her slow, enticing smile was as sensual as any woman ever shared with any man. "You're not the only one who can tell the unvarnished truth, you know."

Unable to resist the lure of all that silken, perfumed flesh, he reached out and traced a slow circle around first one breast, then the other. "If I'd believed you, darlin', I never would have been able to eat dinner."

"Then it's a good thing you didn't believe me." She looked up at him through the fringe of her lashes, giving him the same saucy look that Georgia's most famous southern belle had used to bring that devil-may-care Yankee blockade runner to his knees. "Because you're definitely going to need your energy."

Her scent was surrounding him, seeping beneath his skin and into his blood like a drug. Her flesh was as pale as porcelain, as smooth as satin. His fingers glided over the sprinkling of freckles scattered over the crest of her breasts.

"Sun kisses," he murmured.

Her head was spinning again. She could feel her legs weakening. She thought she'd known what to expect from Cash. After all, they'd been together countless times like this.

But not like this, she amended as she grabbed hold of his shoulders to keep from melting. Never like this.

"What?"

"Your freckles." He dipped his head and skimmed his lips across the light brown flecks. "My mama always told me freckles were kisses left by a smiling sun."

She shivered as his tongue flicked over a taut nipple, causing a spark that shot straight through her to that warm, moist place between her thighs. Her skin, beneath his lips, felt strangely tight. Too tight. And sensitive almost to the point of pain. Her body felt hot and swollen.

She closed her eyes, all the better to concentrate on the tumultuous feelings flowing over her. Inside her. Dazzling lights sparked behind her lids like heat lightning flashing on a distant horizon.

He bit her fragrant shoulder. Then soothed the reddened

flesh with his tongue. Chelsea heard him say something, but
his low deep voice was only a distant roaring in her ears.

He lifted her up, carrying her into the bedroom. He continued to kiss her, the kisses growing deeper and more drugging with each step.

He placed her on the turned-down bed. Although the
room was dark, the light streaming in through the open door
from the living room cast a warm golden light over her. Her
body gleamed like pearls; her eyes shone like emeralds.
Cash stood beside the bed, looked down at her and found
her wonderful.

"You are so beautiful." He shook his head, as if wondering what miraculous trick of fate had brought her to him.

Chelsea held out a hand to him. "What I am," she said,
in a lush, throaty voice, "is lonely."

Cash did not need a second invitation. He began stripping
off his clothes.

Although it took a Herculean effort, Chelsea managed to
keep her passion-heavy lids open to watch him. The sheets
felt cool against her back; his gaze, dark with hunger, heated
her breasts, her stomach, her thighs.

Age had not diminished his sex appeal. During the intervening years, Chelsea had, whenever she thought of Cash,
managed to convince herself that she'd imagined the perfection of his body. But she was wrong.

He was a strong lean man who'd not allowed himself to
soften. There wasn't an ounce of superfluous flesh on his
body; he was all lean sinew and hard muscle. And he ex-
uded a male vitality that made her nerves sizzle like hot
electric wires on a rain-slicked street.

The mattress sighed as he sat down beside her. "You are
so soft." He skimmed a finger up the inside of her thigh.
"So lovely." Excitement crackled along her skin like a flash
fire. As she unconsciously gathered up a handful of sheet

beside her, he took her hand, slowly uncurled her fingers, and pressed her palm against his chest. "Feel what you do to me, Chelsea."

His heart was pounding like a jackhammer. Pleased that she was not the only one so harshly affected, she smiled up at him. "That's amazing."

"It's you." He sucked in a deep breath as she explored this phenomenon further. Her hand slid slowly downward over his rib cage. When she bent her head and pressed her open mouth against his hard, flat stomach, she felt every muscle clench. "Only you."

Her fingers curled around his penis. He was as hard as stone, as warm as a new sun. She tested his weight and thickness and found him thrilling. She felt the tumescent flesh stir beneath her stroking touch and felt a surge of feminine pleasure that she was responsible for such obvious desire.

Chelsea's heart swelled with such emotion she thought it was going to explode right out her chest. Moved, but unable to express her feelings in mere words, she bent her head and touched her lips to the smooth, straining tip.

He bucked beneath her intimate kiss and made an animal sound, deep in his throat. The tortured growl caused sensuality to pump like molten lava through her veins. Encouraged, she flicked her tongue along the length of his penis, and was prepared to take him fully in her mouth, when, sensing her intentions, he fisted his hand in her hair and lifted her head.

"Lord, lady, if you keep that up, we're going to end this in about ten seconds flat."

"I don't care." Her fingers continued to stroke him as her eyes offered a blatant feminine dare. She wanted him. Now.

"Well now, honey, I'm real sorry about that." He

grabbed hold of both her wrists in one hand and pushed her gently back against the pillows, holding her hands together above her head. "Because I want to take my time."

She squirmed beneath his restraints. But in a sensual, erotic way designed to make his temperature and blood pressure soar. "And do you always get everything you want?"

His smile was a wicked slash of white in the purple shadows of the darkened room. "Tonight I do."

Clamping down on his need to take, Cash concentrated instead on his desire to give. To touch. To torment. Lying down beside her, he trailed his hands all over her naked flesh, fondling her aching breasts, scraping over her tingling nipples, creating a spiral of flame down her back before kneading her buttocks.

After her body had warmed to the boiling point, he continued his sensual torment by trailing his mouth over the fiery trail his hands had blazed.

He sucked on her nipples with hot, hungry greed, creating a primal pull deep in her feminine core. His teeth bit into her shoulder, nipped at the tender cord in her neck, closed around an earlobe and tugged. He kissed her stomach, the sensitive hollow between her pelvic bones. His tongue cut a hot wet path through the nest of coppery curls between her thighs. All the time, she was moving restlessly beneath his hands and mouth, writhing on the sheets.

When his lips plucked at the source of all that moist heat, her body bucked, moving instinctively, unashamedly against his mouth.

"Please." Chelsea knew she was begging. But she felt no shame. Her secret places were swollen, throbbing with need. A wild, out-of-control pulse that matched the jackhammer beat of both their hearts was throbbing between her legs.

"Cash." Her voice was half gasp, half sob. "Hurry." She

tossed her head back and forth on the pillow as his tongue slipped into her wet hot center and his teeth began nibbling on her ultrasensitive clitoris. "Please hurry."

"It's okay, darlin'." He put his hands beneath her bottom, lifting her hips off the sheets, pressing her harder against his mouth as he feasted on the feminine juices flowing from her. "I promise not to take you anywhere you don't want to go."

The pleasure-pain escalated, spiraling into a tighter and tighter coil. Just when she thought there couldn't be more, he replaced his tongue with first one finger, then two, reaching deep inside her, stretching her, rasping the tender inner tissues with his deep hard thrusts. His mouth covered hers, allowing her to taste herself on his lips. He held her tightly against him, his fingers deep inside her, his tongue tangling with hers inside the moist cavern of her mouth. This was the way Cash had wanted Chelsea. The way he'd imagined her too many times during too many long and lonely nights during their years apart. Hot and hungry, rising higher and higher toward the dizzying peak of passion.

He released her mouth and tilted his head back, drinking in the sight of her parted lips, her heightened color, the flush, like a fever that covered the lithe body arched against his stroking touch.

His thumb parted the sensitive pink folds, searching for the taut nub above her vaginal lips. When he found it, he pressed down. At the same time he thrust his strong fingers in more deeply than ever before, so deep he was touching the back of her womb.

Her eyes flew open, wide with shock as she felt herself shattering into a thousand crystalline pieces. She cried out his name on a wail of wonder.

He held her, kissing her as the contractions that were

gripping at his fingers, like hundreds of hungry little mouths, slowly subsided.

She was limp. Boneless. The fire alarm outside in the hallway could have sounded and she could not have moved if her very life had depended on it.

"I never knew," she managed to gasp on a ragged, labored breath. "It's never been that way before." Her glazed eyes were puzzled as she tried to focus on his face through the shimmering mist still clouding her mind. "Not even with you."

"And it's just the beginning."

True to his word, he took her higher, again and again, until Chelsea was certain she had nothing left to give. And even then he proved her wrong.

When he finally claimed ultimate possession, surging into her, hot steel into velvet, she tightened around him, drawing him deeper, milking him, matching him thrust for thrust, rhythm for rhythm.

He lifted her spread legs so he could pound into her with a force that rocked the bed and caused fireworks to explode behind her closed eyes in fireballs of dazzling color. Although she would have thought it impossible, Chelsea felt him grow harder. And larger.

He called out her name and went rigid, the muscles of his neck standing out in stark relief. Chelsea felt the explosion deep within as he filled her with his seed, then immediately felt the inner spasms of her own release.

Groaning, Cash collapsed onto her. She wrapped her arms around his back, and her legs around his thighs, keeping him inside her, unwilling to surrender the feel of his hard moist body against hers.

His lips were pressed against her hair and he was murmuring soft, hypnotic words. But because of the wild pounding of her own heart in her ears, Chelsea couldn't hear them.

Chapter Nineteen

Roxanne's only consolation was that it didn't take long. George's sour whiskey-and-cigarette breath, as he covered her mouth with his had made her gag, and his unkempt fingernails had scraped her skin, but after forcing himself inside her, he'd climaxed after two quick pumps. Cursing, he'd immediately passed out.

She gingerly left the bed, grimacing at the sticky semen trailing down her leg. The knife was lying on the quilt, where he'd dropped it sometime during the forced sex. She picked it up, moved it from hand to hand, and looked down at him, fantasizing for a long luxurious moment cutting off his flaccid penis and balls.

Reluctantly reminding herself that this bastard rapist wasn't worth doing hard time for, she instead took the knife and hid it away in her lingerie drawer, then opened the drawer of the bedside table and took out the Smith & Wesson revolver she'd bought last month for self-protection after someone had tried to break in.

She took the revolver into the bathroom with her, where she cleaned up, trying to wash away all traces of George

Waggoner from her body. Although she longed to take a shower, she didn't dare risk getting that far out of reach of her gun. Once he recovered, he would undoubtedly be back for more. And she intended for him to understand that the next time would be his last.

She dried herself, rubbing her inner thighs with a force that reddened her skin. She scowled at the teeth-shaped scrape on her breast. Dammit, he'd broken the skin. The human mouth was dirty at best; she shuddered to think what germs this man's might be harboring.

Deciding that she'd have to think of some reason to talk her doctor into a prescription for antibiotics—although rabies shots would probably be more appropriate in this particular case—she took her emerald green silk robe from the hook on the back of the closet door, put it on, then returned to the bedroom.

He'd rolled onto his back and was sprawled atop her mattress. He was snoring loudly, his mouth open wide. He reached down, unconsciously scratching his groin, which drew her attention back to that limp, flaccid sex. When she viewed her own blood staining her precious quilt, fury surged through her, burning away any lingering pain, searing away her humiliation.

He'd pay for this, Roxanne swore. When she could think up an appropriate punishment. For now, she just wanted him out of her house.

She leaned over him, and pressed the barrel of the gun against his scrotum. "Wake up you son of a bitch," she said. "I want you wide awake when I blow your fucking balls off." Her threat garnered an immediate response.

His eyes flew open. "Roxanne, sugar—"

"Don't you sugar me, you rotten, perverted son of a bitch. In fact, don't you say a damn thing. Unless you want to be singing soprano real soon."

His jaw slammed shut. His eyes were wide, all whites and dilated black pupils. She knew his mouth was dry when he nervously licked his lips.

"You raped me, George." She pressed the barrel deeper into his unwashed flesh. "And for that, you're going to pay. Big time."

"Please, baby." Sweat was pouring down his face. Off his nose, and from the tip of his shriveled penis, like a dripping faucet. His body was slick with the rank moisture. "Look, sugar, I mean, sweetheart—"

"Wrong word, George." She cocked the pistol and smiled down at him. "It's Ms. Scarbrough, remember?"

"Whatever you say. But you used to like being called Mrs. Waggoner," he whined.

"That's yet another thing you've got wrong, George." She clucked her tongue. "This just isn't a good day for you, is it?" She shook her head. "I'm afraid I don't have any choice but to kill you."

"Jesus H. Christ!" His eyes widened even further. He was shaking like a drunk coming off a bender. "You can't kill a man just for forgetting your new name."

"True. But I can kill him for raping me." Her eyes were blue ice, her smile glacial. "Say goodbye, George."

Roxanne was still smiling when she pulled the trigger.

Chelsea couldn't remember ever being so happy. She lay with her head on Cash's chest, listening as his heart, and hers returned to normal. One of his hands was caressing her back, the other was playing in the damp curls of her hair.

"That was amazing," she said on a soft, satisfied sigh.

He kissed her shoulder. "We aim to please."

And gracious, how well he'd succeeded. Beyond her wildest imagination! "Wonderfully amazing," she repeated, still basking in the afterglow of passion. "And surprising."

"Surprising? Are you saying you didn't think I still had it in me to make you fly?"

"Oh, I knew from the moment I walked into Roxanne's parlor you could do that. I just didn't think you—we—could make love so slowly. So beautifully."

She lifted her head and gave him a sweetly serious look that pulled at innumerable cords inside Cash. "I know this is going to sound like a horrendous cliché, but I've truly never experienced anything like that."

"I'm glad." He caught hold of her chin, leaned forward and kissed her. A deep, slow kiss that rekindled smoldering embers.

"I wonder why it was so different?" she mused when the heartfelt kiss finally ended.

Cash was not exactly in the mood for this conversation. He'd finally done what he'd been aching to do for weeks. And it was as good—better—than he'd hoped for. He would have preferred merely lying with her, enjoying the cooling aftermath of their passion. But knowing it was a woman's nature to want to discuss things, he sighed and turned his mind to her question.

"I think it was different because it was different. There's no big mystery involved, darlin'."

"But didn't you feel it? How even though you were burning up, it was still somehow comfortable?"

"Comfortable?" Old shoes were comfortable. The battered, sweat-stained, decades-old cotton hat he wore fishing was comfortable. Old dogs and watermelon wine were comfortable. Sex with Chelsea would never fit that description. "Like boring?"

"Never." She patted his cheek and gave him a benevolent, faintly patronizing smile. "You know what I mean."

"No. I don't think I do. Are you saying you weren't turned on?" Let her just try to deny it, Cash thought.

"Of course not. I was merely trying to explain that in the old days, making love with you was always a little frightening. Tonight, as exciting as it was, I felt perfectly safe."

Safe. Shit. That was even worse than *comfortable.*

"Well that sure gives a whole new meaning to safe sex," he muttered.

"You're not even trying to understand." It was Chelsea's turn to be irritated. She'd been so happy. She'd been floating on gilt-edged clouds of pleasure. Why did he have to ruin it by acting so much like a... She paused, trying to come up with exactly the right word. Man! she decided.

"Oh, I understand, sweetheart." Before she knew what was happening, he'd reversed their positions, and was lying on top of her, his long legs entwined with hers, his body pressing her deep into the mattress. "I was trying to take my time. To let you get used to the idea of us being together again. To make tonight memorable."

He was hard again. She could feel the hot rigid flesh pressing against her belly. He was using his superior strength to hold her to the bed in a way she found undeniably thrilling.

"It was."

"Memorable, but safe." He bent his head and bit her shoulder—not painfully, but hard enough she knew her skin would be bruised in the morning.

"Yes." She'd begun to tremble.

He scraped his teeth down the crest of her breast, enjoying her sharp intake of breath. Then he lifted his head and looked into her eyes, which were darkening with rising desire. "I think it's time for you to understand that what I feel for you isn't always safe. And it damn well isn't always gentle."

His mouth came down on hers, crushing, claiming. His

hands moved roughly on her body, pulling her off the love-rumpled sheets and holding her hard against him.

Then, before she could catch her breath, Cash dragged her into the whirlwind, proving to her that love and unbridled passion were not mutually exclusive.

She had made a tactical error, Roxanne decided grimly. Now her sheets were truly ruined. And unless she wanted her bedroom to reek like a goddamn outhouse, she was going to have to let George use her shower.

She made him leave the bathroom door open, so she could monitor his movements. Meanwhile, after stripping the bed, she changed into a pair of royal purple lounging pajamas with gold piping and a pair of gold mules.

Then she sat down in the wing chair, lit a cigarette, and pointed the revolver at the bathroom door.

"Would you put that goddamn thing away before you give me a fuckin' heart attack," he complained as he came out of the bathroom with one of her monogrammed towels wrapped around his waist. "Besides, it's not even loaded."

"If you think that, why don't you take it away from me?" Her tone was patient, her half smile sly. "Remember the night you got drunk and made me play Russian roulette?" She inhaled deeply on the cigarette, enjoying the harsh bite of nicotine and smoke in her lungs. "But that time, you were the one holding the gun. And I was the one begging you not to kill me."

"Shit, I wouldn't have killed you, Cora Mae. Ms. Scarbrough," he corrected quickly when her lips turned down into a tight frown. "I was just funnin' with you."

"I was terrified," she said on a billowing cloud of exhaled smoke. "The same way you were earlier. It isn't a very nice feeling, is it, George?"

"So that's what that little melodrama was all about? Pay-back time?"

"In a way."

"Fine. Then we should be even."

She shouldn't have let him shower, Roxanne decided, re-alizing she'd made another mistake. He'd been a great deal more docile and desperate with shit and urine all over his ass and thighs.

"Of course we're not," she snapped. "Because you raped me."

"You can't rape your wife."

"The courts feel differently about that these days, George. But it's a moot point. Since we're divorced, dam-mit."

"That's what you keep sayin'. But I notice that you still haven't dragged out the paper proving it."

"I don't know where it is."

"I've seen you work. You don't misplace so much as a goddamn paper clip. You sure as shootin' wouldn't lose a divorce decree."

They were getting off track again. "You raped me."

"That's what you say now. But I remember when you used to scream because you liked it rough. You couldn't get enough. Remember? Not even when you were pregnant."

"I don't want to talk about that!"

She was on her feet, her hand trembling wildly. He shook his head, reached out and took the revolver away. "It's not exactly my favorite subject, either," he muttered.

He opened the gun and spun the cylinder. "Empty. I didn't think you'd do it. A dead man in your bedroom might be a little difficult to pull off, Cora Mae. Even the rich, famous and glib Roxanne Scarbrough probably would have trouble getting out of that fix.

"Now, you can lie all you want, but you can't deny all

those fuckathons made us a baby, sugar. A baby you didn't want.''

''I couldn't be a mother,'' she insisted. ''Not then. I had things to do.''

''Like killin' your stepdaddy?''

''You know I didn't kill him. You did.''

''It probably don't matter which of us swung that hammer,'' he said with a shrug. ''Since in the eyes of the law, the other one would be an accessory after the fact. But there's no point in rehashing it, sugar. Because it's yesterday's box score.''

He tossed the unloaded revolver onto the unmade bed. ''I'm your legally wedded husband, Cora Mae. And it's been a long time since I've been with a woman. And those punk fairies in prison aren't exactly my type, if you know what I mean. So other than my hairy ole palm, I ain't had a lot of sexual companionship these past seven years.''

''Seven years? What on earth were you in for?''

''Didn't I tell you?'' He flashed a dark, evil grin. ''I had sex with a girl on top of a pool table in a Phoenix bar. I say she was willin'. But the goddamn cops called it rape.''

He decided not to mention the little matter of the porno movies. If she thought he might have filmed her, the next time she'd make sure the gun was loaded.

''You really are sick, George.''

''Now that may be, Cora Mae.'' His menacing old ways returned, in spades, as he walked toward her. ''But the way I see it, you're stuck with me. For better or for worse.''

She whirled away, opened the dresser draw and pulled out the knife. As she held it out in front of her, the blade caught the light, making it look like a straight bolt of lightning.

''You're forgetting the line about until death us do part,'' she warned. ''You touch me again, George, and I swear I'll kill you. Even if I have to spend the rest of my life in prison.''

"You'd never do it." His eyes were beady little black marbles. "You've worked too hard for all this to throw it all away and end up on your knees giving head to a bunch of prison dykes in the shower room."

Her eyes were cold steel. "Just try me."

He gave her a long look. Then shrugged. "You were always a lousy lay anyway." Turning his back on her, he strolled over to the smaller of the two closets in the room, opened the door and began looking through the rack of men's clothing that Vern had begun keeping at her house for his frequent visits.

"What are you doing now?"

"I need something to wear," he said simply. "So I figured old Vern wouldn't mind sharing some of his clothes with me. Since I'm willing to share my wife with him."

"That's a $250 shirt," she complained when he chose a blue silk custom-tailored shirt.

"And worth every dollar, too," he agreed, his cheer restored now that the power had shifted back to him.

Vowing that she was going to get rid of this evil monster—and soon—Roxanne watched him dress and imagined slashing the blue silk, and the flesh beneath it. Again and again.

It would almost be worth going to prison, she thought. But she had a horrible feeling that George was like all those monsters in the horror movies. Whatever she did to get rid of him, just when she'd think he was finally dead, he'd pop up again with that evil, devil's grin and try to destroy her.

The trick was to destroy him first.

But how?

* * *

After a long, love-filled night, Chelsea and Cash were having breakfast in bed, when the phone rang. Thinking it might be Roxanne, Cash scooped it up. "Hello?"

His response was greeted with silence.

"Hello?" he tried again.

"I was calling for Chelsea Cassidy," the modulated female voice said. There was enough similarity in inflection to give Cash a very good idea who it was.

"The operator put you through to the wrong room," he said, wanting to spare Chelsea having to come up with explanations she was not yet prepared to make. "Just a minute, and I'll go get her."

He covered the receiver with his palm, earning a curious look from Chelsea. "Is that for me?"

"I'm afraid so."

"Who is it? Roxanne? Surely not Nelson?"

"I think it's your mother."

"My mother?" She unconsciously pulled the sheet up over her naked breasts. "She's calling me here?"

"Seems so. I figured I'd let her think you slept in your own bedroom."

"Thank you." Chelsea had a very good feeling what her mother was calling about. She sighed and held out her hand. "I'd better talk to her. Before she comes to the hotel and begins banging on our door."

"The clerk won't give out our room number."

"The clerk isn't *supposed* to give out our room number," Chelsea corrected dryly. "But you've never seen my mother in action. Hello, Mother." Chelsea forced a cheery, surprised tone into her voice. "How did you find me?"

"It wasn't that difficult," Deidre Lowell said. "When Nelson told me you'd returned to the city this weekend, I simply began calling hotels. I started with the Plaza, then the Four Seasons and the Waldorf. Then I tried the Grand

Hyatt. To tell you the truth, Chelsea dear, the Paramount was very far down on my list of possible choices.''

Her disapproving tone suggested that Chelsea had suddenly taken to wearing leather and turned biker chick.

''I'm sorry you had to go to all that trouble.'' Chelsea dragged her hand through her hair and wondered how it was, that no matter how old or how successful she became, her mother could make her feel like a seven-year-old with scraped knees again. ''I was going to call you.''

''Were you?'' Deidre's tone suggested she didn't believe it for a moment.

''Of course.''

''When? From the departure gate at La Guardia on your way back to Georgia?''

Chelsea closed her eyes as she felt the familiar frustration beginning to build. ''Please, Mother, can we discuss this some other time?''

''There's no time like the present. What's your room number?''

''Actually, it's a suite. A two-bedroom suite.''

''And surely one of those bedrooms has a room number?''

Chelsea sighed, knowing that there was no point in trying to refuse her mother's demands. She revealed the number.

''Fine. I'll be right up.''

''You'll be what?'' Chelsea gave Cash, who was sitting beside her nibbling idly on her shoulder, a panicky look.

''I said, I'll be right up.''

''You're here? In the hotel?''

''Of course. I'm calling from the lobby. The impossible young man at the desk refused to give out your room number. Even after I explained I was your mother.''

Chelsea silently blessed the desk clerk who was obviously made of tougher stuff than he appeared. ''Why don't I meet

you downstairs?'' she suggested. ''We can go out to breakfast. It'll take me a few minutes to get ready, because I still
have to shower and dress—''

''We can talk while you dress.''

''But—''

''Chelsea, you're my daughter. I've seen you without
clothes. I'll be right up. I do hope you've at least ordered
coffee from room service.''

Chelsea sat there, momentarily frozen, the receiver still
to her ear, listening to the hum of the dial tone. Then, she
leaped out of the bed.

''She's coming up here.'' She ran into the adjoining living room and scooped up her discarded dress and shoes
from the floor. ''Now!''

''So I gathered.'' Cash followed her into the other bedroom, watching as she began tearing apart the bed, desper-
ately trying to make it look as if it had been slept in.

She shot him a quick look, groaning when she noticed
that he hadn't bothered to put any clothes on. ''You'll have
to get dressed. And try to keep her busy while I take a
shower.''

''That'll take some time. Maybe you should just throw
on a robe—''

''I have to take a shower! Or else she'll know what I was
doing all night!''

Personally, Cash thought, taking in the sight of her swollen lips, and cheeks reddened from his beard stubble, Deidre
Lowell would have to be blind not to know how her daughter—her adult daughter, he reminded himself—had spent the
night. But since he didn't want to give Chelsea anything
else to worry about, he didn't mention that.

''I'll do my best to keep her entertained.''

''Thank you. You truly are a sweetheart.'' She pulled
some underwear from the zipper compartment of her suit-

case, stopping long enough to give him a quick, heartfelt kiss on the way into the adjoining bathroom. "And whatever you do, don't let her intimidate you. If you give my mother an inch, you'll end up lying facedown on the floor with tank tracks running up your back."

"I'll do my best to survive." He kissed her back, then released her, closing the bedroom door behind him. He'd just managed to pull on some briefs, a pair of jeans and a shirt, when there was a brisk, determined knock on the door.

Buttoning the shirt, he left his bedroom, and although he didn't believe they'd get away with the ruse for a moment, he closed the door to hide any overtly incriminating evidence. Then he opened the door to the suite.

"Good morning, Mrs. Lowell." He bestowed his most cordial smile on the woman dressed in the oatmeal-hued raw silk pantsuit. The style was classic, expensive but subdued. It reminded Cash of the outfit Chelsea had been wearing when he first saw her on television. Although the look had been all wrong for her daughter, he decided it suited Deidre Lowell perfectly.

He held out his hand. "I'm Cash Beaudine. It's nice to finally meet you after all these years."

She looked at his outstretched hand with overt distrust. But good manners prevailed. She slipped her manicured hand into his, barely touching fingers.

"Cash Beaudine?" She frowned. "I don't believe I've heard Chelsea speak of you."

"We knew each other a long time ago." He moved aside, inviting her in. She brushed past him, surrounded by a fragrant, obviously very expensive cloud. "At Yale."

"You went to Yale?" Her gaze swept over him, quickly, judiciously, and although her polite expression didn't waver, he knew he'd just been sized up and found lacking. His sharp eyes noticed the way that little line had deepened between her brows when she took in his bare feet.

"Yes, ma'am. I majored in architecture."

"Architecture?" This time a hint of blatant disbelief slipped into her tone.

"Chelsea has a very strong interest in the subject."

"I wasn't aware of that."

"Oh, she's quite an expert. We used to have many long discussions arguing the relative merits of the early 1900s Eclectic Period versus Post 1940s contemporary housing styles."

His smile was as smooth as whipped butter. Deidre blinked, obviously trying to decide whether or not he was putting her on.

"Would you care for some coffee?" He turned toward the tray he'd brought into the living room from the bedroom. He figured she didn't need to know he'd dumped his and Chelsea's cups back into the pot.

"Thank you." She sat down in a suede-covered tub chair and crossed her legs. When her back remained as straight as every old photograph he'd ever seen of Queen Victoria, Cash realized that it could be a very long morning.

"Cream? Sugar?"

"Just black." She watched him fix the coffee, glanced over at the adjoining door, where the sound of running water had suddenly stopped. "So, Mr.... I'm sorry, but I'm terrible at names—"

"Beaudine," he said helpfully, handing her the coffee.

"Beaudine." She took a tentative sip. Then, apparently finding it acceptable, eyed him over the rim of the cup. "Your accent tells me you're not from New York."

"No, ma'am, I'm not. I was born in Raintree, Georgia. That's a little town about thirty miles outside Savannah."

"Ah." She nodded. "I have some very dear friends in

Atlanta. Martin and Lucinda Callaway. I don't suppose you know them?''

"No, I don't believe we've met."

"They have a lovely home in the Buckhead area. A white Georgian that has always reminded me of that house in that movie. What was its name…?''

"Tara."

"Yes, that's it. It's truly exquisite. And they have the most beautiful gardens. I've often told Lucinda that I would give anything to be able to get things to grow so well at my Long Island home. I suppose it's your climate. All that sun. And moisture.''

"Things do tend to get hot and steamy."

Her eyes narrowed again, as if she suspected him of making a joke at her expense. "Are you employed here in the city?''

"Actually, I'm currently working in Raintree." He couldn't resist tossing his résumé into the conversation. "Before that, I worked in San Francisco. As a partner at Mathison, Tang, Kendall and Peters.''

She arched a narrow blond brow. "That's a very well-respected firm.''

"So I was told when I was hired right out of school. Yale," he reminded her easily.

"Yes. So you said." She took another sip, then put the cup down onto the black kidney-shaped coffee table. "I have friends in San Francisco, as well. Pamela and Ramsey Jennings. Of Pacific Heights.''

Cash nodded. "Them, I know. I worked on an office design for Ramsey's law firm.''

He'd also slept with a very predatory Mrs. Jennings his first year in the big city. Admittedly a fish out of water in the lofty echelons of high society, at first the attention from all those rich, sleek, attractive women had him thinking he'd landed in tall cotton. It hadn't taken Cash long to realize that Pamela and her pampered friends had considered him merely a sexual toy.

"May I ask what you're currently doing in Georgia?"

"I've established my own firm. I refurbish old houses."

"How interesting." Only the faint twitch of her lips revealed that she obviously considered this a step down from his high-profile commercial work in the Bay Area.

"I think so. I'm currently working with Roxanne Scarbrough."

"So is Chelsea. Isn't that a coincidence?" Her deepening frown suggested she did not find it a pleasant or encouraging one.

Before Cash could respond, the bedroom door opened and Chelsea came out, wearing a halter-style dress with a very short flip skirt and white sandals. The fact that the huge white daisies covering the dress had been painted onto a fire-engine red field told Cash that she was not feeling as brave as she seemed determined to appear. More daisies bloomed on the scarlet acrylic earrings dangling from her lobes, and across the wide matching bracelet.

"Hello, Mother." She brushed an air kiss against the older woman's powdered cheek. "This is a surprise."

Deidre's eyes narrowed as they skimmed over her daughter in an obviously disapproving way. "This seems to be a day for surprises. Wherever did you get that dress?"

"At Saks." When Chelsea twirled, like a little girl showing off a new party dress, Cash held his breath, waiting for a glimpse of silk panty, which fortunately didn't quite happen. "I thought it was fun."

"Fun." Deidre's tone revealed her belief that fashion and fun were mutually exclusive.

"Fun." Chelsea tilted her chin. "As in, it makes me feel good to wear it."

"Well, that's what's always been important, hasn't it, dear? That you feel good. Despite how your outrageous behavior affects others."

Cash watched as Chelsea went as white as ice. Then red flags rose to wave in her too pale cheeks.

"What did you want, Mother?"

Cash gave her credit for a valiant attempt to change the subject. But Deidre was not prepared to relinquish control.

"At the moment, I wish to discuss your distressing lack of good taste. You look common. Good heavens Chelsea, you remind me of your father."

Bingo. She'd just hit the bull's-eye. Chelsea rose to her full height, stiffened her spine and looked down at her mother. "My father was far from common. You know, Mother, you've been telling me all my life how much I reminded you of my father. And you know what? I'm tired of all that bullshit."

Ignoring her mother's shocked gasp, she forged on. "I'm me. Chelsea Cassidy. Not Chelsea Lowell. Not Chelsea Whitney. And, thank God, I'm never going to be Chelsea Waring.

"Chelsea Cassidy," she repeated firmly. She poked a finger into the bright yellow face of a daisy in the center of her chest. "No matter how hard you've tried to deny it, no matter how many headmistresses and sadistic Germanic nuns you'll pay to beat those Cassidy genes out of me, I will always be Dylan Cassidy's daughter as well as yours."

Deidre opened her mouth. On a roll, Chelsea held up a hand to stop any interruption. "I'm damn proud of my father. I'm equally proud of what I do. And you're not going to make me feel guilty any more trying to live up to your outdated, impossible standards."

"Since when are good manners outdated?" Deidre asked coolly.

"We're not talking manners here, Mother." Chelsea leaned down until they were face-to-face. "We're talking control. And you've just lost it."

As if just remembering his presence, Deidre glanced over at Cash, who'd gone to stand at the window across the room. "Would you mind, Mr. Beaudine, if I had a few minutes alone with my daughter?"

Chelsea looked capable of handling her mother. Hell, right now she looked capable of handling an entire cast of bad guys from a Sylvester Stallone action film, single-handedly. But he knew, all too well, that appearances could often be deceiving. And the one thing he didn't want to do was desert her the way her Yankee worm had done.

"Chelsea?"

The knowledge that he was offering to stay, to protect her from her mother's icy wrath, gave Chelsea the strength she needed to turn him down.

"It's all right, Cash. This won't take long."

He glanced from Chelsea, to Deidre, then back to Chelsea. "If you're sure."

"Positive." Chelsea crossed the room, placed both hands on his shoulders, went up on her toes and kissed him. A short, but heartfelt kiss rife with emotion. "But thank you for asking," she whispered.

"Anytime." He skimmed a finger down her crooked nose. "I'll be in the next room. Holler if you need me."

She smiled at that. "Don't tempt me," she said in a low voice designed to keep her mother from hearing.

Cash went to leave the room, stopping at the bedroom door. "It was a pleasure meeting you, Mrs. Lowell."

"I enjoyed meeting you as well, Mr. Beaudine," Deidre replied stiffly, obviously lying through her teeth. "Perhaps we'll meet again someday."

"Oh, you can definitely count on that." The smile he flashed at the older woman was as sexy as hell and filled with good-natured humor. Then he disappeared into the bedroom, leaving mother and daughter alone.

Chapter Twenty

Momentarily struck by the force of that woman-killer smile, Deidre stared at the closed bedroom door for a long moment. "Well. So that's the man you've left Nelson for."

"I'm not going to talk about Nelson."

"He's your fiancé."

"Not any longer. In fact, if I never see him again, it'll be too soon."

Deidre sighed. "I don't want to argue with you, Chelsea."

"Fine." Chelsea folded her arms across the front of her flowered dress. "Then don't try to take the worm's side."

"That's a horrible thing to call your fiancé."

"I told you, he's *not* my fiancé. And believe me, Mother, worm is definitely one of the more acceptable words that come to mind. After what he did."

"If you're talking about his little mistake with Heather Van Pelt—"

"His little mistake?" Chelsea's voice went up a full octave. "He was fucking her brains out, Mother. In my bed. In Grandmother Lowell's bed."

''Really, Chelsea.'' Deidre's lips pulled into a tight, disapproving line. ''Must you use such language?''

Chelsea couldn't believe her mother's priorities. On second thought, she could. She felt the fury leaving her, like helium from a brightly colored balloon.

''I see.'' She sat down on a chair facing the sofa. ''It's all right for Nelson to *do* the F-word with my assistant. It's just taboo for me to say it.''

''Nelson is a man. With a man's weaknesses.''

''Believe me, Mother. I'm well aware of all his weaknesses. Including the one he was sticking into Heather.''

Deidre recrossed her legs with an irritated swish. ''You're being purposefully difficult. As always. I don't know why I bother to try to talk with you.''

''Quite honestly, I've often wondered the same thing myself.''

A frustrated silence fell over mother and daughter. Then Deidre tried again.

''You say you admire your father. Surely you don't believe he was faithful while he was gallivanting all over the world?''

''I guess I never thought about that,'' Chelsea admitted.

''Well, he wasn't.''

''And that's why you divorced him?'' She could understand that, Chelsea decided reluctantly. It still hurt, being the one left behind. But at least she could finally understand the reason for her family having broken apart.

''Of course not. A wise woman doesn't let a little adultery disrupt a good marriage.''

Chelsea stared at her. ''I can't believe you actually mean that.''

''It's not a man's nature to be monogamous,'' Deidre insisted. ''I personally believe this behavior goes back to the caveman days, when it was imperative for one man to impregnate several women to keep the species alive.''

''With the exception of drive-by shootings, car-jackings, child abuse and spousal murder, the species seems to be struggling along just fine,'' Chelsea argued dryly. ''In fact, one could argue that adulterous men abandoning their wives and kids is partly responsible for the mess the country's in today.''

''I'm not going to get into a political or sociological argument with you, Chelsea,'' Deidre snapped. ''I was merely trying to explain why a wise woman learns to overlook a man's little peccadilloes.''

''Obviously I'm not a wise woman,'' Chelsea retorted. ''Because I was sorely tempted to cut off Nelson's little peccadillo with a rusty razor blade.''

''I do wish you wouldn't be so crude.''

''It isn't me that's crude, Mother. It's the situation. One that's not of my making. And, even if I was willing to overlook Nelson's sexual betrayal, I will never forgive him for stealing from me.''

''He is not a thief.''

''What do you call cleaning out all my bank accounts?''

''A paperwork mistake. He assures me he's going to get it all cleared up.''

''Excuse me if I don't hold my breath. I was thinking of suing him in civil court—''

Deidre paled beneath her expertly applied Chanel foundation. ''You couldn't possibly be considering parading our private family problems in public?''

''No. But not because of any need to protect our family name. I just figure it'd be pointless. And I'm not real wild about publicly stating what a damn fool I was.''

Deidre sighed, folded her hands in her lap and leaned forward, her expression sobering. ''I can certainly understand how hurt you feel, Chelsea. I even understand—'' she tilted her blond head toward the bedroom door ''—what you're doing with your sexy architect, but—''

"No." It was Chelsea's turn to look serious. "I don't think you do, Mother."

"What does that mean?"

"It means, if you think I'm just having an affair to get back at Nelson, you're wrong."

"You wouldn't be the first woman to seek revenge on an errant mate by going to bed with another man."

"I'm sure I'm not. But that wasn't my motive. I'm with Cash because I'm pretty sure I'm falling in love with him."

"You can't be!" Deidre's hand flew to her throat. She was obviously more than a little aghast at this news flash.

"Why not? Cash is very easy to love. He's intelligent, considerate, loving—"

"Sexy as sin," Deidre interjected.

"True. And that's admittedly a plus. But as reckless as I know you think I am, Mother, I'm wise enough to realize that you can't build a marriage on sex."

"I told my mother the same thing, when she attempted to talk me out of marrying your father."

"And you didn't listen."

"No. And it was the biggest mistake of my life."

Chelsea felt saddened that her mother would refer to something that had resulted in her birth in such negative terms.

"Loving Cash isn't a mistake, mother. The mistake was not acting on my feelings seven years ago. And, if it makes you feel any better, he hasn't mentioned anything about marriage."

"Chelsea, I don't want you to take this the wrong way," Deidre said carefully, "but you haven't told him about your trust fund, have you?"

"Of course I have." Chelsea stared at her mother as the worried tone sunk in. "Surely you're not suggesting that's why he's interested in me?"

"Two million dollars is a great deal of money, dear."

"Nelson certainly thought so. Which is obviously why he was so eager to get back together after he managed to burn through his own money."

Deidre shook her head. "This isn't working, is it?"

"You trying to plead Nelson's case?" Chelsea asked. "No, it's not."

"Actually, I was speaking of you and me." There was something new in her mother's tone, something Chelsea had never heard before. Deidre sighed and stood up again. "I have a meeting at the Hospital Guild. I should be going."

Chelsea knew she should be relieved that the inquisition was over. But instead, she felt the same inner frustration that always plagued her when ending a conversation with her mother.

Why was it, she wondered, things always had to be so damn difficult?

"Please tell Mr. Beaudine goodbye for me."

"I'll do that," Chelsea said, walking her mother to the door.

"And have a safe flight back to Georgia."

"I will." If they weren't careful, they'd start talking about the weather, Chelsea thought miserably.

Deidre was in the hallway, about to walk away, when she turned back. "And Chelsea…"

"Yes, Mother?" Chelsea steeled herself for another criticism.

"Please. Be careful."

With that she was gone. Leaving Chelsea frustrated. And feeling so very much alone.

As if reading her mind, Cash came out of the bedroom and took her into his arms.

Chelsea buried her face against his chest. He rested his chin against the top of her head.

Neither of them spoke. There was no need.

As construction progressed, Chelsea began spending more and more of her time with Roxanne at Belle Terre.

One afternoon, two months after she'd first arrived in Raintree, Roxanne was upstairs in the mansion's master bedroom suite, trying to convince Cash that she truly needed the automatic clothes rack circling the former dressing room turned closet. When Cash insisted it would make the room look like a dry cleaners, Roxanne responded that was just what she wanted.

Growing bored with the argument, Chelsea wandered outside to the smokehouse, which Roxanne planned to turn into a pool house. Although it hadn't been used for over a hundred years, she imagined she could smell the hickory smoke.

The small building was empty; the crew had driven into Raintree for lunch at Catfish Charlie's, which had become the unofficial caterer of choice for the construction crew.

There was sawdust on the floor, which tickled her nose and made her sneeze. She was digging around in her purse for a tissue when she heard the sound of a booted foot behind her.

She turned, expecting Chase. "Oh." Her smile faded. "Hello."

George's yellow smile reminded her of a jackknife blade. His gaze was dangerously feral. "So you're the writer who's going to make Roxanne famous."

"She's already famous. Which is why I'm writing about her in the first place." Uneasy, she went to leave.

"Guess that makes sense." He shifted, barring her way. "What's the hurry?"

"I just remembered something I need to ask Roxanne." Chelsea refused to let this man know he was capable of frightening her.

"She's busy. With her architect."

She moved to the other side. "I really need to—"

"I've been watching you." He moved as well, once more preventing her escape. "Anyone ever tell you that you're a real pretty gal?"

"I'm sorry, but—"

"Yup." He caught hold of her arm as she tried to push her way past him. "I've been watching you sashaying around—"

"Let me go." Fear bubbled up in her throat.

"Now, sugar, you know you don't really want to leave. Not until you and I get to know one another a little bit better."

He stunk of old sweat and cheap after-shave. His words came out on puffs of rank whiskey-scented breath. Chelsea thought if he even tried to put his mouth on hers, she'd throw up.

She was debating her chances of kneeing him in the groin like self-defense experts advised, when the smokehouse door slammed open. Before her eyes could adjust to the blinding shaft of sunlight, George was pulled off his feet and thrown across the stone floor, landing in a pile against the wall.

"Get up and you're a dead man," Cash growled. He put his arm around Chelsea and looked down at her. "Are you all right? If he hurt you—"

"No." She'd never seen such iced fury before in any person's eyes. Not even when Cash had threatened Nelson in the Knickerbocker Club. He looked as if he could quite easily break the horrid man in two without a second thought. "I'm fine. Really," she insisted, when he looked inclined to argue. "I've had worse encounters on the subway."

His muttered curse at what she'd meant as reassurance reminded Chelsea that Cash did not think highly of her home city. But apparently deciding to take her at her word, he turned back toward George, who had, despite the warning, risen to his feet.

"You're fired."

"You can't fire me." George's eyes flashed like two burning pieces of coal. Now that he'd recovered from the surprise of Cash's unexpected arrival, he'd garnered his prison swagger. "I'm workin' direct for Roxanne."

"I can fire you. Or I can kill you. Take your pick."

"You're bluffing."

"Want to bet?" Cash grabbed the front of George's shirt and pushed him up against the wall. "You're outta here, Waggoner. And if I see you anywhere near Belle Terre or this woman again, I won't bother to call the police. Or your parole officer. I'll rip your heart out. And throw it to the gators in the swamps."

During his seven years in the joint, George had been threatened by rougher men than this. "You've got me shakin' in my boots, Beaudine."

The blow was so fast, neither Chelsea or George saw it coming. One minute Cash's hand was at his side. The next instant it was curled into a tight fist and was slamming against George's jaw. He muttered a faint "Ooof" then fell into a heap like a rag doll.

"Figures he'd have a glass jaw," Cash muttered. Chelsea thought he sounded almost disappointed that George had gone down without a fight. He picked him up by his shirt and threw him out of the smokehouse. "Get the hell out of here, Waggoner. And if you're stupid enough to return, I promise, the next time I'm not going to stop with one punch.''

Dazed and defeated, George managed to push himself to his feet and stagger back toward the house, past the crew who'd returned from their lunch and were watching events unfold.

Cash's heart was pounding a million beats a minute as he put his arms around Chelsea. He'd never been so angry in his life. Or so terrified. If anything had happened to her...

"You're shaking," he said.

"I know." Now that she was safe, she'd begun to tremble. "You are, too."

He lowered his forehead to hers and let out a long shuddering breath. "Lord, Chelsea... If you only knew how I felt when I saw that bastard touching you.... I could have killed him."

"I'm glad you didn't." She looked up at him, her heart in her eyes. "He wasn't worth it."

Cash knew she was right. But as they walked out of the smokehouse, he thought back on the raw violence he'd seen in Waggoner's eyes and worried that they hadn't seen the last of the son of a bitch.

After the incident in the smokehouse, Cash tried to talk Chelsea into moving into Rebel's Ridge with him. But sensing that he was only suggesting it to keep her safe from George Waggoner, who was still hanging around Raintree, she resisted.

"Besides," she argued, "this is a small town. I don't want everyone talking about us."

Cash refrained from pointing out that everyone in Raintree was already talking about them. The uptown New York heiress and the sharecropper's kid who made good was a reverse Cinderella story that was proving downright irresistible. And although it frustrated the hell out of him that she refused to move into his house where he could keep her safe, Cash was somewhat reassured by Jeb's promise to watch out for her. And a visit to the sheriff had resulted in a call to Arizona, to Waggoner's parole officer. With any luck, Waggoner—who unsurprisingly had failed to find another job—would be on his way back to the pen any day.

A few days after George Waggoner's aborted attempt to assault her, Chelsea remembered something he'd said to Cash during their brief confrontation. At the time she'd been too frightened for it to sink in. But now that it had, Chelsea found the idea of such a horrible man working directly for Roxanne more than a little curious.

"He's a cousin to an old secretary," Roxanne revealed when Chelsea asked her about it. "Cash told me what happened, Chelsea, and had I known the man was so dangerous, I certainly never would have hired him. I am so sorry you had to experience such a distasteful scene."

It had been a lot more than distasteful, but Chelsea didn't argue. Nor did she press Roxanne, despite the fact that the answer was too pat. Almost, she considered, rehearsed.

One thing this trip had proven, she mused as she entered the courthouse that anchored Raintree's town square, was that her mother was right about one thing. She was *definitely* her father's daughter, she thought proudly as she managed to convince the young, green clerk on duty that, being a journalist, she was entitled access to public records. Surprisingly, the computer age had reached Raintree.

A rush of excitement forked through Chelsea when George Waggoner's name appeared on the screen. This must have been how her father had felt while tracking down a hot story, she thought, enjoying the idea of sharing an experience with the larger-than-life man she'd adored. Chelsea was not all that surprised when a long list of arrests flashed by. Petty theft, drunk and disorderly, and various other crimes all going back to Waggoner's early teens. It crossed her mind that Cash could have turned out the same way; after all, he certainly hadn't gotten an easier start in life. The difference, she decided, was that deep down inside, where it counted, Cash possessed a strong core of integrity.

And yet, she considered, taking in the record of a marriage license, someone must have found Waggoner reasonably acceptable at some time in his life.

"Cora Mae Padgett," Chelsea murmured out loud, writing the name down in the notebook she'd pulled from her duffel bag. "Athens, Georgia."

Unfortunately, the Athens phone directory did not list any Padgetts or Waggoners. She should just let it drop, she told herself. She had enough on her plate at the moment, trying to write two books while exploring her new and exciting relationship with Cash. After all, whoever the horrible man had married had nothing to do with her. Or Roxanne's biography.

No. That wasn't really true. Because every instinct Chelsea possessed told her that Roxanne was hiding something about her ties to George Waggoner. Her mind focused on what, if anything, that could be as she left the courthouse, Chelsea failed to see the person sitting at a picnic table beneath a tree in the courthouse park, watching her with unblinking intensity.

Wanting to reduce her dependence on Dorothy, who seemed to be growing more tense with each passing day, Chelsea had rented a car after her return from New York. It allowed her to come and go as she pleased, and also to periodically escape from Roxanne, who was definitely beginning to lose the aura of calm Chelsea had grown accustomed to.

There were more and more instances of her screaming at workmen and ill-treating Dorothy. She even slapped Jo for not stopping her camera during one such outburst. As if realizing such behavior was definitely beyond the pale, she backtracked quickly.

"I'm sorry, dear," she said, stroking the reddened handprint with her fingertips. "I don't know what got into me. It's been such a stressful day."

"Don't worry, Roxanne." The filmmaker managed a slight smile although her voice did not possess its usually perky tone. "We all have bad days. No harm done."

But as she turned away and began changing lenses on the camera, Chelsea noticed a brittle sheen in Jo's dark eyes.

Later that afternoon, Chelsea drove out to Rebel's Ridge to have dinner with Cash. Although his car was parked in front of the house, he didn't answer when she knocked at the door. Curious, she went around back, where she saw him in the distance, whacking away at one of the tabby slave cottages with a sledgehammer.

Curious, she walked across the field to him. "Hi," she called out.

Cash turned toward her. "Hi, yourself." He lowered the heavy sledgehammer. "I wasn't expecting you for another couple of hours."

He'd taken his shirt off, and just looking at his hard mahogany chest glistening with perspiration made her knees go weak.

"Roxanne was stressed out. I decided discretion was the better part of valor. At least today."

"She's seemed uptight these days," he agreed. "But that's to be expected. Restoration is always stressful. Even the inimitable Diva of Domesticity is probably finding it more trouble than she'd thought when she bought the place and envisioned balls and wisteria-draped verandas."

"That's probably all it is," Chelsea agreed absently,

studying his work. The little house had been reduced to a pile of stone around the foundation. ''What are you doing?''

''Knocking down a house.''

''I can see that. But why?''

His answering shrug was nonchalant, but watching him closely, Chelsea thought she saw a shadow move across his eyes. ''It's a long story.''

''Most stories are down here, I've found.''

He smiled at that. ''It's not that big a deal.'' It was his turn to study the efforts of an afternoon's intense physical labor. ''It's awfully hot out here. Why don't you go on up to the house, have a glass of iced tea or wine, and I'll be with you as soon as I finish up here.''

''Will you tell me what's bothering you?''

''What makes you think anything's bothering me?''

''Are you saying I'm imagining it?''

''Let's talk about it later. After I clean up.''

''Fine.'' She went up on her toes and kissed him. A tender, heartfelt kiss meant to assure him that there was nothing he could ever say to her that would change her feelings for him.

Cash watched her walk away. He admired her long legs, clad in a pair of white jeans, and enjoyed the feminine sway of her hips. Her hair shone in the slanting afternoon sun, making it look as if she were wearing a brushed copper halo. She was still the most desirable woman he'd ever seen. And she was his.

''Amazing,'' he murmured. Then, shaking his head at the idea of the offspring of a bootlegger's daughter and a sharecropper wooing—and winning!—the Deb of the Year, he went back to work, destroying the last physical reminder of his early life in Raintree.

It was several hours before they got around to talking. After Cash returned to the house and showered, they spent a long, leisurely time making love as dusk soothed a skyline fevered by heat. Afterward, they ate a light supper of cold fried chicken and cole slaw from Catfish Charlie's.

Then, much, much later, they were sitting out on the veranda, side by side, on the green glider.

"I can't ever remember being as happy as I've been these past weeks in Raintree," Chelsea murmured, as she listened to the croak of the frogs along the banks of the river, the lonely hoot of an owl in a moss-draped oak.

"You don't miss the big city life?"

She laughed at that. "Although I never thought I'd hear myself saying it, I don't miss Manhattan at all." She thought about how she'd found the empty bottle of antacids in her bag earlier today, realized she hadn't reached for it for a week, and sighed happily.

"Perhaps it's another one of those things I inherited from my father, but I've always been Irish enough to believe in fate. And although it doesn't make any logical sense, I feel as if Raintree is a bit like Brigadoon—a secret, hidden-away place, waiting all these years for me to find it."

She could not have said anything that could have pleased him more. Cash smiled. "I always believed that if you really wanted something, all you had to do was work harder than the people trying to keep you from getting it. I never believed in fate. Until recently."

"What changed your mind?"

"You showing up in Raintree."

It was her turn to smile. "That's exactly what you were supposed to say."

They swung quietly for a time. Chelsea stared up at the sky and felt closer to the huge white moon and the dazzling, diamond-bright stars than the life she'd left behind.

"You promised to tell me what you were doing knocking down that house," she reminded him softly.

She felt him tense. Then relax. Heard his exhaled breath. "I guess you could say I was exorcising the last old ghosts."

"I don't understand." She turned toward him, able to see the way his jaw had turned as rigid as granite. Then she remembered something he'd said the first day she'd come to Rebel's Ridge. "Those were sharecropper houses."

"That's right."

She thought about how his father had died. "You lived there."

"Until we got evicted."

Chelsea closed her eyes, pained by the mental picture of Cash as a young boy, struggling to assure his newly widowed mother that he could take care of her. Take care of them both. At an age when boys she'd grown up with were going off to pricey, privileged summer camps.

"It's funny," she murmured.

"What?" His voice sounded rusty, even to his own ears.

"That we both seem to have been on a journey of discovery. A discovery of forgotten parts of ourselves."

"And you believe those individual roads led us here? To Raintree?"

"Yes." She framed his frowning face between her hands and pressed her smiling lips against his. "Isn't fate a wonderful thing?"

As he drew her into his arms, Cash didn't answer. Not in words. In fact, her blissful statement was the last thing either of them were to say for a very long time.

Chapter Twenty-One

Although Chelsea's days were spent with an increasingly temperamental Roxanne, evenings were reserved for Cash. They'd have dinner. Then make love. Then she'd work on Roxanne's biography, while he worked on the blueprints for an upcoming project he'd signed to do in Savannah. Then they'd make love again. And although progress on her novel had slowed again, she would not have traded a million pages of brilliance for this time with Cash.

Besides, she told herself one morning when she'd reluctantly left Cash's bed to write down a pivotal scene that had been teasing at her mind during her sleep, she was getting so much characterization for her prima donna movie star from Roxanne, that if it took a little longer to finish the Hollywood murder mystery than she'd hoped, her experience in Raintree was definitely worth it. The only problem, she'd explained to Cash, was that approximately fifty pages from what she'd hoped would be the end of the book, the ambitious agent she'd planned to be the murderer was refusing to cooperate.

"I'll just have to find another killer," she said. "Lord

knows, with an entire cast of characters who have reason to hate her, that shouldn't be so difficult.''

"Once again, life imitates art," he drawled, making her laugh as he reminded them both of Roxanne.

Despite Roxanne's increasingly frequent temper tantrums, Chelsea was pleased with the progress on the autobiography. Although it would never win a Pulitzer prize, it was turning out to be a bright and breezy read Roxanne's fans would hopefully enjoy. And, of course, it was filled with all sorts of projects and recipes that Roxanne made look so easy, but Chelsea secretly thought would drive the average woman—like herself—up a wall.

Belle Terre was beginning to show real promise. The wiring and the plumbing had been completed, the walls replastered, new interior drywall installed, and the windows reglazed. The millwork Cash had bought in New York proved even more wonderful than promised, and provided a historically accurate touch.

A muralist from Atlanta had been hired to paint antebellum scenes on the walls of the dining room and ballroom. When Roxanne's artistic vision clashed with the young man's who, despite an impressive portfolio, seemed determined to depict important war battles complete with battlefield casualties, she fired him and found another, more agreeable—and commercial—artist to depict romantic garden and plantation scenes.

"Isn't this better?" she asked Chelsea as they studied the new art.

"It's certainly more restful than the battleground scenes," Chelsea said. Although it wasn't often she found herself siding with the style expert, she'd had to agree that viewing the bodies of all those dead soldiers clad in Union blue and Rebel gray depicted on the dining room wall would have been bound to dull guests' appetites.

"Much more restful," Roxanne agreed. "Let me show you what Annie's sketched in for the upstairs bedroom." She smiled as she gestured for Chelsea to precede her up the stairs. "It's a recreation of Belle Terre's original gardens and it should be lovely. Even if it *is* costing an arm and a leg."

Part of that cost, Chelsea knew, was because the artist, Annie Longview, a willowy, pale, blond girl given to wearing New Age crystals and long flowing skirts emblazoned with moons and stars, had insisted that the ghostly vibes of the poor dead grieving bride-to-be made it too depressing to work. Once Roxanne had offered to tack on ten percent to the original bid, Annie had apparently been miraculously cured of her artistic ghost-caused block.

Chelsea was almost to the first landing when the wood beneath her sneakers suddenly gave way. She reached out, grabbing for the banister, which broke from the weight put on it. The last thing she heard, as she went tumbling into space, was Roxanne's startled cry.

"Are you certain you're all right?" It was the umpteenth time Cash had asked that question. "Positive," Chelsea assured him for the umpteenth time.

"You could have been killed." His expression was grim. His eyes bleak.

"Nonsense. I only fell a few feet."

"Nearly five."

It had seemed like more, Chelsea thought, but didn't say. "The doctor assured me that my ankle's only twisted." She glanced down at the throbbing ankle in question, propped up on a pillow on Cash's couch.

"It could have been broken," he muttered darkly. "You could have been killed." More frustrated than she'd ever seen him, he thrust his hands through his hair. "And it would have been all my fault, dammit."

"That's ridiculous."

"If those stairs were unstable, I should have known it. If the railing wasn't firm, I should have caught it."

She thought about pointing out that he was the architect, not the contractor, and that people had been up and down those same stairs for weeks without mishap. Knowing that he wasn't in the mood to let himself off the hook, she tried a different tack.

"You're right. It *is* all your fault. I don't know why I didn't understand this before. I also realize now that my broken arm falling from the roof when I was five and trying to fly was your fault. And the leg I broke on the ski run in the Alps when I was sixteen, and then, of course—"

"Okay, okay. I get your drift." He sat down beside her gingerly, as if afraid of causing her more pain.

"I won't break," she said pointedly, putting her arms around him. He was still as stiff as a board. She covered his grimly set mouth with hers, her lips plucking teasingly at his as she tried to turn his mind to more pleasurable subjects.

And although it was not easy, Chelsea was nothing, if not persistent.

Jamie Johnson was beanpole thin, with short-cropped hair the color of lemon sherbet, a face covered with freckles and bright blue eyes that observed Chelsea with suspicion and jealousy when he discovered Cash had invited her to join them on their guy's day out.

Although the swelling in her ankle had gone down this morning, Cash had insisted she take the day off work. Roxanne had instantly concurred, suggesting that perhaps she'd be more comfortable in her own home while finishing up the book. Since Chelsea had no intention of explaining that at the moment, she didn't exactly have a home—with Nelson still ensconced in her apartment—she had calmly assured Roxanne that she was quite comfortable at the inn.

Cash had already planned this fishing trip with Jamie a while ago, so Chelsea had had to lobby to come along until he'd finally caved in, allowing that so long as she stayed off her ankle, he supposed it wouldn't hurt.

Although she knew nothing of fishing, and had never so much as baited a hook, Chelsea was looking forward to the scenery, which Jo, who apparently had lived in Georgia for a time with her military father and housewife mother, assured her was something not to be missed.

"I've heard a lot about you," Chelsea said as the trio drove down to the boat dock on the Okefenokee Swamp in the pickup truck Cash used to tow the boat trailer.

The boy's only response to her friendly comment was a shrug. His gaze was directed out the window at the passing scenery.

Chelsea tried again. "Cash said that you played on your school basketball team last year. I know a few people in the Nicks' office. Perhaps, someday you and Cash can come to New York and take in a game."

Another shrug.

"Hey," Cash said quietly, "Chelsea was talking to you, son."

"I don't like the Nicks," he mumbled.

"Of course you don't," she said quickly. "I'll bet you're an Atlanta Hawks fan."

"Yeah."

His flat tone didn't encourage continued conversation, but refusing to give up, Chelsea tried again. "I don't know any Hawks players. But I did make friends with one of the Bulls last year when we were playing golf together at a charity tournament in Phoenix.''

"Who was that?" Cash asked when Jamie stubbornly refused to.

Chelsea smiled her appreciation. Then sat back, let the pause linger a moment and proceeded to name drop. "Michael Jordan.''

That got the boy's immediately attention. When his head practically spun around, Chelsea knew she'd just earned points.

"You played golf with Michael Jordan?"

"And Charles Barkley," she said.

Those blue eyes narrowed suspiciously. "But you're a girl."

"True. And I'm a terrible golfer. But the guys were nice enough to give me a generous handicap. I had a great time. And even beat Barkley on strokes, but of course Sir Charles is a terrible golfer. Although he does tell great jokes," she tacked on as an afterthought.

"I don't suppose you remember any of them," Cash coaxed. Although his eyes were hidden behind his dark glasses, Chelsea could hear the humor in his voice.

"Actually, I do."

For the next thirty minutes she told jokes and spun stories about her day on the links with the basketball greats. By the time they reached the dock and had backed the bass boat into the water, the formerly speechless Jamie had found his voice and was bombarding her with questions about his heroes.

As they cruised the slow-moving, sinuous waterways, Chelsea decided that Jo was definitely right about the scenery being spectacular. The swamp, with its draped cypress, vegetation-choked lakes, and pine islands was a world apart, and although at first it seemed deserted, she began to notice that the rushes, cattails and sphagnum peat bogs fairly teemed with life.

Swallows swooped gracefully, picking insects off the water, white ibis and great blue herons waded along the banks, and a dazzling flock of huge gray sandhill cranes took off with loud, guttural cries as the boat passed by.

Lily pads were scattered over the dark water like flagstones making up a garden path. Mallards streaked low over the lily pads, their honking cries echoing in the steamy stillness.

"This is so amazing." Chelsea spoke quietly, as if she were in church. "I never realized a swamp could be so beautiful."

Her wondrous gaze drank in the tupelo and cypress trees with their huge buttressed trunks, some a man would not be able to put his arms around. A natural garden, as lovely in its own way as the formal English garden planted by Jeb at Magnolia House, bloomed amidst the shadowed water. There were white and yellow water lilies and white clusters of floating hearts, the vine with silky gray seed plumes Cash told her was called old man's beard, the spiked neverwets and the hooded yellow pitcher plants.

A family of otters swam by, sleek bodied and graceful.

"It's the country's largest wooded swamp. Some guy in the 1890s got the great idea to drain it with canals, but he underestimated the project and gave up," Cash said. "See that?"

She followed his gaze to a desolate-looking island of black and silvered stumps and trees. "It looks almost as if they've been burned, but surely that can't be? With all this water?"

"Drought causes the upper layer of the peat floor to dry out and burn," he said. "Which is nature's way of keeping the Okefenokee a swamp, by burning off all the excess brush and dried mulch, which opens it up again and creates more bogs and prairies.''

''The prairies shake if you try to walk on them,'' Jamie piped up. ''That's where it got its name. From the Indian name for Land of the Trembling Earth.''

''But if the ground is unstable, how do the islands support all those trees?''

''Ah,'' Cash said, with a quick grin, ''that's the magic of it.''

And it was magic, she decided, as the day passed. From time to time Cash would cut the electric trolling motor and he and Jamie would cast lines out into the bogs, reeling in catfish after catfish. Although they seemed quite proud of themselves, Chelsea privately thought the fish were the ugliest she'd ever seen.

''Isn't Chelsea going to get a turn?'' Jamie asked late in the afternoon. The slanting sun had turned the water to a molten copper.

''Oh, I don't—''

''Good idea,'' Cash said. He handed his rod to her. ''I've already got it baited. Let's see how you do.''

''I've never fished in my life.''

''Then you've been missing one of life's great pleasures.''

''My dad always said that God doesn't deduct the time we spend fishing in this life,'' Jamie said encouragingly. ''Cash says that, too.''

''That's because I learned it from your dad,'' Cash said. ''Who was a very wise man. Now—'' he turned his attention back to the lesson at hand ''—put your hand here, and your thumb right there on the line, just so.'' He stood behind her, his hands over hers. ''Now, relax your wrist, that's a gal. I tell you, Chelsea, you are a natural-born fisherman.''

''Fisherwoman,'' Jamie corrected.

"Right." Cash leaned forward and brushed his lips against her earlobe as he murmured, "You are definitely all woman, Irish.

"Okay," he said, returning his voice to its normal conversational tone, "now see that little pool over there?"

"The one with the enormous cypress in the middle of it?" It had to be at least thirty-five feet away.

"That's it. We're going to drop this worm right beside that old trunk."

"I hate to ruin a perfect day arguing with you, Cash, but I think the chances of that are slim to none."

"Now darlin', you just gotta have confidence in yourself. And trust me."

"I do." She looked up at him, the warmth in her eyes echoing her words. "But fishing and life are two different things."

"Now that's where you're wrong. Fishing *is* life. The rest is just incidental. Ready?"

She took a deep breath. "All right. Let's get this humiliation over with."

Amazingly, the line whizzed from the reel, the fat night crawler flew through the air, then landed with a satisfying plop exactly in the spot Cash had pointed out.

"You did it, Chelsea," Jamie shouted.

"Cash did it," she argued.

"We did it together," he corrected. "I keep telling you, sweetheart, we make one heckuva team."

It was true. So true, in fact, that these past weeks she'd even begun allowing herself to consider the possibility of a future with this man. Her collaboration with Roxanne was coming to an end. If she followed her original plan, she'd soon return to New York.

But the lush, love-filled days she'd spent in Raintree had her wondering why she couldn't stay right here. With Cash.

She pictured them, sitting out on the veranda of his house overlooking the river, sharing bits and pieces of their day. She imagined sharing the cooking duties in his restored kitchen. The cozy domestic scene was more than a little pleasing, more so, she suspected, because she so seldom cooked. Nelson had always preferred to go out. To mingle with friends, to see and be seen. He'd consider a quiet evening at home with popcorn and a video akin to doing hard time.

She imagined them taking Sunday afternoon boat rides. With their children. Although she'd never experienced the idyllic family life she was envisioning, there was definitely something appealing about building a life and a future and a family with the man you loved.

And she did love him, Chelsea assured herself. Maybe not seven years ago, she'd never know that, for sure. But she had no doubt that she loved him now.

Of course, he hadn't officially asked her to stay, she reminded herself. Then she smiled as she decided that she'd just have to take matters into her own hands. Soon.

As Jamie's sudden shout dragged her mind back from her romantic thoughts of making a life with Cash, Chelsea realized something was causing the line to spin out of her reel.

"Looks like she's hooked Jaws," Jamie said, his young voice literally trembling with excitement.

"You may just be right," Cash said.

"Jaws?" Chelsea echoed. Surely there weren't sharks in this swamp?

"The granddaddy of all catfish," Cash said. "People have been trying to land him for years. Looks like you hit the jackpot."

"Me?" Her voice was little more than a squeak. "Cash, I can't possibly pull him in."

"Of course you can."

The line was still disappearing beneath the water. "Dammit, Cash—"

"You just gotta have some patience," he assured her. "Now, here's what you're going to do…"

Much, much later, Chelsea was listening to Jamie tell the tale to his mother.

"You should have seen Chelsea, Mama," Jamie said. "That old catfish liked to pull her pole right in, but she kept fighting. And then, after she'd landed him, she had Cash take the hook out and toss him right back into the water."

"He'd managed to survive so long," Chelsea explained. "It seemed he belonged in the swamp, instead of on someone's dinner plate."

"That's quite a story," Sharleen Johnson said. She smiled at Chelsea. Cash had introduced the two women to each other when they'd first picked Jamie up that morning. Now they were in the kitchen of Catfish Charlie's, where Sharleen was frying fish for tonight's dinner crowd. "Why don't you and Cash go clean today's catch, while Chelsea and I get acquainted?"

"But, Mama, Chelsea was going to tell me more about Mike."

"Come on, son," Cash said, looping his arm around the thin shoulders. "I think your mama and Chelsea plan to indulge in a little girl talk. Which means you and I just became persona non grata."

"What does that mean?"

"I'll explain it to you. While we're cleaning the fish."

Apparently knowing when he was licked, Jamie stopped arguing and went out behind the small frame building with Cash.

"He's a wonderful boy," Chelsea said, when she and Sharleen were alone. "You should be very proud."

"I am. And relieved, because I thought for sure he was on the road to juvenile hall. Until Cash stepped in."

"He and Jamie certainly get along well."

"Everyone gets along with Cash. But he had to work to win Jamie's trust. It isn't easy on a kid, having a parent pass away. Jamie was angry. And distrustful, and had begun doin' what these days the school administration calls acting out."

"My father died when I was a girl. I behaved so badly, my mother finally threw up her hands and sent me off to boarding school in Switzerland to let the nuns straighten me out."

"That's tragic. To lose your father, then have your mother send you away. Too bad she didn't have someone like Cash."

"Yes," Chelsea murmured, thinking what a difference a supportive adult would have made in her life back then. "It is too bad. But then again, I don't think there are many men like Cash in this world."

"Now that surely is the truth." Sharleen picked up a sharp knife and began cutting a dressed catfish into chunks with swift, deft strokes. "I don't suppose he told you that he lent me the money to keep this place going?"

"No." Of course he didn't. She'd already determined that Cash was not the type of man to blow his own horn.

"I didn't figure he would. He insists it's a gift, but it's important to me to pay it back, so he agreed to accept fifty dollars a month. I figure at this rate, I'll get it paid off in about the time Jamie's kids graduate college."

Understanding pride, Chelsea refrained from mentioning that Cash certainly didn't need the money anytime soon.

Chelsea fell silent, watching the swift movements of the knife as Sharleen prepared more catfish for the fryer. She experienced a momentary regret for the seven years she could have been with Cash. Then, with renewed optimism, decided to begin making up for lost time.

Cash was in the shower when the glass door opened and Chelsea entered, wearing nothing but a smile and a dazzling, gilt-edged feminine invitation in her eyes.

"I read in this morning's paper that the state's expecting a drier than normal summer," she said, plucking the soap from his hand. "That being the case, I decided it was my civic duty to do whatever I could to conserve water."

He watched the lather billow between her palms; his gut tensed, waiting for the touch of those slender hands on his body. "Sounds like a good idea to me." His voice roughened.

"I'm so glad." She replaced the soap in the niche in the tiled wall then ran her hands over his broad shoulders and down his arms. "Did I tell you that I had a wonderful time today?"

"I believe you mentioned that. On the way home from Catfish Charlie's."

"That's right. I did." She smoothed the iridescent bubbles over his chest. Then lower.

The touch of her fingers skimming over his stomach was like flame. Cash discovered, not for the first time since being with Chelsea, that hunger had claws.

"Did I tell you that I admire the easy way you have with Jamie?"

"I don't remember that coming up."

"Well, I do." Her slippery wet fingers curled around his tumescent penis and began stroking it from base to tip.

"Chelsea—" He moaned her name, half warning, half plea. He leaned his head back against the tile and closed his eyes.

"It got me thinking about children." She caressed his wet

chest with her lips; at the same time she took the straining
penis in both hands marveling, as she always did, at his
rampant masculinity. ''Our children.'' She flicked her
tongue across a hard dark nipple and felt him shiver.

She was about to kneel down, to share with this man she
loved the most intimate kiss of all, when he caught her chin
in between his fingers and lifted her gaze to his.

Cash was struggling to comprehend her words. ''Are you
saying—''

''No.'' She laughed and combed her hands through his
wet hair, fitting her body tightly against his. ''Not yet. But,
I was rather hoping that we could change that.''

Cash felt the breath leave his lungs in a mighty whoosh.
At the same time, hunger surged into his groin like wildfire.
The need for her became unbearable. He took hold of her
waist, his fingers digging into her flesh, and lifted her off
the shower floor, impaling her on his throbbing shaft.

When he felt her body opening to him, surrounding him,
caressing him, he nearly lost control.

With her back against the blue-and-white tile, with her
legs wrapped around his hips, and her mouth locked onto
his, Cash took her, standing up in the shower, while the
water streamed over them, surrounding them in a hot,
steamy mist.

Later, after he'd managed to drag her to bed, where they
made love again, and again, he held her tight and marveled
once more at his good fortune to have been granted another
chance with this woman.

''I sure as hell hope you meant that,'' he murmured
against her throat. He was still inside her, enjoying the continued closeness, reluctant to surrender the warmth quite yet.

''Meant what?'' She pressed her lips against his shoulder,
where a purple bruise from her teeth was beginning to
bloom.

"About children." He lifted his head and looked directly into her eyes. "Because if you didn't, we just took a hell of a chance." It was the first time he hadn't thought of protection.

"I love you. And there's nothing I'd like better than having your baby, Cash," Chelsea said simply.

He went still. And was silent for so long, Chelsea feared she'd made a horrendous mistake by being so open about her feelings.

"Cash?"

He saw the worry in her gaze and hated himself for having put it there. "I'm sorry." He smiled and combed his fingers through her still-damp curls. "It's just an amazing thing for any man to hear, Chelsea. I was trying to count my blessings and realized there weren't enough numbers to even come close."

Tension drained out of her. She lifted her hands to his face and knew that whatever else happened in the future, she would always remember this as one of the happiest days of her life.

"Does that mean you like the idea?"

"What do you think?" With his eyes still on hers, he lowered his mouth to her lips. "I love you, Chelsea Cassidy." The words he'd always avoided using came remarkably easily. "As for making babies with you…"

His kiss was warm and sweet and filled with promise. One hand moved between them to knead her breast, while the other slipped under her, lifting her hips to press her more closely against him.

The scent of the Confederate jasmine wafted in through the open bedroom window. Chelsea heard the call of a bird, the distant sound of a boat on the river. As her lips clung to his, she felt him growing inside her again and the outside world faded away.

Her senses became tangled. She heard Cash murmuring sounds that told her his pleasure was as glorious as hers. That his love ran as deep.

She arched against him, flesh against flesh, hearts beating in unison. Their eyes remained open, on each other's face. He laced their fingers together, hands pressed palm against palm as they rode the rising swells together.

And when she heard him call out her name, like a promise, and a prayer, when she felt him pouring himself into her, Chelsea wept with joy.

The piece of paper had been slipped under his door at the River-Vu Motel on the outskirts of town.

The note on the embossed stationery read:

Dear George,
I've been thinking about the old days. And how we were in love and how much I owe you. I now realize I've been unfair to you, because if you hadn't killed Jubal, I could never have achieved the success I have today. But Vern proposed to me last night. George, do you have any idea how much money this man is worth? I've conceived a plan for us to have our cake and eat it, too. But we need to talk. Please meet me at Belle Terre. Tonight, at midnight. You will not be sorry, darling. Destroy this note.

Love, R

George read the paper again. Then once more, to make certain it wasn't a hallucination. Then he threw back his head and laughed.

"I knew she'd see the light." He pulled out the turquoise-and-silver Zippo lighter, lit the corner of the note, then dropped it into the wastebasket. He looked down at his watch. Only a few hours to wait. Plenty of time for a few more drinks before he finally got what was coming to him.

Several hours after joining Cash in the shower, Chelsea sat with him on the veranda, gazing out at the slow-moving river, draped in deep purple shadows.

"Well, if we didn't make a baby, it damn well won't be for lack of trying," he said.

"If we didn't, we'll just have to try, try again." She smiled up at him, her gaze loving and earnest at the same time. "I do so love you, Cash Beaudine."

"Ah, darlin', those are the sweetest words." He kissed her, a slow wondrous kiss that had the blood singing in her veins. "And I love you. So, since we're going to have kids, don't you think we should think about getting married?"

"Absolutely."

He seemed a little concerned about her quick response. "What about your trust fund?"

"If I don't live up to the terms it reverts to charity." She shrugged. "That's probably better anyway, since if I have you, I'll have everything I need."

"Two million dollars is a lot of money."

"So everyone tells me. Will you regret not having it?"

"Not on a bet."

"There you go," she said in an exaggerated drawl that had him chuckling.

But Cash still worried. Just a little. "Are you sure you won't miss life in the big city?"

"You mean will I feel some great loss, awakening to the sounds of morning birds rather than garbage trucks and jack-hammers?" She pretended to think about that a moment. "No," she said with a shake of her head, "I don't think so. Not in a gazillion years, anyway."

"Your mother might not approve."

"So what else is new?" She laughed and was surprised to realize she no longer felt the usual little prick of pain that thinking about her mother had always caused. "Besides, you'll have her eating out of your hand in no time. She'll fall in love with you, Cash. The same way I did."

"I hope you're right about that." He lifted their joined hands to his lips. "I suppose she's going to want a huge three-ring circus of a wedding."

Surprisingly, although she'd been expected to marry Nelson for years, Chelsea had never given any thought to the ceremony. Now she realized that she'd secretly love a big wedding with all the romantic trimmings.

"It doesn't matter what mother wants," she said quickly, not wanting this to be an obstacle to their happiness. "We can elope. Get it over quickly, then—"

"No." He cut off her breathless assurance with a long, deep kiss that had her slipping back into the mists. "You're only going to get married once, Irish, my love. You should do it right the first time.

"I've never been famous for my patience," he said. "So while we're surviving the fittings and caterers and band auditions, I'm going to have to insist that you spend the nights—all night, every night—in my bed."

"I'm already packed."

Cash laughed. Then kissed her again. And again. And again. Until, if they weren't already in perfect accord, he would have had her agreeing to anything.

Chapter Twenty-Two

The night air was so thick it left a metallic taste on the tongue. Lightning crackled overhead, as hot and yellow as molten gold being poured from a smelter. In that flashing sulfurous light, Belle Terre appeared dark and deserted. But as he walked up from the road, where the truck he'd hitched a ride with had left him off, George could make out Roxanne's Mercedes parked behind the house, the polished finish of the luxury sedan gleaming like a piece of hard candy.

He thought of her, as she'd been that night he'd fucked her, smelling of perfume a helluva lot more expensive than the dime-store brand she'd used when they lived together as husband and wife. He remembered her skin, smooth as that silk she'd taken to wearing and thought back on how good it had felt to be pounding into a woman you hadn't paid.

She might have pretended she didn't like it. The same way she used to pretend she didn't like him to hit her. But George knew she was lying.

As the thunder rumbled like Union caissons overhead, a strong, fierce need sparked through his body, sending fire

into his groin. She could tell him her plan to get Gibbons's
money later, George decided as he took a slug from the pint
bottle wrapped in the brown paper bag. After he'd come in
her mouth. And if she didn't swallow, he'd have to teach
her a painful lesson about how to please her man. The
thought made his prick as hard as stone.

The front door creaked as he opened it.

"Cora Mae?"

No answer. The house was as black and silent as a tomb.

"Dammit, Cora Mae, where the fuck are you?"

Again nothing. But listening carefully, he heard movement upstairs. Sticking the bottle in his back pocket, he
climbed the stairs.

She'd obviously been waiting for him. Drawn to the faint
light flickering at the end of the hallway, George stopped in
the open doorway of the room that some of the carpenters
had insisted was haunted. Candles in votive holders, like in
a Catholic church, flickered warmly on the windowsill.

He entered the room, stopping dead in his tracks when
he felt a chill brush over him, making the hair on his arms
and the back of his neck stand up.

"Dammit, Cora Mae," he complained again in a high,
tinny voice, "quit playing games."

He heard the footfalls behind him and turned, determined
to teach her not to scare the bejeezus out of him this way.
He caught a glimmer of the metal head of a claw hammer
descending toward his head.

It was the storm that woke her. Jarred from her dreams
by a crack of thunder, Chelsea reached out for Cash and
found his side of the bed empty.

"Cash?" She sat up and looked toward the bathroom.
The door was open and it was as dark as the bedroom. A
moment later, she heard the sound of a car engine.

She left the bed and went out the French doors onto the veranda. The rain was pouring down from the black sky like water from a boot. She watched as the driver's door of Cash's pickup truck opened. He ducked his head against the storm and ran up the steps to where she stood beneath the low roof.

"Hell, I'm sorry," he said. I didn't mean to wake you."

"You didn't. It was the storm. Then I reached for you and you weren't there."

"I couldn't sleep, so I took a drive."

"In this weather?"

He shrugged. "I do that sometimes, when I'm trying to work out a problem."

"A problem with us?"

"Of course not." He drew her into his arms. She'd commandeered one of his shirts for sleeping and although the hem fell to midthigh, when she lifted her arms around his neck, it rose up enticingly. "I was thinking about a job I'm starting next week in Savannah."

"The governor's mother."

"You remembered."

She nuzzled his neck, breathing in the fresh scent of rain on his skin. "I remember everything about you." She kissed his chin. "I always have." His jaw. "I always will. Do you want to talk about it?"

"What?" He slipped his hands beneath the shirt and cupped her buttocks, lifting her against his arousal. Even after all these weeks together, it continued to amaze Cash how much he wanted Chelsea. How often he wanted her.

"Your problem with the governor's mother's house."

"What problem?"

As the rigid proof of his desire pressed against her belly, Chelsea felt an answering flare of hunger. She laughed, a soft, silky laugh overbrimming with feminine intent.

"I forget." She moved her hips against him, enjoying the friction. Reveling in the heat.

He kissed her hard and deep; she kissed him back just as hard, just as deep. He dragged his hand through her hair, pulling her head back, allowing his mouth access to her neck. When he touched his tongue to the pounding pulse beat at the base of her throat, she sighed.

When he took a breast between his lips and began to suckle deeply, she whimpered, then moaned as his treacherous teeth tightened around a taut nipple and tugged. He slid a finger into the hidden cleft between her thighs and felt her heat, and dampness and need.

A choking noise escaped her bruised and swollen lips. There was something primal in that sound. Something that tore at his already tenuous self-control.

With the rain pounding down on the veranda roof, Cash pulled her down to the green glider, then yanked down the zipper of his jeans. Chelsea helped him drag the wet denim down his legs. He lifted her hips and slammed into her, filling her, exploding almost immediately inside her. While the lightning lit up the sky to a daylight brightness, Chelsea climaxed with a power that had her convulsing in his arms.

Neither had the strength to move. They stayed there, Cash sprawled atop Chelsea, while the lightning flashed and the thunder roiled and the rain continued. Eventually, the storm passed. And then there was only the slight squeak of the glider. The soft sighs of their breathing returning to normal, and the sound of two hearts beating as one.

Back in his bed, Chelsea was enjoying a remarkably sensual dream when the phone rang. Unwilling to completely wake up, she only vaguely heard his quiet murmurs. Then a ripe, vicious curse that caused the lovely dream to shatter.

"Cash?" She watched in confusion as he began pulling clothing out of the bureau drawer. "What's wrong?"

"It's Belle Terre."

"Belle Terre?" The room was dark, with not a hint of dawn's pearlescent shimmer. "What time is it?" she asked, pushing her hair out of her eyes. "I can't believe Roxanne would bother you in the middle of the night over—"

"It's burning."

"What?"

"Belle Terre is on fire. Roxanne just got the call from the fire department. Jo's driving her out there. I promised to meet them there."

"I'm coming with you." Chelsea was out of bed, gathering up her own discarded clothing.

There was no more conversation as each hurried to get dressed. Their thoughts were on the plantation house Cash had worked so hard on. Cared so much about. The house that had brought them back together.

It was even worse than he'd feared. The bright orange flames were literally devouring the house, eating away at the roof, blazing in the blown-out windows. The fire fighters were doing their best, dragging hoses, chopping down doors with the axes, sending streams of water upward. But Cash could tell it was a hopeless cause. The fire, sly hungry bitch that she was, kept dodging the water, leaping from room to room, window to window.

He stood there, hands shoved deeply into his pockets, with the smoke stinging his eyes and the acrid smell burning his nasal passages and literally watched months of his life go up in smoke.

Beside him, Roxanne appeared shell-shocked. Her unmade face was as white as the smoke that rose like billowing ghosts wherever the water hit it. Her eyes were round and dark and empty in that too pale face. Her lips were thin and unpainted and trembling.

Standing beside her, Jo was murmuring words of condolence. Words Cash suspected Roxanne was incapable of understanding.

There was nothing any of them could do, but stand outside the ring of fire trucks and hoses and wait for the inevitable.

Dawn was a teasing pink glow on the horizon when a red car drove onto the scene, orange light flashing atop the roof. It stopped beside one of the pumper trucks. A man clad in jeans and a blue T-shirt climbed out and walked toward one of the firemen.

The two men talked, glancing every so often at the house, then back at the observers, which now numbered about a dozen, most of whom Cash decided were neighbors drawn to the scene out of curiosity.

Both men approached. "Are any of you the owner of this house?"

"I am," Roxanne managed to croak in a frail and fractured voice.

"I'm Marty Cunningham, county fire marshall." He held out his hand. "And your name would be?"

Roxanne ignored the outstretched hand. Chelsea believed she didn't even see it. "Roxanne Scarbrough."

If the name garnered any recognition the man didn't show it. "Sorry to have to meet this way, Miz Scarbrough," he said with genuine, professional regret. "I'm afraid I've got some bad news for you."

"I can see that for myself, Mr...."

"Cunningham, ma'am."

"Cunningham," she echoed distantly. Her voice was as bleak as her expression. "Belle Terre is ruined, isn't it?"

"Well, ma'am that's between you and your insurance company, though I have to admit, it doesn't look good. But the thing is, Miz Scarbrough, we've got ourselves a worse problem here.''

"What could be worse than my life's dream going up in flames?"

"How about a man's life going up in flames?"

She shot him an uncomprehending look. "I don't understand."

"My men tell me that a body was found inside your home."

"A body?" Her gaze whipped from his face to Belle Terre.

"Yes, ma'am. It looks as if the guy died in the fire. They managed to carry him out into the back yard."

"Who is he? What was he doing here? Did he set the fire?"

"That last part's going to be my job to find out. As for who he was, to be perfectly frank, ma'am, I doubt if his own mother would recognize him. But the contents of his wallet weren't totally destroyed, so we were able to make a tentative identification.

"Unless the wallet's stolen," he added. "Would you happen to know a George Waggoner, Miz Scarbrough?"

Roxanne's face turned an even whiter shade of pale as every vestige of color drained out of her complexion. Then she fainted, folding bonelessly to the ground at Cash's feet.

"Can you believe it?" Chelsea asked later, after she and Cash returned to Rebel's Ridge. "What do you think George Waggoner was doing at Belle Terre?"

Cash shrugged. He was exhausted. Emotionally and mentally drained. He wasn't interested in talking about George Waggoner. Dead or alive. "Maybe he was sleeping. He seemed pretty much of a transient."

"Do you think he could have been the one who started

the fire? Perhaps he fell asleep smoking a cigarette? Or maybe he even set the fire to get back at Roxanne for not getting him put back on the payroll and couldn't get out in time.''

"Who knows?" What did it matter? The house was a total loss. "It could have been anything. Spontaneous combustion from painters' rags, kids breaking in to have a beer party and accidently having a cigarette ash fall onto some sawdust. Maybe a firebug who likes to watch things burn. Or even someone with a grudge against Roxanne. It's the marshall's job to determine the cause of the fire. Not mine.''

Chelsea would have had to have been deaf not to hear the edge to his voice. "I'm sorry." She put her arms around him and held on tight, offering what scant comfort she could. "This must come as a terrible blow."

"It sure as hell isn't the best start to a day I've ever had." He backed away and dragged his hand through his hair, which, he noticed, smelled like smoke. "I think I'll take a shower.''

"Good idea." Understanding how devastated he must have felt, watching what she knew had become a labor of love literally go up in smoke, Chelsea wasn't hurt by the way he was distancing himself from her. Cash simply wasn't used to sharing his innermost feelings. She could understand that because she was the same way herself. Such openness would come. With time. And love. "I'll make some coffee.''

"Coffee sounds great."

Ten minutes later, as she watched the water dripping through the automatic coffeemaker, Chelsea thought that Cash must be taking a very long shower. Then she realized that she hadn't heard the water running.

She went into the bedroom on her way to the adjoining bath and found him, stretched out on his back on the top of the unmade bed, sound asleep. She took off his boots, put them beside the bed, and paused to brush a light kiss against his grimly set lips. Then she went back into the kitchen, poured herself a cup of coffee and tried to decide whether she should drive over to Roxanne's.

The writer in her knew she should be at the house with the others. There was no way she'd be able to leave such a devastating development out of the autobiography, and it would be advantageous to observe Roxanne's behavior and emotions now, rather than trying to reconstruct the events later. Of course, she reminded herself, Jo would undoubtedly have it all documented on her video camera.

The woman in Chelsea, the woman who was madly in love with the exhausted man sleeping in their bed, didn't want to be gone when Cash woke up.

Go. Stay. Go. She was sitting out on the veranda, trying to make up her mind, when a car bearing the insignia of the Raintree County Sheriff's Department drove up the dead-end road, stopping beside Cash's pickup. A man wearing the khaki uniform of authority climbed out of the driver's seat and began walking toward her.

"Cash," Chelsea called in to him. "There's someone here. I suppose it's about Belle Terre."

The sheriff was a tall man, about six foot four, she'd guess. He was wearing dark glasses which precluded her from seeing his eyes, and his lips were grimly set.

"Good mornin', ma'am." He tipped his hat. His gray hair was short, styled in a military cut. "I expect you're Miz Cassidy."

"That's right. And you're—?"

"Joe Burke, ma'am. Sheriff of Raintree county."

"What can I help you with this morning, Sheriff?"

"I'm here to see Cash, ma'am. If he's around."

"Of course he is." For some reason there was something

in his tone that had her suddenly feeling uneasy. Assuring herself that it was just a lack of sleep, she shook the feeling off. "I'll go get him."

"That's not necessary," a deep voice behind her said. Chelsea turned around and viewed Cash standing in the doorway to the veranda. "Mornin' Joe."

"Cash. I need to ask you some questions."

"Come on in." His expression was bland. His voice mild. But Chelsea, who'd come to know him well, sensed an undercurrent.

They all went into the kitchen, where she poured the men coffee. "If you want me to leave you two alone—"

"That'd be real nice, darlin'," Cash said.

"I'd like you to stay," the sheriff said at the same time.

The tension in the room was suddenly so thick she could have cut it with one of Roxanne's kitchen cleavers. Her puzzled gaze went from Cash's implacable face to the sheriff's grim one, then back to Cash. Growing increasingly uncomfortable, Chelsea sat down at the table.

For the first five minutes the questions focused solely on Belle Terre. Yes, the wiring was to code. Yes, they'd passed all the inspections, gotten all the required green tags. No, there wouldn't have been any workman at the scene that time of night, which meant that the fire couldn't have been started by a welder's torch as was so often the case. Or a cigarette.

"Would you be surprised to learn that the fire marshall found evidence of flammable liquid at the scene?"

"Not really," Cash said.

"Any special reason?"

"We've ruled out causes of accidental fires. I suppose that leaves arson."

"That's what the fire marshall was thinking. His first thought is that Waggoner might have torched the place.

Since you'd canned his ass— Sorry for the language, Miz Cassidy,'' the sheriff said with a quick glance toward Chelsea.

She nodded and managed a faint smile.

"Anyway, the word among the crew is that you ran him off the job."

"He was a menace. And a criminal."

"A paroled one. Who'd done his time."

"You know as well as I do that doesn't mean squat these days. What with all the prison overcrowding, they probably released the son of a bitch to make room for a check bouncer."

The sheriff didn't deny the possibility. Instead, he rubbed his jaw and looked out the window. "You knocked down the slave cabins."

"Thought it was time," Cash said.

"I reckon so." The older man looked around the kitchen. "You've done all right for yourself, Cash. A fancy Italian sports car, that bass boat with all the high-tech gadgets—"

"Is there a point to this, Sheriff?"

His voice had regained that edge Chelsea had heard earlier. And, she noted, this time he'd referred to the other man by his title, and not his first name.

Chelsea was not the only one who'd caught the challenge in Cash's tone. Joe Burke's square jaw jutted out. "I was just wondering why you'd be willin' to risk it all by killing a no-account drifter like George Waggoner."

When Chelsea gasped, Cash put his hand under the table and squeezed her knee in a reassuring gesture. "I was under the impression Waggoner died in the fire. A fire he probably set for revenge."

"That's what the fire marshall thought at first," Burke allowed. "But that was before the coroner discovered his head had been bashed in. The way we figure it, the fire was set to destroy the evidence.''

''I suppose that makes sense. But what makes me a suspect?''

''How about the little matter of you threatening to kill the guy?''

''Good point,'' Cash allowed.

''And there's something else. A white pickup truck was seen on the river road, headed this way about the time of the fire. You want to tell me what you were doing about midnight?''

''He was with me,'' Chelsea said before Cash could answer. ''In bed.''

The sheriff's eyes narrowed. ''All night?''

''Yes.'' She forced a smile she was a very long way from feeling. ''Believe me, Sheriff, when a woman receives a proposal from the man she loves, she's not likely to let him get away. Until she clinches the deal.''

Burke took that in. ''Well.'' He rubbed his chin again.

Checkmate, Chelsea thought.

''I guess that's just about all I wanted to ask you, Cash. Miz Cassidy.''

He stood up. Cash and Chelsea accompanied him to the door, then stood on the veranda, arms wrapped around each other's waists, watching him walk back toward the white squad car.

''Oh, Cash, one more thing,'' he said, stopping just as he was about to fold his long length back into the driver's seat. ''Don't be planning any trips out of town for a while. Until we get this case settled.''

That said, he climbed into the car, shut the door and started the engine.

''I can't believe this,'' Chelsea said they watched him drive away.

''That makes two of us.'' His voice was as gritty as the gravel river road. ''What the hell did you think you were doing?''

''What do you mean?''

''You know damn well what I mean.'' His fingers curled around her upper arms. ''Why did you lie to him?''

''I didn't lie. Not exactly.''

''You said I was in bed with you.''

''You were. And believe me, darling, I have the marks to prove it.''

''Hell.'' Momentarily sidetracked, he looked down at the faint bruises on her arms. ''I'm sorry.''

''I'm not. And wait until you see your back,'' she advised.

''You don't have any idea what you're getting into. We both know I left here last night.''

''To drive around. To think out an architectural problem.''

''That's what I told you. But how do you know I was telling the truth?''

''Simple. You once told me that you'd never lie to me.''

''Maybe I was lying when I said that.''

''Oh, for heaven's sake.'' Her exasperated breath feathered her curly bangs. ''If you possibly think that I could ever, in this lifetime or any other, believe you capable of cold-blooded murder, even of a loathsome man like George Waggoner, than you're not nearly as intelligent as I know you are.

''I love you, Cash. And I'd do anything for you.''

''Even go to prison as an accessory to murder?''

She gave him a long look. ''Did you kill him?''

''Of course not.''

''There. See? I can't be an accessory to anything. Because the only thing you're guilty of is being fatally sexy.'' She wrapped her arms around his neck. "Now that we've settled that, how about taking a shower with me? We've both got smoke in our hair and it's driving me crazy."

"You want crazy?" Abandoning the lecture about legal jurisprudence, putting aside his fears that Joe Burke was going to be back with a warrant for his arrest, Cash scooped her off her feet and carried her into the shower, where they spent a very long time driving each other to the edge of madness. And beyond.

Chapter Twenty-Three

Her brain fogged with shock, and the tranquilizer she'd taken, Roxanne dragged herself up the stairs, intending to wash her face and clear her mind.

Although it was morning, the drawn drapes caused the room to be as dark as midnight. Roxanne flicked the wall switch, turning on the Tiffany lamp, bathing the room in the soft, flattering glow created by stained glass shading a pink lightbulb.

She paused for a moment, drinking in the sight and scent of this signature perfect, ultrafeminine room.

The bed, discovered at a Charlotte, North Carolina estate sale, was truly a wonder: a towering mahogany pineapple four-poster draped in diaphanous clouds of white netting, covered with snowy Irish lace and piled high with cutwork pillows of her own design. She'd been going to take it with her to Belle Terre. Roxanne groaned as the vision of Belle Terre engulfed in flames flashed yet again through her mind, as it had on the drive back from the plantation house, over and over, like a scene from some late-night cable horror film.

It was as if she were there, watching it again. So caught up was she in the devastating memory, she never heard the footfalls approach behind her. Did not see the chunk of yellow southern pine descending toward her head.

Never heard the thud, like a hammer striking a ripe melon.

A black veil drifted over Roxanne's delphinium blue eyes as she fell, slack, face forward, onto the floral needlepoint rug.

Chelsea and Cash were eating breakfast when the phone rang. "Yeah?" Cash growled without preamble. When he heard the cultured voice on the other end of the line, he closed his eyes and sighed. *Great, Beaudine,* he blasted himself mentally. *That's just goddamn great.*

"It's your mother."

"My mother?" Chelsea stared at the receiver he was holding out to her as if it were a rattler, poised to strike. "Oh, hell," she murmured, her own sigh as deep and resigned as his.

"Hello, Mother," she said in a feigned cheery tone as Cash left the house, going out to pace the veranda. "How did you find me?"

"I called at the inn," Deidre said. "The man who answered the phone suggested I try you at this number. He was very helpful."

"Jeb is that," Chelsea agreed.

"So, that's his name? Jeb?"

"That's right." Surely her mother didn't call just to chat? "Jeb Townely. He owns the inn."

"He's quite charming."

"Yes, he is."

"Is there a Mrs. Townely?"

"No. He's single." She waited.

Deidre did not disappoint. "I don't suppose—"

"No, mother. I have no intention of getting romantically involved with Jeb Townely. No matter how charming he is."

"Well." Deidre half laughed, half sighed. "You can't blame a mother for trying."

Actually, she could, but Chelsea wasn't in the mood for an argument right now. "Was there some special reason you called, mother?"

"Well, of course. I saw the terrible news about Roxanne Scarbrough's house and was worried about you."

"It made the news? So soon?"

"As we've already discussed, the woman has a knack for getting publicity." Deidre's voice dripped with scorn. But beneath it, Chelsea thought she detected a note of honest maternal concern. "When the reporter mentioned something about a body being found in the house, I told myself that it couldn't possibly be you, but—"

"I'm fine."

"You're certain?"

"Absolutely. In fact, I'm better than fine." She took a deep breath, then plunged headfirst into the dangerous conversational waters. "I'm getting married."

"To Cash Beaudine."

"Yes." The smile warmed her voice and lit up her eyes. "To Cash."

"Well." There was a long silence. "I suppose I should have expected something like this, after seeing the two of you together in New York." There was another lengthy pause. "Does he make you happy, Chelsea?"

"Deliriously."

"I'm glad. That's all I've ever wanted for you, dear. That you be happy."

"Thank you, mother."

Just when Chelsea thought they were making progress, Deidre reverted to type. "Of course, I'd once hoped that Nelson would make you happy."

"He didn't."

"So I've come to realize." Another pause, longer than the others. "Oh, Chelsea." There was something new in her mother's tone, something Chelsea had never heard before. "I realize I haven't been the type of warm, earthy mother you would have preferred, but I do love you. If you were having problems with Nelson, I would have wanted to know about them. I would have wanted to try to help."

"You couldn't have done anything."

"I could have listened."

"You never did before." Chelsea cringed inwardly as she realized that she was sounding like a petulant child. "I'm sorry. Maybe you didn't listen because I never gave you a chance."

"And maybe you didn't give me an opportunity because I never gave you any sign that I cared." Deidre sighed. "Oh, dear. I really have made a mess of things, haven't I?"

She sounded so honestly contrite, Chelsea found herself wanting to reassure her. "Of course you haven't—"

"You don't have to lie. My mother was the same way. Cold. Remote. Seemingly too busy to take time to listen to a little girl's hopes and dreams. I always swore that when I had a daughter, I would do things differently."

She sighed. "Obviously, I failed at motherhood. The same way I failed at marriage."

Chelsea was stunned by the unexpected admission. "You weren't any different from all my friends' mothers."

"That's exactly my point. Do you know, I used to envy Tillie terribly."

"Really?" This was another surprising statement in a morning filled with revelations. Chelsea wondered if her mother had realized that the Lowell housekeeper had often seemed more like a mother to her than her own.

"Because from the stories she told me, she and her children all seemed so close. There were times, when she'd show me the photos of another birthday party, or Christmas, or Labor Day picnic, when I nearly wept. Because her family was the one I'd dreamed of having with your father."

"Are you saying you loved him?" Chelsea had never known.

"Until the day he died."

"Yet you divorced him."

"And have regretted it ever since. Unfortunately, I was too much a product of my upbringing. I couldn't be who he wanted me to be. Who he needed me to be."

"And who was that?"

"The woman you've become all on your own. An independent woman. A woman brave enough to remain true to her heart. And to go wherever it takes her. Even if the road ahead seems perilous and unfamiliar."

As she heard the tears thicken her mother's voice, Chelsea felt the moisture stinging behind her own lids.

"Thank you, mother." After promising to call soon, Chelsea hung up. And as she joined Cash out on the veranda, she realized that by giving her heart to Cash, loving him without reservation, she'd finally been able to open up enough to make the emotional connection with her mother that had eluded her for so many long and lonely years.

The house appeared empty when Chelsea finally arrived around noon. Neither Roxanne nor Dorothy's cars were anywhere to be seen. She rang the bell, received no answer and was about to leave when the door opened.

"Oh, hi, Chelsea." Jo greeted her with her usual perky

smile, as if nothing had happened. "Roxanne wondered if you were going to show up today."

"I'm sorry. I was delayed." Chelsea couldn't help the warmth that flowed through her as she thought of how she'd spent the past hour. "Is Roxanne here?"

"I'm afraid not. She had to meet the insurance claims adjuster out at Belle Terre."

"I'll just go out there, then."

"Oh, no. That's not necessary," Jo said quickly. "In fact, Roxanne assured me that she'd be back by lunch. Why don't you come in and wait? LaDonna made some lovely chicken salad sandwiches."

"I guess that makes the most sense," Chelsea allowed. "Is Dorothy with Roxanne?"

"No. Her mother's ill today. Roxanne suggested she stay home and take care of Mildred. Since there wasn't anything she could do around here today. What with the fire," Jo tacked on.

It crossed Chelsea's mind that was unusual behavior for Roxanne. She'd never seen any indication that the life-style expert cared about her employees' personal lives. As for there not being any work, now that the news about the fire at Belle Terre had gotten onto the wire services, the press would begin gathering like vultures. Surely Roxanne would want Dorothy on the scene to run interference?

"Don't ask me," Jo said with a shrug when Chelsea mentioned her concerns. "I just take the pictures. I've given up trying to figure out what makes that woman run."

"She is a little complex."

"There's nothing complex about Roxanne. She's a cold, calculating bitch, pure and simple." Jo's tone was sharp. Remembering the way Roxanne had slapped Jo, Chelsea decided the lingering resentment wasn't so surprising. "But, we had a bad enough night. Let's try to have a better day."

She led the way into the sunny kitchen decorated with gleaming copper pots and pans that Chelsea suspected had never seen a range top.

"LaDonna makes the best chicken salad," Jo enthused. "It's the pimento that makes it special. And I love the way she puts the orange juice in the iced tea. It's delicious."

The chicken salad was as excellent as promised, although Chelsea thought the tea tasted a bit bitter.

"So," Jo said conversationally, as she cleared the table after their shared lunch, "that's really something about George, isn't it?" Roxanne had still not returned and the housekeeper, Jo had explained, had gone to the market in Savannah to do her monthly shopping.

"About him dying in the fire?"

"Yes." Jo looked at her curiously. "Unless you know something I don't know."

"No," Chelsea hedged, "that's what I meant."

She was vaguely relieved that Jo didn't seem to know about the murder. Perhaps the sheriff was going to remain discreet until he had the killer behind bars. She certainly hoped so, not even wanting to think of the media circus the press could make of the story. Despite their new and tentative truce, her mother would undoubtedly be less than thrilled to have her daughter's name linked with a homicide suspect.

"He must have gone into the house to set it on fire, to get back at Roxanne for firing him." Jo mused.

"But it was Cash who fired him," Chelsea reminded her. A headache was threatening. She rubbed her temples with her fingertips. "Not Roxanne."

"Well, sure. But he probably wasn't thinking real straight. I mean the guy was the classic alcoholic. He probably managed to kill off most of his gray matter."

"You've got a point." Little white dots were swimming

in front of her eyes. Her tongue felt thick, making it difficult to speak.

"Chelsea?"

Jo's voice sounded as if she were underwater. Chelsea tried, with effort, to lift her suddenly heavy head and look at her.

"Is everything okay?" Now the words were drawn out, like an old-fashioned 45 rpm record playing at 33 speed. "You look funny."

Chelsea opened her mouth to answer, but she couldn't get the words out. Sweat was pouring down her face, dripping onto the white Irish linen tablecloth, which struck her as strange, since she was suddenly freezing. Her teeth began to chatter.

The last thing she remembered was struggling to stand up, desperate to get to the phone to dial 911. But her watery legs wouldn't hold her and she crumpled, surrendering to the darkness.

Chelsea's head felt as if someone had split it in two with an ax and her mouth felt as if she'd been eating cotton balls. Her eyes were filled with grit. She tried to open them, but couldn't. Tried to pry her lids open with her fingers, but someone had tied her wrists together behind her back, rendering her helpless. Her bound wrists had also been lashed to her ankles, she realized through the thick fog clouding her mind. Someone had tied her up like a stuffed pig.

Now all she needed, she decided on a silent, hysterical giggle, was someone to put an apple in her mouth. Then she could be the entree at a Roxanne Scarbrough luau.

The thought amused her. Enough so that she was actually smiling as she drifted off back into the dark, cold netherworld of unconsciousness.

When she roused again, Chelsea realized that she was in a car, being driven over a bumpy, unpaved road.

But where? she wondered groggily.

And why?

Having no answer, she lost consciousness once again.

The next time she woke, she found herself gagged, tied to a chair in a small, rustic room that reminded her of what the inside of Cash's former slave cabins might have looked like.

Her head was pounding and she feared she was going to throw up. She swallowed down the unpleasant taste that bubbled up in her throat and although it took a mighty effort, she managed to turn her head and take in her surroundings.

The floor was dirt, the walls created of some sort of limestone and shells. The roof was tin. Rain pounded down on the tin, sounding like a snare drum. There was a narrow army green cot in a corner of the room. A single lightbulb hung from the ceiling on a black wire.

Roxanne was lying on the floor beside the cot, similarly bound and gagged. Her hair was a filthy blond tangle around her dirty face. She had two black eyes, and there was an ugly gash on the side of her face. She was a mess. But she was, Chelsea saw with relief, still alive. Her blue eyes, as they met Chelsea's were wide with shock and terror. For the first time since meeting her, Chelsea knew exactly how the life-style expert felt.

"Well, well. Sleeping Beauty is finally awake," the dry voice said.

Chelsea turned toward the doorway, her eyes asking Jo, *Why?*

"I thought I might have killed you," the filmmaker said with a casualness that was even more terrifying than anything else that had happened to Chelsea thus far. To be able to speak so easily of murder denoted either a very evil—or very sick—mind. "Which would have been a shame. Since

you're a very important cog in this little wheel we're build
ing.''

She entered the cabin, tossed some bags of fast food onto
the cot, then came over to Chelsea and looked down at her

"I'm going to untie your gag. But I've got to warn you
you'll be very, very sorry if you scream. Not that it would
help, because there's no one around for miles. But it gets
on my nerves. And believe me, Chelsea, I can be very unpleasant when I get nervous.''

She flashed a smile toward the other bound woman
"Isn't that right, Roxanne?''

Roxanne managed a half nod that made Jo laugh.

When she went over to the cot, picked up her leather
purse and pulled out a knife, Chelsea's blood turned to ice.

"Don't worry," she said, apparently reading the fear in
Chelsea's gaze. "I'm not going to hurt you. Not yet, any-
way.'' She sliced through the thick gag with the shiny blade.
"There. Isn't that better?''

"I don't understand," Chelsea managed to croak. Her
mouth was as dry as sawdust. From fear and whatever drugs
Jo had slipped into her iced tea. "What do you want from
me?''

"What do you think? I want you to write a book, of
course. About Roxanne.''

"I thought that was what I was doing.''

"You're right.'' Jo sighed. "I suppose it would be more
correct to say that I want you to write a tell-all biography
of Cora Mae Padgett.'' This time the smile she flashed at
Roxanne was as lethal as the knife she held in her hand.
"My very own mommy dearest.''

When Chelsea still hadn't returned by late afternoon,
Cash began to worry. He hadn't wanted Chelsea to go to
Roxanne's today. He understood ambition, but, as he'd ar-

gued with her, someone had killed George Waggoner. And set fire to Belle Terre. Someone who was still running around loose.

She'd scoffed at his fears, assured him that no one would have any reason to kill her, then drove away from Rebel's Ridge. Leaving him to pace and worry.

What if George hadn't been the target? What if the perpetrator had gone to Belle Terre to torch it, was discovered in the act, and killed George to cover up his—or her—crime?

What if this person had a grudge against Roxanne? What if he or she tried again?

Chelsea's independent spirit was one of the reasons he'd fallen in love with her. She was more than capable of making her own decisions. But dammit, this one was wrong. Really, really wrong. And there was no way he was going to let her die in the name of feminine independence.

Grabbing his keys from the hook by the door, he climbed into the pickup and took off, scattering gravel as he tore out of the driveway.

Twenty minutes later he was at Roxanne's Tudor house, arriving just as Dorothy was coming out the front door.

"Where is she?" he demanded.

"Who? Chelsea? Or Roxanne?"

"Chelsea."

"I don't know. I thought I'd stop by after bringing Mama home from the doctor's, to see if Roxanne had any work for me to do, but no one was here."

A frisson of terror skipped up his spine. "Chelsea's rental car's here."

"I know. But Roxanne's Mercedes is missing, so I assume they probably took it out to Belle Terre to inspect the damage."

That was a possibility, Cash decided, desperate to have his fears prove unfounded.

"Although there's something that bothers me," Dorothy said, on an afterthought.

"What's that?"

"I found a broken glass of iced tea on the floor of the kitchen. Along with Chelsea's duffel bag. Have you ever noticed how many pens and notebooks she keeps in that thing? I can't imagine her leaving it behind."

Neither could he. Cash cursed.

"I'm going to call the sheriff," he said.

"Why?"

"To tell him we've got a possible kidnapping."

Dorothy's eyes grew wide behind the lenses of her black framed glasses. "A kidnapping?"

"That's right." A fist was twisting his gut in two. "And another possible homicide."

Dorothy's horrified expression echoed his own bleak mood.

He couldn't lose her, Cash told himself fervently as he had no choice but to wait for Sheriff Joe Burke to arrive.

They'd find her. Safe and sound. And he would marry her in some fancy New York church in a three-ring circus of a formal ceremony that he'd hate but would put up with because every bride was entitled to the wedding of her dreams. He suspected he'd be required to wear a morning coat. And drink champagne beneath a striped tent. And smile and make small talk with all her mother's snobby Long Island friends. But he'd do it. For Chelsea. Because he loved her.

And they'd have babies. Lots of babies. With bright copper hair and big green eyes like their mother. And years later, they'd sit together on the green glider on their veranda overlooking the river and watch their grandchildren chasing fireflies, and they'd both agree that they were the luckiest people on the planet. Because they had each other.

Cash did not believe all this because he was by nature an optimist.

He believed it would come true because the alternative was too horrible to contemplate.

He loved Chelsea. She loved him.

Everything had to turn out okay. As the sheriff's car pulled up in front of the house, red-and-blue rooftop bubble light flashing, Cash refused to allow himself to think otherwise.

Chelsea couldn't believe what she was watching. Jo had set up a generator to run a VCR and television in the fishing cabin, subjecting Chelsea to videos depicting Roxanne having sex with Vern Gibbons and George Waggoner. There was also one distasteful episode where Roxanne threatened to terminate Cash if he didn't sleep with her. Loving Cash, and knowing him as she did, Chelsea was not the least bit surprised when he turned the predatory woman down.

She watched George blackmailing Roxanne about her former life, and, it seemed, her stepfather, a man named Jubal Lott. Although it wasn't clear to Chelsea which of the deadly duo had actually killed the man, she could certainly understand why Roxanne had been willing to pay him to keep quiet. It also answered her question as to why Waggoner had been hired to work at Belle Terre.

She cringed at the gruesome scene of George's death. When the heavy hammer came down, crushing his head, her stomach roiled. Bile rose in her throat. With an effort, she forced it back down.

"I don't understand," she said to Jo, "why you killed him."

"Because he was my father, of course," Jo explained.

"That's not true!" Roxanne cried. Although Jo had removed her gag as well, this was the first thing she'd said.

"The videotape doesn't lie." Her eerily serene behavior reminded Chelsea of the calm before a very violent storm. "I can see it's time for a little more show-and-tell." She put in another tape and pushed Play. "You see," she said after the scene depicting George reminding Roxanne about her pregnancy had played. "You can't lie about this, Mama. You and that alcoholic murderer made a child together."

"That's true. But I got an abortion."

"Liar." Jo reached into her purse and pulled out a paper. "This is my birth certificate. And although it has the names of my adoptive parents on it, please notice the date. And here—" she whipped out another piece of paper "—are hospital records showing that Cora Mae Padgett was a patient at the same time."

"How did you get those records?" Roxanne asked.

"You'd be surprised what people will hand over when you tell them you're filming a movie," Jo said. "It was a small hospital, Mama. I was the only baby born that day."

Roxanne stared at Jo as if seeing her worst nightmare come to life. She hadn't looked this bad watching Belle Terre burn to the ground. For the first time, Chelsea thought she looked every one of her fifty years.

"George wasn't your father," Roxanne repeated. It did not escape Chelsea's attention that she did not deny the accusation that she was Cora Mae Padgett. Or even that she might be Jo's mother.

"I *was* pregnant when I married him. But I was afraid the baby might be Jubal's. Surely you can understand that under the circumstances, I had no choice but to get an abortion. Three years before you were even born."

"You're my mother," Jo insisted.

Roxanne let out a slow, stuttering breath. "You may be right. When I was a sophomore in college, I got pregnant again. It wasn't anyone important, just a professor who promised to give me an A in my art history class if I slept with him."

"Beats studying," Chelsea couldn't resist muttering. Her comment earned a hot look from Roxanne and a conspiratory smile from Jo.

"So this professor was my father?"

"Yes."

"Not George."

"No. Not George."

"Oops." Jo giggled. "Looks as if I made a little mistake. She shrugged philosophically and flashed a grin toward Chelsea. "Oh well, the guy was a creep anyway. No one will miss him."

Unfortunately, Chelsea found she couldn't disagree with that statement. Jo turned back to Roxanne. "You were saying?"

Although it was hot and steamy in the cabin, Roxanne was trembling as if she'd been set adrift, buck naked, on an arctic iceberg. "Do we have to do this?"

"If you want to stay alive."

"All right." Roxanne shuddered, took another deep breath and continued. "I'd planned to get another abortion, but I was upset and distracted on the way to the motel where the procedure was supposed to take place and crossed the street against the light. I was hit by a car and ended up with a broken back that forced me to spend six months in the hospital in traction. Since abortion was still illegal at the time, I had no choice but to carry the baby to term."

"So, unwilling to sidetrack your lofty career goals by becoming a mother, you gave me up for adoption and never looked back."

"It was the best thing to do," Roxanne insisted. "For both of us."

"For you, maybe. But not for me."

"That's not true! You've told me all about your parents. Your father was in the military. An officer, I believe. You traveled around the world. Your parents adored you."

"Beneath his fancy dress uniform, my adoptive father was a brutal, autocratic redneck who terrorized the men under his command and beat up his wimp of a wife for kicks. When I got old enough, he beat me up, too. He used to play games. One of his favorite pastimes was playing Russian roulette during dinner. He'd point his revolver at me or my mother and pull the trigger.

"When the cylinder came up empty, he'd laugh. And sometimes he'd put the gun down. Other times he'd try again. Every so often, just to remind us that he *could* kill us, he'd shoot into the wall over our heads. It was a fun life, Mama. Thanks for making it happen."

"How could I have known?" Roxanne argued plaintively. "The woman at the agency—"

"Don't talk to me about that agency!" Jo yelled, displaying her first sign of temper so far. "It was a fucking baby mill. They bought babies, then sold them to the highest bidder. Like you sold me, Mother. For ten thousand dollars."

"I was assured they were good people."

"Don't give me that shit. I know you. I've been living with you for weeks. I've been watching every little secret aspect of your life. You're a scheming, heartless, opportunist bitch. And we both know you would have sold me to Genghis Khan for ten thousand dollars."

She reached into the purse again and pulled out a revolver. "This was my adoptive father's gun. I inherited it when he died when our house burned up. It seems he tragically fell asleep with a cigarette.'' She laughed. ''Which, of course, proves that it's true what the Surgeon General says about smoking being hazardous to your health.''

Chelsea had never seen so much hatred in one person. It was both terrifying and horribly sad at the same time.

Jo put the barrel of the gun against Roxanne's temple. The older woman closed her eyes and cringed. Jo pulled the trigger.

''Well,'' she said cheerfully, when the click seemed deafening in the heavy silence, ''I guess you lucked out this time. We'll try again. Later.''

She handed Chelsea a pen and a yellow legal pad. ''Start writing. I tell you, Chelsea, this revised version of the Roxanne Scarbrough story is going to shoot you to the top of the bestseller list.''

Chelsea had no doubt she was right. She hoped she'd be alive to see it published.

Chapter Twenty-Four

"I gotta tell you, son," Joe Burke said. "Having your lady friend disappear when you're already a suspect in a murder ain't the best thing that could happen to you."

"I didn't kill Waggoner," Cash insisted yet again.

"You weren't home all night with Miz Cassidy, either." When Cash didn't answer that, the sheriff nodded. "That's kind of what I thought. She seemed like a real loyal little gal. But someone ought to warn her that lyin' to a law enforcement officer during a criminal investigation could get her in big trouble."

"I'll tell her," Cash said, his impatience escalating with each minute they wasted. "As soon as we find her."

"That could be a mite difficult. Seeing as how we don't know where to start looking."

"Jo McGovern's got her," Cash said.

"You got any proof of that, son?"

"Yeah." Not worrying whether his actions had been legal, Cash had entered the house and gone straight to the kitchen where he'd heard the faint whirring sound of a camera in the eerie stillness. Opening the pantry door he located the hidden camera.

Jo had documented her crime well. The sheriff, Cash and Dorothy watched the videotape as the young woman stirred the drug into the iced tea. Watched an unsuspecting Chelsea drink it. Then watched as she slid off the chair onto the floor and was dragged, feet first from the room.

The sheriff turned to Dorothy. "You've spent a lot of time with Ms. McGovern. Do you have any idea where she might have taken off to?"

Dorothy shook her head. "I have no idea."

"Dammit," Cash exploded. "She must have said something."

"Mostly she just talked about her film."

"You went sightseeing with her the first day Roxanne brought Chelsea out to Belle Terre," he remembered.

"The day Roxanne got that call from LaDonna?"

"That's it. While you were driving around, filming the local color, was there any one place that she seemed attracted to?"

Cash watched the light of recognition brighten Dorothy's eyes. "Her daddy had a fishing cabin on the Tallatch River."

The river was only a few miles from Raintree, part of the Lower Coastal Plain. It wasn't much, Cash thought. But it was a start. He exchanged a look with the sheriff which told him they were thinking the same thing.

"Do you remember her saying where it was?"

"I may be able to do better than that," Dorothy said. "I believe I can show you."

"You've been there?"

"She wanted to see it. I was irritated because I'd probably be late getting home to fix Mama's dinner. But Jo was so insistent, and Roxanne had instructed me to do whatever it took to make Jo's and Chelsea's stay with us more enjoyable. So I drove her there to look at it. We didn't stay long.''

She shivered. "There was an old alligator sunning himself next to the rickety old front porch. We couldn't get out of the car. Which didn't disturb me in the least, since it wasn't a very nice-looking place.''

Cash picked Dorothy up off her feet and planted a big kiss right on her mouth. "Dorothy, darlin','' he said, when he'd put her back on the ground, "I love you.''

Even knowing that he didn't mean it, not in the way she would have liked, Dorothy still blushed.

"I'll call and have them get a chopper ready for us,'' the sheriff said. "It'll be faster. Do you think you can spot the cabin from the air, Miz Palmer?''

"I think so. So long as you follow the road so I can get my bearings.''

Ten minutes later, the trio, accompanied by two members of the Sheriff's Department SWAT team were taking off from the county airport.

They were going to get to Chelsea in time, Cash assured himself. They had to. Because the alternative was unthinkable.

It seemed she'd been writing for hours. Chelsea's hand was getting cramped. But every time she stopped to massage her aching fingers, Jo would stop dictating long enough to scream at her to keep writing.

Chelsea was reluctantly impressed at how much information the filmmaker had been able to compile. She knew an amazing amount about Roxanne's—Cora Mae's—life. It was only too bad she hadn't known about the earlier abortion. Then George Waggoner might still be alive. Although if she were to be perfectly honest, Chelsea certainly wasn't going to mourn the man.

All the time she was dictating, Jo paced. And filmed the process for her documentary. The dark circles beneath her eyes looked like bruises, making Chelsea wonder how long she'd been in this manic state, and how long she could keep going. She seemed to be operating on adrenaline. And madness.

Every so often, she'd get to a gap in what she knew. That was when she'd turn to Roxanne and hurl the questions at the stricken woman hard and fast. Whenever Roxanne didn't immediately sob out an answer, Jo would hit her. Hard. Then begin to pace again.

As the hours wore on, what had begun as a remarkably detailed accounting of one woman's life became the disjointed paranoid ramblings of a mind that was rapidly unraveling. As Jo grew more and more delusional, Chelsea realized she was also more and more dangerous. One could not reason with madness.

On the other hand, she considered, there was the chance that the crazed young woman might wear down completely. And that was what Chelsea decided to count on.

She began asking Jo to repeat things, which only confused the matter more. Sometimes Jo looked as if she were about to burst into tears. At other times, she appeared to be infuriated by her confusion. It was then Chelsea switched gears, soothing, calming, assuring her that they were in this together. Relieved to have found an ally, Jo would resume pacing. And talking.

Chelsea was not surprised to discover that Jo had burned Belle Terre. But there was one piece of the puzzle she couldn't make fit.

"May I ask a question?"

"Depends on what it is," Jo snapped, looking irritated at being interrupted.

"Did you have anything to do with me falling off the staircase at Belle Terre?"

"Why would I want to do that?" Jo countered. "When I needed you to write this book. Think about it a minute, Chelsea. Who do you think could have felt threatened by you finding out the truth?"

Chelsea immediately turned toward Roxanne, who didn't respond to her probing gaze. But the guilty look in her eyes spoke volumes.

"I didn't mean to hurt you," Roxanne said finally, as the silence hovered over the room. "Really," she insisted when Jo laughed. "But I overheard you asking Jo about my background."

"Fictional background," Jo put in.

"I had my reasons for that," Roxanne snapped, showing a bit of her own spunk. "I kept telling myself that you weren't an investigative reporter like your father, that you'd let it drop. But then you went to the courthouse to look up the old records, and well, I just wanted you to go back to New York. After all, you had enough to finish the book. And if you'd only gone," she said pointing out what Chelsea had already thought of, "you wouldn't be in this predicament now."

"That's enough chitchat," Jo decided. "It's time to get back to work."

Having lost her watch somewhere after being drugged, Chelsea had no idea what time it was. The cabin door was shut and barred, the hurricane shutters closed. The only light was from that single forty-watt bulb hanging overhead.

"I'm so tired," she complained. "And my head is aching. Can't I take a break? I need some sleep. And some aspirin."

"It's not night, yet," Jo snarled. "You don't need to go to sleep."

"What about the aspirin?" Chelsea put on her most conciliatory expression. "You're an artist, surely you understand how difficult it is to be creative when you're in pain. I truly want this to be a wonderful book, Jo." She rubbed her forehead. "But with this splitting headache, I'm having trouble thinking straight."

"There are some aspirin in the glove compartment of the car," Roxanne offered carefully. "If that will help."

Jo spun around. "Why are you trying to help me? What are you up to?"

"Nothing! I'm your mother. As you pointed out, I inadvertently did a terrible thing to you. The least I can do is help Chelsea write you a wonderful book."

Jo looked hesitantly from Roxanne to Jo and back again. She reminded Chelsea of a wounded, trapped animal. "I'm not going to leave you alone in here."

"Where could we go?" Chelsea asked. "We don't even know where we are. Speaking of which," she said, "if I'm not back at Rebel's Ridge soon, Cash will worry. If he comes looking for me and I'm not at the house, he may call the sheriff."

"Let him. By the time they find you, you'll both be dead anyway."

That was exactly what Chelsea had feared. The stakes had just been raised considerably. "I don't think you'd kill me, Jo," she said. "Because I'm on your side. And what good is a dead writer?"

"You don't think Truman Capote still sells?" Jo countered. "Hell, I'll bet his numbers are higher than when he was alive."

Good point. Chelsea tried again. "But if I'm dead, I won't be able to promote the book. Do you have any idea how many people watched my interview with Charles Gibson on "Good Morning America"? All those people are potential readers, Jo.

"If we play our cards right, all of them—millions of viewers—will run out and buy our book and realize how badly you've been mistreated by Roxanne. None of them will ever buy any of her books again. Or her dishes, or her flatware, or her towels. She won't even be a footnote in history. She'll disappear. It'll be as if she never existed. But you need me to help you."

"I'll get the aspirin," Jo decided. "And you can come use the phone in the car to call your boyfriend. But you'd better not try anything funny."

"I wouldn't think of it," Chelsea promised.

As she left the cabin and walked out to the car parked on a strip of bright white sand, the sun was setting, bathing the landscape in a molten copper glow. The rain had stopped, but rather than cooling things down, the steamy air was pregnant with lingering moisture. They seemed to be somewhere similar to the swamp where she'd gone fishing with Cash and Jamie, but the water, rather than black, was a bright tea color. A pair of alligators dozed on the far bank.

"Where are we?"

"That's none of your business." Jo opened the car door. "Make your damn phone call. Then we can get back to work."

Chelsea called, relieved and worried when she got Cash's answering machine. That could mean he had already begun looking for her. Or perhaps he'd been arrested for George's murder.

She left a message, wishing she could have said something clever that would have tipped him off to her whereabouts. Which, of course, would have been impossible, even if she had been able to speak with him, because she had no earthly idea where she was.

She vaguely remembered Cash telling her that the rivers on the Coastal Plain were called backwater rivers. And that their clear water was stained tea-colored by decaying organic matter in adjacent swamps. The salt dunes, she recalled, were on the eastern side of these streams and thought to be wind deposits from the nearby sea laid down some two million years ago.

Terrific. So now she knew she was somewhere on Georgia's coastal plain. Which was only hundreds of miles square. No problem finding her way home, she thought with a sinking heart.

But then again, if she didn't try to escape, her fate was sealed. Because although she might be able to temporarily confuse Jo, she did not believe for a moment that she'd be allowed to walk away from this alive.

Jo frowned as she watched Chelsea hang up. "You know, I never thought of this, but you could have used the phone to call 911."

"But I didn't."

"No. Not this time. Let's make sure you don't." She lifted the revolver and slammed it down onto the console, shattering the phone's plastic casing. "There. That's better," she said with overt satisfaction. "Now let's get back to work."

They were almost to the cabin door when Chelsea stumbled and fell to her knees.

"Dammit," Jo, clearly shaken by this unexpected event, shouted. "I told you not to try anything."

"I fell," Chelsea said on the closest thing to a whine that had ever, in all her twenty-eight years, come out of her mouth. "I told you, Jo, I'm exhausted. I need some sleep."

"You can sleep when the book is done." Something struck Jo as funny about that. "In fact, I promise you, Chelsea, you'll be sleeping for a very long time." She was laughing as they entered the cabin.

"All right." She went over to where she'd left the video

camera on the cot. As she bent down to pick it up, Chelsea lifted the rock she'd picked up when she pretended to fall and brought it down on her captor's head.

Chelsea quickly bent down and tried to untie Roxanne. But the cords were too tight, forcing her to resort to sawing through them as Jo had with her. Unfortunately, she wasn't left with enough cord to tie up her captor.

"We're going to have to get the hell out of here now. I don't suppose you have an extra car key hidden under the floor mat?"

"Of course not."

"Terrific." She dumped Jo's bag onto the cot, rifling through the contents until she found the set of car keys with their gold Mercedes symbol. "Okay, let's get this show on the road."

"Do you know where you're going?" Roxanne asked as she followed Chelsea out to the car.

"Sure," Chelsea answered with exaggerated bravado. "Away from here."

"That's not a very good answer."

"Sorry. It's the best I can do." Chelsea claimed the driver's seat without asking permission, stuck the key in the ignition and turned it. The quiet, unmistakable click was almost deafening. She tried again. Nothing.

"I can't believe this!" She pounded on the leather steering wheel. "This is a sixty thousand dollar car! And the battery goes dead?"

"It can happen," Roxanne replied defensively.

"Shit." Chelsea lowered her forehead to the wheel, closed her eyes and tried to think. They could go back into the cabin and try to hold Jo at gunpoint. But she was honestly exhausted and Jo's insane mania seemed to give her super endurance.

And although Roxanne was calculating and intelligent—

she'd certainly caught on fast when Chelsea had complained of a headache—she didn't want to put her life in this woman's hands, either. Because, if push came to shove, Chelsea knew that Roxanne would save Roxanne. And let her fend for herself.

She glared down at the broken phone. "We're going to have to walk out of here."

"I'm not going to spend the night in some goddamn swamp with alligators and water moccasins and mosquitoes!"

"Fine. Then you stay here and take your chances with your precious baby daughter. I'm getting out while I still can. Besides, there's supposed to be a full moon tonight. That should help."

"There's a toolbox in the trunk," Roxanne said. "It should have a flashlight in it."

Chelsea felt a renewed surge of hope. "That's better than nothing."

The flashlight was a little aluminum Mini Maglite, small, but bright. She was relieved to find at least these batteries were working.

"Why don't you tie her up," Roxanne suggested, still seeking a way to remain safely at the cabin.

"With what?"

"How should I know? A vine, perhaps?"

Chelsea glanced around. "You see any vines around here?"

"There must be some kudzu," Roxanne insisted. "The damn stuff is practically overrunning the entire state."

Before Chelsea could decide whether to risk taking time to look for the seeming ubiquitous vine, the door to the cabin flung open.

"Shit." The opportunity for tying up Roxanne's mad daughter had obviously passed. "I forgot to pick up the

gun." A shot rang out, whizzing past her ear, shattering th
back windshield.

"Come on, dammit," Chelsea shouted at Roxanne, wh
seemed frozen from fright.

Jo fired again, this time hitting the open trunk, joltin
Roxanne into action as she followed Chelsea deeper into th
swamp.

The sun had set in a blaze of fire over the swamp. A
they headed out in the opposite direction, Chelsea praye
that the night would stay clear. The idea of being out her
in the pitch-black dark was definitely less than appealing.

A bloodcurdling scream suddenly echoed across the blac
water.

"What was that?" Roxanne screamed in response.

"An animal," Chelsea guessed.

"It sounded human."

"It was a screech owl," Chelsea, who'd spent most o
her life in Manhattan, where the wildlife tended to have tw
legs, insisted. "I remember reading they can sound remark
ably human. Like peacocks."

"I've never heard that," Roxanne argued.

"It's true." Although her tone carried absolute convic
tion, Chelsea wondered who she was trying to fool. Rox
anne, or herself?

For the first time since the nightmare began, she felt lik
breaking down and bawling her head off. But then the mem
ory of her father suddenly flooded into her head. Her brave
cocky, hero father. If Dylan Cassidy could trudge throug
the jungles of Vietnam and emerge without a scratch, sh
could survive this.

Feeling as if she were literally following in her father'
footsteps, Chelsea kept walking.

The night air was thick with the dank, cloying odor o
rotting vegetation. Fireflies glowed, the marsh grass rustle

as small unseen animals moved through it. There was the nerve-racking sound of crickets all around them, the deep croaking of frogs, the occasional hoot of an owl. The wings of night birds moving from tree to tree whispered overhead.

In the beginning, Roxanne whimpered continually. Then, as if realizing she was only wasting emotional energy, she fell silent, trudging behind Chelsea, seeming more than willing to surrender the power that had once seemed to be so important to her.

Chelsea heard a sound like a log rolling into the water. She turned the flashlight toward the noise and jumped as she viewed the gleaming yellow eyes of an alligator gliding toward them across the water, his back broad and black as he passed by. Relieved that she wasn't a dinner target, Chelsea then gasped in horror as she watched him catch up to a swimming nutria and open his huge mouth. The sound of the furry animal's spine breaking was like a gunshot over the incessant chirp of crickets.

Chelsea glanced back over her shoulder to see if Roxanne had seen the wildlife drama. She had. Her eyes were wide and filled with the shock Chelsea herself was feeling. The two women exchanged a look and, having no choice, continued on.

"Where they hell are they?" Cash demanded, his frustration level rising with every minute the search continued.

"I'm sorry." Dorothy, who'd yet to locate the cabin, was in tears now. Cash knew it was his gentlemanly duty to try and soothe her but right now he didn't feel much like a gentleman.

"It's a big swamp," Joe Burke said unnecessarily. He reached over with his large hand and patted her knee. The comforting gesture only caused a renewed flood of tears.

Great, Cash thought grimly. This was just fucking great.

* * *

The full moon spread an unearthly white light over the land, a glow more eerie than comforting as it cast the trees in deep shadows that seemed even darker by contrast. It had begun to rain again, fat wet drops that soaked through her clothing and ran down her face. Chelsea was considering stopping and trying to find their way out in the morning.

"This is ridiculous," Roxanne complained as she stumbled over yet another root. "Why can't we just rest until morning?"

Before Chelsea could answer, her flashlight focused on yet another alligator sitting on the opposite bank. While she watched, he lifted his head, arched his tail and bellowed. It was not a loud sound, but it shook her to the bones.

"I don't have any intention of becoming gator bait," she said. "If we stop, we're sure to fall asleep."

"We can take turns."

"You might be willing to trust *me* with *your* life, Roxanne. But I have to tell you, I'm not that generous. Especially after you set me up for that fall off your staircase. No, it's too great a risk. We're going to keep walking because I don't have any intention of dying in this godforsaken place."

Chelsea thought of all the things she had left to do in her life. Like marrying Cash. And having his baby. A baby she could be carrying even now.

She thought about how she wanted to explore the fledgling peace she seemed to have forged with her mother. And, despite the gravity of her situation, she smiled at the idea of breaking the news to Deidre Lowell that she was going to be a grandmother.

No, Chelsea vowed. There would be no dying here tonight.

Like Roxanne, she'd already fallen down too many times to count. Each time, she thought about the deadly water moccasins undoubtedly hiding in the grass, remembered the gators, and instructed her wobbly legs to keep on moving.

Behind her, Roxanne was quietly sobbing again. A few minutes earlier, she'd become hysterical when a raccoon had run in front of her. Chelsea had had to slap her—hard—to quiet her screeching and prevent her from running away.

The flashlight's white beam had faded to yellow. The circle had narrowed considerably, and now the light was beginning to flicker. If it weren't for the moonlight streaming in through the tree branches, they'd be in total darkness.

Although she'd tried to remain optimistic, Chelsea felt her confidence sagging considerably. She was reminding herself that she'd never been a quitter, when she suddenly heard a familiar sound.

"Shut up!" she shouted at Roxanne. "Do you hear that?"

The other woman drew in a deep, gulping breath and managed to stop weeping. They both stood statue still, listening.

"It sounds like a motor," Roxanne said. "Maybe a boat?"

"Not a boat." Chelsea concentrated. "Oh, God, it's a helicopter!" She began looking up at the midnight black sky, waving her miserable excuse for a flashlight like a beacon.

Cash was the first to see the dim pinpoint of light. "Look at that," he said, pointing down into the blackness, through the slanting rain.

"Could be St. Elmo's fire," the sheriff said.

"It's too concentrated. It's a flashlight." Relief rushed over him in blessed cooling waves as the pilot focused the spotlight downward. "It's them."

"Seems to be," Joe Burke drawled laconically. But Cash

could hear the repressed excitement in the sheriff's voice. "Got some place we can set this bird down, Danny?"

The pilot swept the spotlight around the area. "That clearing looks pretty safe."

"There you go." The sheriff gave Cash a look that suggested he'd never expected any other outcome. But both men knew exactly how close they'd come to tragedy.

The spotlight from the hovering helicopter was blinding. Chelsea shaded her eyes with one hand, while continuing to wave the flashlight with her other.

"They didn't see us," Roxanne cried out as the copter rose again over the top of the trees. "They're leaving!"

For a fleeting, terrifying moment, Chelsea thought Roxanne might be right. "No," she said, viewing the copter's descent, "they're just finding someplace to land."

When she heard the sound of the rotor whipping the leaves in the trees edging the clearing, Chelsea began running toward the sound.

Cash leaped out of the open doorway and began running toward the place where he'd last seen Chelsea.

He'd come! She'd known he would! Giddy with joy and relief, Chelsea held out her arms.

Feeling like a crazed guy in a shampoo commercial, he lifted her off her feet, covering her wet face with kisses.

She was laughing and crying at the same time. "What kept you?"

"It's a long story." Lord, she felt good! Cash wanted to hold on to her forever.

Oblivious to the others, they shared a long, heartfelt kiss that could have lasted minutes, hours or an eternity.

Heedless of the water streaming over them, Chelsea tilted her head back, smiling up into his wonderful, handsome face. "I do hope this doesn't become a habit. Because I'll be very annoyed if you're late for our wedding."

"Don't worry, sweetheart. I'll be there on time. With bells on."

"That's not exactly the morning coat my mother would undoubtedly prefer the groom to wear," she said. "But it definitely has possibilities."

He kissed her again. Harder. Deeper. With all the pent-up emotion swelling in his heart. With all the love in his soul. She kissed him back as they gained strength from each other. Finally, Cash lifted his head.

"Do you have any idea how worried I was about you?"

"Probably about as worried as I was about myself."

"More." He kissed her again.

"It was Jo," Chelsea told him when them came back up for air.

"I know. We found her body." Cash's smile faded at the memory. "It looked like she stumbled into a nest of water moccasins not far from the cabin."

When she wasn't as shocked as she might have been, Chelsea realized she'd known that all along. Obviously Roxanne had been right about that night-piercing scream belonging to a human.

She shuddered. "That's so sad."

"Not as sad as what she probably would have done to you." His arms tightened around her at the idea.

"She was Roxanne's daughter."

"I know. I saw your notes. I only skimmed the top page, but I got the gist from that."

"It's a terribly tragic story." Chelsea sighed. "But at least I've found an ending for my novel."

His laugh was rough and harsh with pure relief. "There you go." Then he kissed her again because it had been too long. "Let's go home."

"Oh, I'd like that."

As they walked together back toward the helicopter, Chelsea's tangled nerves finally got the best of her. With a mental apology to her father, she put aside the false bravado that was just too heavy to carry any longer.

"Chelsea?" When she stopped walking, Cash felt another stab of panic. "What's wrong? Are you sure you're okay, darlin'?"

"I'm fine," she reassured him yet again. "But I was so worried you wouldn't find me in time," she admitted.

He wasn't about to confess how he'd feared exactly the same thing. "But I did."

"Yes. You did." She managed a wobbly smile and put a hand on his cheek. "And now it's finally over."

"As much as I hate to argue with you, after the lousy night you've had, Irish, you're wrong." Cash covered her hand with his and lowered his smiling lips to hers. "It's just beginning."

A classic story from *New York Times*
bestselling author Sandra Brown.

SANDRA BROWN

"Sometimes I think you aren't real, that you're someone
wonderful that I dreamed up. I love you with all my heart…"

The letters Kyla sent to her husband, Sergeant Richard Stroud,
spoke of a love that stretched across the ocean. But when tragedy
ended their marriage too soon, Richard left behind only a widow with
a newborn son and a metal box filled with his wife's declarations of love.

Trevor Rule had been Richard's best friend. Returning home from
military duty, he was determined to help Kyla move past the tragedy
of Richard's death and convince her of their right to be happy together.
But he was also harboring a dark secret that could tear them apart….

Above and Beyond

Available the first week of March 2004 wherever books are sold.

JOANN ROSS

66849	A WOMAN'S HEART	___ $5.99 U.S.	___ $6.99 CAN.
66821	LEGACY OF LIES	___ $5.99 U.S.	___ $6.99 CAN.
66752	CONFESSIONS	___ $5.99 U.S.	___ $6.99 CAN.

(limited quantities available)

TOTAL AMOUNT	$_____
POSTAGE & HANDLING	$_____
($1.00 for one book; 50¢ for each additional)	
APPLICABLE TAXES*	$_____
TOTAL PAYABLE	$_____
(check or money order—please do not send cash)	

To order, complete this form and send it, along with a check or money order for the total above, payable to MIRA Books®, to: **In the U.S.:** 3010 Walden Avenue, P.O. Box 9077, Buffalo, NY 14269-9077; **In Canada:** P.O. Box 636, Fort Erie, Ontario L2A 5X3.

Name:_____
Address:_____ City:_____
State/Prov.:_____ Zip/Postal Code:_____
Account Number (if applicable):_____
075 CSAS

*New York residents remit applicable sales taxes.
Canadian residents remit applicable GST and provincial taxes.

MIRA®